Praise for Robin Oliveira's *I Alw*

"What a joy it is to be back in Belle Époque Par guided by the masterful pen of Robin Oliveira whose finely crafted language brings to light the complicated relationships of four of the principals of the Impressionist movement—Cassatt, Degas, Manet, Morisot. Only an omniscient narrator has the latitude to disclose the private yearnings and fears of these four as they grapple with issues of art execution, scathing reviews, self-doubt, elusive fame, tempestuous love, and creeping mortality. Here, in beautiful prose, juicy with nuance and depth, is the intimate, heart-wrenching story behind Impressionist art history, with Mary Cassatt at its center. A glorious achievement."
—Susan Vreeland, author of *Luncheon of the Boating Party*

"*I Always Loved You* is a marvelous work, enthralling, illuminating, and beautifully rendered. Robin Oliveira brings Belle Époque Paris and the fascinating artists and writers who walked its streets and filled its salons to the fullness of vivid, fiercely passionate life."
—Jennifer Chiaverini, author of *Mrs. Lincoln's Dressmaker* and *The Spymistress*

"In artfully crafted prose as penetrating and radiant as an Impressionist masterpiece, Robin Oliveira's moving portrait of Mary Cassatt and Edgar Degas is a poignant reminder that beneath the majestic sweep of history and ideas are men and women with yearnings and trepidations as urgent and palpable as our own. *I Always Loved You* evokes, in brilliant detail, the nuances of culture, art, and society in the cafes and salons of late-nineteenth-century Paris while bringing to life the spellbinding whirl of artists, writers, and savants who made La Belle Époque legendary."
—John Pipkin, author of *Woodsburner*

"[This] book is accomplished and well-researched.... Although sometimes [Degas and Cassatt] are completely alienated, they remain linked through their art and love."
—*Kirkus Reviews*

"Oliveira has woven a rich tapestry of the artists' life in Bell Époque Paris, in a close, intimate rendering." —*Library Journal*

"Emulating the powers of observation and expression possessed by the artists she so vividly and sensitively fictionalizes, Oliveira illuminates with piercing insight the churning psyches of her living-on-the-edge characters. This is a historically and aesthetically rich, complexly involving, and forthrightly sorrowful novel of the perilous, exhilarating, and world-changing lives of visionary artists breaking new ground and each other's hearts." —*Booklist*

"Art lovers will fall for this story full of beautiful details about the world of the Impressionists in Belle Époque Paris." —Examiner.com

"*I Always Loved You* is a beautifully composed—and extensively researched—blend of art history, vintage travelogue, and good storytelling." —*The Dallas Morning News*

"A tense romance . . . An imaginative yet faithful story of what might have been . . . This well-told tale will satisfy readers who like *The Paris Wife*." —*Minneapolis Star Tribune*

PENGUIN BOOKS

I ALWAYS LOVED YOU

Robin Oliveira is the *New York Times* bestselling author of *My Name Is Mary Sutter*. She holds a BA in Russian and studied at the Pushkin Language Institute in Moscow. She received an MFA in Writing from Vermont College of Fine Arts and is also a registered nurse, specializing in critical care. She lives in Seattle, Washington.

I Always Loved You

A Story of

MARY CASSATT

and

EDGAR DEGAS

Robin Oliveira

PENGUIN BOOKS

PENGUIN BOOKS
Published by the Penguin Group
Penguin Group (USA) LLC
375 Hudson Street
New York, New York 10014

USA | Canada | UK | Ireland | Australia | New Zealand | India | South Africa | China
penguin.com
A Penguin Random House Company

First published in the United States of America by Viking Penguin,
a member of Penguin Group (USA) LLC, 2014
Published in Penguin Books 2015

THE LIBRARY OF CONGRESS HAS CATALOGED THE HARDCOVER EDITION AS FOLLOWS:
Oliveira, Robin.
I always loved you : a novel / Robin Oliveira.
pages cm
ISBN 978-0-670-78579-7 (hc.)
ISBN 978-0-14-312610-2 (pbk.)
1. Cassatt, Mary, 1844–1926—Fiction.   2. Degas, Edgar, 1834–1917—Fiction.
3. Painters—Fiction.   I. Title.
PS3615.L583I15 2014
813'.6—dc23
2013036813

Printed in the United States of America
1   3   5   7   9   10   8   6   4   2

Designed by Nancy Resnick

This is a work of fiction based on real events.

For Noelle and Miles

I Always
Loved You

1926

Prologue

M ary Cassatt lifted two shallow crates of assorted brushes, pigments, palettes, and scraping knives and set them atop the paint-smeared table shoved under the arched, north-facing windows of her untidy studio. Someone less stubborn than she might have packed up years ago, but she liked to have her tools out and ready, as if at any moment she might turn and begin again, though she had not painted today and would not paint tomorrow and had not painted in some years, the scourge of the continuing betrayal of her eyesight, which she feared had become nearly as bad as *his* at the end. And then there was the pesky matter of confidence, which she'd discovered, to her disappointment, had not solidified over the years as her younger self had expected but had instead revealed itself to be an emotion that was more ruse than intention. The truth was that there was very little she could control anymore, except this one last thing, which made her feel very old.

She turned in a circle, suppressing the unfamiliar swell of panic rising in her throat, an emotion to her so exotic that she wondered how other people—those who yielded daily to weakness or fear—coped.

Oh, where was the damn thing?

She was certain she'd hidden the box among the blank canvases and tin water cans, where no one, not even a sly model bent on discovery, would have guessed she'd secreted the prize. But she was not as keen as she had once been and now feared that both her eyesight and her memory may have double-crossed her. Had she, in a fit of sentiment, concealed it somewhere upstairs in her bedroom in order to keep it close? She dismissed the thought. She could not imagine herself committing such a romantic act.

Daily, light flooded the stone-floored glassed-in studio at the back of the Château de Beaufresne, but now the winter afternoon was fading and her eyes were succumbing to fatigue. Time evaporating. The doctors said she was to prepare herself, meaning, she supposed, that they wanted her to sell her remaining canvases, attend to museum requests, visit relatives one last time—what people *imagined* had been her life. It mystified her that that was what they all thought was important to her. Of course she valued her work, and she had kept careful track as the prices for her paintings rose—prudence required such attention—but did they suppose that in touching brush to canvas she tallied only coin and admiration?

The world blazes along with its critical tongue and shallow impatience, not understanding the *moment*, the *breath*, the *seeing*.

She adjusted her thick-lensed glasses. What a necessary bother they were. Such *goggles*, but it was true that if she were still as careful a housekeeper of her studio as she had been in her youth, she could find what she wanted in an instant. What detritus a life leaves. She would have to call Mathilde to help her if she couldn't find it. Look for *shape*, she scolded herself. The thing is not the thing. It is instead form and light. After all, what are faces but hollows and swells, spheres and lines? She had learned that very young. And now? She removed her glasses and wiped her watering eyes. Oh, to *see* as she once had. Some mornings upon waking, she indulges herself: *Today I will paint the lace on the dress, finish the flowers in the background, and then concentrate on the way the sun plays on the girl's hair.* And then she opens her eyes, and a milky scrim obscures even the bedposts.

Mary replaced her glasses and willed her blurring eyes to focus on the jumble of brushes and palette knives and dismantled easels. Under this purposeful gaze, their forms sharpened and fell away and became the contour and outline she needed them to be. For half a century, she had shifted sight like this at will, though when she was young, when she was first beginning to paint, the effort had pained her. *It is a way of thinking*, her instructors had said. *It is a way of being in the world.*

And with that shift, the half-moon shape of the box revealed itself, protruding from under the edge of the tarpaulin. Kneeling, she felt its rounded edge and exhaled. Tucking it under her arm, she shuffled to the far end of the room, where Mathilde had left the tea tray for her on the table by the hearth, along with the magnifying glass she required.

Mary sank into the chair and opened the lid. It was the kind of box that harbors forgotten photographs or mismatched buttons, so ordinary that after her death they might have tossed it without checking the contents, but she couldn't take that chance. And besides, their curiosity had dogged her all her life; she would not let it dog her death. She was not sentimental, though people believed she was, seduced perhaps by the expressions she had rendered in her paintings. But she didn't know, really, what people thought of her. And she didn't care. Her work, like his, was all the legacy she cared to bequeath to the world.

But she had kept these letters, as he had kept hers, though what they had been thinking, she couldn't imagine. Such recklessness. Private conversations should always remain private. Why should anyone know what they themselves had barely known? And even if something had once been committed to paper, did it mean that it was still true? *Always* true? Unlike the relative permanence of paint, words were temporal. You uttered them and they evanesced, but if you wrote them, they remained, though whether the written word was any more truthful than the spoken was a mystery to her. Only paint was honest. But even a painting could be wiped clean and refined. *He* was forever revising, stealing his paintings back to rework them, everything always unfinished with him.

She fingered the scalloped tendril of faded pink ribbon that bound the letters. She had chosen ribbon instead of string because it reminded her of his danseuses' bright sashes, their pink and green bows, lush and extravagant in their fullness. Somehow, he had made even the sashes seem to dance, though it was the dancers themselves he'd imbued with the verve that now enchanted all of Paris. Motion, captured. Later, after he had painted every position, rehearsal, ensemble, and pose, he began to paint women in the most unflattering way, as if to negate any vestige of the romance his ballet pictures had cultivated. He had been an uncompromising man, stubborn and ironic; hence ribbons, to goad as much as to honor.

At his funeral, she had wept (how could she not?), and even that reasonable grief—had they not been friends above all?—had fanned the old rumors. The whispers about their friendship—their romance, their affair, ask anyone in Paris, they all had an opinion—had not dampened after his death. Nine years now. She had helped to arrange the sale of all his paintings afterward. His studio had been crammed with work, though it seemed impossible, since his blindness should have eliminated any further possibility of his working, as it had her. And yet, they had had to snake through stacks of canvases and unfinished sculptures and wax castings, his collection of paintings by Ingres and Renoir—and even some of hers—crawling up his walls. He had died in those crowded rooms. Happy, Mary supposed now, even though in the end he couldn't see any of his art anymore. She knew—no, believed—that its mere proximity had soothed him, as these letters had soothed her all these years since.

They were all gone now: Pissarro, Manet, Morisot, Renoir. And *him*. Only Monet was still alive, wheezing with illness in his house in Giverny.

She would have arranged the sale of his work anyway, would have been as thorough and competent even had the search for these letters not been her main priority. Half their correspondence. Her letters, which he, too, had kept in a box of old paints tucked into a corner, where no one could reach them, not even his niece, charged with caring for him when he could no longer stumble through the streets of Paris half-blind, searching for scenes to immortalize. Ever the flaneur, the boulevardier. They nestled now beside his in this box, hers also tied with ribbon, though black, as if he had mourned her.

Dear Edgar,
How unkind you have been to me these last months. . . .

She was ashamed now of all her terrible moods, though he should have been just as ashamed of his. He was equally to blame, but what she still didn't understand was whether there was room for love in two lives already consumed by passion of another sort. You would think she would know the answer by now. She had lived a long time, and yet wisdom, the wisdom everyone believed she possessed, flickered like the elusive flame of confidence, just out of reach. People intuit so much that is wrong. She would like to say, *Yes, we chose. Absolument.* Just as we made decisions about the color of light or the tint of a pigment, we made a decision about our lives.

Were he still alive, would he untie these ribbons now? Read the letters one after the other? Revive what they had let die?

Live the life again, and, in memory, alter it?

How brave was she?

The doctors said it was a certainty. As if her mortality had ever been in question, but perhaps they, too, had been seduced by her paintings: If she could create something so exquisite then perhaps she *would* live forever.

Unready, she turned away, lifted the teacup, discovered that the tea had gone cold, the day become night. She could hear Mathilde in the kitchen with the cook, preparing the dinner she would refuse and which refusal they would then report to the doctors and which the doctors would then lament, all of them assigning meaning to trifles.

The candle flared when she lit it with a match. She would not call

Mathilde. No electricity for her—unnecessary when light, so long her friend, had turned its back on her. The night stretched before her, an old woman's night, filled with memories to sift and a life to mediate. Tonight, she would paint once again, though only in her mind; would indulge imagination, though only once. Would believe what she'd scarcely been able to believe then.

Edgar Degas and Mary Cassatt. All of Paris had whispered it, as they had whispered too about Édouard Manet and Berthe Morisot.

All of us keepers of secrets and yearnings and renunciations as impenetrable and ungovernable as our enduring desire to paint.

The ribbon refused to untie, knotted as it had been for a decade. She tore at it with her nails and then the first stack of letters spilled onto her lap and fanned across her dark skirt, great numbers of them, their edges crisp with age, years of quarrel and tenderness and recrimination bleeding into the vellum.

So many pages, you would think they had been in love.

1877

Chapter One

Mary Cassatt was often mistaken for being tall, but she wasn't. She was small boned and finely made, the perception of her height being formed primarily on the force of her personality. People often said that she was beautiful, too, but a careful examination of her heart-shaped face, with its too-narrow chin and unfortunate exaggeration of the forehead, revealed that its most prominent feature, her large eyes, and the other, a pair of sculpted cheekbones, were the deflecting mirage. None of this mattered at all to Mary, who bore her somewhat illusive ordinariness as a kind of weapon. It had served to sharpen her tongue, and when she was lost, as she was now, only her sister Lydia, her mother, and her close friends could detect the terror that coursed through her. To the rest of the world, she remained formidable, and to her friends she was always a stalwart defender of their person, and this combination, along with her lively intelligence, made her the best kind of companion. You loved her or you hated her, and Abigail Alcott loved her. It was a friendship that Mary Cassatt cherished.

Abigail and Mary were attending the last day of the impressionist exhibition on one of the rainiest days of the spring, their umbrellas dripping as they climbed the marble stairway to the apartment on the corner of the Rue le Peletier and the Boulevard Haussmann.

"Paris is raining," Mary said. That was how she spoke about the weather since settling back in Paris: *Paris is raining*, or *Paris is shining*, because the city seemed to dictate weather the way it dictated art.

"It always rains in Paris," Abigail said.

Mary suspected that her friend was vaguely worried that by coming with her today she had crossed to the wrong side of the artistic tracks. The two had met when Abigail had come to study in Paris the year before, two years after Mary's decision to return to the art capital of the world. In the Louvre, they copied paintings in the mornings with the copyists' licenses they had obtained from a pale, sickly clerk officed in a damp little closet in the museum's dungeons. In the afternoons they sketched in the Tuileries, perfecting their drawing. Always, they hoped their work would be accepted at the Salon, the state-sponsored academic art exhibition that was considered the height of artistic success. Held every year under the glass ceiling in the grand Palais de l'Industrie, the Salon was every artist's ambition, for the jury was made up of the most prominent artists in Paris.

Now, they paid for their tickets, bought a catalog, and passed through the turnstile into the apartment that was serving as a temporary gallery. Abigail's thin, vaguely aristocratic face lit with both anticipation and apprehension as they linked arms and surveyed the parlor. This was the renegade artists' third exhibition. Labeled "impressionists" by the hostile critics, they were refugees from the Salon who despised the state system of juries, believing that no judge should separate an artist from the viewer. Today there was no sign of the mocking crowds that had mobbed the exhibition in its first weeks, and Abigail seemed to relax. Despite it being the last day, the apartment was mostly empty. Devoid of any furniture or other domestic trappings, the rooms did resemble an art gallery. Someone had tacked sheets of thin muslin over the windows to keep out the direct sunlight, giving the room a soft, elusive light.

The apartment was large for Paris. Mary and Abigail took a preliminary turn, peeking in from the central hallway through the doorways, checking the numbered paintings against the catalog, noting the canvases they wanted to come back to study: Renoir's sumptuous portraits, Monet's vibrant oils, Pissarro's feathered landscapes, and the stunning canvases of Berthe Morisot, which seemed, on first look, to be spun purely of light.

"Did you know a woman exhibited with them?" Abigail said.

"Yes," Mary said. "She's Édouard Manet's sister-in-law."

"Not *the* Édouard Manet, enfant terrible of the art world?"

"*The*."

Any painter in Paris knew of Édouard Manet. For more than a decade, he had been painting provocative canvases of such notoriety that he couldn't be ignored, which everyone supposed was his object all along. The newspapers printed cartoons and caricatures of him all the time. Last year, after both his paintings had been rejected from the Salon, he'd displayed them in his studio for two weeks, advertising his private exhibition in *Le Figaro*. Unruly lines trailed around the block waiting to see the artist's latest scandalous *taches*, causing an uproar in the neighborhood.

Abigail flipped the pages of the catalog. "Why doesn't he exhibit here? The Salon rejects him all the time."

It was a rare moment of thoughtlessness on Abigail's part. Mary shrugged and looked away. "I don't know."

"I'm sorry. What a stupid thing to say."

This carelessness and Abigail's quick apology were the first hints of any pity on Abigail's part. This year, Abigail's painting, a still life, had been accepted for the Salon, while Mary's had not. Every year for the past four years, Mary's work had been admitted, but now, just when she believed her painting had finally begun to take on a life of its own, just when putting brush to canvas, so long an exercise in study, had become a joy, the Salon had rejected her. But if anyone besides Abigail had received more pleasure from an acceptance, Mary could not imagine it. Abigail had written home to tell her family of her great success. A little oil, of which she was so proud. And why not? In the past, Mary had done the same, had bought catalogs and clipped any mention of herself in the newspaper and sent the notices home, proving her success to her father in the concrete way he understood. And Abigail, after all, had her famous writer sister to compete with. But Abigail had neither gloated over her victory nor patronized Mary, though the rest of the members of the American art community had not been above glee at Mary's failure. At the Palais de l'Industrie, where she had gone to wrap her rejected paintings for the carter, she had seen several of them laughing. Not one friend had come to console her.

"If anyone deserves happiness at being accepted by the Salon it's you, Abigail."

"Why don't we start with Edgar Degas? You know you only want to see him," Abigail said, her voice steeped in the regret of having reminded her friend of her failure. "He has the two back bedrooms."

Degas was the single reason Mary had wanted to come to the exhibition today. She had admired him for years, seeking out his work in small galleries and colorists' shops, always hoping she might stumble onto one of his canvases displayed for sale in a window. Now she followed Abigail down the hall, and upon entering the first of the bedrooms, was overcome. Degas's was a point of view so particular, so specific, so separate from the others' that it struck her once again as modern mastery. Not that he painted beauty. No. The others painted beauty. Degas painted life.

Abigail said, "But you don't want to paint exactly in his style, do you, Mary? You don't want to imitate him?"

"No, of course not, but do you see what he does? Do you see how remarkable the composition is?"

"I see. I think." Abigail cocked her head, studying the painting of a woman seated at a café table, her hand resting listlessly on a glass of absinthe. "*In a Café*, he calls it. Actually, looking at this makes me uncomfortable."

"Degas provokes and reveals our prejudices. Wouldn't you like to be good enough to unsettle someone in this same way one day?" Though "good enough" was a shameful understatement. Instead, Mary wished she had said, wouldn't you like to be *skilled, sensitive, gifted, brilliant, generous* enough, all the things that she, Mary, was not.

"Do forgive me, but I don't see it. I've hardly just begun to understand all that is necessary to paint really well in the old way, let alone the new."

"The Salon would disagree," Mary said, but she said it without rancor.

"Do you mind if I go back and peek at the Renoirs instead? I think I might feel more accord with him."

As Abigail made her escape, Mary began, like the insatiable student she was, to try to discover Degas's secret. For there was one, she was certain of it, and she believed that if she studied each of his paintings one by one, her ravenous eye might discern the workings of his mind, might detect how he translated his vision to his brush, might appropriate his vision as her own. But as soon as she began, unflattering comparisons between her work and his inundated her mind. The anatomy of an artist's heart is a desire for perfection, at least hers was, and barring that, at least the ability to express a certain truth, but now she feared that no amount of hunger would infuse her with the ineffable vagaries that made an artist an artist. It wasn't imitation she was after, as Abigail had suggested. It was that she had been trying for half her lifetime to find her soul, and still she hadn't, while this man painted with his. It was not a lucky thing to want something as much as she did. To fear that no matter how hard she worked, no matter how much she studied, she might lack the essential talent of *seeing*. For true art lay in seeing. This was what she had come to, after years of study. A properly chosen palette, a true sense of proportion, an effective brushstroke: These were not gifts; these were technique, obtainable by tireless observation and practice. But sight? Sight, it seemed, was a gift from God. She stood for a while longer, turning in a circle, then drifted from Degas's room as if she were leaving a funeral.

"Mary?" Abigail asked when Mary found her in the parlor.

"I'll never be as good as I want to be, Abigail," Mary said.

"Every artist thinks that."

"But compared to him, I am nothing."

"I think you ought to meet him. I'll write him a letter," Abigail said.

"You will not."

"Or perhaps you could write to Berthe Morisot."

"No one is writing any letters. Besides," Mary said, distracted by the absurdity of Abigail's scheme, "you know what it's like to try to meet a French person. It's as if you were proposing war and not an introduction."

"We need your sister," Abigail said. "Lydia would charm them all in half a second. Soon you would be fast friends with all these artists."

"Lydia *would* charm them, wouldn't she?"

They both missed Lydia, who had returned home to Philadelphia last summer after visiting Mary twice in the previous two years. Though she was older than Mary by seven years, Lydia never seemed a chaperone. She was instead comfort and conviviality in a city that sometimes overwhelmed. But she was often ill, one day well, the next doubling over in pain. Sometimes Mary wondered whether it was coping with illness that had made Lydia the family's acknowledged center of calm.

They lingered a moment longer, gazing at Renoir's canvases, then wandered back through the rooms, Abigail asking Mary question after question, the two of them marveling at the bright palettes and thickly textured paint, elements so different from the strictures of Salon art that it was as if these artists had set themselves free. Suddenly it was clear to Mary, in a way it hadn't been before, that these artists were *playing* more than they were working, playing at exposing some vision of life that defied convention, exuberant in a way that her painting was not, and could never be, weighted down as she was by the Salon's censorious rule. Nor were these paintings amateur, as the scolding reviews in the newspapers had admonished. Instead, they were lively, inviting, celebratory. After a while, Abigail urged her to return to Degas's rooms. Their arms linked, they strolled past the pastels and oils, awed and speechless, Abigail by the strangeness of Degas's vision, Mary by its mastery. Unlike the other artists, Degas didn't play, though he was not reverent, either, not unless you believed that you honored life by exposing it.

Outside, they unfurled their umbrellas against the soft rain and kissed one another good-bye, French-style, on the cheeks. They were going in opposite directions, Mary to her apartment at the base of Montmartre and Abigail to the attic room near the Tuileries that she shared with two friends. The Parisian evening glow of glistening raindrops and gray light had just fallen, and despite the gutter's accumulation of litter and horse droppings, the scene reminded Mary how much she loved the city and how much she would miss it if she were to leave.

"You're coming tomorrow, aren't you, to opening day?" Abigail said. "I'll need your support."

"I'll be there," Mary promised. "I'll come to the Salon and admire your painting and make everyone look at it."

"Are you sure you don't mind?"

"I promise I'll be there," Mary said.

"And you must promise me you won't go back to Philadelphia."

Mary looked away. "I didn't say I wanted to go home." Though since the rejection, she had been trying to decide whether or not she ought to.

"Paris is the sanctuary of art," Abigail said.

"And its battleground," Mary said, kissing her friend once more. "The place where artists live or die."

"I don't know what those idiots were thinking," Abigail said, squeezing Mary's hand. But as Abigail hurried down the street, Mary knew it wasn't the rejection that bothered her, not anymore. She turned and looked up at the apartment window, now darkened in the gloaming, yearning for the artist's vision she feared she did not have and would never have. She was not being defeatist. She was being practical, a distinctly Cassatt trait, one her father would admire for its resolution even as she mourned its pragmatism. To paint or not to paint. That was the Shakespearean conundrum. Even her father considered this question one of life and death. Once, he had said to her that he would rather see her dead than be an art student in Paris, a statement that had sent her fleeing from the dinner table. And at thirty-three, one had to assess. One had to come to terms. One had to confront dreams. The fading daylight blackened into darkness, and the lamplighter lit the gaslights in succession, and pearls of glassed flame flickered like warm stars.

"Paris is shining," she whispered.

It was then that *he* spoke, in a voice as familiar as her own. *Paint what you see*, he whispered. *Paint what you love.*

Degas's voice, imagined or real, echoed in the splendor of the Paris night. It followed her up the street, away from the Boulevard Haussmann, shimmering now with carriage lanterns and streetlamps, toward the less glimmering butte of Montmartre, where she had made her home among artists, still hoping to become a true one herself.

Chapter Two

The Paris Salon, the great celebration of spring, of art, of taste, always opened in May and always knotted traffic on the Champs-Élysées into a fist. The perpetual congestion of the City of Light drove its denizens and visitors alike insane, but this morning it seemed to Mary that the throng of carriages, wagons, carts, horses, and pedestrians converging on the Palais de l'Industrie was far worse than she had ever seen. She surveyed the clogged arterial from the seat of her hired fiacre and folded the letter she'd been reading into her reticule.

> You desire too much or not enough. I don't know which it is, but this stubbornness of yours is unseemly. Enough, my dear. Time to come home. Come back to Philadelphia and find yourself a husband before it is too late. You can paint here, with much less trouble, far more economically than you can in Paris.

It was a mistake to reread her father's letter, and yet she had done it anyway. The missive had been waiting for her last night when she returned home from the impressionist exhibition. Though it did contain a drab sentence or two of solace, she wished now that she had left the letter behind. It bothered her that he had somehow divined the confusion she found herself in now. Last night she had risen twice from bed to write her father, only to put down the pen and climb back into bed without writing a word. Now she touched her purse, the letter folded inside. How to explain to him what she wanted when she could barely decide herself?

The driver could not make headway, and soon stopped in the middle of the street. Over his objections, she gathered her slim skirts and launched herself into the stalled traffic, ducking between the restless horses and polished equipages, taking care to guard the plumage on her hat, thinking that she wouldn't mind the unseemly scramble so much if she actually wanted to be here.

Up and down the avenue, others, too, were leaving their carriages mid-street, having given up hope of a more elegant debarkation at the doors of the palais. A disk of yellow sun glinted in the soft blue sky, a reprieve from yesterday's gloomy rain, and in celebration fashionable Paris was showing off its regalia; Mary felt underdressed in her simple white blouse and blue skirt. Everywhere nattily attired men in top hats were guiding women draped in spring silk of Naples yellow and vermillion through the crush of conveyances, pausing to untangle ensnared feathers and ribbons from the leather harnesses. Their finery sparkled against the dull bitumen and the ocher dresses of the less well-off, for all of Paris attended the Salon, including laundresses, waiters, liverymen, and hod carriers, who saved centimes all year. Art was the business of Paris, and nothing else in the city attracted this mass of humanity, unless you looked to the recent past and the Communards, twenty thousand of them huddled behind the tombs of the Père Lachaise Cemetery awaiting slaughter after the country's failed and bloody civil war. It seemed impossible to Mary now that the upheaval had occurred a mere six years ago, though just who had wreaked more havoc on this city would ever remain in question: the Communards and their barricades; the invading Prussians, who had preceded them by eight short months; or Baron von Haussmann with his army of shovels, who had first destroyed Paris before reshaping the city to Napoléon III's grand vision. But Mary couldn't say who had most damaged the city; she supposed she wasn't Parisian enough yet to understand the wounded city's heart.

And according to the Salon jury, she wasn't Parisian enough in the way that mattered the most.

Banishing the self-pity from her mind, Mary stepped onto the overcrowded sidewalk in front of the palais, a stone edifice that rose in imposing splendor from the glorious park grounds, a majestic court compared to the modest apartment building on the Rue le Peletier where the impressionists had just mounted their exhibition. Here, the line to purchase Salon tickets stretched fifty people long at least. No doubt Abigail was already inside, awaiting Mary's arrival. She had offered to wait for Mary and admit her free as her guest, one of the perquisites of being an exhibitor, but Mary had not wanted to draw attention to herself. At the ticket window, she paid the one-franc admittance fee and another for the thick catalog. She had to stop herself from searching out the C's, where this year she would not find *Cassatt, Mary*, and the title of a painting into which she had poured all her hopes. Instead, she pushed through the iron doors and climbed the endless rise of polished marble that made up the grand staircase. The building she had visited in shame to collect her rejected paintings just the week before now echoed with shouts and laughter. Artwork in the Salon was arranged alphabetically, in makeshift rooms of temporary walls erected for the exhibition. Mary entered the exuberant throng and made her way to the "A" room, where Abigail stood in a circle of admirers.

"It looks all right, doesn't it? I shouldn't be embarrassed?" Abigail asked Mary after she greeted her, pointing out her picture, hung on the line amid a wealth of canvases that covered the entire wall from floor to ceiling. It was a huge honor to be featured at eye level; it meant that the jury thought the work merited the most advantageous placement. Mary thought Abigail's painting—the rendering of a bowl of fruit, an exquisitely shaped pitcher, and a faithfully reproduced bottle of olive oil—strong, if a bit simple. Though Mary would have been proud if it had been hers, she didn't much care for still lifes. With no emotion to evoke, no difficult hands to reproduce, no flesh to render, they offered little challenge other than light and form.

"Congratulations, Abigail. You should be well pleased with yourself."

A dozen well-wishers crowded around Abigail, and Mary kissed her on the cheek and left her to the ample affections of her admiring friends.

It was now little more than an hour after opening, and the crowd in the palais had swelled by the thousands. People bottlenecked the doorways, then surged into the rooms, sometimes stumbling in the press of humanity, tripping over trains, and catching petticoats in heels. Once safely inside a room, everyone was reluctant to return to the fray. After craning their necks to see the pictures that had been skied out of sight—paintings placed so high it seemed they had been hung in the clouds—the visitors milled about, closing in on pictures they liked and refusing to budge, making the traffic inside the palais as impenetrable as it was outside. Mary assiduously avoided the "C" room but otherwise let the crowd carry her along, taking in the artwork in desultory spurts and starts. There was so much to see—two thousand paintings alone—that they all began to blur, and she hadn't yet reached the statuary or architectural displays that dominated the other wing of the palais. By the time she reached the "M" room, her feet were sore and her spirits low. Someone abandoned a seat on a lone *causeuse* in the center of the room, and she sank onto its edge, contemplating her escape route and hoping that she would see no one she knew.

Edgar Degas stood in a flood of sunlight streaming through the glass ceiling. The harsh light was washing out every nuance of the exhibited paintings, only one of Degas's many reasons for despising the Salon. The jury's selections covered every inch of the high-ceilinged rooms and would, Degas was certain, have been suspended from the ceiling had painters not complained. Most of the artwork relegated to the rafters was invisible anyway, and artists were breaking down at every turn. Here and there clusters of consoling friends surrounded the afflicted, seeking to keep them from committing suicide on the spot. Their disappointment was a pitiful sight. Years before, Degas had written a letter to the director of the École des Beaux Arts, the state-sponsored school under whose purview the Salon lived, suggesting that rather than covering every inch of free wall, the canvases ought to be hung in rows of two at proper intervals so that each could be appreciated on its own merits, but his suggestion had gone unanswered and unheeded, as his uninvited suggestions usually did.

But Degas would not miss the Salon for anything, not only to discover what Corot and Daumier were up to, but also to fete his beleaguered friend Édouard Manet, who was pacing at his side, anxious about his painting's reception. His *Portrait of M. Faure, in the Role of Hamlet,* was good, though not nearly as good as his *Nana,* the other painting he had submitted, which the jury had spurned. Henriette Hauser had modeled for that one. She was a well-known courtesan, whom Émile Zola was also glorifying in a book about her life. In the painting, Manet had included a man at the edge of the canvas observing her toilette. This had seemed to bother the jury, who also did not like the daring Zola, or the infamous Flaubert, for that matter, whose *Madame Bovary* had thrilled all of Paris twenty years before.

"Who is that woman?" Degas said.

"Which woman? Henriette?"

"No, the woman over there, on the *causeuse,* the one who looks as if she is going to murder someone the second she gets a chance."

"Half the women in Paris look like that at any given moment. My Suzanne threatens me daily," Manet said.

"And with good cause, you bastard. If you can't keep your hands off Méry Laurent or your sister-in-law, I might murder you myself."

"Berthe is here?" Manet asked, rising to his tiptoes to search the crowd.

"I don't know. I am not your social secretary, nor do I keep track of your women."

"You injure me, Degas. Berthe and I are dear friends, admirers of one another's work. Besides, all that was long ago. She is married to Eugène now and my brother is my beloved friend. Not that I admit to anything. Ever."

Degas snorted. "Of course not." But he would not tease further. He loved Édouard and besides, Édouard was handsome; the man couldn't help it if women found him irresistible. Degas had yet to meet the woman who did not melt after a mere glance at his friend's rugged blond *tête*. On the street, women openly turned and stared at Manet's passing figure, which was more confident, dashing, and marvelous than Degas's unimpressively round-shouldered and thoroughly unstriking one, though he had long ago given up jealousy; he had moved past that and had voluntarily and officially entered the realm of resigned admirer, for Manet charmed everyone from hack drivers to ballet dancers, and though Édouard frequently cavorted merely out of sport, he, unlike Degas, truly loved people. The tendency mystified.

"No," Degas said. "I meant the elegant woman over there, the one who wears her clothing as if she were the Empress Eugénie herself, come back from England to dazzle us with her finery and impeccable taste. And mind you, leave her alone. I spotted her first." Appreciation spilled from him, and though the woman's eyes were too close together and the shape of her nose was wrong, he admired its misbegotten residence on a face with such magnificent cheekbones. Those were positively architectural.

"News, news, Monsieur Degas is taken with a woman. No doubt you will seduce and then discard her. I don't know why you even try anymore; I don't know a woman in Paris who doesn't despise you for your impotent flirtations. This one will throw you out," Édouard said, but he scoured the crowd for the newest object of Degas's regard while simultaneously catching the glances of half a dozen beautiful ladies and fielding enthusiastic assaults from two flirtatious fans. He didn't like being bested by Degas, especially when it came to women, and it disgruntled him now to have to stand by as Degas planned to exert his rather particular form of charm on a woman he might have been interested in, forgetting, again, that Suzanne, his wife, had thrown the breadboard at him that morning for mentioning a gorgeous laundress he had spied toting a basket of clean laundry down the Rue de Rivoli.

"You are too generous," Degas said, but pulled at his wide necktie, ever puzzled by the convoluted twists of Parisian gossip and its ability to confound truth. What had women been whispering about him now? Were his peculiarly focused attentions such an affront to their unstated wishes that they exaggerated? He didn't know, and didn't like the exposure. Gossip, so often his sword, may have turned against him. But he could not keep his eyes off the woman, even in the crowded room, where the plethora of beribboned hats perched on absurd piles of curls were enough obstacle even without the press of the hyperventilating masses going gaga over Édouard's latest triumph. In *Nana* there was story, suggestion, rebellion, and in this portrait, knighted by the jury, there was merely . . . what? *Taste.* Which was the worst insult Degas could think of. No, the mystery woman was not beautiful. He didn't even think she thought herself beautiful, but her strict self-possession appealed for its singularity alone, as if she cared what no one else thought of her. And her posture, *dear God.* It was as if she fancied herself a Grecian statue, all cool marble and elegance.

Suddenly, the woman rose and just as quickly disappeared into the crush, and not even Degas's sudden wail of frustration could produce her.

"Pity," Édouard mocked.

"Oh, shut up."

"You can hunt for her on the streets."

"She is not the streetwalking type."

"Then she should be of little interest to you. A woman who doesn't take off her clothes on command? Who won't let you paint her juicy bits? Why would you even care?"

Degas turned away. He had already spent too much time with Édouard today, whose persistence in exhibiting at the Salon when Degas and the others had long ago refused to participate in the yearly hypocritical disgorgement verged on disloyalty. That Manet remained his friend despite this betrayal was in part due to the aforementioned charm, but also the man's talent, which to this day overwhelmed Degas, even though he told everyone that Manet was so mannered that he never thought of making a brushstroke without thinking of the masters. Yet Manet's work broke rules even while retaining something of the old elegance, a combination so seductive that no one, not even he, could refuse, though he would never inform Manet of his deep regard.

"Return to your admirers, Édouard. They'll be few enough tomorrow."

"You are only jealous. Admit it. You wish your pictures hung in the 'D' room. You wish you weren't such a stubborn soul. You wish you had submitted."

"If only you weren't so deluded, we could truly be friends," Degas said, and after giving Manet a reassuring pat on his shoulder—for Manet always careened between bravado and terror on opening day—he elbowed his way through the vast warren of rooms, past patrons blocking the passageways, clotting the refreshment bars, and making exit a slow endeavor. He pushed through the "D" room, where he had last exhibited in 1870, and into the "C" room, where he wrestled a square of floor space for himself to scan the wall of paintings, searching for the name Mary Cassatt, whose work he'd once seen. He would very much like to see a painting by her again. There had been something so intimate about that portrait he had admired of hers. *Ida*, was it? His friend Tourny was always saying he was going to introduce them, describing Mademoiselle Cassatt as Degas's secret admirer. Tonight, Degas was going to the Tournys' for dinner, and he would ask, finally, to be introduced. Salon be damned, Degas thought. He could use some admiration.

Shame seeped in, grasping at his weakness. Fame? If he wanted fame, he could easily paint the types of pieces the Salon demanded. And perhaps he should. The failure of the de Gas family bank, revealed only upon his father's death three years ago, had left his and all his siblings' finances in shambles. Even the paltry price of today's ticket had debited him further, making the next payment to his father's creditors, among them the Bank of Antwerp, all the more in jeopardy. He had been reduced to counting *sous*. But he considered it a matter of honor that the de Gas family—or Degas, as he had begun to call himself—repay everything. Monthly, he sent off payments, which involved a humiliating, time-consuming trot down to the bank, discussions of wires and amounts, the painful disbursements from his account, leaving a paltry sum only for his rent, his food, his housekeeper's salary, and enough money for his evenings at the café and his Monday night seats at the Opéra Garnier. In order to raise the necessary funds, he had to paint and sell hundreds of fans and turn out dozens of *articles*. His *articles*, his paintings, had become currency. Oh, dear God, the facts of his life were depressing.

And in the corner some farmer in from the country was oohing and ahhing over some beastly little portrait that any fourteen-year-old with half an eye could execute. Most of the work here was dreck. Why hadn't the Prussians remained after they'd won the war? Perhaps they would have infused some discipline into the brains of the ignorant, though he immediately shook off the unpatriotic thought. Dear God, the Prussians and that awful winter. Oh, the cold. The coldest winter Paris had seen in a long time. It was amazing he even had any eyesight left at all. This morning his right eye was particularly bothering him. He dabbed at it with his handkerchief, then looked up and glanced across the room, where the woman he had been admiring was approaching the doorway. Unable to control himself, he raised his hand and called, "Madame! Madame!"

At that moment, a patron sidled alongside him and said, "Monsieur Degas, are you exhibiting? Have you seen Sylvestre's painting? It's enormous."

Degas would not sanction enormity as a value, even more so because Sylvestre had won the Prix du Salon. As a matter of principle, Degas despised awards.

"Shut up," he said, then turned and called, "Madame, madame," but the woman slipped through the crowd as if she couldn't stand to be in the palais one minute longer. Degas shouldered through the chattering tourists and gossiping Parisians, following the gay plume of the woman's hat as it weaved ahead of him in the crowd.

Descending the grand staircase, he dodged arriving patrons, causing at least a dozen to curse at him. Upon reaching the sidewalk, though, he could not find her. She had been swallowed up by the horde of art lovers come to drool over the parade of canvases the idiots at the École had deemed worthy for viewing this year.

This was it, Degas thought. He was losing his mind. He was forty-two years old and he had actually chased a woman onto the street. Perhaps the toll his disastrous finances were taking on him was more than he had estimated. And now his eye was acting up again. The little black hole that had appeared mysteriously one day on his visit to see his brother in New Orleans flickered in his vision, no doubt brought on by the sudden sunlight. He shut his eyes, waiting for the blight to disappear, but when it did not, he swore and set off for the Café de la Nouvelle Athènes.

He did not mind the long walk. He loved the city, loved its poverty and wealth, its ugliness and beauty, its history and future jumbled together in a welter of humanity. But the city was changing; the Paris of old had been a vessel for his life, and Haussmann was erasing it.

At the café, Degas pushed open the glass doors with the familiar absentmindedness of long habit, a gentleman returning home, confident of welcome and comfort, expecting to be greeted by his friends, who often met here in the evening, eager for talk after a day of working alone. But the café was devoid of anyone he knew. Neither Monet nor Renoir nor Caillebotte nor Pissarro was holding forth at a table littered with the remains of a shared meal. No one. Not even Émile Zola was here as he usually was, scribbling in a corner in a notebook.

Jean, the waiter who always took care of them, rushed forward and steered Degas to a table. Degas removed his silk top hat and put it on the chair beside him and ordered a bowl of onion soup and a glass of wine. He ate disconsolately. Lately, Degas thought, his café evenings had felt depleted. His youth was disappearing, or had already disappeared, which he only acknowledged on evenings like this one, when his eye was bothering him. No more the raucous evenings of the Batignolles at the Café Guerbois, when they had been young and life had seemed a far more open field. Degas swallowed the last of the wine, the dregs sour on his tongue, spoiling the piquant aftertaste of the soup. No matter; he was off tonight to the Tournys', who would feed him well.

Outside, Montmartre shimmered in the setting sun. Above the encroaching city, the wind was turning the *moulins*; he could hear the windmills' blades slowly whispering as they traced their eternal paths. Beneath them murmured the tintinnabulation of cattle bells, the trill of a piano keyboard, the hollow click of a key turning in a lock, an escaped sigh of pleasure from a bedroom window. Degas stood transfixed, the chatter from the café, banal and urgent, falling away as he strained to hear the *other*. This aural innocence—the *sonnettes* and a door slamming and amorous silences and the melody of moulin dance halls offering seduction— seemed to Degas something essential. But he feared that no matter how many years he had left before his eyes failed him, he would never be able to capture on canvas the hole these simple sounds tore in his heart tonight. The landscape of yearning was always the next brushstroke away, a vanishing eternity no desire of his, no matter how ardent, could ever produce.

The thought that perhaps this longing had nothing to do with the limits of art, he refused to entertain. And then the *other* receded, and he turned back to the city and his evening engagement just as the city's lights began to flicker on.

Chapter Three

Édouard Manet had spent the first day of the Salon fielding praise from his friends and suffering the criticism of the ignorant, all the while surreptitiously scanning the crowd for Berthe Morisot, his brother Eugène's wife. In the afternoon, he had sent his own wife, Suzanne, away almost as soon as she arrived, as she had grown restive and shrill in the burgeoning crowd. Now, at this hour, four o'clock, most of the patrons at the Palais de l'Industrie had drifted off to the outdoor gardens for tea and glaces at the pretty little tables set up under the chestnut trees, where the ladies could be assured of propriety and the men could be seen to be indulgent before they turned their thoughts to their evening plans. But on this pleasant afternoon, as waiters ferried *thé-complets* and glasses of beer out to the tired patrons scattered under the low flowering branches, a hint of lilac wafting from the garden beds, Édouard strolled among the tables, battling the indignity that forced him to make this display of himself. If Berthe hadn't come to the opening, then she had broken his heart with her unkindness, and if she had come but not made herself known to him, then she had broken his heart yet again.

She claimed survival. He declared her cruel. This was their eternal conversation.

Oddly enough, it had been propriety that had forced the match between Eugène and Berthe, a practical answer to their impossible problem. It was Berthe's mother who had finally decided the matter. Berthe, as her mother had contended in a letter to Berthe's sister, Edma, couldn't spend her life mooning over Édouard when his perfectly acceptable brother—acceptable but regrettable—could offer Berthe at least rescue. And she, Cornélie, wasn't going to live forever, she told Edma, wasn't going to be able to provide Berthe home and protection after she died, which she did two years after Berthe married Eugène in a black dress at the *mairie*, marrying him while she was still mourning her father. Perhaps it had been the surprise of mortality that had nudged Berthe into the practical, or perhaps it had been that he, Édouard, had encouraged the match, had told the weeping Berthe that she needed to be cared for, that a woman of her elevated social standing couldn't be on the loose forever. He repented this cavalier assertion as soon as the words were out of his mouth, but in that moment of betrayal he had tied the knot of his own undoing, having seeded Berthe's mind with a tortuous logic that no amount of his later pleading could undo.

Now, two and a half years later, Édouard strolled the palais grounds, trying to appear contemplative in the sea of society and its show of finery and *arrivisme*, even as his sense of longing grew into an ardent panic. Once again he felt himself unseated. He didn't like to feel this way, but that assertion, he knew, might just be a lie. There was something so enlivening about his persistent boiling need and the secretive glances and the perpetual denial that at times he thought it might be desire he loved and not Berthe.

Berthe had to be here, he thought, in the gardens, or perhaps hiring a cab. It seemed impossible that she could hide herself, even in this crowd, for she looked like no one else in Paris. Her beauty hypnotized: a bounty of raven hair pinned into soft waves that fell about her face, haunting black eyes that seduced despite her natural reserve, and a complexion so pale it startled everyone. People had been known to gasp when they first met her, an occurrence so embarrassing that she avoided parties and evenings where she might not know some of the guests. But he couldn't find her. He made one last sweep of the grounds, hoping that his gaze appeared bored enough to convince anyone who knew him that he was merely exhausted from the day's feverish throngs. And he was tired. His legs were bothering him. All day he had nursed them, shifting his weight from heel to aching heel, trying to assuage the dull numbness that had appeared from nowhere. The doctor had recommended water treatments, which his wife was eager for him to take because it meant a summer in Austria, which suited her idea of how a summer ought to be spent, but Édouard did not like leaving Paris, even though he had once begged Berthe to.

Placing his hat on his head, he limped toward the Champs-Élysées and the long cab line, where he hoped he might find her. He would feign astonishment, offer his protection, which, in public, she would have to take, for fear of fostering even more rumors. But the snaking queue yielded nothing of Berthe, so he waited for his own cab to the Nouvelle-Athènes, where he hoped Degas, if he were still there, might favor him with more of his condemnation regarding his disloyalty and ill-placed aspirations, effectively stripping Berthe from his mind.

Berthe Morisot was seated at a little table quite distant from the palais doors when she saw Édouard weaving between the tables. She opened her parasol to hide her face and only lowered it when, peeking from behind its lace ruffle, she observed him hobbling toward the Champs-Élysées. She had worn a new dress for the opening, one he didn't know, and she was grateful that her little disguise had worked. This morning, Eugène had wished her well, pretending that he didn't know where she was going, saying how glad he was that they would go together to the Salon tomorrow, and ignoring the pink heat radiating from her severe cheekbones, which he had long ago noticed appeared only on certain occasions, usually Thursday nights, when they saw Édouard at his mother's evening.

And it was Eugène's spousal generosity—or ignorance—that had kept Berthe from Édouard today, when she had dared to arrive unescorted to the Salon. Hiding behind a fan, jostled but concealed by the throngs, she had watched Édouard and Degas from across the crowded "M" room, alert to Édouard's distinctive face, uncertain as to whether he was disappointed or relieved that she wasn't there. If Édouard only knew his brother's forbearance, he, too, might feel ashamed, but she had long ago learned that shame was not in Édouard's vocabulary. The little dance she played with Eugène—he ignoring her confusion, she pretending not to be confused—made up their *gentile* life together, one of agreement, placidity, and resignation. Some days she thought she was winning. Hours could go by and she wouldn't think of Édouard, but then some shameful vestige of the old passion would revive—prompted by what, she never knew; rapacious justice, perhaps—and the desire would spirit her into the past, into the months before she married Eugène, when a different future had still been possible.

She did not know what had possessed her to come to the Salon unescorted. Now she would have to walk home alone, a breach of propriety that would have made her mother faint, were she still alive. But Berthe had traveled a long road, one her observant mother had discerned and that had led to the maternal machinations that had ended in Berthe's respectable, if less than satisfying marriage.

Berthe gathered her things and began her circumspect stroll up the Champs-Élysées, her shoes pinching her tired feet, the sunshine falling on the parasol she unfurled to avoid unwanted male attention. When she reached her apartment, housed in a grand new building on the Avenue d'Eylau, where she and Eugène had moved after her mother had died, Berthe pulled off her gloves and unpinned her hat and thought, I have found a good man who will forgive me anything, even the gossip of others. Even the truth. What, then, was love? The incessant whisper of passion, or the tedious murmur of caring? The ragged tear at your heart, or the gentle caress that rendered you safe? Perhaps there was no one thing that was love. She would like to know, though, if there were, to quash uncertainty, to understand which way her life had turned out. What was true? If she had risked everything and run away with Édouard, would she be happy now? Or, in choosing Eugène had she gained a happiness she did not yet appreciate?

Her mother's lifelong complaint: *You don't know how to be happy, darling.*

But, Mother, she always asked, *what is happiness?*

Chapter Four

My dear Mademoiselle Cassatt,

I have heard through the inevitable gossip that the Salon jury turned down your paintings this year. I propose something, or rather someone, to cheer you. May we call at your studio this afternoon, perhaps at three, which is early, but I hope after you have finished your work for the day? You will be pleased, I believe, though if you are not, forgive this admirer for hoping to lift your spirits by making a small offering to assuage your sadness. My wife says that I am being forward, but I am an old man now and believe I am permitted to take such liberties if it means the happiness of someone I hold dear. Don't forget that I promised your mother when we were all in Belgium that I would look after you.

Forgive my reticence about my gift, but I do love a surprise.

Respond by return post as to your acquiescence regarding my unforgivable cheek. It is well meant, my dear.

Amitiés

M. Tourny

Chapter Five

When the door opened to Mademoiselle Cassatt's studio and it was she who greeted him—the woman from the Salon, the one he had made a fool of himself over—Degas summoned his Parisian soul, relying on the French masculine misapprehension that women were, above all, expendable.

"Dear God," he whispered to himself, enough to make Tourny glance at him and murmur, "Not today, Degas."

Tourny had warned him of his affection for this *américaine*, this foreigner whose accent he described as abominable, but whose artistry made up for the inexcusable deficit. It was Degas's duty as a friend, Tourny had said, to squelch his tendency toward mockery and find it in himself to be, for once, charming. Degas thought this preemptive remonstrance supremely unfair, given that he had agreed to come—was, in fact, eager to meet the woman who'd painted that stunning portrait he'd admired four years ago. He still did not know how she had found a way to convey in a pair of eyes, in the tilt of a head, in the rendering of flesh, an inner life of such profound sorrow and tenderness that he had felt envy upon looking at it. That she and the woman before him were one and the same seemed an impossible gift from the heavens, heavens he would never paint and didn't believe in, but a gift all the same, one he uttered silent thanks for now in case he was mistaken. Today, instead of the simple blouse and skirt she had worn at the Salon, Mademoiselle

Cassatt wore a viridian green dress of elegant cut and line; not a Worth, as far as Degas could tell, but an excellent copy nonetheless, one that highlighted her heavenly posture. Standing in her doorway, she held herself with the grace of a dancer onstage, an attitude so appealing that his hand instinctively searched his pocket for a pencil to sketch her.

"Here is my surprise for you, my dear," Tourny said, taking Mary's hands and kissing her cheeks. "May I present Monsieur Degas? Monsieur Degas, Mademoiselle Cassatt."

Rarely did such moments of pleasure occur for Tourny anymore. His age had crept up on him. He had met Mademoiselle Cassatt a few years ago in Antwerp, where she had spent several months copying Rubens in the museum there. Madame Tourny and Mary's mother, who had come to Europe to accompany Mary to the Belgian city, had become fast friends while Mary and Monsieur Tourny spent time in the museums refining their touch and sight. Then, he had felt young, but just a few evenings ago he had reached for a glass of wine and discovered that his hands, with decades of granite and marble flecks wedged into their crevices and cracks, were no longer deft but frail. Overnight, this had happened. He hadn't been paying attention to the wicked passage of time, its selfish stealth. So it was a pleasure now—a lark, really—to introduce these two artists, a moment reminiscent of his youth, when whim and not deliberation had connected lives. At dinner the other night, how alive he had felt when Degas insisted that he introduce him to the American artist. Yes, Tourny said, he would be thrilled to, and told Degas where Mademoiselle Cassatt lived, even as his wife glared at him across the table. His wife was fond of saying that Degas growled like a bear. They had known Degas since he was nineteen and lived with them while he copied the masters in Italy. That boy was now a man in his forties, more than capable of deciphering his wife's look, but Degas graciously ignored it and instead ruminated at the dinner table that it was odd that he and Mademoiselle Cassatt hadn't met before, considering that they lived so close, just a block apart. And Paris was a city of artists, he said;

on the streets in the morning, wasn't it true that one saw nothing but art students in their rough blue suits hurrying in the dawn chill to their glass-roofed ateliers, their easels and paint boxes clasped under their arms, a kind of starving eagerness about them?

"Monsieur Degas?" Mary said now, her hand lingering in Monsieur Tourny's. "Monsieur Degas is my gift?"

"Mademoiselle Cassatt." Degas dipped his head in an aristocratic bow. He would not reveal that he had seen her at the Salon. He would summon discipline; after a certain age, it was all one had left. "Monsieur Tourny says you are an admirer."

"As am I," Tourny interjected, wishing Degas could have at least said something more courteous, even if it was only a dull recitation of his pleasure at meeting her.

Outside, the clopping of the omnibus horses on the Boulevard de Clichy funneled down the narrow Rue de Laval. Mary tried to reconcile this commonplace noise with the surprise of Monsieur Degas in her living room. Degas was nothing like Mary had imagined. He had a narrow face, round, droopy eyes, receding brownish hair heavily streaked with gray, and pale cheeks blotched pink above a groomed white beard. He had a funny way of tilting his head and staring, too, as if he were concentrating very hard, though even with this particular affectation he could have passed by her at least a dozen times on the street and she wouldn't have noticed him. She was fairly certain that he was older than she by at least a decade.

Finally, Mary's Pennsylvanian upbringing emerged. Trying not to reveal the tidal wave of nervousness that washed over her, she said, "Do come inside."

Degas thought her studio beautifully appointed. It seemed to be a combination of parlor and atelier: Turkish rugs carpeted the walls, four elegant chairs surrounded a dining table, two bergères of gilt and green were nestled in a far corner. In a drying stand, overlapping canvases in varying forms of finish composed a colored wainscot. An easel angled toward the window. Though crowded, the space was uncluttered, unlike Degas's rooms, in which he bobbed around like a cork, trying to find his work amid the piles of canvases and drawings. Here, only a chest of drawers betrayed any sense of disorder, spilling over with tubes of paint, numerous brushes, a tin of walnut oil, another of turpentine, a clean palette, and assorted jars, knives, and rags. It was a disciplined spill, though, of tidy proportions. On a coat tree hung her painter's white smock, barely streaked with color. Degas smelled turpentine in the room, though the windows were open to the narrow street. The sunny afternoon showed signs of promise that the dreary spring had finally ended, though one could never be certain in Paris. Degas had half a mind to flee to Italy, but then he remembered his money troubles and that he couldn't flee to Italy, and he felt again, for half a moment, how unfair the world was.

Tourny, who had removed his top hat, turned and took Degas's and handed them both to a hovering maid, who disappeared down a hallway with them, a small dog nipping at her heels. Tourny looked from one to the other of the new acquaintances, waiting, but the silence in the room confounded his expectations. Mary Cassatt was not her usual self-possessed self; she had not even offered them seats. Degas, ever the witty, clever man, had lost his tongue. Perhaps, Tourny thought, he had been too coy, but he had wanted to surprise her. Perhaps his wife had been right again. *Why keep Mademoiselle Cassatt in the dark?* she had asked. *She'll need armor to make it through tea with that man. You know how disagreeable he can be.*

"Perhaps we should all sit?" Tourny said, drifting toward the round dining table set for tea, but Degas seemed not to hear. He remained as rigid as a peasant summoned to see the emperor, and Mademoiselle Cassatt, who always seemed empress-like to Tourny, displayed none of her smooth grace. Tourny wondered how he could have miscalculated so badly. The maid entered with the steaming teapot, but Mary still did not invite them to table.

"I saw your most recent exhibition on the Rue le Peletier, Monsieur

Degas," Mary said, speaking slowly. Lately she had become self-conscious about her French. Her vocabulary and grammar were excellent, but her accent seemed to make everyone cringe. Often she had to repeat things to be understood.

Degas shifted his gaze. "Then perhaps you would do me the honor of showing me some of your work? Anything you might wish to show me? Anything at all?"

"Why don't we begin instead by having tea?" Tourny said. Such a misguided beginning, though he ought to have known. Degas never behaved in the way one would wish. Tourny herded them both to the table and poured a cup for Mary, who took it from him and then set it down, while Degas ignored the cup Tourny held out to him. Tourny gave up and took it for himself.

"Your work," Degas said. "The paintings the Salon rejected, perhaps."

"I say now, Degas," Tourny said. "How can you ask her this?"

Mary looked from one man to the other. "You told him, Monsieur Tourny?"

Tourny sighed. "It was well meant, my dear."

"I have not come out of pity, Mademoiselle Cassatt," Degas said. "I have little pity for anyone, least of all you."

Mary had hardly slept in the past two weeks. She spent whole nights trying to decide whether or not to leave Paris, to give in to her father's desire that she renounce the life she had been hoping to live. Last night, rereading his letter one last time, she decided to book her steamship tickets this afternoon at the booking office in the Gare du Nord; she spent part of the morning calculating the price of the one-way ticket, first cabin, intending to drown herself in comfort. An added incentive was that the steamer *Mosul* was sailing, which she heard was more stable than some, and she was hoping its steadiness might stave off her usual debilitating seasickness, possibly alleviating the pangs of her failure. But then Tourny had written this morning and now Degas was standing before her, asking to see her work. Why was it that life's true moments never announced themselves? Why did they pounce dressed as a quotidian date for tea?

"Monsieur Degas, I need to ask you a question," Mary said. "Do you believe that talent is a gift? That God bestows it on some artists and not on others?"

"Gift? Rubbish. What have those idiots on the jury done to you? Art does not arise from a well of imaginary skill, obtained by dint of native ability. The sublime is a result of discipline. Art is earned by hard work, by the study of form, by obsessive revision. Only then are you set free. Only then can you *see*."

"Then you do not invoke the divine when you work?" Mary asked.

"The gift you speak of is nothing but your own devotion to attention, to deliberation, to study. Only this will help you transcend your own measly abilities and create something extraordinary, something that doesn't depend on you at all."

Mary was suddenly aware of every bone in her body, the inexpert way she occupied space, the way she no longer fit in this room where she had lived and worked so hard. "But I have studied for years. I have never achieved transcendence."

"Tell me the truth, Mademoiselle Cassatt. You indulge in doubt, but you have had such a moment. I know you have."

Tourny was staring. He believed he could get up, put down his tea-cup, ask the maid for his hat, and leave, and neither of them would notice. He could even slam the door and they wouldn't hear it. Outside, a fish-monger was crying, "Haddock!" and a woman was calling to him from her open window across the street, but neither Degas nor Mademoiselle Cassatt seemed to notice.

"But the eye," Mary said.

"The mind is the eye. It can be trained." Degas turned his head then, looking at her out of the corner of his eye. His features, less impressive on first meeting, now seemed dignified and refined. Mary could see that he had not been a beautiful man in his youth. His eyes were too closely set above his long nose, but this defect was fleeting—registered, then forgotten.

Across the street, the woman leaned out of her window, her fleshy arms draped over the windowsill, the tall shutters rendering her in shade.

"*Combien?*" she called.

"*Un franc, madame,*" returned the bodiless voice.

The woman withdrew into her rooms, presumably to descend to the street to buy the expensive fish. Tourny marveled: the banal and the ethereal, juxtaposed, separated by only a narrow lane.

"We could argue forever, mademoiselle, or you could just let me see your work," Degas said.

Degas was studying her—judging her—before he had even seen a thing; gauging, Mary thought, the quality of her mind not by her rejected canvases, but by whether or not she would expose herself to him. The canvases were still wrapped in their paper and secured with twine. The carter hired to fetch them from the Palais de l'Industrie had dumped them inside the front door of the building. She had returned from a date at Abigail Alcott's to discover them left for anyone to have carried away. She had hauled them up the stairs, set them in the corner, and tried to forget them.

She cut the twine with a pair of scissors, the tight weave fraying before it gave way with a snap. The subsequent tearing of the paper sounded like the earth opening beneath her feet. She turned away because she did not want to see Degas's reaction; she deserved at least this last protection. While he studied her canvases, she fixed her gaze out the window, where she could see her neighbor gutting a fish on the windowsill, throwing the offal into the gutter below.

"You hate these, don't you?" Degas said.

Tourny rose from his chair. His wife would have his head. "I apologize, my dear Mary."

"Don't you see?" Degas said. "Of course she hates them. She has all the tricks right. She has confined her expression to the academic values. The background is dark, the figure classically beatific, the dimensions beautifully flat. In order to paint these, she laced her heart up in a tight Salon corset so that she couldn't even breathe." He turned again to Mary. "You couldn't breathe, could you? You were afraid the whole time you were painting."

Mary thought he might as well have said that he had seen her at her bath, had seen the imperfections of her figure, had spied the most personal things about her. Instead, he was undressing her mind and rummaging around in the pleats and folds of her brain, a voyeurism more intimately invasive than any physical violation would have been.

"But just there," Degas said, leaning into one of the canvases, his finger hovering above the bodice of the dress, "is where you strayed. The loose brushstrokes, the play in the rendering of the silk, the way you captured the light. That's what the jury hated. That's why you were rejected. And it's the best thing in the painting."

Mary nearly buckled under Degas's praise. She reached for the back of a chair.

"I am not in the habit of flattery, mademoiselle," Degas said, "but I will tell you that I have admired your work for a long time. I saw a painting of yours once that has never left me." Not, he thought, just for the way the lace mantilla in the portrait shimmered with light and color, but for the thoughtful face it framed. *C'est vrai*, he remembered thinking at the time. *This is true.* "Tell me, would you like to join our group, Mademoiselle Cassatt? Exhibit with us next year? You might find a home with us."

"Exhibit with you?" Mary said. "Next year?"

"You will no longer have to subject yourself to the parsimonious Salon jury; you will paint what you wish to paint; you will show what you wish to show."

Mary looked from Degas to her paintings, which now seemed the muted muddle of all her hopes. "I accept," she said.

Tourny uttered a little gasp.

"Ah. Good. You will see, mademoiselle; you will see," Degas said, and sat down at the table and took a sip of tea.

Chapter Six

After taking leave of Mademoiselle Cassatt, Tourny and Degas walked down the narrow Rue de Laval in the direction of Degas's studio on the Rue Frochot.

"Take care with her, Edgar," Tourny said. "She is not French; she is American, with American values and a mother and father who care about her. Unlike the other women you violate with your attentions, this one is defenseless."

"Don't be absurd," Degas said. "You've been listening to rumors again. And she is not at all defenseless, just pummeled a bit."

"I mean it, Edgar. I made her mother certain promises in Belgium, and I intend to follow them."

"You completely mistake her. That American is perfectly capable of taking care of herself. Did you not read her carriage? She is made of steel."

"She is both vulnerable and serious and I do not want her hurt."

"If you didn't want me to know her, then why did you introduce us?"

Why, indeed? Tourny tried to think now of why he had thought this was a good idea but he couldn't recall his reasons. Not all connections were good ones, and though he loved Edgar, his artist's temper could sometimes turn savage.

"Be kind," Tourny said.

The problem, Degas thought, with cultivating a reputation as a man of severe wit was that people believed it. He did not mean to batter; he traveled around Paris with all the good intentions of genuine interest, but people could be so *disappointing*. What did people do with their intelligence? It mystified him.

"She is a fellow artist, Tourny."

"And you don't want to take her to dinner?"

"No."

"Nor to bed?"

"This one wouldn't go to bed."

"But you won't ask?"

"Dear God, Tourny, I haven't gone insane."

Recently, Tourny had heard that Degas had bribed an attendant at the Saint-Sulpice baths to let him observe women at their ablutions through a peephole, and that many of his pictures—the awkward poses, the absolute honesty of their unflattering positions—had been sketched in that dark wall space while the women, unknowing, washed themselves, believing themselves to be alone. Tourny supposed the ugly rumor had begun because Degas was fond of saying he liked to look through keyholes. No doubt Degas had been deliberately misleading, to titillate, but he didn't really know. Edgar wasn't puerile, or at least Tourny didn't believe so. But he was in many ways unknowable, unpredictable.

"I've heard things, Degas. But this one is special, you understand?"

"You wound me, Tourny. You of all people know who I am."

Tourny's steady gaze turned back up the street toward Mademoiselle Cassatt's flat. He wanted to believe Degas.

Degas cocked his head, his right eyelid drooping as he examined his friend. "I need to ask permission, then, to talk to her? To speak to her of the everyday? To ask her how she is, what she thinks of the new minister from the United States?"

Tourny put on his hat. "I will see you soon."

"Or maybe," Degas said, following, "whether the weather is treating her well? Has she been to the Opéra? What kind of soap does she use? No, perhaps that's too personal. Who is her butcher? Am I allowed to ask her that?"

"Oh dear God, you can be a bore," Tourny said, glancing across the Boulevard de Clichy, hoping to dine in peace at the Nouvelle Athènes before he returned to his afternoon of polishing his latest sculpture, a bust from a piece of marble so glorious that its pink undertones shimmered with every swipe of his polishing cloth.

"I am never boring," Degas said. "That, my friend, is a far worse insult than all the other injustices you just flung my way."

"I apologize."

"But still you must pay for your insults."

"Don't you have work to do?"

Degas stopped dead in the street. And without even saying good-bye, he hurried up the Rue Frochot to his rooms.

In her studio, her little Brussels griffon at her feet, Mary Cassatt picked up a palette knife and stared at the Salon canvases upon which she had lavished so much hope. During the past twelve years, she had felt at home nowhere, not back in the States, not in Paris, not even in the sunlit hills of Tuscany, where she had studied for a year after the second time she'd left Philadelphia, before she'd returned to Paris. Hers had been a peripatetic, self-crafted education in search of an excellence that had eluded her most earnest efforts. At least Degas had not said *that* word. Her father had said it once. *You are so earnest, my dear.* As if to aspire to excellence was a capital offense. Earnestness carried with it the scent of amateur devotion, the shame of which had dogged her from the first moment her father had uttered that insufferable word.

Her return home to Philadelphia after she had first moved to Europe had been forced on her because the Prussians had begun bombing Paris. She'd lived in Europe for five years, cobbling together an education after the ateliers of Paris had disappointed her. She studied in Ecouen, outside

Paris, painted in the Alps, and finally, accompanied by her mother, studied in Rome, always dragging with her her paint box and easels. But the Philadelphia homecoming in 1870, rather than being a triumph, had turned out to be an endurance test of head tilts, nods, and condescension forced on her by her parents and their friends.

Well, at least you've spent some time in Europe. And you have some finished pictures. Bravo! I could never have done that. You should be proud of that accomplishment, my dear.

Or, *Oh, would you draw me? I'd love to have a little sketch to hang in my bedroom.*

And she'd complied. Like a circus animal, a trained seal. In despair, she'd fled to Chicago with her work after Goupil's in New York had not been able to sell it and the galleries in Philadelphia had refused even to hang it. One night in Chicago she awoke to screams and smoke and a maid pounding on her door; the city was engulfed in a conflagration so fast, so hot, that she'd only had time to escape down the stairs of her hotel with a coat over her nightdress and a handkerchief pressed to her nose. Her artwork was irretrievable, locked in the jewelry store that had agreed to display it, and as she ran, she imagined the paint bubbling and boiling off the canvases. She had avoided the Prussian army lobbing shells into Paris, but halfway around the globe she was running through raining cinders, gasping for breath, jostled by crowds who ferried their mattresses and trunks and crates of squawking chickens while she had left her work—her work!—to the omnivorous scarlet and purple flames painting a vicious midnight sunset. People had grabbed her elbows and carried her along eastward to Lake Michigan's edge, where drifting embers singed their clothes, set the mattresses on fire, and drove them all across the railroad tracks and into the lake to splash water into their eyes.

If only she had thought to capture that memory on canvas, she would not now be staring at canvases dull enough to make Degas wonder if she had been *afraid* when she'd painted them. True fear had been running through the streets of Chicago. But what she feared now was that he had diagnosed instead a deficit of imagination, a much worse diagnosis than fear, one he had probably been far too considerate to point out. One she believed might be the true problem of her work. The true problem of *her*.

Would she ever truly see?

She stared at her canvases, remembering her blunders, the inadequate corrections, the agony over proportion, the francs and francs paid to the unremarkable models, the hours invested, the renunciation of friends in order to work. A dedication as earnest as her father had surmised. She shut her eyes and opened them again, and thought, *Truly, these paintings are not bad. They are even good.* She could say this without irony, as someone educated enough to see that she had employed the academic techniques she had learned, had rendered light, shadow, expression, emotion, all that she had been striving for. No one, not even she, could say that she hadn't achieved technical competence.

But transcendence?

She fingered the palette knife. What care she took with her instruments. How faithfully she cleaned them. Meticulous is what her father had called her, a rare admiring comment.

She stabbed the first of the two paintings, slashing its center. Then she picked it up and ripped the cloth from the tacks. Slowly, methodically, she tore the painting into smaller and smaller pieces. The second picture, with its thicker paint, took longer. Flakes of pigment floated like colored ash to the floor. She had destroyed canvases before, but none this good. She squinted at the ruin: All her work was now a formless collage of color and light.

Scraps of the destroyed artwork clung to her silk dress. Mary brushed them off and called for the maid to bring the broom. She took it from her, swept the pile of her past into the dustpan, and dumped her work into the trash without explaining anything to her maid, Anna, who watched open-mouthed from the corner and wished, beyond anything, that her mistress would have given her the canvases, for she couldn't remember ever having seen anything so beautiful in her life.

Chapter Seven

Days later, Berthe Morisot alighted from the omnibus at the Gare
Saint Lazare. She had written Édouard a note requesting a private
audience because she needed to tell him something in person. At least she
told herself that it needed to be said in person, that a mere letter wouldn't
do, that friends did this sort of thing all the time, that the fact that she
missed him had nothing to do with this sudden need to see him privately.
The note was a necessary precaution because Édouard loved to have visitors while he painted, gossiping as he worked, his paintbrush flying as fast
as his tongue, entertainer as much as artist, beloved and revered by both
the demimonde and the erudite writers who came to see what the irreverent Édouard Manet might say while he painted the portrait of some half-
clad girl or actor. But Berthe did not want to be discovered in his studio
by anyone or to share him with anyone else, either. There were already
enough whispers. In his review of the impressionist exhibition at the Rue
le Peletier, Karl Huysmans had accused her of being Édouard's pupil
when she never had been, and Albert Wolff had written that she suffered
from a frenzied mind, possibly from her close association with the rebellious Édouard Manet. Berthe's husband, furious, challenged Wolff to a
duel, but Wolff apologized and Berthe persuaded Eugène to accept this
unusual concession from the famously pompous critic. The world had
cultivated an opinion of her relationship with her brother-in-law, and today she did not want to feed the ravenous dogs.

Berthe circumnavigated the train station and headed toward the Rue de Saint-Pétersbourg. Below, to her left, an open bay of tracks extruded from the roofed sheds of the station. Locomotive steam billowed in the cool morning air. The ubiquitous rumble of the engines frothing to be gone always made it feel as if a subterranean monster were going to consume this section of Paris, and some days Berthe wished that it would, that something would prevent her from ever alighting at this station again to make the walk she traced in her sleep at night. But the familiar path to 4 Rue de Saint-Pétersbourg, though less than half a kilometer, did not clear her head. She had made many such resolutions in the past, firm, clear resolutions of inarguable good sense. But the memory of her dead mother's despair proved futile, gossip she tried to ignore, and not even Édouard's expression of satisfied triumph when she knocked on the door could dissuade her from entering.

"I needed you at the Salon," Édouard said, after opening the carved door that marked for Berthe the entrance to both heaven and hell.

"I came the second day with Eugène. You know I did," she said, relieved that Édouard had not seen her the first day. She lived by these little lies of omission, withholding the fullest truth, preserving the delicate gauze of her tenuous life. She removed her gloves and laid them on her purse, which she had set on the table by the door. Little had changed since she'd last been here. The long red curtain still decorated the high far wall; the brocade armchairs for Édouard's guests still occupied every corner not taken up with drying racks and supplies. The piano occupied center stage, next to a freestanding cheval glass. Paintings massed together hung in Victorian splendor on every inch of wall: Degases, Renoirs, even hers, a small oil that he had hung on the line. A dozen Turkish rugs were scattered about, giving the place a rakish air, even among the marble tables and crystal lamps that made Édouard's studio feel less like a workplace and more like an opulent café.

"I meant the first day," Édouard said.

"You knew I couldn't come alone," Berthe said. "Besides, you weren't showing your *Nana*." That painting, after its summary rejection and subsequent residence in a shop window on the Boulevard des Capucines, now hung on his wall among all the other pictures he was unable to sell, infamous canvases that exuded rebellion and panache, *Olympia* and *The Luncheon on the Grass* and *The Balcony*, for which she had modeled. That painting was hung high up, as if to simulate the balcony it pictured, and Berthe's painted eyes followed her now as she made her way to a chair to sit down.

"I didn't show her because the jury didn't admit her."

"She is so beautiful," Berthe said.

"You have come to compliment me? For this you requested privacy? Or have you come to tell me that you love me still, no matter that the Salon hates me? Eva Gonzalès refuses to come to see me now. I think she believes me too radical to associate with. Soon, I shall be all alone." Eva had been Édouard's student, and in Berthe's eyes had already spent far too much time with Édouard.

"Please, Édouard, no one believes that you will ever be alone."

His sleepy, smiling eyes were enough to undo her even without the reddish-blond curls that crowned his head like a halo. Berthe longed to touch those curls. Perhaps it had not been a good idea to come to see him; she already lived in an odd world in which she pretended that her husband, who looked like Édouard, was Édouard, a world in which she prayed that one day Édouard's soul would miraculously surface in the body of her husband.

It was three years ago, the summer that her father had died, that Berthe and her mother went north to Dieppe to spend July and August at the beach in the breezes of the North Atlantic. Édouard had been ordered to stay away, to not even visit for a day, on pain of serious maternal rage. Instead, it was Eugène and his mother who joined Berthe and her mother at the idyllic seaside haven. There was a problem to be solved, and the mothers, apparently tired of the dallying of their misdirected progeny, planned to solve it in an imposed exile disguised as a summer retreat. That Eugène looked like his older brother was only to the advantage, Berthe's mother told her, a boon that would go a long way toward concealing Eugène's deeper problems, not the least of which was that he had no profession and lived off his family's money. But she declared the gangly young man with minimal prospects to be the single unmarried answer to Berthe's marital question. Paris, she scolded, was filled with men, and yet somehow Berthe, admired for a Spanish beauty that no Parisienne could rival, had failed. Not to fall in love, but to fall in love with someone *possible*. So she arranged for Berthe and Eugène to be much thrown together, aided by glorious weather, a circumstance that encouraged long hours outside at twin easels, where Eugène, lacking talent, praised Berthe's, and made good use of their unchaperoned isolation.

At least, Madame Morisot said, the young man knew when and how to take advantage of privacy.

For Berthe, the marriage had been not a capitulation, but rather a subsidence. Something over which she did not exert even the slightest bit of will. She simply would do as her mother wanted because all the light had gone out of the world. But before she married Eugène, she enacted one last rebellion. On their return to Paris, Édouard declared that he wanted to paint her one last time, and Berthe acquiesced. Every morning in October she left her mother's house on the Rue Guichard in Passy to catch the omnibus. Her mother's warning screed followed her out of the house and down the still-countrified lane. "Haven't you made enough of a fool of yourself over that man? What will Eugène think if you continue? Will you jeopardize everything?" It wasn't enough, it seemed, that Berthe had given in and finally agreed to marry. No, her mother wanted her to be happy about it too, the insistence upon which seemed to Berthe to be more than unfair.

The dress Édouard chose for the portrait was black bombazine, with a sharp V-neck that showed off her décolletage, unlike the dress she had worn when he had first painted her four years earlier. That dress had been as virginal as a bride's, high-necked, white, embroidered with miniature rosebuds. This dress was nothing less than brothel chic, fit to be worn in public only by a café chanteuse.

When Édouard presented it to her on the first day of the sitting, he said, "I went to your dressmaker. She had your measurements."

"Bombazine? The cloth of mourning?"

"You are in mourning for your father."

Berthe spent the sittings reclined on the divan, holding the pose though her muscles ached to move. This repose was his last gift to her, Édouard said, before she ruined her life.

She wasn't ruining her life, she said, she was trying to find it, though she held her expression as he wielded his palette and attacked the canvas.

Édouard's plump wife often swept in with a market basket over her arm, always knocking over stacks of blank canvases in her haste. After relaying some triviality about her youngest brother, Léon, she would venture, "That is quite a dress, Berthe. Whomever did you persuade to knock off such a tarty thing?"

Édouard would roar at her to get out and Suzanne would leave, but not without an accusing glance over her shoulder at Berthe.

Sometimes, Suzanne would sneak in and stand quietly in the corner, but Édouard had a feral sense about her, and after a short while he would mutter, without turning around, "What is it?" and Suzanne would claim that Léon wanted to ride to the *bois* with him, to which Édouard would always answer, "Tomorrow." Suzanne frequently slammed the door on the way out, and Édouard would sigh, "Why does she care *now*?"

Berthe said nothing. Édouard believed that his flirtations had no effect on anyone, and that his serial desertions, for her, for Eva Gonzalès, for Méry Laurent, were none of Suzanne's concern, or Berthe's. Berthe's eyes often drifted to the door as she tried to recall how many times she had fled a room, a party, a gathering, the gnawing grip of humiliation and shame hobbling her. A hundred times she had sworn that she would turn away from him, that she would never again allow him to charm her.

"Lift your chin," he would say.

She would.

"Higher. Now look at me that way you did that one time. After the ball at the Opéra, when we had so much trouble with your dress."

"That look is no longer for you."

"My dear Berthe, that look will always be for me."

"I hate you."

"There. Just so."

And so their days had gone.

Now Édouard leaned on the table, his long, languid body lazy as always, waiting. He had had to wait for so few women in his life that he affected patience as a matter of courtesy. "Where does Eugène think you are?"

"Please don't be vulgar."

"Why did you come?" he asked. "What do you want?"

"I came to tell you not to give up," Berthe said. At the Salon, from across the room, she had seen the dismay on his face as the acclaim his portrait failed to garner instead washed over Sylvestre, who had won the Prix du Salon. The crowds marched past, indifferent, as Édouard's manner escalated from ebullience to bravado, teetered on hilarity, then crashed into melancholy sorrow once Degas had left him. She had wanted to run to him, had wanted to hold him up, to stand by his side, to declare to passersby the damage their ignorance was causing. "People don't understand," she said, "what they see."

He started then, all semblance of composure fading. His gaze fixed on hers. "Ah, my Berthe, if only it was you I came home to."

"She is beautiful, your *Nana* is; she is fearless. You should be the same. Don't let them say things that hurt you. They don't know what they are doing. Or perhaps they do and say it only to hurt you. I don't know. But they are wrong, in every case. There is no greater artist than you alive today."

"You are alive."

"I am not you."

"I could never have painted *Nana* if it weren't for your painting of the girl in the cheval glass. Such command of light you have. Such delicate glimmers of beauty."

"You are the one who shines."

"My love—"

"I'm going now." She picked up her purse and gloves.

"But no one is coming today."

"Please," she said, holding up her hand. Sometimes, all it took was a mere glance from him for her to surrender, but she had made resolutions.

"Then let me walk you."

"No."

"I will hire you a cab."

"No."

"Don't tell me you came on the omnibus again. Your departed mother will haunt me if I allow you to travel like that. To say nothing of Eugène."

"I'm caged enough as it is, Édouard. Let me go."

"I looked for you, that first day," he said. "I needed you. No other."

One hand on the doorknob, she turned to face him. "I was there."

"I don't believe you."

"Degas chased after a woman."

A ghost of a smile broke across Édouard's face. "You *were* there," he said.

She nodded. And was gone.

Chapter Eight

The day after Degas met Mary Cassatt, he made a visit to his oculist, Dr. Maurice Perrin, at 45 Rue Saint-Placide, and suffered the usual interminable delay before the doctor called him in from the waiting room. For days and days, the little black hole had floated in the center of his vision. He had talked to it, begged it to go away, then ignored it, thinking perhaps he was conjuring the thing from fear and that if he paid it no attention, it would disappear and give him back the clarity he needed. But at Mademoiselle Cassatt's, the hole had sometimes obscured her head. He had had to turn to look at her out of the corner of his eye.

The doctor took a seat and opened his notes. "Which eye, again?"

"My right. Don't you remember?" How many times had he told the man that his problem had begun long ago, even before he had turned twenty? It was the cold, he had told the doctor. When he had first moved out of his father's house, he'd rented an attic atelier that leaked rain and cold on the winter nights. And then six years ago, defending Paris on the artillery lines during the bone-chilling winter of the Prussian War, the incessant cold and wind had numbed his eyes. Surely the two together had damaged something?

"I have many patients, monsieur," the doctor said.

"Light hurts my eyes too," Degas said. "The light problem started in New Orleans."

"Light and a black hole?"

Degas considered the possibility that the doctor might think he was crazy. Even to him, the affliction sounded contradictory. He suffered from dark, yet he could not tolerate light. And this beastly plague was such an inconstant caller. If he could only discern a pattern to its visits, he might discover the cause and find the solution, but the thing never announced itself or behaved in an orderly fashion. He didn't even know what to call it. The black sun. The opposite of light. An eclipse of sight. The hole stole everything from him: time, sight, confidence. He might vanish into it, if the hole had its way.

On the wall above the doctor's head floated a diagram of an eye.

"Such an elegant invention, the eye," Degas said.

"Not too elegant if it fails, is it?" the doctor said. Once, the doctor had held an eye in his palm, the cool jelly-like grape with its tangle of tissue and tentacles that communicated with the brain. The retina, the macula. What did all these layers do? Names certainly didn't help, not the painter, at least. The doctor could not impress the painter with anatomy alone. The painter wanted clear vision.

The doctor conducted an exam, first separating the painter's eyelids at the window, so that he could better peer at the conjunctiva. He dropped belladonna into each eye, lit a table lamp, and held his new ophthalmoscope before each eyeball, first evaluating whether or not the lenses had clouded and turned cataract, but they had not. He could see no other abnormality. The painter denied any foreign object having scraped or pierced his eyes at any time.

The doctor set the ophthalmoscope down and sighed.

"You can help me?" the painter asked.

"I have an idea," the doctor said. He would not say he could help him because he was not certain that he could. He knew the painter was anxious, but he could not measure his affliction as he could the simple parameters of refraction or the functional abnormality of a cloudy lens. This was something else. This was something hiding inside the eye, or perhaps hiding deeper, in the mind. An absence of light at the center of his vision. This was what the painter always described. The doctor did not doubt him, but what he could not see and what the painter did see equaled frustration for both men. Some eyes were too mysterious to understand.

He prescribed glasses to wear in the daytime that might obscure the absence. Purple lenses to hide the black hole. The painter would try to believe that the glasses were working, and so he would not turn up again on the doctor's doorstep for several weeks at least. He could prescribe different color lenses for a long while before the artist caught on. Later, if the trick of the lenses did not work, the blindness might be something out of the doctor's control, but he hoped that would not be for a long while yet, and perhaps by then someone would come up with an answer for this odd complaint that yielded no anatomical clue.

After the appointment, Degas followed the doctor's directions to an ophthalmic shop on the Rue du Faubourg Saint-Honoré to have the glasses specially made, and when he returned a week later to retrieve them, he emerged terrified into the Paris noon drizzle, for the glasses turned the world purple, an unfair distortion given that he already had to *remember* hues, shades, tone. Recently, he had interrogated his colorist, Jérôme Ottoz, as to whether or not the man had changed his grinding or his composition, ashamed of his suspicion but alarmed at the way the very light had seemed to be shifting. Jérôme's small shop was on the Rue la Bruyère, just around the corner from Degas's old house on the Rue Blanche, in a little cubby of a shop with a glass door, but its proximity was not what Degas loved. He loved the purity of the colors, their absolute reliability. It frightened Degas that even this certainty might be pulled from underneath him. He implored Ottoz to remember that color was perennial, imperishable, and that to alter even the slightest tone was to violate the laws of physics.

The doctor claimed that light was a wave, but in New Orleans, where Degas had gone to visit his brother René, the light had been a battering ram, an all-day assault that left his eyes feeling taut and naked. He had been able to paint, but only after weeks of contending with the flat gulf light. He always marveled that Monet and Renoir worked outdoors, in the uncontrollable elements, in the blistering wind, *en plein air.*

Degas adjusted the colored glasses, pinching them lower and then higher on his nose, searching for the black hole in the purpled light. The doctor had been entirely too happy about the eyeglasses. In fact, the man was entirely too happy about everything, in Degas's opinion, which was why he tried hard to keep from believing too much in the doctor's ability to help him. It was too much to believe that his eyes might be helped by curved and colored glass.

The Damoclean sword of blindness, for a man whose work was to see. All he knew was art. When he woke in the morning, his hands were already moving, as if his unconscious mind were dictating his work. If he'd been sculpting, they would be kneading wax; if painting, his right hand would be making brushstrokes of his dreams; if drawing, his head would be angling for the line. What would he do, if blind?

He stood on the corner, watching the altered world pass by, muted in a lavender hue. He waited a long while, until, at the center of his vision, the hole reemerged, now tinged a deep purple by the useless glass.

Chapter Nine

Across town, Mary Cassatt readied her studio. She had written her father a letter, explaining that she was going to stay in Paris and, understanding that she was flouting his wishes, wanted to inform him that she was also renouncing her allowance. She had saved some money, but only a little, and as soon as she posted the letter she could hardly suppress her terror. How would she support herself, an American woman in Paris, alone? She supposed she could paint plates, or teacups, or even lampshades for that little bric-a-brac shop in the Galerie d'Orléans in the Palais-Royal, which the souvenir-hunting Americans visited by the omnibus-ful, but she feared she would be paid only a pittance.

Nevertheless, she had made plans to visit the boutiques when a reprieve came in the form of Miss Mary Ellison. A friend, she was one of the contingent of American girls sent over from the States in the years after the Civil War to learn French, to absorb a sense of style, and to obtain that indefinable je ne sais quoi needed to become highly desirable and therefore marriageable. She lived at Madame Del Sarte's Pension for Young Ladies with Mary's other young friend, Louisine Elder, who also loved Degas's painting and had once managed, on her own, to buy one of his pastels. Mary still barely managed her envy. At tea with them last week, Mary had related her new circumstances, and within a day Miss Ellison had sent a telegram to her father explaining that Mary Cassatt was the only artist in Paris she wanted to paint the portrait her father wanted her to have done.

Now Mary laid out her walnut palette and knife, boar bristle brushes, and the new tubes of paint from her favorite shop, Maison Édouard, on Rue Clauzel. She'd been so excited by purchasing the new colors that she'd forgotten an appointment with Abigail Alcott for tea, and had had to send a note explaining her truancy. *I've fallen in love with color. Please forgive me, but the attraction was irresistible.* Abigail had readily forgiven her, and would forgive Mary anything, Mary believed, now that she had decided to stay in Paris.

But Mary had yet to experiment with the new colors, her first foray into the impressionist style, and she worried that Miss Ellison's father, who was paying the commission fee, might not like the surprise. She feared that the Ellisons might be expecting a dull Salon portrait, the kind she had vowed to never paint again, and touchy sitters—and their paying fathers—sometimes grew furious afterward and withheld payment. His reaction mattered. If he liked what she had done, he would recommend Mary to other Americans on their grand tours seeking a portrait to take back home as a souvenir. And if he didn't, she would be painting bric-a-brac.

Miss Ellison arrived in a high state of nervous excitement. It was something to do with the fiacre driver's accusation that she had misdirected him with her poor French and he was therefore due an extra fifty centimes. Mary seated the girl on her rose velvet couch, trying to calm her. On the wall she tacked the studies she'd made two days ago when Miss Ellison had sat for the preliminary drawings: the line of her neck, the shape of her eyes, the curve of her hands.

It occurred to Mary while she worked that she had not heard from Degas since he had come to see her three weeks ago, nor had she seen him passing on the street. She had come to believe she might have imagined his visit, his invitation to show with them, everything. She wondered whether it was possible that he could have forgotten his proposal. She didn't know enough about him to know whether or not he kept his promises. She hoped he did, because now there was no going back.

The sitting lasted only two hours, but when the chattering Miss Ellison left, Mary was exhausted. She studied the painting, walking away and returning again. She was not concerned with form. Form she had conquered in the early sketches, perfecting Miss Ellison's small shoulders and round, as yet innocent face. It was instead the color, more dazzling than she had ever applied, ultramarine and permanent rose painted directly from the tube, the colors so saturated and pure that their intensity was a deeply visceral surprise. Tears sprang to her eyes. Without help, without instruction, without anyone telling her how, she had achieved the beginning of something new.

Cleaning her brushes at the stand in the back of the building, Mary planned the next few days. How impatient she was to paint the lace of Miss Ellison's dress, how thrilled to attempt her articulated hand holding her embroidery hoop, how pleased to render a portrait she knew the Salon would undoubtedly reject.

Chapter Ten

Sunday Evening

My dear Mademoiselle Cassatt,

Would you do me the honor of accompanying me to the Manets' Thursday night soirée, where you will meet people far more interesting than I, if you can tolerate their idle chatter and nonsensical opinions about art? I think it is time you met a few of the brigands with whom you will be exhibiting; that should give you plenty of time to repent your decision to join us. There, you are warned.

Thursday, June 7? I will call for you at seven. They feed us there, but poorly. Dress as you would for an evening at the Opéra. Do you enjoy the Opéra? One of the many mysteries to unravel about you.

Yours,

Edgar Degas

The slightly flirtatious note arrived with the Monday morning post in the first week of June. Mary laid the letter on her writing desk. She'd been living permanently in Paris for three years now, and not once had she ever been invited to an "evening." The French rarely invited Americans to their homes. That was why the American colony—the expatriates, the low-level diplomats, those in town doing the season—crafted their own social events, entirely separate from the French, excluding the occasional open-invitation balls at Versailles and the Presidential Palace. These, however, were off-limits to those who hadn't sufficient money for the required regalia of resplendent evening dress and diamond tiaras. Mary no longer followed the notices in *Galignani's Messenger*. The colony, on her rare early ventures into its jaws, had proved insular, a provincial small town in Paris rife with gossip and nonsense. Mary's evenings consisted of tea with other art students in their shared rooms, or an occasional night at the Opéra, obtained through a cultivated friendship with one of the ticket sellers, who provided her with a seat on the mezzanine for the price of the third-tier balcony.

In her reply, Mary did not want to mimic Degas's flirtatiousness, though formality somehow seemed wrong for the casual air of his invitation. In the end, she simply thanked him and said that she was looking forward to it, an understatement that amused Abigail Alcott very much.

"Looking forward to it? It's what you've been dying for," Abigail laughed. Louisine Elder's family was visiting and had lent Louisine their suite at the luxurious Grand Hotel, on the Place de l'Opéra, frequented by Americans who loved that the entire hotel staff tolerated their poor French. Louisine had arranged for a belated birthday celebration for Mary: dinner served in her family's suite.

Abigail recovered herself and said, "He'll introduce you to everyone. I'm a prophet—didn't I say you ought to meet them?"

"Will you tell Monsieur Degas how much I admire him?" Louisine said.

"I'll probably be too terrified, to tell you the truth. What if I make a fool of myself?"

"You?" Mary Ellison said. "Never."

"You are formidable. Remember that," Abigail said. "At least I find you formidable." She smiled and laid her hand on Mary's forearm. "Aren't you glad you stayed in Paris?"

After dinner, when she returned home, Mary studied the portrait of Miss Ellison, which was curing before she shipped it to the girl's father in Philadelphia. While not masterful, the portrait nonetheless glimmered with change, especially the heightened palette, which she was pleased to see was retaining its vividness in its finished state. In the past few weeks, the transformation she was making in her work had exhausted her. It was as if in trying to paint in the new way, she was rearranging even her muscles and bones. Her right shoulder had grown stiff because of the different way she was holding her brush. Her mind throbbed; she was learning and letting go at the same time, having to *unsee* everything.

On Thursday evening, Degas called for her promptly at seven, impeccably dressed in a tailcoat and top hat. She had worn her best dress, as Degas had instructed, a white silk with fringe dangling from the bustle that she hoped wouldn't be out of place at a house party. Degas helped her with her wrap, then went before her down the spiral stairway, remarking only on the unevenness of the stairs and his gratitude for the candle he carried to illuminate their way. They rode in a hired equipage to the neighborhood that skirted the Gare Saint Lazare, the new Place de l'Europe, with its surrounding streets named after foreign capitals. Tonight it was ablaze with gaslight, a bright contrast to their more humble neighborhood. He warned her to pay homage to Édouard's mother at some point in the evening because even though she hid herself in the corner, Madame Manet was the true host of the party.

When she stepped into the flat at 49 Rue de Saint-Pétersbourg, it was only half past seven in the evening and already blue smoke was settling like an ocean fog in the close confines of a parlor populated mostly by men. Degas had led her astray. The few women were attired not for the Opéra but in less showy gowns of muted tones. Mary took off her wrap and handed it to the maid, who took it along with Degas's top hat, but not before conferring a smirking glance on the splendor of Mary's dress.

"Degas! Mother will be furious with you. How rude you are to bring a guest you haven't warned us about." A man barreled toward them through a widening path of guests, a glass of champagne aloft in one hand. "And when she is so well dressed, too."

"Édouard Manet, may I introduce Mademoiselle Cassatt? She is a painter. She is joining us next year for our exhibition, which, if you weren't such a bourgeois fool, you would do too. But of course you won't." He turned to Mary. "Mademoiselle Cassatt, this is Monsieur Édouard Manet, fearless rebel of the art world and our host for the evening."

"It is lovely to meet you, Mademoiselle Cassatt. It's a shame you are here with Monsieur Degas, but you are very welcome." Manet's was a welcoming kind of handsome, all wrapped up in a reddish beard and snapping blue eyes and a gaze of such scrutiny that Mary nearly blushed.

"Thank you, Monsieur Manet," Mary said, conscious of the covert glances cast their way. A quiet hum had replaced the cacophony that had greeted them; everyone had lowered their voices to eavesdrop on their conversation. "Monsieur Degas didn't tell me he had invited me illegally. I would be happy to leave, if that would suit you."

Quiet titters filled the room.

Édouard laughed and said, "Only an American would suggest such an unhappy solution."

Relieved that Édouard had understood her joke, she smiled, but there was only one way he could know she was American. "We Americans can't quite seem to get the French *e*'s or *r*'s properly out of our mouths. A fatal flaw, I fear."

"I forgive you! Not the rest of your countrymen, but you, certainly. Come in and let me introduce you or at least force Monsieur Degas to do the honors now that he has exceeded the bounds of my hospitality."

"Hush, Édouard, or you'll frighten Mademoiselle Cassatt," Degas said. "She will think I have no manners."

"You don't have any manners," Manet said, placing the palm of his hand on the small of Mary's back and escorting her deeper into the parlor.

Across the room, Suzanne Manet was hiding behind the half-open door of the kitchen, observing the newly arrived Degas and his guest, a woman of severe posture, whose fashionable dress was cinched at the bustle by an enviable amount of fringe that shimmered in the candlelight. The dress came, to Suzanne's sharp eye, not from the house of Worth, but instead from one of the eagle-eyed but less expensive seamstresses of the Rue Volney, who did reconnaissance at Worth's elegant store at 7 Rue de la Paix, committing to memory the shapes of bodices and sleeves.

"This Mademoiselle Cassatt is very American, isn't she?" Suzanne said.

"She is overdressed," Berthe Morisot said, self-consciously smoothing her pale blue dress, its worn beauty no prize next to the magnificence of the newcomer's. The two sisters-in-law stood with their heads inclined toward one another, inspecting the woman, agreeing that the blazing candelabras heightened the dark caverns under her cheekbones and emphasized the whites of her rather prominent eyes. They examined, too, the throng crowding the long, narrow room. Claude Monet, who was beginning to resemble a bear with his heavy muff of black beard, was eyeing Mademoiselle Cassatt suspiciously from a corner where he, Pissarro, Renoir, Caillebotte, and Berthe's husband, Eugène, were suffering an endless rant from Monsieur Zola, the writer and art critic. Monet was sometimes mistaken for Zola on the street and once had had to persuade a fervent fan that he was not the famous writer, an idiocy that had infuriated him. Renoir had already shifted his attention from the querulous Zola to Mademoiselle Cassatt, who was accepting a glass of champagne from the hovering Degas. Pissarro was demanding to know why Zola had devoted only two sentences to him in a recent review. Eugène, catching Berthe's eye, lifted his chin in invitation, but she made no motion to join him.

Madame Manet, Édouard's mother, was presiding over her party from an armchair, a glass of untouched champagne at her elbow. She wore black, as she always did, in perpetual mourning for her husband, dead more than twenty years. Gustave, the youngest of the three Manet brothers, was seated at his mother's side. His presence could usually mitigate the wide gulf between his two brothers, but he rarely made it to these Thursdays, as his interest in art paled in comparison to his interest in advancing as quickly as possible through the hierarchy of the French bureaucracy, a desire that entailed religious attendance at the Thursday evenings of an influential magistrate. Suzanne's younger brother, Léon Leenhoff, also kept Madame Manet company, but he appeared as bored as any young man might in the face of family obligation. Though it was rarely said outright, and never discussed in the Manets' home, everyone believed him to be Édouard's son, conceived more than a decade before their marriage, even though Édouard had spent the boy's entire life denying the rumor. It did not help dim suspicion that Édouard and Suzanne had raised him, nor that he looked just like Édouard, with the exception of the ruddy Dutch skin he shared with his "sister." Neither Madame Manet nor Léon rose to greet any of the guests, though they eyed the door whenever it opened, turning now as the artist Zacharie Astruc and the poet Stéphane Mallarmé entered, sweeping off their capes in a dramatic entrance they hoped would be noticed.

In short, Berthe thought, the evening was proceeding as usual, with the exception of Degas's guest.

Suzanne agreed that Mademoiselle Cassatt was rather finely dressed for so pedestrian an occasion. Recently, the ravages of age had begun to settle in uneven mounds around Suzanne's belly, something she did not want to bring to Berthe's attention. This very morning she had been mistaken for a fishwife when her mother-in-law had sent her out to execute the errands the maid certainly should have done, a grievance Suzanne added to the long list she kept of her mother-in-law's serial cruelties. Despite her critical eye Suzanne didn't go in anymore for fine clothes, not like Degas's guest or Édouard, who tonight wore a finely cut dinner jacket perfectly tailored to his svelte frame. Shame was the current price of marrying a beautiful man too many years her junior. Well, only two years, but time had been crueler to her. How she envied her husband his stylish aplomb, his good looks, his still youthful face, though no amount of envy could ever diminish her affection. She had loved him since she had first taught him to put fingers to ivory. An indifferent piano student, he had found other, more delicious uses for his deft fingers, ones that Madame Manet never failed to punish her for.

Tonight Suzanne would play the piano as she always did, grateful that she had something to offer, because one could disappear in this group of gifted misfits, though she supposed since she helped to feed them she could say that she was at least saving them from starvation. Monsieur Renoir had practically disappeared before their eyes for several years, turning more gaunt with every passing day, and she'd heard that even now Claude Monet and his family were living on such extended credit that no one would lend him another centime. She knew why, of course. The fools gave up food to buy paint. Claude and Camille had had to move to the country so that they could feed their little son out of their garden, and Renoir was so poor he begged for money from all his friends, living with the Monets off and on for years. Everyone knew he was besotted with Camille, a transgression Claude somehow forgave, though lately it appeared that their friendship was cooling. Earlier, she'd overheard Claude whisper travel plans to Édouard that he didn't want mentioned to Renoir, who still had the look of the starveling about him, though perhaps it was his great height that gave that impression.

Having abandoned Zola's conversational circle, Renoir now occupied the blue chair in the darkest corner of the room, his long spider legs thrust before him, his narrow face and shock of red beard, clipped to a rectangle, lending him the appearance of a hunted scholar. Catching

Suzanne's eye, he smiled in his benign way, no doubt making something beautiful in his mind of her face. Suzanne often wished that he would paint her. Degas had savaged her—as he savaged all women he painted—in that portrait Édouard had destroyed in a fit of spousal loyalty. She would ask Renoir if he would oblige her. Just once, she would like to look like the adored Camille, a plain woman if there ever was one, but who glowed in his canvases like a radiant flower. Of course, he loved her. That was why he made her look so beautiful, but she would ask Renoir anyway, hoping for the same treatment. And she would make Édouard pay him so the poor man could eat. It would be revenge for all those portraits of Berthe, her dark beauty smoldering off the canvas.

Suzanne said, "It is a beautiful dress. But taste doesn't make up for her face. Too thin at the chin, eyes too prominent, and the proportion of her cheek to her forehead is too steep. Édouard would never paint her." Suzanne realized that she had paid Berthe a veiled compliment, but she was nothing if not resigned to the enviable truth that no woman could hold a candle to her sister-in-law.

"It's curious, though, isn't it?" Berthe said, skirting the danger of Suzanne's largesse. "Degas treats this one as if she is made of china. Have you ever seen him dote on anyone with such singular attention before? Why, he's even brought her a drink. Look how he takes her by the elbow. Look how he makes Édouard pay attention to her."

"Do go see to her, would you, Berthe? Who knows how she'll fare once the men get going. I'll deal with the maid. Degas will bite off my head if I don't have food on the table soon. One would think the man hardly eats, the way he pretends to faint from starvation when he doesn't consume his dinner by seven."

Berthe crossed the room to join Édouard and Degas and to welcome his guest. Eugène joined them. As his arm encircled her waist, Berthe greeted the gesture with a slight shudder.

"Ah. Madame and Monsieur Manet," Degas said. "May I introduce the lovely Mademoiselle Cassatt? I should warn you, Mademoiselle Cassatt, that this Madame Manet is best known as Madame Morisot. There are far too many Madame Manets in this family. And we wouldn't want Mademoiselle Cassatt to mistake Berthe for your wife, would we, Édouard?"

Mary, who had spent the last few minutes listening to Édouard Manet and Degas good-naturedly insult one another, noticed that Berthe flinched slightly.

Édouard said, "Tell me, Degas, weren't you recently raving to me about a woman in the Salon so impressive that you went hunting for her? I believe you said you made a fool of yourself over her, didn't you?"

Degas gaped at Édouard and stated that he had no idea what Édouard was talking about.

"Welcome to our unruly Thursdays, Mademoiselle Cassatt," Berthe said. "Monsieur Degas, you've been remiss. You must introduce her to everyone or I will do it for you."

Degas placed his hand on Mary's back, and in the crowded parlor, this possessive movement of Degas's caught everyone's attention.

"*Messieurs et mesdames*, I present Mademoiselle Cassatt. I have invited her to exhibit with us next year. May you all abandon your bad manners to welcome someone whose talent exceeds all of yours. Especially you, Édouard; see if you can be hospitable to a woman who draws better than you ever will."

In the silence that followed, while everyone appeared to assess what she thought of his bad manners, Mary fought not to betray the chagrin that flooded through her. The performance at the door, it seemed, had not been enough; she would be forever judged by what she said next. This was the way of intellectuals—Philadelphian or French, no matter: You had a moment, no more, to establish yourself. And Mary had been in Paris long enough to understand the clannish nature of Parisians, their intolerance of foreigners, their disdain of the Americans invading their boulevards and museums, clutching their Baedeker guides and immolating the French language. Nor did it matter that she was an artist. In this crowd, there would be no easy acceptance.

"You must ignore Monsieur Degas," she began, "who seems tonight to possess the tongue of the devil. I claim neither talent nor pride, only honor at being here tonight. My thanks to Madame Manet"—ignoring Berthe Morisot, Mary looked about the room until she spied the figure of the older woman, seated in a chair, who nodded in reply—"for forgiving my cheek in accepting Monsieur Degas's invitation. I am most grateful to be in your home tonight."

This crowd adored cheek. Combined with the false humility, of which everyone approved, her cheek turned out to be irresistible, apart from the abominable accent that they collectively decided to ignore, choosing instead to embrace her Americanism with a generosity they extended to no one else, except James Whistler, whom they all knew from his early days studying at the atelier Gleyre, and who, when over from England visiting, was beloved because he traded witty barbs with Degas all night, thus freeing the rest of them of the burden of sparring with him, if only for an evening.

No one noticed when dinner sailed out on the tarnished silver trays. All the guests surrounded Mary, though Claude Monet held back. Of the many things he disliked about Degas, he especially didn't like him always dragging new artists into their midst in an attempt to balance out the landscapists. An American? Degas, he decided, was going out of his mind. She probably painted teacups or something, by the look of her. Renoir stepped forward and kissed her hand. Lately Monet had been snubbing him, and tonight Renoir decided to show his old friend what it was to be a gentleman in the presence of a lady, as this woman undoubtedly was, since the silk alone in her dress had probably cost her a fortune. Renoir was an expert on anything to do with silk. Édouard, stung by Degas' comment, was challenging everyone to a drawing duel, declaring that he would run to his studio to get them all lead and paper, though he moved only enough to admit Mary's new admirers into the fold. Émile Zola merely bowed in Mary's direction. Gustave Caillebotte, tidy and handsome, smiled and kissed her hand. Zacharie Astruc and Stéphane

Mallarmé made chivalrous comments and promptly turned away. But Monsieur Pissarro took Mary's hand in his and smiled without reserve. Next to the extravagant black beauty of Berthe Morisot, who had extracted herself from her husband's arm and taken Pissarro's elbow, he seemed like light itself.

"Mademoiselle Cassatt, as you have discovered, our dear friend Monsieur Degas, while a genius, is not always kind. To say nothing of his arrogance and presumption," Pissarro said.

"It's true. Monsieur Degas has abandoned me in public several times," Berthe said.

"Though you are never without an escort, my pet," Eugène said. "Not if you want one."

Everyone waited for Berthe to reply, but she didn't. It was easy, Mary thought, to overlook Berthe's husband. He looked a great deal like his brother, but there was something of the shade about him. His features failed to compel and his voice had a petulant quality.

Into the void Degas said, "I resent your comment, Pissarro. I am never presumptuous and rarely arrogant. And I am very fond of you, Berthe, as you well know."

"You are always arrogant, Degas," Pissarro said. "I apologize for him, Mademoiselle Cassatt. Mostly, we men forget that we are not in a café and therefore behave abominably."

"Monsieur Pissarro never behaves abominably, do you?" Berthe said. "Madame Pissarro won't mind if I steal you, will she?"

"I would mind," Eugène said, but everyone ignored him.

"I'm terribly afraid she will mind," Pissarro said. "I've left her behind for the week in Pontoise with the children, and when I return home, I'll be made to repent my abandonment. Perhaps I am as unkind to her as Monsieur Degas was to you."

Suzanne Manet, strands of loosened hair straggling about her reddened cheeks, toured the room, saying, "Oh, do come and get your plates, everyone, before the fish is hopeless."

The fish was hopeless. Gustave Manet quietly slipped out as people queued for plates, thereby avoiding the fish entirely. Degas endured the buffet line twice to bring Mary a plate and another for himself. He sighed and said, "At least it's not swimming in butter like the asparagus." The collective sighed too. It was awkward standing about with china and cutlery, a glass of champagne balancing on the nearest ledge, subject to thievery and spillage. Mary Cassatt set down her plate, her half-eaten food congealing on the china, while Berthe didn't even touch hers.

Soon after, all the men abandoned their plates for the candlelit corner next to the piano, where a few rested their elbows on its ebony skin and the rest sprawled in armchairs, twirling their delicate flutes of amber champagne, which they held by their stems. No one spoke, but they eyed one another as if waiting for a starting gun, boredom and anticipation warring on their spectral faces as the flickering candlelight painted shadows on the wall. Someone lit a cigar. Mary moved to join them, but Berthe motioned to her to sit beside her on a brocade love seat away from the men.

Stéphane Mallarmé brought the tips of his fingers together and leaned forward into the ring of men, a serious but quizzical smile on his face. "Monsieur Zola," he said. "Do you think your book *L'Assommoir* deserves its success when your prose, usually so evocative, is lazy at the oddest junctures? Sometimes I think you are getting careless."

Mallarmé's voice betrayed no mockery as he lobbed this bombshell, but instead affected an urgency of inquiry, as if he'd been worrying about this regrettable flaw of Zola's for a long while and was happy to finally have the chance to discuss it.

"Zola has been dodging him forever," Berthe whispered to Mary. "Stéphane wants a literary duel, albeit a civilized one, but Zola won't give him one."

Mary whispered back, "This is what you call a party?"

"No," Berthe said. "This is Paris."

This is Paris. People were always explaining things to her by invoking the city, just as she was always declaring that Paris was shining or raining. One couldn't help it, she supposed, if Paris held a magnetic spell over all its inhabitants.

"If I may, Mademoiselle Cassatt," Berthe said, "I think that some of this posturing has to do with you. Forgive me, but no matter how welcoming everyone was, you should know that you are at a disadvantage. Monsieur Degas is always dragging in strays."

"Strays?"

"New painters," Berthe said. "I don't want to be unkind, but Degas seems to think that anyone he discovers is wonderful, and we don't always agree with him."

Mary tried to forgive Berthe the cruelty of the word *stray*, though she was finding it hard to reconcile the suddenly unsympathetic woman beside her with the extravagantly feminine paintings she had exhibited at the Rue le Peletier.

"I see. And how did you prove yourself?" Mary said.

"I'm married to Eugène. And I paint."

"As do I," Mary said.

"They will exclude you until they approve of your work, and maybe not even then." *They* will exclude, as if Berthe were including her now. And maybe she was. Maybe this was the way French women made friends. They warned you of the hurdles ahead and then sat back to see how you fared.

"How did you meet Monsieur Degas?" Berthe said.

"He begged the introduction; he apparently has admired my work for some time."

Berthe looked away, but Mary felt her small victory.

In the corner, Zola had commandeered the end of the piano, the place of power, his bulk leaning against the instrument. He had emitted only a low growl of a sigh in response to Mallarmé's taunt. Degas, seated beside him, eagerly took up the gauntlet. "Unfair, Stéphane, when Zola imitates life in art so clearly that he defines realism. The triumph of his mimesis trumps whatever lazy prose you accuse him of."

"You realists band together," Mallarmé said. "I agree Monsieur Zola is the definition of modern, as are you. And Émile knows I admire him. But excellence is a responsibility. It's fine to describe a sky, and you do it well," he said, turning to Zola, "but the character's contemplation of it has to have some connection to the narrative. Some reason why it exists in the novel. Nothing can be superfluous."

"Excuse me, Stéphane, but a novel is not a poem," Zola said. "You are mistaking the two genres as one."

"Nothing is superfluous in a poem," Mallarmé said.

"Watch," Berthe whispered. "Now Monsieur Zola will insult Monsieur Mallarmé."

"All poetry is superfluous," Zola said.

"*See?*" Berthe mouthed.

"You mistook my meaning, Émile," Mallarmé said. "And you lack curiosity."

"I will mistake your meaning every time you tell me how to write a novel when you are capable of composing only twenty or thirty lines. You write neat little rhymes, but nothing of scope," Zola said. "And besides, nobody understands what your poems mean anyway."

"Density is not a fault," Mallarmé said.

"But clarity is a virtue," Zola said. "And besides, everyone looks at the sky, so why not include a little description of it? It hardly ruins the narrative."

Degas, feverishly rolling his empty glass between his palms, said, "Let's apply your argument to you, Émile. If what you say is true, that Stéphane is unqualified to critique you, then how are you qualified to critique art when you have never painted a picture?"

Zola made a show of pulling his pocket watch from his vest. He always left the Manets' Thursdays early so he could attend his own

Thursday salon, which everyone knew didn't begin until ten o'clock, after his friends had left the theater or the café chantants and were in need
of a watering hole and companionship until two or three in the morning.
Several guests here would migrate there this evening, after Suzanne finished her first two piano pieces, drifting out with nods and apologies and
spilling with relief onto the street, where they would shake off the pall of
Suzanne's need and head to the Gare Saint Lazare, where they could easily find a hack to whisk them to the more convivial Zola's.

   "Oh no you don't, Émile!" Degas roared. He turned to Berthe. "What
time is it, Madame Morisot?"

   "Nine o'clock," she said, consulting the clock on the table that Degas
could just as easily have consulted, but hadn't, to make his point.

   Degas raised his eyebrows at Zola.

   Zola feigned nonchalance and secreted his watch back inside his vest
pocket. "One must eat, as you well know, Degas, and they pay me for
those articles, and in my defense, and to my visionary credit, I insist you
admit that I have defended this group when everyone else has attacked
you. Where is your gratitude? Besides, have you never decorated a fan,
say, to feed yourself?"

   "You know I have, but I don't paint a critique of your writing to make
money."

   "Here is the difference between writers and painters. You are handicapped by your medium, paint, whereas a writer is a savant of sorts, using
our more facile medium of words to inquire about and observe any subject. In fiction, we present a mirror; in critique, an opinion. The medium
is the same: words. Just try to use paint to present an opinion. Our medium encompasses everything. Words reign."

   "As in poetry," Mallarmé said, but neither Zola nor Degas paid him
any attention, and Mallarmé sank into his chair, usurped.

   "*My* medium is words," Zola continued, pressing his point. "Yours is
paint. Your medium is more limited than mine."

   "*My* media are paint and pastel, clay and copper, ink and press, a far more extensive arsenal than yours," Degas said. "I look. I observe. I create. Opinion and mirror, both, about any subject I should wish to expose. What is my painting *In a Café* if not an opinion about the same people you write about in *L'Assommoir*? Or Édouard's *Nana*, named after your character? The downtrodden workers, seduced by absinthe? But if you claim yourself a savant, I therefore declare *In a Café* a critique of *L'Assommoir*."

"That's absurd. You painted that picture first. And I'll have you know I think a great deal of that picture. Truth incarnate."

Degas leapt up and made a sweeping motion with his hands. "*Messieurs et mesdames*, may I present Émile Zola, the most intelligent art critic in France," he said, bowing as laughter filled the parlor, pleased with himself for having extracted a compliment that Zola had had no intention of bestowing, and even more pleased that he had confounded Mallarmé, whom he liked very much, but who could bore.

So this, Mary thought, was what it was to be a woman at a party in Paris. One either fed the men or was consulted about the time, but was not expected to speak beyond pleasantries. And now she was a *stray*.

She rose. "Messieurs Degas and Zola. I pose a question."

Silk and spring wool rippled in the room as everyone turned to stare at Mary. Berthe touched Mary's hand, but Mary folded her hands in a deliberate parody of acquiescing womanhood.

"Isn't it true that to parse mediums like this is to claim territory? How different is your argument than the one the Salon uses to exclude my art or Monsieur Monet's or even Monsieur Manet's? If you examine what you think are your moral positions, you will see that they are probably no different from what goes on in the Salon hanging committee."

Degas said, "I only said that Zola claims the impossible when he says he is sovereign of both writing and art."

"Monsieur Zola has achieved fame for his novel *L'Assommoir*, while you, Monsieur Degas, were reviled by the critics for your *In a Café*, even though both novel and picture addressed the same subject. Each was accepted differently by the public. In my opinion, Monsieur Degas, your portrayal of the drunkenness of the despoiled and downtrodden is so evocative that the public, horrified, has to look away, while Monsieur Zola's medium, words, is less vivid, and therefore more acceptable."

Zola sputtered from the piano bench. "My novel? Not vivid?"

Mary turned to the author, who had snubbed her earlier. His wine-flushed face blushed an even deeper shade of vermillion, suggesting the blood orange of sunset. "I am using conjecture, Monsieur Zola, about what appeals to the masses. For the sake of argument. Using your medium. Words. But I have read your novel and quite like it," she said.

"*Quite like it?* She quite likes it? She is American, isn't she?" Zola said, turning to the group, seeking accord.

Berthe waited to see whether or not Eugène or Édouard or Suzanne would manage Monsieur Zola, and when they did not, she rose from the love seat and glided across the room. "Please forgive me, if you can, Monsieur Zola, but earlier I misread what time it was. Don't let my error keep you from your guests. We've all been selfish to delay you. No doubt they are knocking at your door at this very moment, wondering where their dear Monsieur Zola is, hoping they won't be deprived of your company."

As Berthe nimbly guided Zola to the door and into the night, Degas came to Mary's side and said, "Adroitly done, Mademoiselle Cassatt. Monsieur Zola will spend the rest of the night trying to understand what just happened to him, a prospect that gives me great pleasure."

"Berthe implied I had to prove myself."

"We are all wondering what we did without you now," Degas said. "Even Claude, though he'll never tell you." He smiled with pride and interest, but Mary felt exhausted, though she had to admit that the interlude had exhilarated her. Not one of her American friends was as alive as these people gathered here tonight. Abigail Alcott was as dear to her as Lydia, and darling Louisine was more sister than friend, but they were neither of them as provocative as this group.

"Do you always test people in this way, Monsieur Degas?"

"Test? I don't know what you mean."

"Don't be coy," Mary said. It was warm in the room, especially near the kitchen, and she could hear the maid banging pots and pans in the sink. "Will you tell me what Monsieur Manet meant earlier? About the Salon?"

Degas reddened. "He's a scoundrel. Don't listen to him."

"But his joke angered you. It must mean something. Berthe said everyone is angry with you because you bring in strays. Am I your latest stray?"

Degas took her by the hand and pulled her into the far corner behind the dining table, near the serving dishes of the drowning fish and wilted asparagus. "Édouard was referring to the opening day of the Salon. I saw you in the crowds. I tried to reach you to introduce myself, but I lost you. I didn't know who you were. When Monsieur Tourny introduced us, I hid my surprise. And all this nonsense seems to have amused Édouard very much. I did warn you, didn't I, that you might repent your decision to join us?"

"You did," she said.

"Well, then?"

After a time, she said, "The fish really was awful wasn't it?"

A smile played on Degas's lips. "Yes it was," he said.

Suzanne Manet, having overheard the comment about the fish, breezed past them with a disapproving air, her hair irretrievably wilted. With an insulted flick of her wrist, she cleared a path through her guests, mounted the piano bench, and opened a piano score, flipping pages one after the other until she found the music she wanted. At the first notes, Degas steered Mary back to a gilded armchair to listen to the exquisite tones of the Handel sonata, played by Suzanne with skill and feeling. Berthe settled into a wing chair, her husband standing guard beside her. Édouard, restless, hovered nearby, dividing his attentions between Berthe and his wife until he drifted away, slipping quietly backward.

The mellifluous tones filled the parlor, and Mary closed her eyes, sinking into the soft cushion of the chair, thinking how much she loved Handel. She thought she felt Degas's hand, its dry fissures stained with ink and graphite, graze her shoulder lightly. She opened her eyes, surprised, but it was only Berthe Morisot passing, tracing Édouard's path into the depths of the flat.

Chapter Eleven

The Manets' maid, Eloise, gaped as Édouard dragged Berthe through the back doorway of the kitchen and into the stairway that led to the maid's quarters. When the door closed behind them, Eloise shook her head and whispered to herself, "But the bedrooms are down the hall."

Halfway up the stairs, Édouard leaned in, smelling of wet wool and the failed fish. Berthe still couldn't get used to the smells of rich food. The excess seemed obscene. During the siege of Paris, when the Prussians had strangled the city and rat had been on every restaurant's menu in town, she'd lost perhaps twenty pounds, and now she believed that the stringent asceticism had affected her forever. She'd dreamed then of food, but now, when she could have anything at all she wanted to eat, she measured it out spoonful by spoonful, a daily ration, just as she had measured out increments of Édouard, each hour an uncertain, suspect gift, because it always ended in his leaving and going back to Suzanne. Her mother would have said that her abhorrence of food had come before the siege, just about the time that Berthe had lost her mind, the moment she fell in love with the married Édouard.

"You let him love you." Édouard's voice caught in his throat.

"You think Eugène is my consolation prize."

"He lacks imagination. He has always wanted what I have. To paint, to live like I live."

"But you don't have me. Not anymore."

Édouard hooked a finger under her chin and inserted his knee between her legs with a gentle pressure, as nonchalantly as if he were saying, "*Ça va?*" Her knees parted to let his in. It had started this way, in small gestures, a long time ago.

"You don't have to love him," Édouard said.

"What am I supposed to do? Cry every night?"

"Suzanne likes her willful ignorance."

"But I do not. I want a child, Édouard."

Struck, he said, "That is low."

"None of us is an idiot, Édouard. We know Léon is not Suzanne's younger brother. You should tell the boy."

"I would rather have a child with you."

"You would ruin me rather than let me try for even a chimera of happiness."

"We could run. Italy. Spain. My mother would help—"

"You are spoiled, Édouard, by your looks and your charm. You believe people will love you no matter what, that you will have infinite second chances. But everyone is not me. They have much better sense than I have."

"We don't speak Italian. No one would know who we are."

"Europe is a small town, Édouard. An artery runs from Paris to the rest of the world. Exile is not a private place. It is a state of mind. And you are too weak to endure it."

"He isn't worthy of you, Berthe." Édouard toyed with the tiny black bow where the bodice of her dress closed in a series of buttons, his other hand pressed against the wall above her head. "Why do you stay with someone as weak as he is? As prideless?"

"You revile me for wanting a semblance of normalcy."

"There is nothing normal about having my brother as your husband."

"*He* asked *me.*"

"Every male asks for you every second of every hour of his life."

"You told me to marry him. And besides, my father was dead,

Édouard. I had no other choice. I was already old and tired. No one else wanted me. These are practical considerations you have no understanding of." Though he did. What was more practical than marrying your piano teacher eleven years after you'd impregnated her, as Édouard had?

Édouard released her hand and twined her jet-black curls around his fingers. "Some days I think I will die without you."

"We are brother and sister, closer than ever."

"Don't say such a hateful thing."

"Let me go, Édouard."

"To hell. I will let you go to hell."

Why had she followed him? She was a fool. She laid her hand on his chest. It took only the smallest pressure to push him away. "Go back to Méry Laurent. Rile her keeper again and get your head handed to you. Or make Eva Gonzalès your lover. There was a time when you couldn't keep your hands off her." By hands she meant paintbrush. But he couldn't paint Eva. It had tortured Berthe to hear that Édouard scraped the paint off the canvas at the end of each session, believing that he did it only so that he could call her back again to prolong their intimacy, but harboring hope that he couldn't paint Eva because he was thinking of her. "Or seduce anyone on the street. One of your models. You can take her behind the screen in your studio, once, twice a day, as much as you like. You can call it making a study."

He slapped her across the cheek. Once. Very hard. Then he bounded out of the stairwell and into the steamy confines of the kitchen, the wedge of vapor and light blotting out when he slammed the door.

Berthe bent over, her hand to her cheek. Flesh upon flesh, this time in anger, though the better times came back to her as they always did, his hand grazing her cheek, tugging her hair, caressing the curve of her waist, the hard pull of his hand at her shoulder blades, drawing him to her.

Her mother had once said to her, "Your beauty does you no good."

At the corner of her lip, Berthe could taste salt and blood. She wiped it with the back of her hand, but only a small vermillion teardrop appeared. She stood upright to steady herself. No mirror to ascertain the state of her dress, her hair, or her cheek, but with Édouard, reflections lied. In his eyes the world was remade, and she had once believed in his ability to change anything into what he wanted it to be: love, his marriage. But no longer. No matter the state of her appearance, immaculate or disarrayed, everyone would know she'd been with Édouard again. She might as well tear her clothes off or kiss him in front of everyone. Eugène, however, would not see. Berthe sighed. He would fail all his life because he did not know that nothing was ever as it seemed.

She would say she had run into a door. That she'd been careless. But only if someone asked, and they wouldn't, not after seeing Édouard emerge from the same door, even if it was only Eloise, who knew more about them than anyone in Paris, and would pass the gossip along to Madame Manet the next morning.

Chapter Twelve

Degas called for Mary the next week, on a Wednesday, inviting her to accompany him to the Musée d'Artillerie to solve, he said, a problem of light. He wore a black silk top hat, wrinkled linen coat, and lavender pince-nez that Mary had not seen before. He had sent no note, arriving just after she had finished her breakfast.

"You wish to solve a painting problem at a museum of war?" she said, standing in her studio, her apron tied around her dress, her palette in her hands. She had been just about to squeeze out her paint.

"You'll see," he said. "Unless you wish to work, in which case I am sorry to have interrupted you."

"Do you often take outings in the middle of the week?" she said.

"Never."

Outside, she picked up her skirts as they walked toward the omnibus; the backstreets that led to the Place Pigalle had evaded Haussmann's cleansing pick and shovel and today the gutters were running foul. They rode *imperiale*—on the top deck of the omnibus—in the row of open seats, changing conveyances at the Arc de Triomphe for the slow parade down the Champs-Élysées under the horse chestnut trees, their white blossoms fluttering in the late spring breeze. At the Avenue d'Antin, they disembarked to stroll toward the Pont des Invalides, past the gardens of the Palais de l'Industrie. Degas's top hat occasionally bumped the tips of her parasol as he walked hunched forward, his gaze roving as they approached the river teeming with steamboats, omnibus boats, coalers, barters, and rowboats jockeying in the narrow channel. The river ran fast and muddy, buffeting an ugly island of floating baths anchored on the right bank. Mary thought they must have opened the locks upstream to accommodate the spring runoff.

"Tell me," Degas said, "why do all you Americans come here to study? Don't they allow artists to live in the United States?"

"The history of art in America is only a second long, whereas here it is the whole of time."

"I've visited your country. The light was horrid."

"New Orleans," she said.

He raised his eyebrows.

"Your *Portraits in an Office*," she said.

"You know that painting?"

"I know most of your paintings."

They walked along the left bank, toward the gold dome of Les Invalides. Open fiacres rumbled along the quay, their passengers decked in summer finery. A laundress hurried past with her delivery basket, bluing staining her arms. Degas turned to watch her, then said, "Aren't you the least bit worried about what people might say?"

"I beg your pardon?"

"About being seen out together. The two of us."

He had caught her off guard. "People will talk?"

"My dear, this is Paris."

She looked down the street toward the direction of the abattoir, from which a breeze was bringing the metallic scent of blood. "We will tell them we are forging better Franco-American relations. To improve your opinion of the light in America."

"Ah, yes. You are Benjamin Franklin, a diplomat, but for art's sake, not war."

"And you are whoever he persuaded to arm us," Mary said.

"Revolution! Though I shouldn't say that too loudly or someone will build a barricade. It takes very little provocation around here for people to build barricades. After all, this is Paris."

They resumed walking and in a moment the esplanade of the Hôtel des Invalides opened before them, and with it the great gold dome of the chapel floating above the hulking stone edifice. The sun was at its height, and a glare shone off the square. *Paris is shining*, Mary thought as Degas advanced across the cobblestones. She had to hurry to keep up with him on the uneven stones, and only when they entered the dim confines of the first *salle*, where suits of armor glimmered in the diffuse light, did he slow his pace. He removed his glasses and placed them in his jacket pocket.

"And what problem of light are we going to solve?" Mary said.

"I'm painting a picture of bathers for Monsieur Faure, the singer Manet painted for the Salon. The light, you see, for the copper basins?"

The armor, curved and smooth, seemed to make something strange of the luster filtering from the high windows; one could imagine men wandering through these dungeon rooms in these suits of armor.

Degas said, "It's like touching time, isn't it?"

"And you ask why Americans come here."

"I'm thinking of using gold paint over pastel," he said. "I've been badgering my colorist to see if he can grind a paint that imitates the Italians."

"Gold paint, to capture the light," Mary said. "Of course." Yes, that would be the answer. How brilliant. The shimmer would be implied, the surface at once matte and luminous. Mary had never before tried to paint metal; differences in cloth were difficult enough to render. She tried to imagine the technique, how the paint would need to be applied so as to brighten the pastel and reflect the metal's smooth curve, intimating its metal-ness while catching the light, though she imagined the hue would have to be subdued, for in a bathhouse the light would be ambient, arising only from a candle or muted sunlight filtering through the slatted wallboards.

"The light could work thematically, too, couldn't it? Intimating a lack of privacy, mirroring the viewer's voyeurism?" Mary said.

"Just so. It isn't really just about the light alone. It's the context of the entire picture," Degas said. "The classicists eschewed the viewer, shying away from the implication of intimacy, but I want to expose our natural curiosity."

"It's a question of how one sees life, isn't it?" Mary said, turning, but in that instant Degas had disappeared.

She found him outside, leaning in shadow against a pillar in the damp arcade, his head bowed, his hat tipped low over his forehead, its brim shading his glassed eyes from the scatter of the bright May afternoon.

"Did I say something?" Mary said.

Degas sighed and straightened, readjusting the glasses on his nose. "Nothing to do with you, Mademoiselle Cassatt. A failed experiment on my part, I'm afraid. I apologize. It was rude of me to leave you alone. It's these eyes of mine."

"Your eyes?"

"Some damage during the siege. Berthe Morisot stayed too, you know, during the war, when most men fled. She can hardly eat, poor girl. She nearly starved to death. She and her family stayed in Passy and the bombardment there was horrific."

Mary hardly knew how to respond. His eyes? God, what terror. "Hence the glasses?" she said.

"My doctor tells me not to worry."

"But you still do."

"A little," he said. "More than a little. A black hole appears as if from nowhere. I don't know why. I cannot tell what brings it on or what makes it go away. I capture light for a living, and now it is sabotaging me."

He did not want to go back in. They walked out of the courtyards onto the esplanade and the shimmering cobbles. He cupped his palm as if to scoop up and measure the weight of the ungoverned light, calculating, it seemed, how much harm this vital component of his work could do to him. And then the light dulled, the incursion of a cloud, perhaps, or the rotation of the earth away from the sun. Degas let his hand drop. "It's gone."

"What is?"

"The black hole." He blinked once, twice. "Yes, gone completely." He turned in a circle, taking in the square, the gardens, the plane trees. "I'm going to switch oculists," he said.

"Yes, perhaps that would help. A different color glass."

"I fear I am in line for a rainbow of eyeglasses, none of which, I'm certain, will change anything."

"Perhaps. But you might find an answer."

"It's a question of time, too, you see. How much time I have left to paint."

"The hope of the eternal," Mary said. "Of what will survive."

"Yes," he said. "The immortal."

Mary looked away and then back again. "You keep your promises, don't you, Monsieur Degas? Because I decided to stay in Paris because of you. Not you precisely," she said, suddenly embarrassed. "But you meant it, though, didn't you?" She sounded more earnest than she wanted to, but he had said nothing about the exhibition.

"I rarely make promises," he said, "because I find them so difficult to keep. But I made you no promise that I recall. I did, however, make you an invitation to exhibit with us. And I would never withdraw an invitation."

He reached for her hand and held it for a moment before he let it go. Each barely registered the physical touch, but felt instead the way the light loosened something inside them, their twin reserve dissolving in the lambent glow of the newly benign esplanade. Degas offered Mary his elbow and they walked out of the square toward the river. They were each aware of the other in a way they hadn't been when they walked this way an hour before. Even the tawdry traffic on the Seine seemed beautiful now, an aberrancy that even Degas celebrated, for the day had turned out very fine indeed, the light an ever resplendent halo, now so beneficent and shimmering, so pale and beautiful, that Mary and Degas both longed for a brush to record it before it slipped away.

Chapter Thirteen

Berthe Morisot's studio occupied a back room of her apartment, bordering an interior courtyard with views of the building's maids gossiping amid a tangle of water pipes and clotheslines. Paintings, many of which Mary had already seen at the Rue le Peletier, hung one on top of the other on her studio walls, which were flooded with light. Whether landscape, interior, or portrait, the paintings vibrated with femininity, in feeling as in color, the brushstroke so loose and lively that even when the palette included black, applied not as shadow but as color, the pictures radiated an ethereal aspect unmatched by anyone else. Mary thought them glorious. She was especially fond of *The Cheval Glass*, a portrait of a woman dressed in a slip and black neck ribbon, regarding herself in a mirror.

"Did Monsieur Manet influence you?" Mary said. "About the black, I mean?"

Berthe was standing by the windows. It had been two weeks since the salon at the Manets'. This morning, Berthe had sent Mary a note to ask her to please come to see her at her home on the Avenue d'Eylau. Mary had hesitated, then acquiesced. She still carried with her the hurt of Berthe's *stray* comment, with its implied declaration if not of war, at least of its threat. Now the soft light from the windows fell on Berthe in such a way that the deep black of her raven hair glimmered with indigo and ivory. She stood very still in her white lace dress. A red sash was tied in a large bow around her waist.

"Yes," Berthe said, "though Édouard uses it far more than I. I don't know why. It's as if he courts death with that color."

Mary turned back to the canvases. "*The Cheval Glass* reminds me of his *Nana*. Do you ever collaborate with him?" Mary again turned to her hostess, whose face, in the light, so beautiful a moment before, had taken on a pained expression.

Instead of answering, Berthe sat on the long couch under the wall of paintings, indicating that Mary, too, should sit. Above Berthe's head, a sweet pastel of her in blue and ink was signed "É. Manet." She rang for tea. The maid, who must have been hovering outside the door, hurried in with a tray. Berthe poured and handed Mary a porcelain teacup, its thin edges nearly transparent.

"Mademoiselle Cassatt, I invited you here not to talk about my paintings, though I am grateful for your careful observations." Her face was unsmiling as she poured milk into her own teacup. The heightened bon vivant, the coquette, the sociable hostess from the salon had disappeared. "I invited you here because I wish to warn you, with respect, that Monsieur Degas can be mercurial. You haven't known him long enough to know that his regard can easily be withdrawn. You must understand, he is not fickle as much as he is paradoxical. One really never knows what he intends when he says or does anything."

"Are you saying his offer to exhibit is insincere?"

"What I am saying is that you must be careful. I do adore him," Berthe continued, appearing to erase all her life's earlier *adores*, all the truth of that perilous word. "But he can be terrible."

"I'm not sure I understand," Mary said, in as even a tone as possible, unwilling to commit to betrayal on so little evidence.

"What I mean is that you should own yourself. Don't rely on Monsieur Degas. And besides, he is French, and he is a man, and on that basis alone, a woman should take care."

It was impossible to discern Berthe's motive. It seemed that one moment she was attacking, and the next merely trying to be of some help, as if she believed that an American woman afoot in Paris could benefit from this kind of cryptic guidance.

"I am not enamored of him," Mary said. "I merely admire his art."

"Well, he admires you. He could speak of little else the last time I spoke with him."

"Is that true?" Mary said. She held herself very still.

Berthe nodded. "I hope you'll forgive my intrusion. I think women owe one another this, rather than condemnation."

A furtive confession, Mary thought, or perhaps an inquiry to see whether or not she suspected anything. She wouldn't have, not at all, but for Berthe and Édouard having disappeared during Suzanne's performance.

"It is always wrong when women judge one another in situations where they, too, might slip, given the chance," Mary said. She meant the sentiment, but not that she would ever be in that kind of danger herself. Berthe's dark hair, spilling over her shoulders, was caught in a loose ribbon tied at her neck. Mary thought she now knew why Édouard Manet loved black.

"I don't know why I said anything," Berthe said. "A woman who can stand toe-to-toe with Degas, a man whose withering wit exhausts even the most caustic man in the room, is due a kind of reverence."

"Is she?"

"I mean the concern kindly, Mademoiselle Cassatt. I get carried away when the men are sparring. They are so cruel to one another. It can change the way I behave. Forgive me?"

"Only if you explain to me how you keep your brushstroke so light and yet communicate so much."

Later, from the parlor window, Berthe watched Mademoiselle Cassatt stride toward the Place de l'Étoile, feeling certain that she had not done her new acquaintance a service at all by falling into the oblique. But what could she have asked that the woman would have answered with any amount of truth, especially after she herself had been so careless as to reveal herself? What could anyone have asked her about Édouard that she would have answered, oh so many years ago, when she had been too young to know the consequences? In the end, it was you who suffered anyway. You, who had to keep on living.

Chapter Fourteen

The single vellum envelope in her mother's hand arrived on a Thursday at the end of June in the early morning post as the street sweepers and night soil carters trudged toward the outskirts of Paris, lugging the city's refuse and litter with them toward their new slums, having been excommunicated from their old ones by Haussmann's scythe. Mary was often up as the city shed its nighttime identity, greeting the postman, awaiting her maid Anna's stumble down the stairs from her room in the building's eaves, marking the pink light of dawn as she drank a first pot of tea.

June 15, 1877

Darling Mary,

Your father has ended his dithering and decided once and for all that we are to give up our home here and move to Paris. He says that if you won't come to us, we will come to you. That we are leaving behind our grandchildren, your father does not seem to consider an impediment. (I believe he longs to be closer to your brother Robert's grave, in Germany. His death is so long past, twenty-two years now, that I think of him only as an angel who visited us once.)

I know it is a lot to ask to take time from your painting, but could you please find a suitable apartment for us all, including our darling Lydia, of course, preferably near the Champs-Élysées, in the new American quarter, if you can possibly manage it for a decent rent? We would do best, I think, with five rooms, considering how you have crowded yourself into that tiny studio where you work, too. The turpentine! We should faint if we had to suffer such smells all day long. Your father is pressing me now to tell you that in our newly reduced circumstances we cannot possibly pay for the rent on your studio in addition to an apartment, and since your father has decided that we will continue to pay your living expenses—a not unwelcome burden, my darling—it is imperative that you alone pay the lease on a studio from your earnings.

Mary met this news with ambivalence. She was furious that her father had refused her declaration of independence in favor of more control, but on the other hand, though the commission payment from the Ellisons had come in, it was by no means enough to ensure her financial autonomy.

Your father believes this new state of affairs will force you to focus and thereby guarantee your success. To date, we have engaged passage on the *St. Laurent* of the General Transatlantic Line on October 4th, and will arrive on the 14th; from Le Havre we will then take the express train to the Gare du Nord and hire a hack to whichever address you eventually engage. Please send the address as soon as you can so that we can ship ahead. As you know, my French is excellent, but all the same I shall write down the address for the driver, who

should be able to find it but they can sometimes feign
ignorance as I remember from my last visit—

In the early morning silence, Anna was bustling in the kitchen,
making another pot of tea, slicing bread, spooning jam. These domestic
clatterings were the only sound Mary heard in the dreamy haze of morning, before she began to work. Today, before the postman had delivered
the letter, she'd been staring at a blank canvas, preparing herself, agoniz-
ing over tone and hue, brushstroke and subject, perspective and line.
Maybe she suffered from her subject matter, as Degas had recently suggested after another evening at the Manets'. *Paint what is real*, he had
said, *what you see before you, the grit life is made of, not some formal ide-
ation. Paint the men and women who travel up and down the street; paint the
hod carriers. Or better yet, paint what people hide. What people hide is more
real than what they show.*

She had to give up this constant thinking of him. She liked to believe
that whether or not Edgar Degas had ever entered her life, she would
have changed the way she painted in the end, perhaps not as soon, but
eventually. His encouragement might have been the reason she had decided to stay in Paris, but she would have gone on painting in Philadelphia, though whether or not even this was true was a question she might
never answer. But she was not stupid. She knew the extraordinary when
she saw it. Edgar Degas painted in a way that negated all art before it.

Careful, dear. You are exaggerating.

*But if you don't devote, if you don't commit, then is anything really worth
doing?*

Of course not, but do entertain some perspective.

Already her father's voice was in her head, before he was even in
France. She imagined suffering his daily scrutiny, his unwelcome opinions, his scorn. What might he make of the Manets' salon, of Renoir's
less than genteel poverty, of the tangle of the Manets' familial relations
that both Berthe and Degas had alluded to?

And what might her father make of Degas? Neither he nor his paint-ings shied away from the brutal: nudity as professional uniform for the demimonde in the most unflattering postures; ballet dancers more strangely ugly than beautiful. He had shown her more of these last Thursday, when he'd invited her to his studio and apartment on the Rue Frochot, his studio two railroad rooms separated by an alcove, up a spi-ral staircase off the building's entry. The first room was a dim place fraught with chaos: unframed canvases three and four deep lining the wall on the floor, stacks of notebooks and portfolios teetering on tables too small for their burdens, sketches and drawings toppling from the fireplace mantel, studies pinned to the walls, their subjects drawn over precisely graphed penciled grids, others spilling from half-open drawers, their triangle corners draped over the bureau hardware. Shutters cov-ered the casement windows and the close confines smelled of turpentine and oil paint and dust, a miasmic cloud of familiar scents that made Mary feel at home, though the disorder confounded. As she looked about the room, Degas hung back, his tweed coat threadbare at his wrists, his smile an invitation of agitation and pleasure. He'd removed his glasses when they'd come in and he peered at her now to see how she was taking the shambles.

She said, "How do you find anything?"

He shrugged. "Frightening, isn't it?"

Through the alcove, a second room opened to a wall of windows that betrayed mean balconies opening onto an alley, where neglected pots of straggly carnations and limp baby's breath suffered on the edges of bro-ken flagstones. Cardboard boxes of sculpting wax dominated the space under those far windows. Two easels, their wooden poles like masts at sea, supported two paintings, but they were turned, so Mary couldn't see the canvases. A small intaglio press, its drum and wheel glinting in the noon glare, was pushed against the wall.

"You do prints," Mary said. It wasn't a question, but a memory, rising. The work her friend Louisine had purchased had been a monotype, enhanced with pastel and gouache, the shock of color against the black and white an astonishing surprise.

"Tourny taught me. I'm surprised he didn't offer to teach you."

"Have you seen the Japanese prints at that new shop on the Rue de Rivoli?" Mary said, turning. "Off center, color-blocked, flat perspective? They're stunning."

"I haven't. You'll show me. We'll go together."

They returned to the first room. He offered her a seat, not bothering to dust from the deflated seat cushion the powdery residue of months of scraped paint. In his old studio on the Rue Blanche he would have had his sitting room and its luxurious appointments to welcome her—well, he wouldn't allow himself the pity. One made do, and one didn't complain, because you couldn't change anything, especially the actions of careless parents. How could his father have calculated so badly? And not to tell him. Such a mess.

He did not open a window to let in light or fresh air. Instead, he lighted a lamp, its dusky wax intimating the musky skull of the sperm whale that had donated its life so that Degas could see. Hunched over, he began to flip through the thicket of canvases lining the wall.

"I used to have an Ingres and a couple of de La Tours. Not Fantin's, you understand, but two gorgeous pastels by Maurice-Quentin de La Tour. You know him, don't you? He drew Voltaire and the Marquise de Pompadour, Louis the Fifteenth's mistress."

"Of course I do."

"But I had to sell them," Degas said, as plaintively as if he had said, *I had to sell my children.* "When my father died, I discovered that he was not as skilled a banker as he had led me to believe. You don't suspect these things will ever happen. These are swords falling from the sky. And now I find myself hindered. We, my sisters and brothers and I, are shackled to grubbing for money to pay my father's creditors when all I wish to do is make art. One of my sisters might have to move to Argentina to live just to be able to feed her children. Can you imagine? My Ingres fetched a great deal of money, but not enough, it may turn out, to keep her here. And oh, how I miss my Ingres. It hurts me to be without that perfect drawing. As if someone had lopped off my finger. I don't understand money. It just disappears into a great maw, somehow, and you are left with nothing in the end, not even your family."

He pulled from the jumble a canvas, presenting it to her cradled in his arms. The painting was a landscape of plowed fields, interrupted by three bare trees and two figures walking into a November horizon and the advent of an endless winter. "Do you know whose this is?"

She didn't.

"Pissarro's. Splendid, isn't it? I'm fond of neither peasants nor land-scapes, but there is something so real about this. And look at this one." After more hunting, he produced a canvas of peasants riding atop a brimming hay wagon drawn by two horses down a lane. "What I love in this one are his lines: intersecting, askew, varied." He gazed at the un-framed canvas, held now at arm's length. "I could learn to love land-scapes if only Monet would paint like Pissarro. God, what Monet could learn from him if he would only pay attention."

"You don't like Monsieur Monet?"

"His brushstroke is lazy."

"Then why do you exhibit with him?"

"Because the Salon won't have him."

"Are all these canvases by other artists?"

"No. Most of the rest are mine."

"And you don't hang them?"

"God, no. If I had to look at them, I'd rework them all and never begin anything new. I see every mistake of composition, of brushstroke, of line. They are all flawed, every one of them." He sighed. "I am weary. I will never finish anything." He pulled from among the stacks images of the ballet: rehearsals and performances, prints, sketches, oil paintings, pastels, an obsessive profusion of devotion. On more canvases, laundresses scrubbed linen, jockeys rode horses; his much-referred-to hod carriers were not hod carriers at all, but jockeys and laundresses and ballerinas. The pictures lacked any specific romance: The laundresses were workaday rather than glorified; the ballet scenes objective rather than sentimental; but what they both captured was movement, as if Degas were not capturing the memory of the moment, but the viewer instead. And it was more than brushstroke, more than color, more than the play of light, the instruments of his colleagues; his perspective obliterated separation. The viewer was *in the room, the audience, the bathing room* with the subject, as if there were no distance at all between the viewer and the viewed. *As if the canvas didn't exist.*

"How do you do this?" Mary's throat was raw, the scorch of desire so strong that she could hardly get out the words. "How do you make the figures move, the canvas disappear?"

"Gesture."

"Held?"

"No. Made. Repeated. Modeled."

"From life?"

"Yes and no. From what I observe on the streets, primarily, here and there, dinners, cafés, anywhere. I watch how people move; they have no idea that I am raping their lives. Then I make my models reproduce the gesture I want over and over again while I render it on paper. When I finally have it, I trace and retrace it until I can draw the line from memory. Voilà: movement."

"Nothing spontaneous? Nothing from the moment?"

"Nothing in my art is ever from the moment. Nothing about it is ever spontaneous."

"And yet it looks as if it is. As if you have deciphered the heart of motion." Mary was near tears. Her pictures implied motion, but it was the motion of imagination—contrived, fanciful, false. His was the motion of life. "It's extraordinary. It looks effortless."

"Effortless?" Degas's placid expression twisted into a fiery swirl of pursed lips and forehead. "What do you think? That this is easy for me? That I could decide to paint something and then it magically appears from my hand? That I have some gift, that my work arrives finished, that this is not a struggle for me?"

"No. Not at all, but—"

"It's an insult for you to think that I do not work. That I do not have to earn every painting, every print, every drawing I produce."

"I didn't mean to insult you. I was merely asking—I was admiring—"

"You're not stupid. Don't say stupid things."

"I wasn't."

He turned away, the tails of his coat brushing a stack of tracings to the already littered floor. His sudden fury seemed to have enervated him, for within seconds he turned to face her, his shoulders drooping with regret, but Mary was already pulling on her coat, lunging for the stairwell, for escape. Up the echoing spiral of stairs, laughter floated from the street, where people were meeting for lunch, for coffee, going about their days, concerned only with the simple needs of their lives.

"Wait. Please," Degas said.

Mary could not name what tide of emotion rooted her in place. Dust motes danced in the yellow light of the stairway; the clatter of a passing carriage made them shiver and shimmy in arabesques of beauty.

"You must know that if you treat me as everybody else does—as if I am not real—then we are lost, you and I," Degas said.

"You are wrong. We are lost if you mistake my intentions. It is not an insult to wish to paint as someone else does. To admire someone. To be in awe."

"Your adulation will give me a power over you I do not want to wield."

"Desire is not deference. Admiration is not capitulation."

"It always has been in the past. And it always curdles to envy."

She turned. "I promise you, nothing terrible will happen between us because I admire you."

"You must speak to me differently," Degas said. "As if you are accomplished. As if you need nothing from me."

"But I don't know how to do what you do. And I want to know, more than I want anything."

"You must understand. Every day I awake and wonder how I'm going to get through the day. I have to draw and redraw endless lines upon endless lines, tracing within grids to get the perspective right, to perfect the proportions, to establish the composition. And even then I get it wrong. I have nothing of talent. I have only desire and dogged work. I doubt myself every moment. If you do not allow me my weaknesses, if you do not acknowledge my pain, then I am alone. Do you see?"

"You're not alone. I feel the same."

"But you won't believe that I do."

He was right. The something, the leap an artist makes so that his painting is more than its technique, he had already achieved. And she wanted that. She wanted his brain to seep inside hers, his vision to be her vision, his skill to be her skill. She wanted to hear him talk about everything, and by doing so, help her make that elusive jump. Was that wrong? Perhaps it was, if she couldn't offer him anything in return.

No master in need of disciples he, only a man afraid of being alone. How different he was in private. She could hardly reconcile the public man of banter and repartee with the pleading man before her. She thought about what Berthe Morisot had said to her, and decided that Berthe didn't know the real Edgar Degas, who was as needy as anyone.

"Skill is only an accumulation of attentive work," he said, his hands falling to his side. "I cannot teach you how to work. I don't know how to save you from the pain of it."

"I don't want you to tell me how to work. I want to divine the mystery."

"But mystery is indefinable, and therefore divine."

"This moment. This is all I want. To speak of the divinity of art," Mary said.

"The precipice of eternity—"

"Is where artists work."

His gaze sharpened as he assessed her, calculating, she thought, how much credit he might give to her for divining his thoughts, for finishing his sentence, for understanding him.

Degas gestured then. A simple but elegant turn of his wrist, almost balletic in its grace. "I just want to lay my head somewhere."

"What do you think salvation is if not respite?" Mary said.

He held her gaze a long while, a perfect light now falling through the tall windows of the courtyard, a light to covet, a light to work by, a light to compel an artist to rush into the street to hire a model, anyone, to take advantage of its beauty; he said, "Would you sit for me?"

The rasp of the charcoal on the sketching paper, the tear of the sheets and their falling to the floor, his furious crumpling of paper, his exasperated shouts of frustration, his terse orders to hold, goddammit, he wasn't getting it, could she do it again, the turning of her head, the dropping of her chin, the smell of dust and turpentine in the sunlit studio, the plaintive wail of an infant across the alley resolving to a gurgle of pleasure, the hour in which he could look at her as intently as he liked and she could allow him to do it, even the fatigue of sitting on the stool, the undoubted cramp in his hand—all this carried them beyond intimacy. She remained clothed; he asked for nothing.

It seemed as if she had known him forever.

Maybe she had always been hurtling toward him. Maybe her endless arguments with her father at the dinner table in Philadelphia had always had as their end that moment, when the dust of pretense fell away and she surrendered. She turned her mother's letter to the next page, certain that Degas would not have mourned this development as she was, certain now that having lost his father, he would cherish his company if he could only have him back, despite his financial troubles. Her father's primary motivation, it seemed, was money, yes, but life did come down to economics, as Degas had so brutally learned. In France, the exchange rate was five francs to the American dollar; living here was cheaper than in America. And Lydia, *darling Lydia*, would be back—not forced, like Degas's sister might be, to move to Argentina to be able to eat.

Since returning to America from her visit to Paris last year, Lydia hadn't been well. The French doctors seemed better able than the Americans to hold Lydia's malady at bay. Back home, her illness had flared and retreated without reason, much like Degas's eye problem. But their parents, particularly their father, had wanted Lydia with them. He could be so selfish, her father, with his daughters' lives, no matter that they were grown women. For medical reasons alone it would be better for Lydia to be back in Paris, to say nothing of Mary's happiness at once again having her sister's company. And since they would all live together, Mary would only be responsible for her studio expenses. And her mother had never failed to be lively, good company. It might not be too bad, Mary thought. But then she tried to imagine her parents and Lydia at the Manets' salon and sighed.

—and so you will arrange for our lodging as soon as is convenient for you, won't you? Which I hope is very soon as it would be very expensive to have to spend a fortnight or even a week in a hotel upon our arrival, and since we are moving to Paris to conserve money, we (just you, I'm afraid) must be vigilant on our behalf. Oh, and if you could please have the new apartment furnished before our arrival? Your father will wire you the money for this task as soon as you've found us an appropriate domicile and I do trust you, darling, but not any furniture that is too dark or too heavy, and if you could, something beautiful but not too dear? I do hope that you will enjoy this distraction from your painting, which I know cannot occupy you all day long or your eyes will suffer as I know you know. More to come very soon, but until then, keep us

posted on all the arrangements and your father will send the
money for the lease as soon as you have everything firm.

Your loving Mother,

Eager, as ever, to see you again, and soon, with no more
separations to suffer. I am so happy, darling Mary.

She would have to explain Degas to them.

She would say, *He is my colleague; he is part of the new school of painting; he is brilliant.*

But she would not say, *He is someone I suddenly* need. *I cannot live
without him.*

And then she realized she would have no way of explaining him.

She folded the letter, placed it in its envelope, and secreted it in the
desk drawer where she kept her correspondence.

Chapter Fifteen

The residence Mary chose for her parents rose in splendor from the Rue Beaujon just off the Place de l'Étoile, the neighborhood her parents had requested. The increasingly fashionable charms near the Champs-Élysées had lured American expatriates from their traditional stronghold of the environs of the Palais-Royal. The Étoile neighborhood was so new that the tongues and grooves of apartment buildings thrust themselves into neighboring empty lots waiting to be attached to new facades. The rent was forty-five hundred francs, or nine hundred dollars, for the year, but Mary persuaded the reluctant *portier* to let it month-to-month, uncertain whether her parents would approve of the expense. She could never anticipate her father's moods, and did not want to commit to a flat that her father might dislike, whatever his reasons.

But surely, her father could not object to the gold brocade couch, elegant wing chairs, and the round Louis XIV dining table that graced the sunlight-filled rooms. Her mother had written before their departure to say that Lydia had again fallen ill, and that she feared the ocean voyage would be hard on her, so Mary decided that Lydia should have the bigger, brighter bedroom that fronted the street and she the smallest bedroom in the back, with only the dim courtyard to illuminate its claustrophobic confines; she installed a shade to ward off the inquisitive glances of the neighboring building's maids, who spent their days gazing out the kitchen windows into neighboring apartments while scrubbing pots and preparing meals. To her parents, she assigned the large bedroom at the end of the center hall, with its two sets of windows along the courtyard and the street and a long wall that accommodated two wide wardrobes. While installing them, the movers had scratched the parquet floors, and poor Anna, eager to make a good impression with the extended family, had spent an afternoon rubbing varnish into the unsightly scratches with a rag.

All July and August, Mary despaired of finding a new studio whose light and situation were conducive to work. The long months were an odyssey of grumbling *portiers* who tended promising buildings with glorious facades that turned out to harbor shabby, ill-lit apartments. At 6 Boulevard de Clichy she finally found a large room on the top floor of a squat building that nonetheless included tall windows to the north, promising good light, though the omnibus clopped outside the door and shouts from the street reverberated against the plaster ceiling. It would have to do, though. It was all she could afford. Until she made more money, Mr. Ellison's check would have to stretch for a year, and her old apartment studio was far too expensive.

Her summer of diligence was interrupted by several outings with Abigail Alcott, who was soon to leave for London to study watercolor, hoping, too, to find a better market there for her paintings, because, she told Mary, they were in the same boat. An artist had to face fiscal reality. Louisa's money wouldn't last forever. Her sister's success with *Little Women* had provided the kind of financial help Abigail had needed to study abroad, but it was limited, though now there was some income from Abigail's own book, a guide for art students in Paris. But Mary suspected the move had far more to do with poverty than Abigail was letting on, though Abigail glittered with happiness; at thirty-seven, she said, it felt as if life was finally beginning. And, she said, they were kinder to Americans in England, especially if they painted in watercolor.

"But you are deserting me," Mary said. "You must stay in Paris. Think how upset you were with me when I said I might go home. Whom will I talk to who makes as much sense as you?"

"Perhaps Monsieur Degas?" Abigail said.

"He is away for the summer."

"You're being careful, aren't you?"

"Oh, Abigail, there is nothing to be careful of," Mary said, but she guarded her voice. Degas had decamped to the country, to Ménil-Hubert-sur-Orne, whence he wrote complaining that the weather was damp and cold. She received a letter from him every week, detailing the impossibility of painting while visiting people in their country homes and counting the days until he was back in Paris, where, he said, she was.

"Good," Abigail said.

"But it's true," Mary said.

"Then all is well. But soon you will have Lydia, and in her fine company, you won't miss me at all."

As soon as Abigail and Lydia had met, their affinity had been immediate. Lydia loved fashion, as well as art, and could wax poetic on the various fashion houses where a starving artist might kit herself out for a small sum, information that Abigail, on her tight budget, had appreciated. Though the proceeds from Louisa's book had provided the money for study, they had not provided much for a Paris wardrobe. The gift had been made bittersweet, however, in that Louisa's health, damaged when she had nursed at the Union Hotel hospital during the Civil War, had not allowed her to come visit her more cosmopolitan sister. They had that in common, Mary and Abigail: sisters they adored who were ill.

"How is Lydia?" Abigail asked.

"Mother says she's not at all well," Mary said. "But Lydia spares me her sadness, you know, as her younger sister."

"Hardly that young," Abigail said, smiling. Abigail was four years older than Mary, making her closer to Lydia's age than to Mary's; Lydia was turning forty this year. "Though by all rights you are the baby. She should spare you."

They made the most of the summer. On especially warm August nights, they drove to the Bois de Boulogne, the old King's hunting grounds, with its newly installed lakes and paddleboats providing watery respite from the stifling confinement of a summer spent in the city. Only toward three did they make their way home, the eastern sky threading pink with the earliest hints of dawn. On one of Abigail's last days in Paris, they hired a carriage for an entire afternoon, sketching all over the city in the early September sunshine, directing the driver to stop at corners so that they could draw benches and lampposts, passersby, storefronts, and houses, recording all of Paris for Abigail to remember.

In late September, Mary saw Abigail off at the Gare du Nord, her trunks and easels piled around her. As she tearfully kissed her friend good-bye, Mary's only comfort was that Lydia was coming soon.

Chapter Sixteen

On a blustery day in mid-October, Mary climbed into the fiacre she'd hired to fetch her parents from the station and tried not to dwell on the fact that since she'd engaged the studio, no new work had sprung from her mind. She had hung her tapestries and carpets, filled the room with her easels and paint box, arranged the bureaus and paint-splattered tables, her basins and tins, discerned the best hours of light on days both sunny and dim, and yet, she had garnered no commissions. Her head ached so much that some days she could hardly get out of bed. But she did, Anna tiptoeing in to announce the time and prod her from the covers with newspapers and croissants. After breakfast, she took the omnibus to her studio. How she missed rising in her small apartment, reveling in its isolation. Not even visits from Louisine and the ever joyful Miss Ellison erased the cloud of worry. They often came together, bearing gifts of Darjeeling tea and *macarons* from Ladurée.

One afternoon, taking in the new studio, Miss Ellison said, "How do you get your ideas?"

"One imagines," Mary said, "and then one constructs. One sees, and then remembers." *One tries*, she thought, *and often fails*.

Now, traveling down the Rue la Fayette, she bristled. People were always asking artists that inane question. *Don't ask me how I do what I do*, Mary thought. But hadn't she asked Degas the same thing in his studio? It was the question her father asked of her, though he asked it in a far more fiscal way. Yesterday, a letter arrived that he must have posted a few days before they were to leave, listing an agenda of items to discuss upon his arrival.

> We'll outline your business plan for selling your work, also peruse your budget, including any completed sales for this calendar year and projections for the remainder. A debit and credit ledger will be prudent, for accounting purposes.

As if art were a railroad timetable, or a commodity to be traded on the stock exchange. Not that she was averse to selling, not at all. She wished she could persuade her father that she had a healthy respect for money, that it was only the being checked on that galled, the watching over her shoulder, the assumption that she could not manage things herself, but there was also the bald truth that despite her efforts, she might always be reliant on them economically. How she would much prefer to welcome them to Paris on her own terms, as an independent woman of means, supporting herself, able to be gracious without the pall of her father's suspicion.

Outside the *salle des bagages* in the Gare du Nord, having already waited an hour, Mary paced in front of the doors to customs, wondering whether perhaps her parents had missed the train from Le Havre. She was trying to decide whether or not she ought to telegraph the hotel there when her parents and sister emerged, trailed by a harried porter pulling a handcart heaped with trunks. Her father was leaning on a cane, breathless and appearing far older than when she had last left them in Philadelphia. Lydia walked beside him. Even accounting for the exhaustion of the journey, Lydia was very pale. Her mother was shepherding the two of them, efficient and brisk and stolid, turning back often to make certain that the porter hadn't lost them in the crush.

"Oh, my darling! But weren't we coming to you?" her mother said, her eyes alight, embracing Mary with a sigh of pleasure. Her mother's soft skin, cross-hatched with time, was nonetheless pink with health. She always appeared ready for a brisk walk anywhere.

"I wanted to surprise you," Mary said. "Aren't you surprised?"

"Of course I am. You are wonderful. But it was a nightmare about the baggage. The customs men move as if they are dead. And poor Lyddy isn't well; the passage was miserable. Days of storms. You know how that can affect a person. If you'd been with us, you would have made them turn the ship around."

Lyddy, as she'd been called forever, managed a rebellious declaration of health through a smile that nevertheless grew quickly wan. In the gray light of the echoing train station, she appeared far older than her forty years, an alarming change from the last time Mary had seen her. Her cheeks were puffy and an unmistakable patina of exhaustion dulled her skin. Mary fought back a sudden well of tears.

"Don't cry, Mary," Lydia said. "We're here."

"I'm not crying," Mary said, wiping her cheeks with the back of her hand. She took her sister by the shoulders. "You should see your room. I had Anna fill it with flowers."

"Mame." *Mame.* Her father whispered his affectionate nickname for her as he embraced her.

Mary gestured at his cane, which he dismissed with a shake of his head. Since she had last seen him his hair had grown completely gray.

"I'm perfectly fine, darling Mame; this is nothing but a necessary nuisance. But do get us home; we're all on the brink of collapse. You have a fiacre, don't you, waiting for us? Trying to hire one now with everyone vying will be difficult." He looked over his shoulder at the pressing crowd, and this small action sparked a memory from a long time ago, when Mary was six and she and her family had first come to live in Paris. She remembered walking along the platform beside the train, grasping her father's warm and solid hand, terrified as the steam blasted from the locomotives. It was she who had been anxious then, not her father.

"I've taken care, Father, not to worry. And Anna is making us a lovely dinner."

The look of relief on his face shamed her even more. The six years since she had last seen her father seemed a century. He was seventy-one years old now, and the vibrant competence of her mother, ten years his junior, revealed how the tide of time had dragged on him. All this time she'd been thinking their arrival would mean that they would expect her to accompany them about Paris in pursuit of their interests, dismissing her need to work, or that they would disapprove of the Manets and Degas, but it was clear now that these would be the least of her worries. She feared her parents—even her energetic mother—were far less vital than they had once been, when they had regularly changed residences on a whim from Altoona to Philadelphia to Paris, living for four years in Europe when their children had required schooling and governesses, relocations that had demanded energy and stamina and ingenuity. And now her father was fretting about a fiacre, and Lydia looked as if she needed to sleep for a fortnight.

She took each of their hands in hers and kissed their cheeks three times, formally welcoming them in the French way, ignoring her father's embarrassment and the porter's impatience, before leading them out to the conveyances and helping her father into the cab.

Chapter Seventeen

That night, Degas waited in the wings at the Opéra, biding his time until his chosen *petit rat*, his dancer in training, Marie van Goethem, changed out of her costume. He had recently been awarded a backstage pass, which he guarded in his pocket as if it were gold. Tonight he was joined in the wings by a dozen other men, all dodging the scene shifters removing the wooden tavern and *balcons* that had made up the background for tonight's last performance of *Coppélia*. All the men were waiting for the young dancers to finish changing from performance tutus to street clothes. But unlike the *abonnés* striking poses of aloof indifference, hoping to conceal their pedophilic intentions, Degas was fingering the wing's curtains. How many times had he painted this heavy velvet without ever once having the chance to observe the play of limelight up close? Not yet snuffed after the night's performance, the greenish light still flared in the bank of footlights, the flickering shadows undulating on the folds of the velvet like an articulating flock of birds. He was instantly dismayed as he thought of all the canvases on which he had painted the falling light wrong. It was nerve-racking, discovering one's mistakes; exposure at every turn. To approximate reality necessitated reality, and though he usually remembered his way through his work, he liked his imagination grounded. Like, he supposed, the *petits rats*, the scampering girls vying for a place in the ballet corps, their mothers peering over their shoulders and sitting through rehearsals, pushing them to succeed so that their families could eat, ignoring the desires of the men who in the evening took the girls home with them, and perhaps fed them before consuming them, and who, if things worked out, might one day fall in love with them and take the girls off their parents' hands.

Giddy, the girls emerged in a swarm from an iron balustraded stairway from the cellars, having navigated the tortuous passages from the crowded dressing rooms they all shared, face paint still smeared on their soft cheeks, their overextended limbs twisted and gawky in the ghostly half-light of the wings. One by one, they sheered off from the group to be taken up by the waiting men. Marie ran to Degas and he embraced her, full of affection and praise for her performance, though she had stood in the back row and her only task had been to keep her hands raised in an artful *V* as the *étoiles*, the stars, danced a pas de deux.

"You are not too tired?" Degas asked, emptying into her waiting hands the sweets he always carried in his coat pockets when he visited the Opéra.

"Only a little." She had spent the day in class, then rehearsal, then performance, but she showed no fatigue as she trotted alongside him past the other male patrons to the stage door, where he engaged a fiacre to carry them the brief distance to Montmartre. Marie was young, fourteen, and her breath came in little gasps, though he had not yet said or done a thing even remotely seductive, had merely touched his hand to the small of her back as he guided her to his studio from the blare and clamor of Pigalle's cafés, where he'd directed the driver to stop. He supposed he could ascribe her breathlessness to the exhaustion of her night, but it was clear that the young thing was simpering. He didn't know what the girls said to one another, or what the mother had said to the girl, though all the girls knew what the *abonnés* were after. He wondered what she expected, what she had heard. *When a monsieur takes you home.* Marie could not have asked her mother; she had long since left the Opéra house, having negotiated a good price for her daughter's services, the nature of which she had not questioned.

Sweeping into his studio on a dizzy cloud of euphoria—sweets and a fiacre ride!—the girl kicked off her street boots and flopped onto the velvet divan, throwing her arms above her head in anticipatory surrender. Degas took his time removing his overcoat and top hat, hanging them with his black scarf on the coat tree by the door. He shuttered the windows, then fumbled with a match and lit a single candle, which he set on a table far from his tins of flammable turpentine. He considered lighting the sperm oil, but tonight he did not want its bright glare. It would set the wrong mood and thankfully tonight his eye was cooperating, no floating, blurred cloud to confound his vision.

After stoking the stove and kindling its flame until the room began to warm, Degas leaned against the curved arm of the divan, taking stock of his latest acquisition. She was indeed a specimen. A fringe of long lashes smothered her inexpertly kohled eyes, and her cheekbones sliced up and away from a pouting mouth. Her bare arms, while still plump, exhibited the tight muscles born of her punishing daily exercise. The candle's soft shadows sharpened them, lending her the look of an overworked peasant. The rest of her was buried in her froth of an evening gown, no doubt sewn by her ambitious mother, who wanted everything and more for her daughter.

"*Ma chère fille,*" he said, making a dusting motion at the hem of her evening gown. "Shall we begin?"

He swept the white foam of her petticoats up to her knees, then pushed them higher, to the middle of her thighs, where garters secured her black stockings. He unsnapped the garters and inched the smooth silk from her taut thighs and calves to the ends of her callused feet. Then, after slipping his hands inside her thighs, he pushed them apart. He did not look at her face because it was not her pleasure he was after, a fact she would discover soon enough. Her skin was luminous. In this low light, her flesh reflected every color: pink, yellow, and, surprisingly, cerulean, though he also detected a hint of olive and orange.

On their way home in the carriage from her first visit to the Manets',

Mary Cassatt had confessed to him her disappointment that they had not talked about painting. He wanted to please her and so he confessed that for him flesh was the most difficult thing to paint, that it remained his ever-present challenge.

Like God. Like trying to create life, Mary said.

Yes. Each time, he had said, surprised again, as he had been at the party, by her astute observations.

Degas wondered now what Mary would make of this scene. She had no basis upon which to mount an objection, unlike any of Édouard Manet's paramours, all of whom had sound cause to burst in on him. Degas had been careful, though it was possible that the letters he had composed this summer to amuse Mary may have been a tad affectionate, but that was because he had been surprised by how much he had missed her. Words had flown from his pen, just as they had begun to flow before he had left for his extended summer away from Paris. It became his habit to stop by her studio on his way to the Café de la Nouvelle Athènes in the evenings. Of course, she knew that her studio was out of his way, but she never mentioned that indelicate fact. In the late afternoon, around four-thirty or five, she welcomed him with a pot of tea at a small round table she had placed next to her open window—their private café—and he told her all the little odd bits that he had thought of throughout the day. These interludes reduced the stock of bon mots and incisions that he usually unleashed on his colleagues, all of whom had begun to remark on his later arrivals and relative silences, but this did not trouble him. Mary was an alert audience, penetrating and witty.

It was on one of those afternoons that she had told him that her family was moving to Paris. The shock had been significant. He had come to think of her as his and could not imagine her with other loyalties. It felt then as if time was short, and he had taken leave of her with some apprehension. In his letters, he had responded with sympathy to her complaints of rents and the unreasonable demand of her father that she give up her studio. He had signed his letters *Yours.* He had, he believed, perhaps revealed too much. Upon his return, she had been distracted, busy with the arrangements for her family's arrival, and he had not been able to see her. He did not like that now she lived so far from Montmartre.

Sighing, he lifted the girl's right leg, studying the colors and the reflection of the candlelight. As if she were onstage, Marie extended the leg and pointed her toes. He grasped her heel, then ran his hands from her extended ankle along the knotted calf over the knob of her knee to the sinew of her thigh, probing with his fingers. He had been thrilled when he had first learned that it was the lesser muscles that levered the leg upward, the strength coming from the hamstring and not from the quadriceps. It changed the way he drew the girls, though the alteration was subtle, perhaps noticed only by him. He turned out her right leg, rotating it in her hip socket, into a side battement, observing the stretch and contraction of the complementary muscles, quantifying the ratio of ankle to knee to hip. Finally, he pushed the legs together and laid them side by side on the divan.

"Point your toes again," he said, and she articulated first her ankles, then the balls of her feet, then the toes, until her legs were one single limb, as firm as iron. He pressed down on the tops of her feet, feeling once again with his right hand along her thighs, for the way the muscles separated as she pushed against his hand.

"Stand."

She stumbled to her feet.

"Take off your dress."

She turned. Expertly, he undid the buttons and the dress fell to her feet.

"Your corset next."

She nodded, mute, as he unloosed the ties, but he made her draw the garment away from her body herself.

"Turn around."

She did, slowly.

"Remove your garter and panties."

Silent, she slipped her thumbs under the silk garments and worked them down her muscled legs.

His gaze traveled up and down her body. "Rise to your toes."

She turned out her feet to first position and pressed the floor away from her.

"Now perform a port de bras."

Her back muscles engaged, causing her arms to float upward. Degas circled her, inspecting her buttocks, her back, her flat stomach, the tiny floating orbs of her young breasts, the way her neck elongated as her shoulders settled and anchored her in space. She had such a gnarled body, limbs like poles, as gawky as a boy's. When her hands met a half inch apart, he asked, "Can you hold that position?"

Wordlessly, Marie nodded.

He retrieved the distant candle, lit a dozen more, arranged them before her on the floor to imitate the flare of limelight, pulled his latest tablet from its pile, and began to draw.

"Do it again," he said.

"Do what?"

"Lower yourself, then rise to your toes and perform the port de bras. Over and over again, until I ask you to stop."

He drew her from behind, from the side, from the front, observing the musculature as she raised her hands above her head. He drew her thighs as they pressed together, tried for the curve of her shoulders as her arms rose, all sinew and muscle, the grace of the hands as she floated them upward. He believed art was an exaggeration and a distillation both, but when he was working, he doubted everything. My God, it was just an arm. Why couldn't he get it right? His hand flew over the paper, his eyes on the girl. He would stay here a hundred hours if he had to.

Marie complained of pain. She lowered herself from en pointe, stretched, entwined her hands behind her, thrust her jaw forward as she arched her back, and placed her feet in fourth position. There was something so bestial about the move, so ugly, that Degas was enthralled. A gift of sudden sight. He didn't understand how the elusive sometimes came from his hands; he only knew that if he was stubborn enough, if he stayed at his work, something sometimes condescended to flow through them.

Banker's hours. Perhaps it was his father's influence. The single paternal gift.

He tore off the last drawing from his tablet and said, "Don't move," as he retrieved another.

At three or four in the morning, he steered the exhausted girl up the steep Rue Lepic to her laundress mother, who was on guard outside the door of their hovel, her chapped hands cupped around a mug of coffee long gone cold. He handed the girl's mother two francs, the standard modeling fee, and she grunted and slipped the money into her coat pocket. What the mother thought he'd done with her, he didn't know, though he'd been very clear. She asked neither him nor the girl, who yawned and stumbled through the door in anticipation of a few hours' sleep before returning to the Opéra for class. Degas knew that ultimately the mother wanted her daughter to be taken care of, something he could not offer her, unlike an *abonné* with money to spend. Degas hoped that the evening's combination of surprise and disappointment would keep Marie silent, as it had kept all the girls silent before her. He hoped that she would one day understand that he had spared her.

The studies had poured out of him, and though he should sleep, he would go back now and pin them on the walls and look at them, the dawn light offering a cleansing clarity that the night had not. The fever was on him now, and nothing, not even a lack of sleep, would keep him from it.

Chapter Eighteen

I s this what it means to be an artist in Paris? You can be late to dinner parties?" Robert Cassatt snapped the black-and-white pages of *Le Figaro* and continued trying to read the newspaper by candlelight, having eschewed the complicated problem of lighting the gas jets by lighting a match instead. "Have you begun to indulge such terrible habits too, Mame? Is this what has become of manners in Paris?"

Mary attributed her father's vile mood to his campaign to improve his French. After two weeks in Paris, he was feeling incompetent next to his fluent wife and daughters, whose facility outshone his. To repair this, he had begun reading the French newspaper instead of *Galignani's Messenger*, the English-language newspaper published for the benefit of the American colony. Tonight, President Grant, his term recently ended, was in town and Robert wanted the details of the visit, but he was having trouble deciphering the longer sentences, and his exasperation was trying everyone.

"You know you love Paris, Father, and you yourself said that Haussmann made a jewel out of a stone." Mary set her glass of sherry on the marble table at his side and sat next to him, hoping to mollify him. His raised voice would carry his surly impatience into the hall, which would reach Degas even before he stepped through the door into the foyer.

"You exaggerate, Mame," Robert said. "I can't imagine having lived through the city's destruction. I don't know how you did it, dodging piles of debris everywhere."

The family had moved from Paris to Germany, then back to Philadelphia just before Haussmann had begun to transform the city, and Mary could not help but wish that the work had been finished when she'd returned to the city the first time to live on her own, in 1865. But all the upheaval had been worth it. When her family arrived two weeks ago, riding in from the Gare du Nord, they had traveled down the Boulevard des Italiens, their many bags trailing behind them in a luggage cart, its driver standing against the dash so that he wouldn't lose them in the evening traffic. It had been out of the way to go by the Boulevard des Italiens, but Mary had wanted to show her father the city's newest showpiece. Even Lydia, her most recent visitor, gasped as they rounded the Place de l'Opéra, where the Opéra Garnier glimmered ivory in the gloaming, the arched and colonnaded facade set ablaze by the newly installed electric lights lining the place and the boulevard.

"Paris is shining," she said. "Isn't it glorious?"

Even her father couldn't hold out against such magnificence. He wrapped her hand in his and said that it was glorious, indeed.

Paris, no matter its inconveniences, could charm anyone, and she was pleased that it had charmed her father all over again, but it wasn't long—two days, to be exact—before the unreliable water pipes in their new apartment made her father lament their move, failing to appreciate that they had indoor plumbing, tricky as it was, while eighty percent of Paris still filled buckets at the public fountains. The apartment kitchens even had gas stoves, which meant that no coal smoke seeped through the floors and walls to choke the flat with fumes, and yet this improvement was somehow not enough to render her father happy. Even though the whole family had exhausted themselves in helping to arrange the apartment more to their father's liking, shifting rugs and tables and rehanging curtains, he had remained cross. And now he was furious with Degas before having even met him.

The evening was not beginning well on any account. Anna, as yet inexpert on the lighting and timing of the gas oven, had been resuscitating the roast chickens for half an hour now, basting and putting them in and pulling them out of the oven at intervals to try to keep them warm, while the roasted potatoes shriveled and the last of the season's kale grew more bitter with every passing moment. Lydia still had not recovered from the voyage and had dressed today only for dinner. Their mother, Katherine, had spent the day trying to pry from Mary details about just who Edgar Degas was.

"Tell me again," she said to Mary now, "about this new friend?"

"Is he an actual person, Mame?" Robert looked at her over the top of his newspaper, his glasses slipping to the end of his nose, his forehead furrowing in anticipation of an answer that would appease him. "You didn't make him up, did you, to play a continental joke on your poor old father? To see how far you could push him? To further convince him that to have moved to Paris was a foolhardy choice? Because we haven't gone over your finances yet, and I'm beginning to think that you're making everything up. Your studio, your work, your friends."

"Oh, Father," Lydia said. "You're being unkind. We're going to see Mary's studio tomorrow." Lydia sat breathless and pale at the far end of the divan, but she couldn't be persuaded to rest throughout dinner. She had informed Mary that she was going to meet Degas because Mary had hardly spoken of anyone else since their arrival.

"That isn't true, is it, Lyddy?" Mary had said that afternoon, bringing Lydia tea as she rested.

"I remember you admiring him before. And now you are his friend?" Lydia had said, taking the teacup and smiling at Mary. "I'm not going to miss this dinner for anything."

"Well, if the man doesn't show in the next five minutes, I'm going to eat that chicken before it tastes like death," Robert said now.

"He has moved, Father, and is just now settling in," Mary said. Recently, Degas had fled the alley life of the Rue Frochot for a new apartment on the Rue Lepic, at number 50. He had sent out an announce-ment to all his friends, with the words "Belle Journée" inscribed on them. "Something must have happened. He is never late." Which wasn't quite true.

"Never late? Then we're special. How wonderful."

"Father, this is Paris. The traffic is always difficult, but in the rain it is a nightmare. You know this."

The rain had begun lightly at first, in the afternoon, but now water was coursing down the gutter in the center of the street. Even from high up in the apartment, she could hear the tributaries slipping across the cobbles to join the river raging down the trough. Or perhaps she was imagining the violence of the deluge, making excuses for Degas's ab-sence. She hadn't seen him in months, not since July, when he had left for his extended exile in the country. Though his letters had grown intimate as time passed, full of gentle teasing and amusing confidences about his hosts, she imagined now that they could have been written to anyone. Per-haps it had not been the best idea to invite him to meet her family, though propriety—her parents' expectations—demanded the introduction.

The knock at the door startled them all.

Mary rose to answer, and her mother said, "Please let Anna get that."

"Anna can't hear every knock when she has to cook dinner, too, Mother. It's nothing to answer a door," Mary said.

Rivulets ran from Degas's umbrella, and his coat was drenched. Mary took his top hat, beaded with rain, and handed it to Anna, who had run from the kitchen, wiping her hands on her soiled apron. The coat they let drip on the rack and the umbrella they opened and left on the landing.

"Thank you for this," Mary said to Degas.

His eyes, even shielded by the lavender glasses—he had taken to wearing them even at night—radiated that inquiring gentleness that she had missed in his absence. No one but Degas looked at her like that. No one in her life had ever looked at her like that.

"I'd forgotten how lovely your face is," he whispered, leaning in to kiss Mary's cheek.

"Come in before my father shoots you," she said.

"How pleasant," Degas said. "Does he own a firearm?"

He had had to wait a long while for an available seat on the omnibus, as all of them had arrived at his stop fully occupied. This explanation hardly mollified Robert, who sniffed as he stood to shake the artist's hand. Degas carried a velvet bag, inside which several small gifts were wrapped in colored tissue paper and bright ribbons. Nor did the gifts appease Robert in any way, even when his wife and Lydia gasped as they opened two exquisite silk fans that Degas had painted for them, he said, as soon as he'd learned Mary's family was coming. He handed Robert a similar package, and he opened it to find a cravat of silk paisley "for the Opéra." Robert wondered what such intimate gifts could possibly mean. No man in America would ever give another man such a personal item, nor would anyone but a close male relative give a woman such a romantic present as a fan.

Partaking of sherry and preliminary talk was abandoned to speed them to the dinner table and the roasted fowl, but not even the good wine could disguise the culinary disaster. The poultry had that twice-cooked rubbery taste and the potatoes had withered into hard pellets. Anna whisked the dismal meal on and off the table within the space of fifteen minutes, producing in its place a dessert tart of Normandy pears. She poured cream over each generous portion and served walnuts, too, with a pot of fresh coffee to finish, then withdrew into the kitchen.

"Are your paintings selling, Monsieur Degas?" Robert asked, after the polite talk of their ocean voyage and the stress of their move had been dissected while they devoured the exquisite tart, the pastry crust so flaky that not even the heavy cream drowned out its buttery lightness. Occasionally, Mary had to translate Degas's rapid French for her father, but he was able to negotiate the conversation if no one strayed too far into the irregular verbs or conditional tense. But her father could be, with his limited capacity, just as rude in French as he was in English. Mary set her fork on the table, a drop of cream falling onto the white linen tablecloth, newly unpacked from its trunk that morning.

"Father, you cannot ask Monsieur Degas such a personal question."

Degas, seated across the table from Mary, shrugged and said mildly, "How does a man live as an artist? An important question, indeed," but he said nothing more as the grandfather clock, adjusted this morning by the clockmaker, ticked in the ensuing silence.

Robert, used to being heeded and obeyed, waited for a longer explanation that did not come. Mary knew that a question like that from anyone else would have earned a resounding storm of mockery from Degas. She turned a pleading gaze on her mother to take up the mantle of conversation before her father could untangle the evasion and realize that he'd just been handled by a guest in his own home.

With a barely perceptible nod toward Mary, Katherine said, "Monsieur Degas, why don't you tell us about your family? I'm sure we'd love to meet them."

"Madame, my parents have died. I have four siblings, one of whom lives in New Orleans and has a family there. I went to see them several years ago. I very much liked visiting your country. Have you been to New Orleans?"

"We haven't been to the South," Katherine said. "We travel to Europe instead. No decent Northerner can abide the South after the war, but I suppose our quarrels didn't affect a Frenchman on tour."

"You are here in Paris as many years after our war with Prussia. Have our recent troubles affected you in any way?"

"I suppose not," Katherine said. "Though I do miss the glorious Hôtel de Ville and the Tuileries Palace. So lovely, those buildings."

"I thought the Communards here had some basis, you understand, for their fury, perhaps as your Southerners had basis. After all, you did destroy their way of life."

"I beg your pardon?"

"The war changed everything for your Southerners, did it not?"

"You cannot tell me you condone slavery?"

"Not at all. You mistake me," Degas said, avoiding looking at Mary. "It must be the language difficulties."

"I've lost no French," Katherine said, bringing a napkin to her lips and appealing to Mary.

"I should have warned you that Monsieur Degas says things he doesn't mean just to roil the conversation," Mary said, fixing Degas with an imploring gaze, which he returned with a blank stare of innocence.

"Then he should hardly have any difficulty answering my question," Robert said, his French suddenly more fluent than it had been all night. "On average, Monsieur Degas, what do you think you sell—how many paintings a year?"

"Why don't you just pull out your ledger and show him our finances, Father?" Mary said rapidly in English. "Or better yet, empty your pockets and let him count your coins, and then he can do the same so you'll be satisfied as to his economic circumstances." She switched to French and turned to Degas. "I'm sorry, Monsieur Degas. My father's interests in art, as they are in anything, are mercenary, not aesthetic. He doesn't believe in buying art, so I don't know why he is asking."

"I like a good argument, mademoiselle, just as it seems your father does," Degas said. He addressed Robert: "I don't keep records, Monsieur Cassatt, if that is what you are asking, so I cannot fulfill your request. To keep me eating, I do portraits in the afternoon. Tell me, didn't Mary say you were in railroads? What will you do in Paris now that you are *re-traité*?"

Mary flashed Degas a grateful smile for the expert diversion.

"Mary's brother Aleck is the one in railroads. I'm in stocks. Or was."

Robert took a sip of coffee. "Maybe I'll take up painting in my spare time. I'll have nothing else to do."

Degas's smile turned brittle. "My dear Monsieur Cassatt, you will find that painting is not very difficult when you don't know how, but that it's very difficult when you do. But, you're right, take it up, as you might horse racing. It's a pleasant enough pastime. Anyone with a brush can do it. Or perhaps we could exchange occupations. I could go into stocks," Degas said. "Would an hour of instruction from you suffice to prepare me? That seems plenty for such a straightforward endeavor."

The evening was threatening to end in outright war. Mary was grateful when Anna carried in a bowl of cut apples doused with brandy, a smattering of pecans and figs, and the morning's leftover brioches on a tray. She set the brandy ablaze, then smothered it with a cloth and spooned the caramelized fruit over the stale brioche. Mary watched the girl march away with the tureen, astonished at her timing and resourcefulness.

"We Cassatts are a practical bunch," Robert said. "Mame is our first artist."

"Mame?" Degas said.

"My endearment for our Mary. I confess I don't understand why she should continue working if she can't sell what she paints. What is the purpose of any endeavor if not to make money? And how does an artist tell whether or not he is successful? For that matter, how does one know whether or not she is any good at all, or whether she is just daubing at canvases and deluding herself?"

"Father, you insult our guest, and me," Mary said.

"It's a valid question. As your father, I have a responsibility to ask whether or not you are wasting your time."

"Don't ask Monsieur Degas. Ask me," Mary said.

"Do you believe, Monsieur Cassatt, that Mary will only be a great artist if she makes a lot of money?" Degas said.

"In business, that is how we define success." Robert turned to Mary. "You cannot pretend that you do not want to sell your paintings."

"Of course I want to sell my paintings."

"Then why is it so terrible that I asked?" her father said.

"Because you are talking about *money*."

"We in France despise money," Degas said. "We despise its necessity, having to run after it, to think about it, to have to acquire it, to settle accounts, to owe people things."

"Thank God the world isn't run by artists," Robert said, seemingly unable to think of a further reply to a man who didn't appreciate the value of money.

"No artist wants to run the world," Degas said.

"More is the pity," Lydia said, breaking into the conversation in her honeyed voice. They all turned to her now, as if remembering for the first time that she, too, was at the table.

"Just so, mademoiselle," Degas said. "Tell me, the North Atlantic didn't undo you, I hope? When I crossed, the waves were terrifying." He asked more questions about her plans and whether or not she would sit for her sister, complimenting her on her command of French and promising to escort her to the Louvre, showering such chivalrous attention on her that the rest of the evening passed without incident.

Degas took his leave toward eleven, before the omnibuses shut down for the evening. Anna had dried his hat by placing it on a napkin in the kitchen near the stove, but his coat was still damp and someone had stolen his umbrella from the landing.

"If you wish to never see me again," Mary said, "I will understand."

"On the contrary. Your father matches Zola in his ignorance. Why would I deprive myself of such fun?"

"You were good to my father, but he had no right to your charity."

"Oh, but he is your father, mademoiselle," Degas said, and placing his hat on his head, he strode onto the landing and down the echoing stairwell, its walls already peeling paint, toward a rendezvous with some friends at the nearby Cirque Fernando, where he liked to watch the elephants, jugglers, horse riders, and the performer Miss La La, who executed the most bizarre skills while suspended from the ceiling by a rope gripped between her teeth. Some people accused Degas of being a recluse, but Mary had no idea how that rumor had ever begun. He was out every evening, either at a café concert, in his seat in his loge at the Opéra, eating dinner with friends, haunting a salon, or taking in the spectacle of the circus, delighting in every diversion, low or high, that filled the dark winter evenings and the sublime summer twilights, dreaming always of what to paint next, unencumbered by parent, wife, or child, free of every obligation save that of repaying his father's debt.

"Mame?" her father called.

"Coming," Mary said, and shut the door.

Chapter Nineteen

The doctor, a Monsieur Girard, emerged from Lydia's bedroom, his black bag in hand, and walked briskly into the parlor, where Robert and Mary awaited him. Mary had gone that morning to the Hôtel-Dieu de Paris, on the Île de la Cité, to beg his presence, which had required a wait in his reception of two hours and a promise of double his payment if he would come directly to their home that evening after his clinic. She had not had to exaggerate to persuade him. After Degas's visit, Lydia suffered all night long from a headache she described as an expanding balloon in her head. Overnight, her hands and face swelled so much that the skin was as tight as a leather glove. Katherine and Mary stayed up all night with her, plying her with laudanum to relieve her pain, and now, as Katherine followed the doctor down the hall after chaperoning his visit, a grim pallor washed across her fatigued face.

"It is, I think, a problem of, if I may speak frankly, her elimination," the doctor said. "Her urine is dark and frothy, which does not bode well. My prescription is that she must eat no meat, no poultry, no fish, just vegetables and fruit, but no sour fruit. Not a grain of salt is to be had. And no more laudanum, Madame Cassatt—and no wine, either. She must be stringent, for any careless indiscretion of diet may do her great harm. I must emphasize this rule most carefully. Any indiscretion can harm her irreparably."

"I hurt her, didn't I, with the laudanum?" Katherine said.

"It was the alcohol in the laudanum that was injurious to your daughter. I will get you the oil of poppy for her instead, to relieve headache, should it recur. She will help herself immensely if she can maintain discipline. But you must speak to your cook. You must insist. No salt in the food. No broth. No egg or bacon for breakfast. No bread. Just vegetables and fruit."

"For how long?"

"For a while."

"But she cannot live on that forever."

"No, she cannot."

"But she will live?" Katherine said.

"She must follow my prescription. She must also drink fresh blood daily at the abattoir, as soon as she is able. The one behind des Invalides provides a facility with clean glasses and the blood is always fresh. I will return tomorrow and every day after until she is well, then weekly after that."

Katherine and Mary exchanged looks. "Blood?" Katherine said.

"It's very helpful in cases such as these," the doctor said.

"Shall I go and fetch it for her now?" Mary asked. "If it will make her better?"

"No. It will coagulate by the time you bring it to her and will be useless. She must take it there."

"But what if she isn't well enough to go?"

"Patience, mademoiselle. I will be back tomorrow. Give her coffee to rid her of the fluid that is making her swell. It will help her headache, too. I would bleed her, but the coffee will do for now. She is my patient and I will do everything I can to keep her from harm. You did well to come find me. How did you know to ask for me?"

"I didn't. I asked at the reception and the man there recommended you."

"Then you are lucky. Someone else might have killed her."

The grim words impaled Mary's heart.

"Should we have moved her from America? Was it too much for her?" Robert said.

"Perhaps. It is impossible to know. *Bonsoir*," he said to Mary and Katherine. "Do not worry. Worry never helps," a sentiment that Mary thought distinctly French.

When Robert and the doctor stepped outside to conduct the unsightly transaction of payment, Mary said, "She has visited Paris many times before, Mother. It cannot possibly be because she traveled here again. None of this is your fault."

"Was the dinner overly salty, do you think, last night?"

"Lyddy hardly ate anything."

"She never does. Or she doesn't when she doesn't feel well. I should have noticed. Ask Anna to make coffee, would you, please, Mary? Oh, I'll do it. You go sit with Lyddy. But don't tell her about the blood. That will just make her ill all over again."

In Lydia's bedroom, a low candle burned in lieu of the gas. She lay in a tangle of sheets, her cheeks so swollen her eyes were nearly shut, her right forearm thrown across her forehead.

"Mama is bringing coffee. The doctor says it will help with the pain."

"Everything is swimming."

"It's the laudanum. No more for you."

"I hate it, anyway. It makes the pain go away but I am so dizzy and stupid that I can't utter a decent word. I'm sure the doctor thought I was simple."

"No one would ever believe you simple."

"Am I to live?" Lydia said.

She would not have asked, Mary thought, but for the loosening of her tongue by the laudanum. Mary's throat caught and she could not answer.

"Is it that bad?" Lydia said.

"No."

"You should never lie. You're terrible at it."

"The doctor claims he's brilliant."

"Is he?"

"Of course." He seemed brilliant, anyway. Or at least confident, and at this point that would have to pass as brilliant. "The French are gifted at medicine. Moving the family here was my conspiracy to get you near the best doctors. I arranged it all," Mary said.

"You just defeated your own argument. You didn't want us here and you know it, Mary. And now I am ill and making things worse for you. I promise I will get better so that you can paint again and you won't have to spend your days chasing after doctors and your nights taking care of me."

"It is Father I mind."

"He may grumble, but he doesn't steal your days by keeping you up all night."

"If you apologize one more time, I will make you eat dinner alone with Monsieur Degas."

"Hardly a punishment." Lydia lifted her arm and turned her head toward Mary. "Is he your beau?"

"No."

"Then what is he?"

Mary shrugged. "I cannot say."

"Well, he is not from Altoona."

Mary laughed. "Oh, darling Lyddy. What have I done without you?"

Lydia yawned. "What you have done since I was last here: tried to get work done. Didn't you say there was coffee?"

Mary rose. Lydia was still pale, her skin dry and taut, but nothing, it seemed, not even illness, could alter her essential good nature, and it was this, Mary thought, more than diet or animal blood, that might save her. Abigail Alcott she missed, but Lydia was goodness itself.

She shut the door behind her and went into the kitchen to try to hurry the coffee, where she found Katherine making lists for a weeping Anna, who had to be restrained from throwing the saltcellar out the window.

The sole care of the family was deemed too much for Anna, and within days Katherine Cassatt hired a German woman, Mathilde, to help her.

1878

Chapter Twenty

Within a week, Lydia's health improved; she made daily forays with Robert to the abattoir to drink a glass of blood, releasing Mary to go back to work, but this release was preempted by her family's expectations regarding dinnertimes, family outings, dress shopping, and the vagaries of French plumbing. Not even her mother's and sister's previous extended visits had prepared Mary for her family's constant presence and many demands.

In the first week she repeated, "I can't; I'm working," so many times that that was all she seemed to say anymore, which meant that she left home in a terrible mood, arrived at her new studio in a terrible mood, and then first had to light the little stove because the room was bone cold. There had been so many advantages to living, essentially, in her studio, advantages she had lost in the move. She spent the mornings shivering until the coal warmed the air, preparing the many canvases she had purchased for the months ahead. It was now only six months until the fourth exhibition of the impressionists. Six months! How was she to produce the plethora of canvases she needed to make a presence? She couldn't paint just one or two and submit them, as she had for the Salon. No, she needed at least eight, perhaps more, and she hadn't ever produced that many original paintings in a year, let alone six months.

Mary begged her mother to model for her, and hoped that once Lydia's health stabilized she could paint her, too. It would be a new beginning, painting her family, after the long drought of preparing for her parents' arrival. Family cost nothing, unlike models, and the time they spent together might ease their disappointment with her dedication. Even her father said that he would submit to the brush. He had given her expenses a thorough going-over and praised the economy she'd shown in choosing the modest studio for its reduced rent, though he remained utterly indifferent to its drawbacks, strict in his belief that Mary must do everything to keep herself within budget, even tolerate the mess of horse and gutter that was the countrified Boulevard de Clichy. And so, once the Christmas and New Year's festivities passed, with their bags of oranges and exchanges of gifts, her mother rode with Mary on the omnibus crowded with clerks and shopkeepers bundled against the wet Parisian chill to the bitter cold of her studio, which they mitigated with hot tea brewed on the spirit lamp while the coal gathered strength. Far from Robert's impatient probing, they spoke of Lydia's health, Mary's brothers, Aleck and Gardner, and the news Katherine read in the newspaper, propped open on her lap while Mary worked.

Sometimes Degas stopped by. "It is memory," he said to Katherine. "Mary is remembering you. It is all the life and love you have given her that she uses to paint you."

"Memory?" Katherine asked.

"If an artist reproduces only what he sees, then where is the artistry?"

Degas seduced Katherine's warming regard with a display of impeccable manners on his subsequent visits, which were suitably brief, and which Katherine thought showed a respect for propriety. Since that first disastrous dinner, there had been other, better evenings, with suggestions of joint summer excursions to the Bois de Boulogne for the horse races, to seduce Robert, who was a lover of racing, as was Degas. He even invited Robert to his studio to see some of his paintings of horses, which Robert, not knowing what a great exception this invitation represented, had yet to accept.

When Katherine's portrait was finished, Mary painted Lydia, who had recovered sufficiently by February to both sit for her portrait and get about town, accompanying Mary to the Opéra, where the gilded chandelier and searing limelight ameliorated the oppressive dark of winter. Mary, in need of ever-widening subjects, carried a small sketchbook in pockets she had sewn into her evening dresses for the purpose. Sometimes she and Lydia met Louisine Elder and Mary Ellison there, who forgave the rasp of Mary's pencil during the performance as she sketched the theatergoers, the embellished ceiling of painted cherubs floating in a blue sky, and the ornate curves of the crystal chandelier from their box, composing pictures in her mind, bending over her book to finish even as the performances ended and people stood to applaud. Mary avoided Degas's night, which was Monday. She did not want to greet him on the fishbowl of the grand staircase, where every turned head was remarked on, and every whisper repeated the next day.

Lydia loved the portrait that Mary was painting of her. In it, she wore her most daring evening gown and a string of tight pearls, and she was being painted as if she were seated in a loge at the Opéra. She had begun to feel much better, despite the loathsome visits to the abattoir, though she didn't like the bemused and sympathetic expression on the doctor's face even when she was feeling her best. Mary insisted that her skin shone with such luminosity that she would certainly be better now for all of time. Lydia hoped that was true. The swelling in her hands and face had exhausted her and the headache had felt like death. In the weeks afterward, it had been difficult to go out, for she could hardly appear in public when her face took on that chipmunk puffiness and her stomach swelled to twice its normal size. And she descended into such a *fog*. But it was true, all the dullness in her skin had disappeared, and she was happy to be in Paris again.

"Is my picture to be an answer to Monsieur Degas's danseuses?" Lydia said. "Degas paints the dancers and you paint the audience?"

"Not as an answer, no," Mary said, hoping that no one else would draw the same conclusion, though the picture was an answer, of sorts. One had to paint something, and she could not draw cafés or bathhouses as the men did, nor did she wish to impinge on Berthe's glorious dressing rooms. The answer had come to her one night as she despaired. She didn't want to sit women in chairs forever and paint them as if they spent all their lives embroidering. Her portraits needed a context, and the Opéra was perfect. But Lydia's painting was taking longer than usual. For the first time, Mary was painting a detailed background: It wasn't just a picture of Lydia; it was a picture of Lydia *at the Opéra*. And she was still learning the new technique. The style change mystified her family, who had been schooled by Mary to believe that academic art was the ideal art and that all her training had been leading her toward success in that realm. Mary had fueled that belief over the years by sending home newspaper clippings of her triumphs at the Salon. Now she was declaring that she'd been set free from the prison of the Salon. She talked on and on of rendering form by indicating it with color rather than establishing it with line, of lightening her brushstrokes and palette, of abandoning the formal for the informal. She detailed the best ratio of poppy seed oil to paint, varying it as she painted layer upon layer, pushing the pure colors out of the way with her wet brush laden with yet another color, juxtaposing tones so that she could render high and low lights. Day after day she talked of applying the new techniques she was finally inhaling from her conversations at the Manets' Thursdays, where she had given up being the polite newcomer and cornered Pissarro when he was in town, or begged Renoir to discuss tones and values. Her family had yet to go with her. Robert said he would rather die than suffocate in a parlor of writers and artists, and Katherine claimed that she was still too American to plunge into such a bohemian crowd.

Winter gave way to a warm, if wet, spring, and across Paris artists were once again in the clutches of Salon fever. For the first time, Mary was not at the mercy of a jury, but the impressionist exhibition was scheduled for June and by the beginning of April she had only four canvases ready: a

portrait of her father, one of her mother, and two of Lydia. She was beginning to despair. What else to paint? She was not Degas. She couldn't
find a thousand ways to paint a woman in a loge. They would always be
elegant, always coiffed, always caged. Daily, the sense of panic widened.
Unable to afford a model, unable to paint outside in the rain, unable to
think of another pose for her family, she fretted her time away in the
studio. She set her easel at the window to try to capture the street scene,
only to fail miserably. She stalked people in the Place d'Anvers, hoping
someone would sit so that she could sketch them surreptitiously, but everyone flew past in the blustery wind. She even considered visiting a
café, but the horror of being a woman alone defeated her.

To distract herself, Mary went with Lydia to the Opéra on a Monday
night, the only night that week that Mary could obtain cheap tickets.
During intermission, they ran into Degas in the doorway of the grand
foyer, a strategic location from which he liked to observe the ascending
and descending patrons on the grand staircase, with their stunning
dresses of silk and brocade, their headdresses bobbing in the shimmer of
the thousand candles that graced the crystal chandeliers set high above
the staircase. One had only to stand and gaze at the architecture to be
amazed; the dancing and singing onstage were mere dessert.

Degas took one look at Mary and grasped her by the elbow, steering
her to a balcony overlooking the grand staircase, out of the crush of patrons crowding into the foyer in search of mid-show sustenance in the
form of champagne. Lydia trailed behind, but turned her back on them,
enacting the faithful blindness of sympathetic chaperones throughout
time. She gazed over the staircase and sipped from her own flute of sustenance, bubbling water in deference to the doctor.

"What is the matter?" Degas asked Mary. "Are you ill? Or is it something worse?"

"I don't know what to paint. I can't do another portrait of my family
or I shall go mad. Not that I don't love you, Lyddy dear," she said over her
shoulder.

"Of course not, darling," Lydia said. Chaperones might be blind but they were never known to be deaf. Besides, she wasn't certain she wanted to sit again for Mary. The brief spate of good health she had enjoyed in February seemed to be abating. It was little things, noticeable only to her. Her rings too tight on her fingers, the darkening of her urine. It was embarrassing being ill with such an indelicate malady, one so private that she felt shame even with the doctor, who examined her with a serious but furtive air, and who studied the contents of her chamber pot even while she was in the room. Coming to the Opéra with Mary was a way to forget, as well as to appease her mother's worries over the nature of Mary's friendship with the French artist she feared might hurt her daughter, but about whom Lydia had no reservations. Besides, it was nice to be out and pretend she wasn't ill; she told no one, but she counted every day as possibly her last, a grim yet realistic approach Mary would consider too dire and dramatic. Mary wanted Lydia to believe, and so she pretended to believe, to make Mary happy.

"I have no money to pay a model," Mary said to Degas. "I don't know what to do."

"You must find your subject."

Mary said, "Like yours? Ballet, horses, brothels?"

"Obsessions are an artist's gift. Obsession is poetry," Degas said.

The intermission chimes rang and they parted, but not before Degas asked Lydia about her health, pressing his hand into hers, taking from her the champagne flute and hunting down a waiter so that she wouldn't have to be bothered.

Chapter Twenty-One

Édouard and Eugène Manet were seated on a bench in one of the many alcoves along the vaulted hallway of the Île de la Cité hospital, awaiting Édouard's turn with Monsieur Siredy, the family's doctor friend who would no doubt have come to the house had Édouard asked. But Édouard had not wanted to alarm Suzanne, who could be impossible when she was frightened, and he deemed it better, on the whole, not to arouse trepidation in a household full of women who might feed his barely contained panic. He was having a hard enough time as it was. His note to Eugène had been deliberately cryptic. Would Eugène meet him, please, on the Pont Neuf, the following morning at nine o'clock? Eugène had only learned of their destination after Édouard had picked him up and given further directions to the hack driver.

The pain had attacked one morning when Édouard had been wandering down the Rue de Rivoli, following a fetching laundress he had spied. He'd been enjoying the undulations of her hips and the plump strength of her arms when a lightning bolt struck his leg, traveling from his hip down the inside of his leg to his ankle, a pain that caused him to buckle and cry out as the girl swayed away, oblivious. Two passing men leapt to help, asking whether he'd been shot and where was the blood, but there was no blood, only the sharp memory of pain.

It happened again a week later, a violent assault that, because he feared its return, terrified him. Once was an aberrancy, but twice was a warning. The pain inhibited Édouard's favorite aspect of life in Paris. The pleasure of Paris was to be outside and to walk its narrow streets and wide boulevards, to swagger along the Rue de Rivoli and peer into the shops, to wander the quays of the Seine to look down onto the river and the sequestered lovers on its shores, to navigate the places and squares on his way to a café, to experience the delight of the women of Paris—to look at them and dream of them and flirt with them.

The pain struck a third time one day as he stood at his easel, painting. A third time was a prophecy: It would happen again and again. To deny it was to invite destruction.

He told no one but Eugène, and only just this morning. To display his weakness to his younger brother was the kind of odd development that the pain was engendering. But he could not have sat so calmly in the bedlam of the hospital were it not for Eugène's diffident company. If Eugène suspected Édouard's love for Berthe, it did not seem to impinge on his brotherly sympathies. They sat waiting together, Eugène stalwart and present, for the better part of an hour, until the doctor called him in. Eugène went into the surgery with him. If the doctor thought the brothers unusual for coming together, or for coming to see him at the hospital rather than requesting that he see them at home, he did not say.

Édouard told his story, and Eugène, unaware of the multiple occurrences of the attacks, listened with an impassive yet attentive affect. When Édouard was finished, the doctor asked a series of questions. Of late was he particularly irritable? Was he prone to ideas of grandeur?

Édouard shook his head and the doctor looked to Eugène.

"He is a painter," Eugène said, shrugging.

Monsieur Siredy pulled a rubber hammer from his coat pocket and tapped Édouard's knees. His legs flew off the table and swung back in a display of limitless exuberance. The doctor asked more specific questions. Had his speech changed? Had he become forgetful? Had his muscles weakened and that was why he had fallen?

"No and no," Édouard said. "The pain made me fall."

"Are you having trouble forming sentences?"

"Do I seem it?" Édouard said.

Again the doctor looked at Eugène.

Eugène said, "I have never known my brother to be at a loss for words."

"And, how often, my friend," the doctor asked, "do you visit the brothels? Have you had any rashes, any sores? How long ago? Did you ever lose your hair? Think, now. This could have occurred some time ago." Though the police regularly examined the brothel denizens for venereal disease, there was always the chance a prostitute could blossom into fulminant contagion the second she stepped outside the doctor's surgery. It was a chilling thought, one that sobered every Parisian male whenever the prospect was mentioned, and it was mentioned often, usually in asides and whispers, whenever an entertaining night on the town was proposed.

With a rush of terror, Édouard understood what the doctor was implying. His father had died of Neapolitan disease; he had suffered enormously. But how did a man remember a rash? When it appeared, its nature? When he'd been young, when his father had banished him from art to force him to find a more respectable career, Édouard had joined the merchant marine. They'd sailed to Rio. There had been the carnival, the freedom. And afterward, there had been Paris and the brothels, Suzanne, and other willing women. But he was careful. Some of the time. Most of the time.

Édouard said, "A man lives. You understand."

The doctor nodded. "We can watch this. It's possible there is another explanation."

"Something benign?" Édouard said.

The doctor pressed his lips together. "Come to see me if the pain recurs." He turned to Eugène. "Are you having the same troubles?"

Eugène shook his head, and Édouard thought that it must be the first time in Eugène's life that he was happy not to have imitated him.

Outside, Édouard said, "Don't tell Berthe."

"She would only worry," Eugène said. "Will you tell Suzanne?"

"And suffer her hysteria?"

Édouard took the carriage, but Eugène crossed the Pont Notre-Dame on foot to catch the omnibus that ran along the Rue de Rivoli. Édouard envied his brother's galloping gait. Who would have thought after all these years that Eugène would be the lucky one in everything?

Chapter Twenty-Two

Several days after Mary and Lydia had seen Degas at the Opéra, Mary received a note at her studio.

My dearest M,
Are you alone?

D

She paid the urchin a sou to return her brief answer.

Oui.

Less than half an hour later, Degas was knocking at the door of her studio, holding the hand of a little girl he hoisted into his arms as they stepped inside. The girl flung her arms around Degas's neck and peeked at Mary from the safety of the folds of his plaid woolen scarf. He untied the child's hat, revealing a mass of dark curls that cascaded down her back.

"You brought a chaperone?"

"I did. You said you were alone."

"Is she yours?" Mary asked. She had never seen him with a child before.

He laughed and petted the girl's curls. "She belongs to some friends. But she likes me very much—don't you, sweetheart? Eloise, meet Mademoiselle Cassatt. Mademoiselle Cassatt is very nice, but she is very sad because she doesn't know any little girls in Paris."

Eloise squirmed in his arms and he set her down. The coal stove hadn't yet heated the studio, so Degas unwound his scarf and gave it to the girl. She dragged it across the floor and climbed onto the blue armchair Mary had brought from the apartment after her father expressed his distaste for its tufted flowered upholstery. The girl dangled her legs, her expression a cross between patience and boredom. Mary's dog circled the chair, then huddled into a mop near the stove.

"When I said I was going out of my mind at the Opéra, I didn't mean that I was pining for a child," Mary said.

"You should paint her," Degas said.

"Paint her?"

The girl's coat had scrunched above her knees, and she was kicking her legs, sprawled on the seat of the blue armchair, one hand propped behind her head, the scarf entwined about her waist. Mary set down the sketchbook in which she'd been struggling to devise an idea, any idea. She'd been staring out the window when she'd received Degas's note, wishing she painted cityscapes, landscapes, anything, just so that she could begin.

"Tell me the truth. Did her parents ask for you to do her portrait?"

"Yes, but I told them I would do their darling child no justice and that I had a friend who possessed the most sublime ability to express a child's spirit."

"You want to *give* me an obsession? Obsessions aren't adopted. Obsessions seize your soul," Mary said.

"I have no control or concern over what you paint next. But this child is beautiful and she deserves your brush."

"But I've never painted a child before."

Eloise was playing with Degas's scarf, singing to herself, calling to

the dog, who sidled up to the chair and collapsed at her feet. Despite the
cold, she threw off her coat, revealing a white dress and petticoats, and
then slumped back again, dragging Degas's scarf across her dress. The
tartan clashed with the upholstery in a beguiling contrast.

"Will she hold a pose?"

"Realism, my dear. How do children really behave? You don't need to
lie. That's the problem with bad art. It lies."

The exquisite terror of beginning flooded through Mary as an idea
formed in her mind: something new, not quite a portrait, but something
else, something about being a child in an adult world.

"It will be about the girl. It will be about the chair. Or rather—"

She broke off, finding it impossible to express what she saw only in
her mind, what she didn't yet have words for, what describing in detail
might destroy. The idea had to simmer inside her, find its own truth, even
as she was seeing Degas's dancers, endless numbers of them, his pictures
portraits more of moments than of the dancers themselves. Repetition
and variation, forming a story larger than each figure's individual life,
inducing a tremor of recognition in the viewer, who would understand
the larger meaning without even recognizing that the parts expanded the
whole. The inchoate vibrated in Mary's mind, as she dreamed the picture
her imagination was painting. But she felt, too, a wash of sadness, for that
sensation happened rarely for an artist, and was in turn fleeting. How
quickly it would devolve into the punishing discipline of hard work. The
vision she was entertaining would require technical prowess she was not
yet certain she possessed or ever would possess. And the clarity of this
moment, the glorious moment of the idea, would fade into doubt of the
value of the idea itself, and she would be left working and reworking a
canvas upon which her dream seemed as banal as her fear of failure, and
which in turn seemed far more certain than success. This gift of Eloise,
she knew, had been meant to spark just this moment of joy, but it was also
a betrayal, because soon she would suffer a surfeit of agony.

But in this first moment Mary dismissed, as all artists do, the pain to come. She kissed Degas's cheek, an unconscious effusion of gratitude she wouldn't remember after he and Eloise had gone, though for the rest of the day Degas would touch his hand to the place where her soft lips had grazed his skin.

"I'll bring Eloise and her mother tomorrow," he said.

"How can I repay you?"

"Someday, I'll need you." He gazed at her a long while. "Come, Eloise, we're off to return you to your mother. How would you like to come to see Mademoiselle Cassatt again tomorrow? She will paint you and you will be remembered forever."

The girl skipped to the door and he tied the ribbons of her hat and hoisted her once more into his arms, where she contemplated Mary with a gaze that was serious and patient, still clutching the scarf in her hands. Degas took it from her and wrapped it around Mary's neck once, twice, and said, "A gift."

When they had gone, Mary brought the scarf to her face and breathed in the scent of turpentine and oil and the chalky essence of a newly opened box of pastels.

Degas.

It was soon apparent that the little girl could sit still for only a few moments at a time. It was like capturing the light at sunset. She wiggled and squirmed and twisted in the chair until her mother declared her spent and scooped her up with an apology and a promise of better behavior the next day. But the promised better behavior never materialized. After concentrating on the girl's face, getting the features just right, Mary then had to work fast, faster than she ever had, and this limitation forced from her hand a light, breezy portrait that somehow radiated both charm and the boredom Eloise had suffered in the sittings. It was the limitation that helped Mary. She wondered how Degas might have fared, with his deliberate technique of drawing and redrawing and beginning again. He might love children, but whether or not he could suffer their peripatetic dances was another thing entirely. But within a week Mary believed she had breathed life into the girl. All else in the picture she could paint without her.

But it was the rest of the picture that gave Mary trouble. She had sworn off plain backgrounds of no distinguishing feature. A good portrait was a picture in context, the background as important as the person, defining who they were. Just as she had painted Lydia at the Opéra, she was determined to make something more of this picture than any of her previous ones. The composition she had already imagined. She would repeat the blue chair as Degas repeated dancers, but she would vary its position, its appearance. Doing so would require forced perspective, a technique she had not yet mastered to her satisfaction. The prospect terrified and thrilled her. She could move the chair, rearrange it and paint it from either side, but there was the even trickier background of the room, the windows, baseboards, and walls—all derived from her imagination, for she had no similar room to model it after.

For two successive mornings, she stood before the canvas, eyeing the chair, eyeing the canvas. She thought, *I will crop the chairs except the one that holds the little girl.* But how large to make the room? How to draw the eye to Eloise? She had placed her to the side of the canvas, but that would not be enough if she didn't paint the chairs just so. Balance and emphasis. All of art was balance and emphasis.

She painted a second chair, then a third, not as a chair but as a couch. Variation. And then a final chair, painted almost as a doll's chair, forcing the perspective even more. And she had to place the chairs in a real room, with a floor and windows. What color for the walls? How much detail? In a picture already rife with flourishes and bright pigment, how would she make the whole work?

One day as she stood at the canvas, her little Brussels griffon fell asleep on the chair. She took the gift. His brown coat would echo the scarf and the little girl's socks, which she had painted to echo the tartan. The dark colors grounded the two figures in the frothy sea of blues and oranges, anchoring them with an arabesque of contrast.

She studied the tone of the background, which she had primed gray and which now seemed too gray. The darker brown needed echoing too, but the hue had to be lighter. She wanted Eloise's white dress to surprise. So yes, brown, but light brown, with an undercurrent of red to echo the orange in the chair. No wallpaper on the walls. And the windows a wall of light. She saw it all, but her paintbrush would not move.

A day passed. She went to the studio intending to work, but after an hour gave up and instead took the dog for a long walk. She did not want to admit that she was paralyzed, but she was. This painting was much more ambitious, much more complex than anything she had ever attempted.

Her walk took her home, where she made the excuse that she was ill, and felt ashamed when Katherine doted on her all afternoon. The next morning, she returned to the studio in the April drizzle and found Degas waiting for her at the door.

"How are you getting on?" he said.

She opened the door with her key and let the dog run in before her, holding the door open to let Degas see the painting aloft on its easel. Inside, he removed his hat and overcoat and studied the canvas. She stood behind him. The stove and spirit lamp could wait. She was cold, but warmth was not what she needed.

"The background is giving you trouble, yes? The perspective?"

She nodded.

He pointed with his finger. "There, the walls will intersect. There, the baseboard will run. Windows?"

"Yes," she said.

"Then start here, behind the chair, and then next to the couch."

"I can't begin. I can't find it."

"Yes, you can."

"I literally can't."

He regarded her for a long moment, then took up her palette. "Tell me which," he said.

"I thought terre de Sienne, some white, vermillion, too."

"Yes." He squeezed dollops of paint onto the palette and mixed. He held it out for her approval.

"Yes, just that, but more poppy oil," she said. She wanted a thinner wash for the back. At least she knew that.

"I will paint the lines. Remember, it is always line. Whenever you are stuck, go back to lines." He took up a thin hogs hair brush as she hurried to pour him some turpentine.

He painted eight lines. In less than a minute his judicious brush had created an entire room.

"Do you see the windows now? Where the floor ends?"

"Yes."

"I can go now, yes?"

"How did you know?"

"Because we all suffer, *ma chérie*," he said.

"Thank you, Monsieur Degas."

"Oh no. Not anymore. I am Edgar." He leaned over, kissed her cheek, donned his coat, and left as quickly as he had come.

Chapter Twenty-Three

Mary Cassatt, Gustave Caillebotte, Claude Monet, Camille Pissarro, Berthe Morisot, and Eugène Manet all watched Degas pace from one end of Caillebotte's well-appointed parlor at 77 Rue de Miromesnil to the other. Mary thought the chosen meeting place odd; the Caillebotte family had suffered a spate of recent deaths and it seemed unkind to invade, but Degas had assured her on the way over that Gustave's mother had offered her parlor in hopes of enlivening their spirits. But when they arrived, there was no sign of her. A downcast maid greeted them at the door, and a dark pall hung over even the home's exquisite furnishings and brocade draperies.

A formal letter outlining Degas's concerns had arrived at the Cassatt home a week ago, causing Mary's father to roll his eyes and say, "This is what happens when you withdraw from official exhibitions and entrust your welfare to renegades."

The assembled group, huddled on armchairs and divans, was depleted. Though he was still committed to the group, the relentlessly impoverished Cézanne had removed to Aix, his family home, to reduce expenses. However, he was not missed, because he rarely socialized with anyone other than Zola, his childhood friend. Mary had met Cézanne on several occasions, and even in his best moments he looked like a beleaguered skeleton, his red-rimmed eyes ever roving. Renoir, also absent, had recently clashed with Degas over his dictum that anyone who submitted to the Salon must forgo exhibiting with the group. It was a matter of principle, Degas had said, to which Renoir had replied that it was not a matter of principle, it was a matter of money. He needed to make some, and no one with money had ever hired an impressionist to make his portrait. Not that Renoir's defection had done him any good. The Salon jury had rejected both his paintings.

Degas would not engage with Mary in the carriage, though she had pressed her argument, crafted over the past week, as forcefully as she had dared. Now he paced, preparing to recount his fears to the group, which he had already summarized in his letter. Though Degas rarely had trouble expressing his opinion on anything, he seemed unusually nervous.

"It is foolishness even to try," he began.

They were scheduled to open their exhibit in two weeks, on the first of June, in a different apartment on the Rue le Peletier. A deposit had been paid. Frames had been purchased. Posters had been printed. But Degas was concerned about the World's Fair, the Exposition Universelle. The fair was not a surprise; the city had been preparing for it for months, but the extent to which it had engulfed the city had shocked everyone. Day and night, workers destroyed sleep and rendered life miserable. Construction of a brick palace atop the Trocadéro and fair buildings on the Champ de Mars had rendered the seventh and sixteenth arrondissements din-filled arenas. Thuds and shouts infiltrated every home, mean and stately, in the two districts. Electric arc lights burned all night long. An overabundance of spring mud made the *champ* a quagmire: Carts and *camions* overloaded with materials plunged into bubbling sinkholes. Even mourners at the Passy Cemetery had had to contend with the hubbub drowning out priests' remarks. And now that the exposition had opened, traffic strangled the city; every fiacre and omnibus overflowed with visitors.

"It's difficult enough to compete with the Salon, let alone a world exposition. That irresistible circus is smothering everything in the city. I propose that we cancel our exhibition. Even the Salon is opening late this year," Degas said, shamelessly using the Salon he despised as a supporting argument.

"Forgive me, Degas," Caillebotte said, "but all you've talked of all winter has been your search for a venue, of printing the necessary posters, of Mademoiselle Cassatt's debut. And now you want to abandon all of it? Paris is teeming with visitors from all over the world. We could surpass all our previous attendance by the thousands."

Mary nodded in agreement. She barely knew Caillebotte, but she liked him very much. His lean build and sharp, carefully groomed beard conveyed a disciplined personality that appealed in the midst of the slapdash garb of the other men.

Before Degas could answer, Pissarro leaned forward and said, "If I may, Degas, didn't you just tell me the other day that you have no canvases to show? Isn't that really why you want to put off the exhibition? Because you are not ready?"

"Nonsense," Degas said. "I don't know what you're talking about."

"Is that true, Degas?" Caillebotte said.

"It is not true. What is true is that visitors don't know Paris. They won't know how to find us. We could paper all the kiosks in Paris with fliers and no one would come. For that matter, we are the only Parisians left in the city. Most everyone else has fled. They've sublet their apartments for twice, three times the rent and escaped to Dieppe or Nice for the summer. Paris has turned into nothing but a huge hotel. And I can assure you, foreigners who visit expositions are not art lovers. They go to fritter away their time on the fairgrounds in the interest of being seen. We would be wasting our time. No one will come to see us. At this late date, we can't retrieve the deposit for the apartment, but we can at least save half the rent."

"But, Degas," Pissarro said, "you told me you have nothing ready to show."

"That is not relevant. I'm trying to be prudent."

"So prudent you forced Renoir from our midst?" Caillebotte said.

"With your silly rule, you made him desert us. And he is one of the best of us."

The argument was veering off course. Of late, the group, which Mary had at first believed so singular in its objectives, seemed to be nothing more than a loose association of opinionated individuals who rarely agreed. She would never admit it to her father, but his suspicion of the group no longer seemed unfounded. She said, "What if we double our efforts at advertisement? We could distribute fliers at the fair—"

"And look as if we are amateurs or gypsies?" Monet said. He sat slumped in a straight-backed chair set apart from the rest of them. His face was ruddy from having spent the spring painting outdoors. He held his glass of wine precariously in his callused hands. "We might as well set up our canvases on the streets leading to the Trocadéro and let people peruse them there. Besides, the Champ de Mars is too far from the ninth arrondissement to induce attendance."

"Berthe," Mary said, "what do you think? You and Eugène could find us a space there, couldn't you, since you live so near? Or at least you could suggest one? There is no rule, is there, that our exhibitions have to take place in the ninth arrondissement? Why not the sixteenth or the seventh? Why not look near the Trocadéro? Why not pitch a tent near the *champ*?"

The Manets had arrived at the same time as she and Degas, but they had spoken only for a moment. Tonight Berthe looked wan and pale, thinner than usual. "I—" she began, but before she could finish, Monet said, "That's already been done."

"Give my wife leave to speak, Claude," Eugène said.

"Forgive me, Madame Morisot," Monet said. "Have you anything to say to enlighten the American?"

"Enough, Claude," Caillebotte said. He turned to Mary. "I'm afraid Claude is right, Mademoiselle Cassatt. The last time Paris hosted a World's Fair, Édouard rented a tent just off the *champ*. He set his pictures on easels, laid a carpet on the wooden floor, furnished it with armchairs, and even had a maid serve refreshments. No one came, even though Zacharie Astruc wrote an article about him in the newspapers every day. The whole thing was a huge failure. Édouard lost so much money his mother nearly disowned him. Isn't that right, Eugène?"

"It was her money, of course, that he'd used," Eugène said.

"There are more of us this time," Mary said. "Together, we could attract more visitors; we could share the costs."

"You are forgetting, mademoiselle, that the relevant point is that we could not charge admission," Degas said. "So it would be an outlay with no return. Unless Monsieur Caillebotte sees fit to throw his money away."

They all turned to Caillebotte, who met their inquisitive gaze with an impassive one of his own. He had, over the years, lent them all money, never asking for its return. Unlike the others, family wealth sustained him, but he did not acquiesce now.

"You see? Far be it from us to follow in Édouard's failed footsteps," Degas said. "So, are we agreed? We abandon this year out of practicality? Or put it off till autumn?"

"Will you have canvases then, Degas?" Pissarro said.

"I did not say I did not have canvases."

"But this capitulation is premature," Mary said. "We haven't yet exhausted every idea."

"I believe we have," Degas said. He looked around the room. Sidelong glances confirmed that everyone, or almost everyone, agreed. "Then it's settled. Perhaps autumn. But not June."

Mary colored. Everyone else rose from their chairs to find their way to the drink trolley to refill their glasses. No one came to talk to her, not even Berthe, who hovered near the doorway with her glass of sherry.

"Try not to see this little interruption as a failure," Degas said, bringing Mary a glass of wine and sitting beside her. "Manet is beside himself. He has to move studios because his landlord is still furious about that little stunt he pulled with his private exhibition. This is nothing like that."

"Only a little interruption?"

"Nothing public matters. What matters is what happens inside the studio. Your work. That is where genius lies, where it is born, where it is played out. It is not born on the walls of an exhibition. That I *can* guarantee. Besides, the press destroys us every time. Not because they are right, of course, but because they are stupid. Think of this as a reprieve from your inevitable public flogging. They will ridicule you just as much as they ridicule the rest of us."

"Don't patronize me, Edgar."

"But weren't you worried that you didn't have enough canvases to show?"

"And aren't you just being selfish? If what Monsieur Pissarro says is true?"

"Be thankful you have more time," he said, ignoring her accusation.

"It would seem that now I have an eternity." The wine was tannic. Mary bit her lip. "You are giving up. All of you. We could have made people come. There is always a way."

"But you have a picture showing at the fair. A juried show, I might add. What more do you want?"

In late March, a letter had arrived for Mary. The printed letter, addressed to *Sir*, though the envelope itself was directed to *Miss* Mary Cassatt, stated that the "Committee for Selection of Pictures by American Artists in Europe for the Paris Universal Exhibition" was soliciting artwork from American artists in Europe to supplement the work they had already collected in America. American artists resident in Europe were to be allotted one-eighth of the available gallery space. Given the limitations, it was advisable to send but one painting for consideration. Oil or watercolor only, sent to the Fine Art Department of the United States by 15 April, inclusive, labels included, their blanks to be filled out and affixed to the case and back of the picture, sent to a suite reserved at the Grand Hotel in Paris.

Mary sent two: the one of Eloise in the blue chairs and another recent drawing, of the head of a woman done in yellow pastel on blue paper.

The rejection did not arrive heralded via yellow envelope, as did rejections from the Salon. It did not even arrive via post. It arrived in the dirty hands of the carter she had hired to carry her work to the hallowed halls of the Grand Hotel.

> Mister Cassatt,
>
> Thank you for your submissions to the Committee for the Examination of Works by American Artists, Resident Abroad. We are returning your canvas of the painting of the little girl in the blue chair, "Portrait of a Young Girl." We regret that due to space restrictions we have had to be very rigid in our selections, having been charged with selecting art that best represents the American character. We will, however, be exhibiting your "Head," which exemplifies that fine attitude of American optimism we wish the world to admire.
>
> Yours most sincerely,
>
> Mr. C. E. Detmold,
> Mr. Augustus Saint-Gaudens, and
> Mr. D. Maitland Armstrong

While she was pleased to be represented, one drawing was not an exhibition.

"What more do I want?" Mary said now. "I want you to try."

"That's not what you want. You want recognition, my dear," Degas said. "You and Renoir should pout together outside the door of the Salon

hanging committee and beg for medals when they answer their door."
His tone had grown sharp and mocking.

"That is unfair," she said.

"So your father was right. You do paint for others."

Mary set down her wineglass. "Why do you paint, Edgar?"

"I paint to make art."

"As do I. We are no different."

"Oh, yes, my dear, we are. You want the world to admire you, which
means you think too much of it. I, however, think so little of the world
that I don't care if it ever admires me."

"Then why exhibit at all?" Mary said. "Why not hide in your studio
and make art and ignore everyone? Why ever let anyone see what you've
done?"

Degas shrugged. "In a perfect world that would be my preference."

"I don't believe you."

"You are too bourgeois for your own good, just as your father is."

Caillebotte, listening from across the room, said, "Degas, there is no
need to attack the lovely Mademoiselle Cassatt because she disagrees
with you."

"Degas can attack her all he likes," Monet said. "Her proposition is
ill-founded. She thinks because her family has money that money is an
obstacle for no one. I can't risk a centime on so shaky a prospect."

Mary's hands were trembling. "We don't have the kind of money
we're willing to throw away. And none of you has the courage to do what
is necessary. The world is in Paris. Let's show them who we are."

Monet turned away and muttered, "'We'? She hasn't even exhibited
with us yet."

Mary waited for Edgar or Caillebotte to say something, anything, to
defend her against Monet's attack, but no one said anything.

She rose. "If I may, Monsieur Caillebotte, could you please ask the
maid for my wrap?"

"Certainly," he said.

Degas said, "Wait. I have to call for the carriage."

Mary started for the door. Berthe hovered near the entryway curtains. Mary did not look at her as she passed. When she reached the door the maid handed her her wrap.

"Allow me, mademoiselle," Pissarro said, appearing beside her. In a moment they were outside, on the street, where he was somehow able to hail a cab before Degas could rush after them.

Mary blinked back the hot traces of her anger. The street pulsed with silence. Rain splattered the windows of the carriage. As the cab twisted through the dark streets, the slap of the wheels on the water began to work on her like a lullaby, an effect she first fought, then surrendered to, wiping the spill of angry tears with a handkerchief. Pissarro looked out the window, pretending fascination with nocturnal Paris as street after street slipped by.

After a time, he said, "We didn't have an exhibition in '75; you know that, don't you? It sometimes works that way."

"Yes. But it's possible, isn't it, that there might never be another exhibition? That you could all decide not to show together ever again? That your differences will divide you forever?"

Pissarro sighed. He did not even try to dissuade her. In his measured silence Mary knew that she had set her heart on a dream, and that now ruin might come from such unreasoned folly.

She pulled her wrap tighter against the infiltrating mist. "Have I made a mistake, Monsieur Pissarro, in trusting all of you?"

"I'm afraid it depends, my dear, on what you are after."

"It was the first time Edgar has ever spoken to me like that," Mary said. She could not come to terms with the man who had just embarrassed her in front of everyone: the man she so admired, the man who had given her the gift of Eloise, the man who had brought her disagreeable father a silk cravat.

"If I may, mademoiselle? Guard yourself. I have too many other things to worry about than your heart."

"No wonder Berthe adores you," Mary said.

Pissarro alighted from the fiacre with Mary on the Avenue Trudaine on the pretext of the pleasure of walking back to the Rue des Trois Frères, where he kept a cot in his studio. He insisted on paying for the cab, too, which mortified Mary, but she let him, resolving to convince her father to purchase one of his paintings in repayment. He kissed her cheek and glided away; his rounded shoulders, out of place on so tall a frame, marked him as an artist, but he could easily have been mistaken for a gentleman down on his luck, for he wore his thin corduroy coat and woolen scarf with great dignity.

She would have asked him in, but she was exhausted and it was late, and besides, her home didn't feel like her home anymore. Her father, having found much to complain about the apartment she had chosen for them, had embarked in January on a mission to find somewhere else to live. His purported excuse had been to return Mary to the ninth arrondissement and her life in the shadow of Montmartre, but she believed his dissatisfaction had more to do with the insular nature of the American colony. Mary had tried to warn her parents, but they hadn't listened, and soon Robert had discovered for himself the infighting and shallowness of the expatriates, who were always vying for an invitation to a ball at the Élysée Palace or the numerous fashionable Quai d'Orsay balls and receptions at the French Ministry of Foreign Affairs. And at colony dinners, the conversation ran to inanities like the resplendent décolletage on display on the nine p.m. train to Versailles, or the impossibility of the hours spent waiting in coaches at the Élysée Palace for everyone to debark and be announced. After a month or two of barely concealed disdain, Robert had turned his back on his fellow expatriates. Better, he said, to become completely Parisian and die of loneliness—for his French still foundered—than to remain American and die of inflicted idiocy. And though Mary shared his impatience, his rejection of the apartment negated all the time she had taken to find a place for them in the precise part of town they had requested, time she had needed for her work. And the move to the Avenue Trudaine had taken up even more time, first to find the apartment, then to negotiate the impossible French bureaucracy, and finally to mollify the angry *portier* at the Rue Beaujon who had counted on them for a year. Once again, she'd had to find movers who wouldn't destroy everything, and in the end her father rejected most of the furniture she'd chosen anyway. Their new apartment remained sparsely furnished, because no carter could be procured to deliver new furniture now that every conveyance in Paris was needed to transport visitors to the Exposition. They had moved to the Avenue Trudaine in the beginning of March, and though the change was arguably better for her—she could now walk to her studio instead of riding the ponderous omnibus—the cost in time had once again been punitive. The Avenue Trudaine, leafy and less showy than the Rue Beaujon, was not even quiet. The students of the nearby Collège Rollin frolicked on their way to and from classes, creating a ruckus several times a day, setting even the calm Lydia's nerves on edge.

In the rain Mary looked up at the apartment building, readying herself for the five flights of stairs and the look of *I told you so* in her father's eyes when she relayed the news. Now her father could say that her opposition to the inconvenience of the move had been unfounded. What had it cost her, he would say, when there wasn't even going to be an exhibition? And Abigail Alcott had married. There had been a letter today from England announcing her news and a move to the outskirts of Paris. It was hard not to compare her situation with her friend's: Abigail had achieved everything she wanted, while Mary had achieved nothing. She had trusted the renegades and now the renegades had failed her.

The nearby Place d'Anvers, peaceful and deserted, beckoned, but she opened the door and went in to face her father.

Chapter Twenty-Four

July 12, 1878

My dearest Mary,

I believe I've been unkind. No, worse than that. I've been an imbecile. No doubt you've been thinking of me in those apt terms. When you did not answer my previous two letters, I knew that I had offended you in the most indecent way. Of course you were disappointed. It was blind of me not to understand this. You possess that American optimism that believes anything is accomplishable, while we poor French succumb too often to our laziness, though I do hope you realize what great hurdles would have been in our future had we dared to climb the battlements, considering Manet's earlier, dreadful defeat. We have used up all our store of rebellion in opposing the Salon, and have none to spare, which undoubtedly makes us cowards, but I promise you that I will work hard for another independent show as soon as the exposition is over. I owe you that much after inviting you to exhibit with us and then marooning you in a welter of time. Can you forgive this irritable man? May I still call you friend, my dear, dear mademoiselle?

E. D.

"It is a very graceful note," Lydia said. She was curled on the window seat before the open sash. Degas's letter, read and reread, was now folded in the open pages of the book on her lap. The slight summer breeze was ruffling the maple trees that rose from the abyss of the Avenue Trudaine, its gas lamps spilling circles of evening light onto strolling passersby. Upon moving into the flat, Lydia had seized the window seat as her own and no one ever challenged her. "You must admit that, Mary."

Mary looked up from the new writing table, delivered yesterday by a carter whom she'd had to bribe to deliver the desk before his profitable day of ferrying visitors to the Tourville gate of the fair. In the height of the summer, prices for hotel rooms and vegetables had doubled, fiacres had become even more scarce, sidewalks were unnavigable, and the unending trumpet and drum of daily life seethed at a volume not unlike, people said, the invading rockets and bombardments of the Prussians. Italians, Spaniards, Orientals, African princes, and bewildered Americans roamed Paris with an eye toward experience, stumbling exhausted from the surfeit of the exposition into the attractions of a city already exhausted by the visitors' poor French and worse manners.

None of this had benefited any of the impressionists. Tonight, Mary was writing a letter. An art dealer in Philadelphia had been recommended to her, a Mr. Hermann Teubner. He was a restorer of old works, well known in the city, and open to receiving as many of her paintings as she wished to send him, under consignment for twenty percent commission, as befitting the recommendation of his dear friend, Lady Mitchell, to whom he was indebted for the connection, etc., etc. He directed Mary to send the unframed works as soon as possible, though he did require that someone she trusted meet the shipment at the dock in Philadelphia, as his days were taken up with a great deal of work. Lady Mitchell had mentioned that Miss Cassatt had a brother who might be a good intermediary? He was hers most sincerely.

Mary was listing the inventory she was going to send, nearly everything she had, save her most recent work of the past year: fifteen pictures to be properly packaged and entrusted to the shipping company. She was specific in naming the prices for her work; Mr. Teubner was to charge neither more nor less, and to communicate with her about potential sales. The negotiation was as bourgeois a transaction as existed; her father would be proud and Edgar would be horrified, but she had no other choice.

"Monsieur Degas apologized, Mary," Lydia said. "You are too hard on people."

"He was awful to me," Mary said. "He was mocking and unkind."

"You could remind him that the picture of the blue chairs was rejected. Would that be retaliation enough?" Lydia said.

"He has no respect for other people's opinions."

"He has written you a lovely note, one you ought to acknowledge if you are not to die an old woman, miserable and mean."

"I am not going to die an old woman miserable and mean, because you will be at my side to save me from myself," Mary said.

"You'll write to him? Because if you don't, I shall write for you and will apologize endlessly, saying how sorry you are that you couldn't see his point of view and that you were only thinking of fame and glory and that you have been beside yourself with worry that you have lost his dear friendship and that it means more to you than a missed exhibition and that it was only pride—"

"You're feeling better to tease me so."

"I am. I feel wonderful."

"I'm glad. But you don't understand, Lyddy."

"Friends hurt one another, you know, from time to time. They can't all be as kind to you as your devoted sister."

Mary picked up her pen, then put it down.

"Why did only Monsieur Degas disappoint you?" Lydia said. "Everybody else agreed with him, even your beloved Monsieur Pissarro, and yet it is only Edgar with whom you are angry."

"He was vicious. You weren't there."

"No one cares for you as much as he does."

"You suggest romance because you want me to have one, but there isn't one. At least not now."

"You questioned his courage and veracity. He was hurt."

"I only spoke my mind."

"As did he. Write the man a nice note and drop your silly pride, for your sake as well as his, or I shall send him flowers and say that they are from you, with love."

"You'll do no such thing. And besides, he hates flowers."

"Likely I won't, but I do feel well this evening, and I see that that lovely little flower shop on the corner is still open, and I am in need of some exercise, and—"

"You will not betray me."

"Betrayal is your favorite word. I was only teasing. You are too touchy, my dear sister; it will cause you infinite trouble if you do not rein in your pride."

"I'll write."

"Today?"

"Today."

"Good."

"But he was unkind."

"Of course he was, but that is not the point."

"What is the point?"

"The point is that you're both stubborn."

"That's not true."

"Of course it is," Lydia said, returning to her book.

Chapter Twenty-Five

But she didn't write to him. A month passed. Two. She composed a hundred letters in her mind, failing each time to arrive at the perfect tone to communicate the depth of her hurt, so she sent none of them.

Instead, she worked.

She rose early in the morning to the dawn light stippling her bedroom wall. While the rest of the family slept, she made her ablutions, the dog prancing at her feet. Anna served her coffee and a roll for breakfast and packed her a midday meal of sandwiches while they whispered about the day's shopping and housekeeping before Mary scooped up her dog and escaped down the spiral stairwell.

She loved the brisk walk to her studio through a wakening Paris that was full of the limpid beauty the city seemed to conjure from the dew. In this corner of the city, far from the Champ de Mars, the uproar of the exhibition was muted, so that the usual morning pleasures of Paris—the brush of the street sweepers tidying the sidewalks, the bakers unfurling their striped awnings, the clop-clop of the milk wagon on its deliveries—still soothed.

At her studio, her steps echoed on the dull tile. The dog alighted to sleep on the blue chair, the housekeeping and the other demands of family life fell away, and Mary was left with only the anticipation of work.

Lately she had developed a ritual of not looking at the canvas she was working on until she had donned her apron and set out her brushes and turpentine and poppy seed oil, squeezing out the paints onto the walnut surface of her palette before she readied herself to face the unfinished work. Always, in the moment before, an unbidden terror arose: Was the painting as good as she thought it was? She disciplined herself not to answer, for her opinion of her work, rooted as it was in emotion, was unreliable in the vulnerable gulf of time between what she wanted the canvas to be and what it currently was. Self-pity did not help, and she found that if she denied herself that indulgence and instead simply began, keeping her brush moving, the bristles and wooden handle soon became an extension of her unconscious, where the truth about a work really lived. Technique—studied, practiced, perfected—birthed freedom, and her years of apprenticeship now began to cohere in a tornado of work. The muse, so stingy the years before, visited and revisited like an enamored lover, as new canvases—watercolors, oils, pastels—began to line the floors of her studio to dry and cure.

At the end of each day, she dropped her brushes into a tin can and ferried them to the *portier*'s closet in the hallway, where she washed them with turpentine in a spattered sink. It was now that she had to shutter her ears to the suddenly voluble critic, who awakened as she emerged from her reverie. The persuasive voice harped alternately that she was posing, or that her work was hackneyed and flat, or that she lacked the soul of an artist and was therefore incapable of imparting truth, or that she would never hear again from the art dealer in Philadelphia, who had probably stolen all her canvases anyway, or that she ought to give up, or the worst, that Degas would think nothing of her work. The voice blathered on and on, taking advantage of her fatigue as she rinsed and re-rinsed her brushes and rubbed from her chapped hands the ocher and rose splatters of paint that decorated her wrists and knuckles. She had no idea where she would ever show her work now that she had broken with Degas.

Back in the studio, she fell on the sandwiches and fruit that Anna had packed for her, looking out the window to the busy boulevard, where the late afternoon bustle washed away the perverse workings of her doubting mind. The effort of spurning the ugly voice exhausted her, and only when she was certain it had quieted did she turn to study the canvas before she locked the door and started for home.

In this way, the summer of the Exposition Universelle passed: the cold, rainy July and the disconsolate oven of the brutal August, when wealthy Parisians traveled to Dieppe or Provence while her family spent the summer seeking relief in the shade of the Bois de Boulogne, hiring fiacres to transport them from the city to the cooler environs of the park.

One afternoon at the end of August, Degas came toward her on the sidewalk of the Rue Frochot. His linen suit was wrinkled, his top hat was moist at its wide satin band, but his gait was as certain and sure-footed as always. In the bright afternoon he wore his lavender glasses. The reflection on the glasses made it impossible to read his eyes. She thought for a moment that he might pass her by.

"Mademoiselle Cassatt," Degas said, stopping at the last moment.

"How are you?" she said.

"Quite well, thank you."

He was never well. He always had a complaint. "You have not gone away for the summer," she said.

"I will vacation in October."

"So there is no possibility of an exhibition this autumn?"

"None."

"I see."

"How is your family?" Degas said.

"We have suffered here."

"Give them my regards, Lydia especially," he said, tipping his hat.

He walked past, his shoulders set, his stride resolute.

"You are never this polite unless you do not care for the person you are conversing with," she said, turning.

He stopped. "You do not seem to care for the truth, or for my apologies."

"You must admit you were wrong. We could have dropped sugar cubes and people would have followed them to our exhibition."

Degas shrugged.

"You are indifferent?"

"You are the one who did not answer my letters. I am not so in need of friends that I force myself on someone who doesn't care for me."

"I was hurt."

"I believe I said I was an imbecile."

"You *were* an imbecile."

The cobbles had absorbed the sun's heat during the day, but now the sun dropped behind the gables of the buildings, and the wretched glare diminished. In the reprieve of shade, Degas removed his glasses, and Mary studied his eyes, hoping to find the spark of interest he had always carried for her. They were cool, but not angry. Assessing.

"You're a bulwark when you're angry," he said.

"And you are glib and unkind."

He would have to walk away to end it. Her pride would sustain her in this; she would stand here through dinner, through the night, all the way to the morning, if necessary, though there was little satisfaction in it.

"I will not tell you that I am sorry," she said.

"You owe me no apology. Just an acceptance of mine."

A sliver of light penetrated a break in the buildings' facade. Degas winced, but did not put on his glasses, concentrating his piercing gaze on her and what she would say next.

"We are adept at wounding one another," she said. "But can we not? I would rather have you in my life."

A small smile lifted the corners of his mouth. He said nothing, but took her parasol from her, shut it, and hung it over his forearm, then folded his glasses into his coat pocket. He reached for her hands and wrapped them in his. Like hers, his were reddened and roughened by the scourge of turpentine, shaped by the dexterous manipulation of brush and palette knife, tinted by pastels and oils fast nestled into crevices. Mirrors, their hands.

"I don't want to have to spend my life defending my aspirations nor my right to speak. Not to you. Not to my father. Not to anyone," she said.

"I thought I'd lost you," he said.

"Would you come see what I've done? It's new, and I'm not sure." Though now, in his presence, she was sure. It was solid work: new, bright, and veracious. "If you come, it won't take more than a moment," she said, but it would. And he wouldn't mind. He would abandon whatever friends he was on his way to meet now and would come back with her and look at all her paintings and exclaim over them.

"I looked for you," she said. "Every day. On the street. I never saw you."

"Except today."

"Yes. Except today."

Chapter Twenty-Six

S o, you have what you want at last," Édouard said. He stood in the drawing room of Berthe and Eugène's apartment on the Avenue d'Eylau, holding his hat in his hands. It was a warm September, and his suit was wet with perspiration. Berthe had not yet offered him a seat.

"You blame me for wanting a child," Berthe said. "How like you."

She was lying on the rose-colored divan in her rose-colored salon. She wore a white dressing gown, its grosgrain ribbon secured with a bright bow under her breasts, hiding the swell of Eugène's child beneath. Berthe's face had grown more angular since she'd been with child, but to Édouard, that severity only made her more beautiful. She had been ordered to rest in her apartment for the duration of her confinement. The doctors were adamant; at thirty-seven she was old to have a child, and there were dangers.

Édouard shifted on his feet. "You know as well as I do that your child could have been my child, if I had wanted, if I had pressed."

"Did you come to make me unhappy? Was that your plan this morning when you left your house?"

"Eugène tells me he believes he will have a son." Eugène was away in the South of France in search of a job, which was why Édouard had chosen today to visit Berthe.

"You misdirect your jealousy."

"Léon is not mine," Édouard said.

"Why do you persist in telling such an ugly lie?"

"Why do you press me now, Berthe, on such an old story? Léon is grown, he is happy, I was a father to him—what do the details matter?"

"Because I am to have a child, and I want to know who his true cousins are."

Édouard clutched the back of the armchair next to the divan. A sheen of perspiration sprang to his forehead. The pain came in waves now. Lately, just being alive had been exhausting enough; add to it the trauma of being forced to move out of his beloved studio, and well, some days he wasn't certain he had the energy for anything. He limped around the armchair and sat down. "I didn't come to argue with you, Berthe. I came because I have something to tell you. And I needed to tell you alone."

Berthe blanched against her pretty couch.

"The doctors tell me I have ataxia," Édouard said. "Neapolitan disease. It is possible that Rio is to blame, when I was in the navy."

She drew her hand to her throat. "Such dreadful things you tell me."

"You will be all right. I asked the doctor. Suzanne has been fine for a very long time. I believe I am the only victim. The doctor has prescribed mercury baths. Calomel. Potassium iodide." His voice broke. "The same treatments Monsieur Maisonneuve ordered for my father."

"What about my child?"

"I repeat, the doctors have no fear for you."

Outside, the sky grew suddenly gray; the wind turned cool. The sheer curtains ballooned. Édouard rose and shut the window. As he hobbled back to his seat, the dull light made pale marble of his hands. "Suzanne claims she is not to blame, but it is difficult to know."

"Your father? And Suzanne?" Berthe said. She sat very still. "No wonder your mother despises her."

"My mother devised it all. She diverted funds to Suzanne when she could no longer give piano lessons; she concocted the lie that Suzanne was not the boy's mother. She protected everyone. Herself the most, I think."

"Now you tell the truth."

"After such a long time, a lie feels like the truth."

"So, Léon could be your brother, not hers; your father's son, not yours?"

"I don't know. Perhaps."

"Will Suzanne never tell who is the true father?"

"I don't think she knows. Though I try to believe she was faithful to me, after she and I began." What must his father have thought, as he lay dying of the pox? Did he blame Suzanne, as Édouard tried not to do now? They had each used her, but Édouard didn't think that Suzanne had minded. He had decided long ago that she loved him best, decided that was why she had agreed to marry him as soon as his father had died, decided that was why she didn't mind the manufactured confusion about the paternity. It made it easier to glide over the messiness of her past. "Perhaps my father got it from someone else and gave it to her, and she to me. Perhaps I picked it up along the way. Or perhaps it was Rio, after all."

Berthe said, "You don't know?"

Édouard shrugged. "I don't remember when the signs appeared." Worse terrors circled now than the pain. The mercury the doctors had prescribed was said to deprive its takers of memory and sense. Already, in conversation, his wit could be struck dumb; nightly, froth bubbled from his mouth and he had to shed his nightclothes after sweating through them. The potassium iodide promised help for the pain, but he still experienced debilitating attacks, often when he was out and about on the streets. Sometimes, he had to stagger to a building and lean up against it until the pain abated. More than once, he had fallen. And always, his father's fate loomed. Paralyzed, an invalid. *Congestion cérébrale*, the doctor had called it, in an attempt to eradicate the shame of the diagnosis by diction, but no euphemism had saved his father from death. His illness had occurred too late to alert Édouard to the dangers. And Suzanne never really had said. Why would she, given the awkwardness of being mistress to both father and son? If she truly had been?

"Not quite incest," Berthe said.

"It was love."

"Love is always the excuse for shameful behavior. Claiming it is such a shabby ploy."

"Did Eugène not mention any of this? I asked him to go with me to the doctor, so he knows. I thought he might have told you, to make you love me less."

"Do not disparage Eugène. He is the innocent, either way; he is the goodness neither of us deserves." A wave of nausea washed over her. She had been faithful to Eugène since her marriage, but barely.

"The specter of mortality, evoking shame," he said.

"You will destroy my happiness yet."

"You won't miss me too much, will you, darling?"

"Don't invite death," Berthe said.

"Death will come."

The tainted future, too, would come, and bring with it this memory of sadness. Berthe shook her head, trying to erase the indelible, blighted past.

"I will need you, dear Berthe, in the end."

Relieved of his burden, he took his time, stroking her cheek as he kissed her, caring nothing for her tears as he left, for he had seen them often enough.

1879

Chapter Twenty-Seven

The soft taps of hammers, murmurs of consultation, and occasional trills of laughter wafted through the apartment on the Avenue de l'Opéra, where Mary Cassatt stood in a bedroom, the door closed so that she could have a moment to herself. Soon, people would begin arriving for the private party on the eve of the opening, and she wanted to savor the miracle. Of the seven new artists that Degas had invited to exhibit with the group, only Mary had been allotted a room of her own. While not the Salon, the private room seemed to Mary to surpass it in every way. Eleven of her canvases decorated the walls, hung as she wished— not skied out of sight by a querulous Salon hanging committee, but arranged by her, to her taste, to show her work at its best. She peered at the exuberant paintings that had sprung from her hands these past two years and marveled at the perseverance it had taken her to get to this moment—hour after hour, day after day, year after year of faith and hard work and sheer strength of will, all of which had often failed her.

The door opened behind her, sending a great whoosh of air into the room. The gaslight flickered behind the sconces, causing yellow shadows to dance on the windowpanes blackened with rain. It had been raining for days. She'd had to pay the carter extra to place her crated pictures under a tarp for the trip from her studio to the apartment. Now Edgar removed his hat, glistening with raindrops, and surveyed her work, which he had already seen a dozen times. In the past week, he had even helped her to choose some of the frames, though he had chafed when she had chosen red for one and green for another. He preferred white frames, because he believed they were neutral and did not detract from the work, but she had insisted because she liked the complementary effect of the colors on the artwork, and because green and red were her favorite colors. Edgar thought it a travesty for an artist to fall in love with specific colors. Color was a utility, he said, that one ought to deploy discriminately, but Mary had ignored him.

"Not a bad canvas among them," Edgar said. "You did well, my dear. Even if you were impatient."

"A year late," she said, smiling, taking the opportunity to tease him about last year's debacle.

"But here you are," he said, "with more canvases to show than you otherwise would have had." He did not hide his self-congratulation. The profusion of exquisite canvases that Mary had been able to produce was more proof that he had been right about the cancellation. "And it is such magnificent work."

"Do you think so? I'm suddenly nervous. I spent half the day in bed with the covers pulled up to my neck. I could hardly get dressed. I wasn't even sure I wanted to come."

She had dressed, though, and early, because Abigail Alcott, newly married and now named Nieriker, had come for dinner to introduce the entire Cassatt family to her husband, Ernest, a Swiss businessman, whom she had met in England. While Robert and Ernest discussed Ernest's new appointment as inspector general of a mercantile house, Abigail explained privately to Mary and Lydia that he had been of immense comfort when her mother had died, having the effect of endearing himself to her more quickly than she otherwise would have allowed. When Ernest had to relocate, they decided to marry rather than endure a separation. She'd had to explain this to friends when she'd returned to Paris, as hasty marriages usually indicated a pregnancy, but this was not the case, though Abigail was hoping, she confessed, despite her age, to have a child yet. At dinner, Ernest revealed himself to be a kind man who adored Abigail, and their mutual affection and admiration of Mary and her accomplishments had distracted Mary from thinking too much about the evening to come. After dinner, the Nierikers had escorted her to the exhibition early so that she could make one last check before the party. They were outside now, having a look before the place got too crowded, though so many people had come ahead of time that the apartment was already a hive of laughter and flurry.

Gustave Caillebotte stuck his head in the doorway, his gloved hand rimming the jamb. He still wore his hat and coat, though he had arrived several hours ago. Since then he had not once stopped moving. "Degas! They said you were here. Where are the rest of your things? I've counted only three of your canvases. *Three*. We open tomorrow. Have you gone insane? Of course you have; why am I asking?"

Edgar had listed twenty-five works in the catalog, but the walls allotted him in the parlor and dining room were still mostly blank, adorned by only one portrait of a laundress and two pictures from his series on the École de Danse.

"Gustave, you will develop a headache if you continue badgering everyone. Why don't you let Portier manage all this?" Edgar said. Alphonse Portier was Edgar's neighbor on the Rue Lepic, a colorist who wanted to begin dealing in pictures. He had been hired as manager, but Caillebotte, who had rented the apartment and whose money was at stake, could not let go.

"Just bring them, Degas."

"Oui, *maître*." Lately, Edgar had taken to calling Gustave *maître*. *Master* this, *master* that.

"When?" Gustave asked.

"Soon."

"I—" Gustave began, but the pretty woman who had been recruited from a local shop to sell tickets interrupted him. A competent young thing, she nevertheless appeared beside Gustave with an expression of great worry. "Can you come? The turnstile is here and they want to know where to install it."

"Convince him, Mademoiselle Cassatt, would you, please, before *I* go insane?" Caillebotte said, his chiseled face shadowed with the usual stubble.

The tails of his military-style coat whipped behind him as he led the ticket taker toward the apartment entrance and the problem of the turnstile.

Mary said, "Why haven't you brought in your work?"

Edgar threw up his hands. "It can't be helped."

It could be helped, but Edgar didn't want to help it, and when Edgar didn't want to do something, he didn't do it, something Gustave knew as well as Mary. It would be hopeless to try to cajole him, and so she didn't try. They were all exhausted. Putting together the exhibition had been a nightmare. Many of the original group had "turned traitor," as Edgar put it: Monet had been too discouraged over his recent work to send anything, so Caillebotte had written everyone who owned one of Monet's paintings to send it in on loan; Renoir had been accepted to the Salon and so was banned; Cézanne had decamped even without acceptance to the Salon; and Berthe hadn't worked since the birth of her daughter, Julie. Miffed at the multiple defections, Edgar had invited new artists, whose excited murmurs were now breaching the door. They were unknown to Mary—Marie Bracquemond and her husband, Félix, Jean Louis Forain, Paul Gaugin, Henry Somme, Albert Lebourg, and Federico Zandomeneghi. Also this year, Degas had declared that they would banish forever the foul appellation of "impressionist" by leaving out the word "independent," as if the critics had somehow misread the title. This year the catalog had been printed with the bland heading of "*Catalogue de la 4e Exposition de Peinture.*" The complicated politics could drive someone crazy, Mary thought, but tonight she let them go. She was in an exhibition, she had eleven canvases, and despite the lump in her throat, on the other side of the door champagne corks were popping.

Edgar was standing in the center of the room, studying her. "Despite your nerves, you are happy," he said.

"I am both thrilled and terrified," she said.

He went to the door and shut it. In the gaslight, the last of the raindrops clinging to his coat sparkled like jewels. "I should have asked you for permission to shut the door, but I have something I wish to say to you. I also should have spoken earlier this week, but you were busy. What I have to say is not, perhaps, what you want to hear, and I do not wish to diminish your happiness, my dear, but I want you to be prepared."

Mary shifted as bile began to rise in her throat. God, what an impossible thing it was to debut. Not that this was her first exhibition, but it was the one that mattered most, the one at which she could not bear to fail. All the others—the Pennsylvania Academy when she'd first begun, her Salon appearances—were nothing compared to this one.

"I want you to know that after tonight, everything will change for you, and not necessarily for the better. These last two years, you've been able to paint by yourself, for yourself, with no one caring or knowing what you were doing. But tonight is the eve of everything. In a few days, a dozen reviews will be published, and another dozen the day after that. Everyone will have an opinion of your work. They will say, on the whole, very stupid things. They will be extraordinarily mean and personal in their attacks. They will care not a jot for your hard work or your artistry. They will endeavor to make you suffer. They will claim that your style parts too much from standard taste, and in their ignorance will disparage you without reserve. Not every critic, but most. And these are people who cannot even mix a color, let alone render something as simple as an apple on a canvas. But they will believe themselves right and influence the public for the worse. They will be wrong, of course. What I want you to understand is that you should not allow their ignorance to destroy you."

How different Edgar's tone was than last year, when he had canceled the exhibition and spoken of public flogging and intense ridicule. She crossed the room and lifted her hand to his face. He smelled of graphite and oil and turpentine; he smelled of work, of Paris, of all of art, of everything she wanted. He had helped her. Nothing on these walls would have been made if not for him. He had drawn it out of her by believing in her.

Edgar lifted her hand from his cheek and kissed her palm. He peeled back the lace at her sleeve and kissed the inside of her wrist. His lips traveled up her sleeve to her elbow. Years of practiced decorum, of discipline, of restraint slipped away as Mary closed her eyes and touched her cheek to his. His beard was rough and wet from the rain. The edge of his glasses grazed her cheek.

He said, "I once made a promise to Tourny to be careful with you, and I have been. Do you still want me to be?"

A small moan escaped her mouth, an assent she had not known she would make.

He hesitated only a moment, then touched his lips to hers. Hers parted for his, just a breath. It had been so long since anyone had kissed her. The dalliances of her youth—single kisses stolen behind doors at the Pennsylvania Academy, brushed lips on horseback rides with neighbor boys before anyone caught up with them—had not prepared her for this. She had been so long untouched that she had forgotten what it was to be caressed. Her fingertips grazed his cheek as he kissed her. His hand on her shoulder pulled her to him. They sank into one another. The noises of jubilation beyond the door fell away. There was only the roar of breath and heartbeat.

When the kiss burned away, they parted, hands entwined. Neither of them spoke. The surprise of it, the rightness of it, were equal. No youths they, but the pleasure still made them smile. The world outside the door gradually came back to them, but they did not hear the door open.

"Mary—oh, I'm sorry," Abigail said.

Mary released Edgar's hands, embarrassed, but relieved that it was Abigail and not her mother who had interrupted them. "Abigail. Wait.

Please come in. I would like you to meet Monsieur Degas. Monsieur Degas, my dear friend Madame Nieriker."

"It is a great pleasure to meet you, madame. Mary has spoken of you often."

"And she of you," Abigail said. "For a very long time."

"Come," Edgar said. "Before someone else bursts in on us and thinks we are all flirting." With his hand to the small of Mary's back, he guided the two of them out the door and into the party.

"You cannot tell me you don't know this story," Edgar said.

"Tell us, tell us!"

The Cassatts, Degas, and Abigail and Ernest Nieriker were standing in front of one of the many blank spots in Degas's section of the exhibition. Edgar had been explaining that one of his missing pictures was a portrait of the art critic Edmond Duranty, whom he had painted in his book-lined study. Mary's parents and Lydia, who had arrived in fashion in the new carriage that Aleck had recently purchased for them, had been teasing Edgar about his empty walls, if you could call Robert's stunned silence at Degas's tardiness teasing. "They are where?" he had said, shaking his head at Edgar's airy excuses for the canvases' absence.

"I tell you," Degas said, "this story is famous. A few years ago, Édouard Manet didn't like something Duranty wrote about him. So Édouard slapped him in the face at the Café Guerbois. Duranty demanded that Édouard apologize, but of course he wouldn't, so a few days later the two of them boarded a train to the Saint-Germain-en-Laye forest with a pair of seconds, and there dove at one another with their swords. Right off, Édouard inflicted a nasty scratch on Duranty's chest, the seconds called off the match, and they all rode home together, friends again."

"You're lying," Mary said. She had grown gleeful. As the evening had worn on, it was as if someone had exchanged Edgar for someone else. He had become a maître d', a bon vivant, a host extraordinaire. From time to time, the memory of the kiss revived itself, and she had to keep herself from taking Degas's elbow or otherwise giving herself away.

"I am not lying," he roared. "Émile Zola was Édouard's second. Ask him."

"He wasn't!" Lydia said, laughing. Tonight she had drunk two glasses of champagne, worrying Mary, but Lydia swore that any medical upset would be worth the celebration of Mary's triumph.

"My dear Lydia," Degas said. "You missed everything by meeting me so late in life. You should have known me a decade ago. I was excitement at every turn."

"Attempted murder is certainly one way to handle the press," Robert said, shaking his head, mystified as he always was by the antics of the French. Ernest Nieriker colluded with him in disapproval; they had already agreed that they were out of their element.

"We will smite them all, Robert, just as Édouard did." Degas shifted his champagne glass and called Édouard over, who had escaped the cloying crowd and lodged himself in the far corner, where he was draining a third glass of champagne. His expression was one of irritation; tonight he had had to explain a dozen times why he wasn't exhibiting with his friends.

"Édouard. Come over here. Tell them what you did to poor Monsieur Duranty."

Édouard hobbled through the crush of guests toward the knot of Cassatts, enduring the pitying looks of those who had heard that it was now confirmed that he had the Neapolitan disease. It could not have remained secret much longer; he walked now with a cane. It was difficult maneuvering without knocking himself or someone else over, so he took his time, stopping to accept the affectionate kisses of sympathetic admirers, all women, all beautiful.

When he reached their little circle he stood slightly tilted, leaning on his cane. His cheeks had grown ruddy in the stifling apartment.

Someone had opened a window, but little of the night's cold breeze penetrated the crowd.

Manet said, "I claim no victory," though secretly he had loved the excitement of the thing, the harsh clang of the swords, the thrill of fear when he thought for a moment that he might have killed his good friend after all. The police had wanted to arrest them both, but when they learned that Duranty had needed not a single stitch, both of them had been released without even having to pay a bribe. "It was the right thing to do," Édouard said. "Duranty never wrote a cruel thing about me again. Rather like how you dispatched Monsieur Zola when you first met him, Mademoiselle Cassatt. He'll never write a thing about you now. He wouldn't dare."

"Have you been arguing with critics too, Mary?" her mother asked. Tonight Katherine, attired in a new gown, looked every inch a well-outfitted Parisian dowager, albeit more trim than most. She and Lydia had embarked on a walking campaign for Lydia's health, abetted by the freedom that their new carriage—a gift from Aleck, who was now more successful than his father had ever been—afforded them. Daily, they strolled the Rue de Rivoli, their arms entwined and parasols unfurled, shopping the windows of dressmakers and bookstores. And Robert, too. Lately, he had been able to give up his cane.

"I merely asked Monsieur Zola some questions and gave him my opinion on one of his books," Mary said.

"You did?" Abigail said. "When?"

"She chased him away. He lives in Médan now," Degas said, "in a pile of a house that *L'Assommoir* bought him. He rarely comes to Paris anymore, though he did write me a note, Mademoiselle Cassatt, to beg me to make certain you won't be here next Tuesday, when he plans to come see the exhibit."

"He did not," Mary said, laughing and looking about the crowd. Excepting Zola, the cream of Paris intellectual life had crowded into the new apartment on the glittering Avenue de l'Opéra: Alphonse Daudet, the great descriptor of Parisian life; Paul Gachet, the celebrated physician who attended nearly everyone in the room with the exception of Manet and Lydia; Antonin Proust, a member of the Chamber of Deputies who loved fine art; Stéphane Mallarmé, the pursuer of Zola; the art dealer Paul Durand-Ruel, whom Mary hoped might one day represent her; the artist James Tissot, who had abandoned his adopted London to visit Édouard but who was now flirting in the kitchen with Méry Laurent; James Whistler, also in from London; and the writer Edmond de Goncourt. Even Guy de Maupassant was holding forth with Pissarro in the dining room. Anyone who mattered in society was here tonight, but more important, anyone who mattered to Mary was here tonight. Satisfaction flooded through her. Her parents were at ease in the luminous crowd; Lydia was laughing with Edgar; Abigail and Ernest had easily fit in; and Edgar, from time to time, touched the small of Mary's back and smiled quietly at her. But even more gratifying, a thousand compliments had come her way tonight; everyone had sought her out to tell her how much they admired her work. In all her life, no other night had matched this one. The pinnacle had been achieved, everything glorious at once: the promise of love, the promise of recognition, the promise of success.

Berthe and Eugène arrived and made their way toward them through the tight assemblage. Eugène towered above Berthe and scowled at anyone who bumped into her. Not quite wan, but not quite well, Berthe exuded fragility. It was her first outing in practically a year, having been released only a week ago from her confinement.

Édouard kissed Berthe on the cheek and greeted Eugène with another. "You look glorious, Berthe. Doesn't she look well, everyone?"

She didn't look well, but everyone exclaimed over her robust health and general beauty and asked about the baby. Introductions were made, Abigail quietly elbowing Mary when she learned that it was Berthe Morisot she was meeting.

"It's as if everything we said that day at that exhibition has come true," Abigail whispered to Mary. "And you owe me an explanation of just what was taking place in that room."

"I don't know what was taking place," Mary whispered back.

"I think I know," Abigail said, a teasing smile playing across her lips.

"Tell them what you told me the other day, Madame Morisot," Degas said when the chatter died down. "Tell them what you said about Bibi." Bibi was the nickname Berthe had given to her daughter, and everyone had adopted it.

"I beg your pardon?" Berthe said.

"You remember. You said that Bibi looked just like her uncle."

Berthe blanched. Édouard looked away, out the window, over the heads of the crowd, as if he were stifling a second urge to duel.

"What did Degas say, Mame?" Robert said. "I didn't hear."

Lydia, too, looked to Mary for an explanation, as did, for some reason, everyone, including Berthe, whose doleful gaze fixed on Mary. The noise of the room fell away as Mary sought her footing. A moment ago, Edgar had been nothing but charm, and before that, nothing but intoxication.

"I think what Monsieur Degas meant is that Eugène and Édouard look so much alike that Eugène's daughter could not fail to look like a Manet. Her father and uncle have such similar countenances. Really, Father, don't you think they look alike?"

The brothers, weary of the scrutiny that had been foisted on them since they were children, nonetheless struck a pose on opposing sides of the circle: chin up, shoulders back. Evidence in court.

"Yes, they are quite similar," Robert conceded.

"Yes, they are," the Nierikers agreed.

Berthe, unsteady, said, "They overwhelm all the Morisot in my Bibi. There is nothing of me."

But Berthe had made a second mistake. She should have said *Eugène* overwhelms all the Morisot in her Bibi, and she knew it. Her pale face blushed a bright vermillion.

Mary said, "Berthe, will you indulge me and let me show you my work? Excuse us, everyone." Before Berthe could answer, Mary took her hand and plowed through the tightly knit crowd clogging the hallway to the bedroom where her canvases hung. She shooed everyone out and shut the door.

"Degas is terrible," Berthe said.

"Yes."

"You're not going to defend him?"

"Of course not," Mary said. "Why would I?"

"Aren't you—?"

A chill ran through Mary. "No, we are not," she said in a flat voice, shuddering to think what she would have said an hour ago. *We might.* Or, *Soon.*

"Ah. Then the gossip is wrong."

"There is gossip?"

"Of course. This is Paris. You didn't think his attentions to you would go unnoticed, did you?"

"But why would you listen, Berthe?" Mary said. *You, of all people*, she wanted to say.

"I'm sorry. I've been cooped up with the maids too long." Berthe's hands flew to her flushed face. "Why does he persist in making me miserable?"

"I don't think it's you he's teasing. I expect it's Édouard. They might be outside killing one another right now."

"Sometimes, I think I should never show myself in society again. All that time at home, in bed, isolated, waiting for Bibi . . . it was a less exposed life."

Mary hesitated, but tonight had altered any intention of restraint she might have exercised even a few hours ago. She feared that Berthe might consider what she was about to ask her cruel, perhaps as cruel as Degas's jest had been, but Berthe had tried to warn her a long time ago. In fact so many people had warned her not only to take care, but that Degas was not as he seemed, that now the kiss, in all its splendid beauty, seemed an act of immense folly.

"Tell me, Berthe, do you regret anything? I'm sorry to ask. I mean no harm, truly. But has it been worth it?"

Rain and wind lashed at the window glass. Berthe looked around the empty room as if searching for an anchor in the deluge.

"Live without having loved? I don't know if I would have wanted that. Sometimes, though, the shame is too much to bear. I can hardly believe I allowed it to happen. And Édouard has been so cavalier. So many women, while I . . ." She looked away, her gaze running over the pictures her mind was not yet registering. "But for me, he was the only one. And I can't help that I love him. I wish that I could, but no amount of wishing has made it so." In her despair, she was very still. "I can't help you, Mary. I thought once that I could, but I know what it is to be lost. I am no model, no seer, no lighthouse. Nothing I can say will get you home, except that at least Degas is not married."

Yes, Mary thought, at least there was that. But he was cruel and facetious. She wasn't sure she wanted to be with a man who would break someone's heart for the fun of it, especially someone he claimed to love, as he said he loved Berthe.

"Do you still have time?" Berthe said. "To reconsider?"

Mary nodded.

Berthe took Mary's elbow. "Good. Then let's forget our sadness tonight. Show me everything. Show me what you have done."

Shaking off her confusion, Mary introduced each canvas, telling Berthe the problems she had had with each, the challenges she had overcome, her terror at how they would be received. They were all there: Eloise in the blue chair, the portraits of her family and a second one of Mary Ellison, a series of pictures of women at the Opéra, two commissioned portraits. At some point, a knock came at the door and Eugène, his cravat askew, stepped inside and listened too. He followed them about the room, taking time in front of each of the canvases to study them.

When Mary finished, Berthe said, "They are all beautiful. Every one of them."

"Mademoiselle Cassatt paints just like you, doesn't she, darling?" Eugène said, directing his conversation to his wife, as he often did. "Your touch is a little lighter, Berthe, but Mary's impasto is brilliant."

"What a lovely compliment, Monsieur Manet," Mary said, thinking that Eugène might be too dim to be able to silence Degas and too in love with Berthe to believe anything bad of her, but that he was entirely adept at kindness. "Tell me, how is your darling baby? Is she wonderful?"

"Yes, she is. I've gone mad with love—haven't I, Berthe?"

Berthe smiled a vague, far-off smile and said, "Yes. Mad."

"Are you tired, darling?" Eugène said.

Berthe smiled a weak assent and Eugène took her by the elbow and guided her out the door into the party. As Mary watched them go, Eugène attentive and careful, Mary thought that the art of love might just be blindness: the willingness not to see the truth of anything, to blur life's sharp edges and drift on an impression of one's own making, to act as if the life you lived was the life you wanted.

Later, after the harried ticket taker had finished wiping up the spilled champagne and lugged the empty bottles to the dumbwaiter, she held out the keys to the apartment to Edgar and Mary, who were the last to leave. It was past midnight. Mary's family and the Nierikers had taken their leave an hour ago. Caillebotte, exhausted, had left in anticipation of the next day's ordeal, as had Portier. Degas snatched the keys from the girl and pocketed them, promising that he would lock up and return in the morning in time to open the door. "Now, off with you."

"Monsieur Portier will not be happy with me if something goes wrong. You promise you'll be here?" the girl said.

Apparently, she had noticed whose pictures were still missing and had drawn her own conclusions as to Edgar's reliability.

"Yes, yes," he said.

The sound of the front door shutting echoed in the empty apartment. The girl's retreating footsteps clattered on the marble stairs, the only sound penetrating the apartment turned gallery. Mary and Edgar had been arguing when the girl had interrupted them. They began again now.

"If you wanted to have your little joke, you could have just said something to Édouard alone. You put me in a terrible position, having to make up an explanation that anyone could see was a wild concoction."

"I didn't put you in that position; your father did."

"But it was you who brought it up."

"It isn't a secret, is it, what's been going on between them? Berthe certainly knows. And God knows Édouard does. You Americans are too prudish when it comes to such things."

"My point is that you were thoughtless. It was not a small thing for Berthe. She was devastated."

Now that the party was over, the apartment had grown cold. Edgar would admit no weakness, but his hand traveled to his watering eyes, naked tonight of their glasses. "This meddling of yours comes from my unbridled affection for you. Obviously it caused too much liberty of opinion. Now you think you can say anything to me."

"But how can I trust you?"

Edgar appeared unmoved. "I might be mischievous—"

"Mischievous? You should have seen Berthe. Whatever happened between her and Édouard is not for us to know, and certainly not to advertise or for you to use as a weapon for your personal amusement."

"As I was saying," Edgar continued, "I might be mischievous, but you are guilty of crimes too. You reveal little of yourself. You can be formal, withdrawn, self-possessed. You sometimes seem as if you need no one. You certainly don't need me."

Mary was exhausted, suddenly. What had that kiss been but need? "Tell me," she said, "do you love anyone? Anyone at all?"

The flickering shadows of the gaslight revealed the charcoal outline of Edgar's face, but nothing of what he wanted. Four hours ago, she had touched that face, had found comfort in his arms, had believed that he loved her. Now she felt battered and alone.

The gas hissed and blinked in the jets. Edgar stood very still, all the warmth washed from his rigid frame. He said, "How are you getting home?"

"The family carriage is waiting for me. The Nierikers took everyone home."

Out in the hallway, Mary pulled on her coat and descended the marble stairway while Edgar pretended to have trouble with the lock. The carriage was well away before he emerged from the building. Or at least this is what Mary assumed, since she would not look back.

Chapter Twenty-Eight

The exhibition was worth seeing for the same reason that one would go to see an exhibition of pictures painted by the inmates of a lunatic asylum.

Impressionism has arrived. It is of today, so to speak, of the period; it is the chrysalis of a butterfly.

Madame Mary Cassatt enters boldly into the ways of impressionism. This is all fine, but why is the décolletage of a young woman in a theater her primary interest? I assure you, madame or mademoiselle, this was quite unnecessary.

Mary Cassall exhibits ingenious, extremely interesting portraits set in boxes at the Opéra. One, of a young red-haired woman in a box, has as a background a mirror in which the hall is vividly reflected; it is the picture of this painter that most boldly strikes visitors to the exhibition. The reflected flesh is a revelation of a most particular talent.

Mary Cassatt should not forget that the one thing in the world that is particularly sweet, fresh, smooth, and transparent as dew is the skin of the woman, so why paint it as if she were plastering a wall, thereby obliterating its velvety delicate freshness?

A new watercolor by Mary Cassatt merits attention for its fine tone and boldness of key.

The work of Madame Mary Cassatt betrays a preoccupation with attracting attention, rather than an attempt to paint well. Her study of a woman with a fan, of a woman in a loge, indeed all her canvases provoke laughter. But if I place twenty meters between myself and the work, I can distinguish something: I perceive a shimmer, in the shade, the air, the hint of a subject, again, this subject is disgusting; but really, is it necessary that I have to look at a picture from twenty meters, neither more nor less, to find anything that is not mediocre?

An American, Miss Mary Cassatt, aims also for the strange, and forces herself to appear more eccentric than she is at heart.

Decidedly, Raphael can sleep well in his tomb; Rubens in his.

We admire Mlle Cassatt's paintings and pastels, her soft and exquisite tones, and serious rendering of form. We note especially *Woman in a Loge*, in which the woman's head and shoulders are reflected in a mirror with astonishing accuracy.

Now, for the fans of a good joke, we will post a picture by Madame Cassolt. (Wherein a caricature follows.)

In such sublime company (Degas's), it is necessary to cite M. Mary Cassatt. She shows a portrait of a woman in a loge that

is too horrible. The poor woman has shoulders direct from
Zola's *L'Assommoir*, and behind her can be seen gilded boxes
where the gilding has been replaced by an egg yolk that
threatens to splash on her shoulders. And, she surrounds this
victim with a green wooden frame. A second supposed masterpiece is adorned with a red frame.

Seated around the dining table, the Cassatts traded the papers in a
circle, reading only the good reviews aloud, endeavoring to hide from
Mary's ears the cutting words she was nonetheless reading for herself. For
long minutes, nothing was heard except the rustling of papers, the *schwep*
of pages turning, and the occasional sigh accompanied by listless waits
for the next paper to be passed. From time to time, Robert asked the
meaning of a certain word, and it was always some terrible reminder of
the mayhem, like *mediocre* or *eccentric*, nothing that shone with the bright-
ness of the rare positive remark written on Mary's work. That morning,
after breakfast, Robert had gone out and gathered all the papers, braving
yet another deluge of April rain, a paternal duty and privilege he exercised
with taciturn diffidence. Returning, he set them on the table and com-
manded, "Shall we begin?" Mary hoped he might absent himself to spare
her his judgment, but he pulled out his chair and sat at the head of the
table, presiding over the reading as if he were conducting a meeting. His
officious presence exacerbated the unease Mary had suffered since the
day after the party, when the exhibition opened. Half the attendees broke
into laughter and the others shook their heads, asking, "Why is this considered good?" and their companions tittered that it wasn't. She had fled
to her studio, where she hadn't been able even to prepare a canvas, let
alone think of painting another thing. But the reviews were ten times
worse, permanent words of disdain that she could never escape.

Now, Mary dreaded her father's comments, certain he would revive
his tired argument that to be an artist was to embark on folly. "Have I
seen them all?" she said.

"I think so," Katherine said. The sterling silver coffeepot and an untouched plate of croissants were marooned next to the island of untidy and creased newspapers heaped in the center of the table. Two dozen papers, at least. It had been only five days since the opening, and there were still all the art journals and the weekly papers to come. "At least the exhibition wasn't ignored," Katherine said, in an effort to make some sense of the disaster.

"Two reviewers misspelled my name. Some think I am married. How can they claim to know anything of my art if they can't even get the simplest details correct? My name is in the catalog. *It's in the catalog.*"

Katherine and Robert exchanged glances. Mary would be impossible for the rest of the day, and when Mary was impossible, life was impossible.

"My dear, if I may, you said Edgar warned you," Katherine said.

"Oh, Edgar. What does he have to worry about?" To no one's surprise, his reviews had been laudatory. *Brilliant and exquisite in his truth and execution. Provocative and bold. Monsieur Degas is, as always, one of the stars of the group.* Envy swelled. It was awful to be compared to him, to be reviewed as *horrible* while his work was deemed *exquisite.* Since the party, he hadn't sought her out, and wouldn't, not even to console her, not now, not after *the question.* But she didn't even know whether she could have faced him anyway—or anyone, after this. All her armor, all her pride, was not equal to the humiliation of being publicly belittled. *Le tout Paris* would read these reviews, at least those who cared about art, which was everyone in the city. And no doubt Edgar, in his cavalier independence from critical judgment, would read none of the reviews, would remain unaware and unaffected that he had been praised above everyone. No wonder he could tell her to disregard the reviews; it was easy enough to do if you were the critics' darling.

"You mustn't act as if Edgar emerged unscathed. On the whole, they loved him," Lydia said. "But not *Le Figaro.* Mr. Wolff eviscerated him."

"As I recall, Mr. Wolff didn't even mention me. I was lumped in with '*les autres*.' Not even worthy enough to mention. It seems my fate is to be either ignored or attacked."

"They didn't attack just you, Mary. They were equally as unkind to Monsieur Caillebotte. And they called Monsieur Forain a cretin." Lydia touched Mary's hand. "At least they weren't that cruel to you."

"Wonderful. I lie somewhere between cretin and exquisite. Right in the middle, where mediocrity resides." Mary rose and paced around the table. Her little dog trotted at her heels, following her with mincing steps, her button eyes anxious and uneasy. "One of them used that word, didn't they? *Mediocre*?"

"Another said you were ingenious," Lydia said.

"And another that I was strange."

"You sold a painting to Alexis Rouart," Lydia said. "If that isn't success, what is?" Rouart was a wealthy industrialist and an old friend of Degas's who had been taken with one of her pastels. Mary had been thrilled, but now that victory seemed small in the light of this merciless drubbing.

"'Her canvases provoke laughter—'"

"Stop it, Mame. That's enough self-pity," Robert said. He stood, resting his hands on the edge of the dining table. "What is the matter with you? If you are going to abandon your work because someone speaks ill of it, then it has never really been your work, has it? It becomes theirs. You give it up. Do you want to do that? Your work is different; you declare it so; you want it to be so. But you cannot expect the world to understand when you ask them to look at work that is different than what they are used to seeing. The human mind is not equipped to adapt so rapidly. People have been told for so long what is good by the École des Beaux Arts that when something new comes along, they cannot adjust their thinking. Your work doesn't look anything like what they have been told is good. Ergo, your pictures must be bad. It's confused logic, but logic nonetheless. And it will alter with time. You must give it time. Why yield your confidence to a bunch of jackals?"

Mary, Katherine, and Lydia stared at Robert, who sat down, took a sip of his coffee, then replaced the cup in its saucer. His posture, ever militaristic, was even more so this mid-morning, his white cravat tied as beautifully as if he were going to the Élysée Palace, his jacket brushed free of lint and gleaming black in the morning light despite his earlier dash through the deluge.

"The truth is," he continued, "you cannot fight logic, ill-conceived or otherwise. You must simply wait until the formula changes by exposure. This is what your exhibition is for. You are exposing the world to something new until at some point, it will no longer be new. Until that time, you are different and therefore unacceptable. But not to everyone. You had some glowing comments. It is upon these you must focus. Forget the rest. They mean nothing."

Mary put her hand to the back of a chair, to bolster herself. "You are not ashamed?" she said. The question, hoarded for two decades, simply appeared, voiced by her heart.

"'Revelation of a most particular talent.'" Robert lobbed this lovely phrase across the dining table. He had lingered over the words, exquisitely turned in the French, and as he had translated it in his mind into English he had memorized it, to use it as a weapon, but he had not imagined having to use it so soon, nor having to use it on Mary. He had imagined smiting the press with it, or defending her honor at dinner parties, or writing letters to American newspapers, quoting the generous appraisal as one might quote a stock price.

The truth—the truth Mary just revealed that she knew—was that he had often been ashamed of Mary. Few parents in Philadelphia had had to contend with the kind of single-minded stubbornness that Mary had exhibited almost from the moment she was born. And it had only gotten worse. He had never believed that sending his daughter to the Pennsylvania Academy would result in her desiring to become an artist. It was only meant to finish her, to give her something to do, to distract her until she married and had children. When she had insisted on traveling through Europe on her own to study, when she wouldn't listen to reason, when his concerns were dismissed with a roll of her eyes and endless arguments about whose life hers was to lead, he had foreseen this moment, when her welfare would be disregarded by savages, when the fabric of her soul would be riddled and torn, when she would be discussed publicly as an entity to be dissected and examined and declared wanting. What did a father live for, if not to protect his daughter? And what did a father do if his daughter refused protection? He had had no weapons other than to forbid, and that, he had learned long ago, had been an impotent sword. He had long believed that it would have been better had Mary been born a man. She could have gone into business, would have been as successful as her brothers, running a railroad like Aleck or trading stocks at Cassatt & Company like Gardner, saving herself from this tenuous occupation with its dependence on subjective yardsticks wielded by envious and misinformed critics. To succeed in art? The endless question continued to haunt him. How was he or anyone to measure her success? He had long given up the standard of sales. Those seemed elusive, uncertain, improbable.

"I don't understand what you do, Mame; I don't pretend to. But if you let go now, it will be as if you never understood anything about yourself at all," he said. "And if you let this nonsense deter you from your work, then I *will* be ashamed of you."

This moment of grace, this moment when Robert Cassatt surrendered so that his daughter wouldn't, was met with a barely audible gasp, a release of years of tedious rebellion and steely resolution and the enduring sorrow a daughter suffers when her father denies her heart. A few years later, her father would try this trick again on Lydia, believing in its power, but he would fail—there would be no moment of grace; the gasp exhaled would be another kind of letting go, one that would age him by a decade. But now Mary rounded the table and tangled her arms about his neck. He smelled of soap and happiness, the scents of her young childhood, before they knew how to make one another

miserable, before she understood that filial desire could sabotage paternal love.

To Katherine and Lydia, the awkward engagement of arms and elbows and pats on the hand appeared a Degas painting, truthful in its
inelegance, redemptive in its ungainliness. Mary took a seat beside her
father, a place she did not usually choose, and through glassy eyes gazed
at the disarranged papers. She took a deep breath. "But what do we do
with all of these?"

Robert shrugged. "Cut out the good reviews, send your brothers copies, and burn the rest. Don't say a word about the poor ones to anyone,
and I won't either. I'll tell your brothers you triumphed. The bad reviews
no longer exist. And let's go away. Let's travel this summer. You've
worked hard for two years. What do you say? You've traveled with Lyddy
and your mother. Now let's you and I go on a trip."

"My work—"

"Aren't you tired? Couldn't you use a break? Let's travel to Switzerland. Perhaps we could go to Italy, too. You can introduce me to all your
artist friends in that little Italian town you love so much. It's time I
learned a thing or two about your gypsy life."

A life he had refused to finance and one she'd had to hide from him
in order to preserve the tenuous ties that bound them.

"I don't want it to appear as if I am running away."

"From your excellent reviews? The only ones that exist?"

Her father's face betrayed no irony, no mockery, no unkindness. Having just performed the fatherly miracle of replacing her pain with pride,
he now managed to alter their history and make her believe that a daughter and father could reconcile, given enough understanding.

"I would love to," she said.

"You're sure, Mary?" Katherine asked, before she was able to stop herself. The tectonic shift in the family geology felt to her as ominous as if
the ground really had moved. She could not imagine the two of them
traveling together, not with their history, no matter this reconciliation.

Robert eyed her with a dull stare. "What would she not be sure of, Katherine?"

"Only that she is more tired than she thinks. We could get a house in the country, couldn't we? Isn't that what Parisians do?"

"Go to the added expense of renting a house somewhere else just so we could stare at one another all summer long like last summer?" Robert said.

"Traveling is tiring," Katherine said. "Mary just said she was tired." She would not ask again for Mary's opinion, would not put her daughter in the position of having to refuse her father, not after she had already agreed to his plan. *Oh*, Katherine thought, *why do I always make myself the mediator?* Because it was the future she saw, the future she feared, as all mothers do.

"Either would be lovely, wouldn't it?" Lydia said, and with the mild question performed the healing ritual incumbent upon her role as the pliable daughter. No one had thought to include her. Had anyone asked, she would have preferred a long journey, like her father, rather than a country house, preferably a journey with an undefined end, fine vistas, and beautiful hotels. She couldn't remember the last time she could think of undertaking such an adventure. Tired as Mary might be, her concerns were not doctors and medicines. Hers were only the perpetual questions of familial nuisance; Lydia alone knew what a privilege those were.

Mollified, Katherine relinquished her worry about Mary and turned to the maternal task of reading Lydia's mind. "Perhaps you and I could plan our own little trip this summer, Lyddy. We'll find somewhere beautiful to stay. Would you do that for me? So we won't be so bored, you and I, cooped up in Paris?" She didn't mention how happy she was to have this opportunity to take Lydia to the south for the waters. Her ever-present fear for her daughter's health rarely had the opportunity for so practical an outlet, hampered as she was by Robert's needs. It was one thing to have lost one child, but it would be quite another to lose a second. How quixotic grief was. Decades later, and the memory of her lost son, Robert, could still cause almost unbearable pain.

"We'll all be gypsies," Robert said, rising, putting an end to the endless feminine tangle of parsing feelings and ascertaining accord. How he longed for his sons, for the plodding masculine practice of reason and sense. "Will Anna and Mathilde never announce luncheon?" he asked, and stalked out of the drawing room.

Chapter Twenty-Nine

Degas wiped his face with his napkin, bid adieu to Jean Louis Forain, whom he had found bolting his food in a corner and who could not stop complaining about his unfair reception by the critics, left payment for his abstemious noontime *salade et soupe,* and trudged the two and a half blocks from the Café de la Rochefoucauld to his studio to gather his paints to take with him to the home of his latest client. The studies for the newly commissioned portrait had not gone well; the woman he was painting had insisted on examining the sketches for approval, which, unsurprisingly, she did not approve. Without being direct, she implied that she wanted Degas to correct with his paintbrush her many years of gustatory overindulgence. After suffering all her comments, Degas said that he understood her completely, then barred her from examining the work in progress, which he had covered with a tarp tagged with a telltale string should she dare remove it. The portrait, he would make certain, would convince no one of her imagined asceticism. That he might not be paid when she confronted her true self on the canvas did not concern him; he would not lie in art, not for the concerns of petty vanity, and especially not for money. Dodging the beastly concierge, Degas unlocked the door to his rooms, thinking that later his commission could hire Renoir if she was displeased; that man would prettify anyone for enough coin.

The magnificent sum of 439.50 francs was each artist's share of the earnings from the entrance fees for their exhibition after repaying Caillebotte, who had regained his full investment along with his own artist's share. Degas was delighted with the financial success, for it reinforced his belief that they might one day conquer the ridiculous barriers the Salon erected around art. Despite the malevolence of the press, *le tout Paris* had come to the Avenue de l'Opéra, and the astonishing accumulation of francs had enlivened them all. This was the first time they had realized money from their exhibition, and Degas felt vindicated, for they would have incurred a dreadful loss had they tried to compete with the Exposition Universelle last year. The monetary exoneration was especially sweet too, because Cézanne and Renoir, those two traitors, were already fuming about losing out on the profit, though Renoir hardly needed it. He had made a huge commotion at the Salon with his portrait of Madame Charpentier and her two small children, which had earned him a thousand francs for his efforts. All winter long, he'd been toasted at their Monday salon, where he was their new pet, rendering Édouard Manet, who had long been the center of their attention, more than a little jealous. Claude Monet had been particularly delighted with the proceeds. Portier was sending him a draft for the full amount and they all hoped that the money would be of some help. Monet was said again to be on the brink of ruin and to be begging for francs from anyone he could find.

For Degas, the exhibition had been even more profitable. Caillebotte, for all his harassment about Degas's tardiness, had coveted one of the largest paintings, the *Portrait of a Dancer,* and was now making noise about purchasing it. Durand-Ruel was interested in another, a pastel, *Aria After the Ballet,* but so many of Degas's other *articles* had been commissioned or purchased beforehand that most of his work had not been for sale—not even the fans, whose owners had despaired of lending them for the exhibition but had finally given in. Mary had claimed the sole available fan before the exhibition had even opened. Still, he had made good money and could continue his devotion to the Opéra and to the Cafés de la Nouvelle-Athènes and de la Rochefoucauld without ration, a prospect that pleased him immensely.

Do you love anyone, Edgar? Anyone at all? Mary's question came back to him now, as it had multiple times a day since she had uttered it. He woke with that question and went to sleep with it. He was glad Portier was in charge of the finances so that he, Edgar, was not obliged to correspond with or visit Mary, because he would not be able to endure it. Her question enraged him. Of course he loved someone. He had adored his father, and despite the financial grave into which he had flung his son, he remained in Degas's heart as the man who had bequeathed to him the gift of an inordinate love of the Opéra. And he adored his sisters, too, whom he did not see often enough. And despite the complicated entanglements his brothers had fallen into—bankruptcy for René and a petty, ridiculous crime of passion for Achille—he loved them, too. As to Édouard and the conversation Mary had objected to, women never understood the ribbing men conducted with one another. Oddly, though, Édouard had said nothing to him that night in return, when a year ago he would have pounced. Edgar was beginning to fear for his friend, who lately was looking quite ill, though he didn't believe it possible that Édouard could be as doomed as everyone said. Half the men in Paris were suffering from one form or another of any number of ill-gotten diseases. When Edgar pressed, Édouard revealed nothing, neither confirming nor denying the lascivious rumors of the cause of his discomfort, which made Edgar even more worried. But that did not mean he would spare his friend a good joke when it made itself available.

What Mary had meant, of course, was whether or not he loved her. From a kiss to love, in one evening. Did she understand nothing about men? Had she not spoken in such accusatory anger, he might have been able to answer her, for he had begun to wonder himself if what he felt for her was love or some other stirring not quite love but more than common affection. Why not love her? Why not say it? What had quickened when he had kissed her had at least been lust. But he was not a romantic man.

He never lied about that. Knowing Mary was to know more of himself, an astonishing development at his age. Few knew him as she did, and fewer loved him, of that he was more than certain. Right now he could not even name a woman other than Mary whom he could tolerate for longer than a few minutes. Or perhaps it was the other way around. Perhaps he was too harsh, or too crude, or too truthful for a woman to tolerate, none of which had ever mattered until now.

He could not remember why he had come into his studio. He turned in a circle, trying to recall what it was that he had wanted. His newest project was hidden under a sheet toward the rear of the studio. This—what would he call this latest? a sculpture? a confection?—was different from anything he had ever attempted, and therein lay its scintillating challenge. He was having to make up the technique as he worked. He had already incurred so many disasters that he had been reluctant to speak of it to anyone. Not even Mary knew what he was doing.

Not even Mary.

Ah! His paint box. He retrieved it and locked the door, hurrying down the stairs to the lobby, his footsteps echoing on the iron stairway, forgetting that the lurking *portier* would pounce on him the moment she heard him to waylay him with some trumped-up complaint, like her last about the stultifying odor of turpentine emanating from his rooms. He was nearly across the lobby when she appeared like a hunchback from the shadows, waving an envelope she had pulled from her apron pocket.

"Monsieur Degas. I am not your *postier.*"

"What are you squawking about?"

"You have had a visitor. Some man. I told him I didn't know where you were."

"I was eating where I always eat. Direct my visitors there, you worthless woman." He seized the envelope from her hand and hurried out the door.

The letter was from Félix Bracquemond. Before the exhibition opening, he had offered to help Degas with printmaking, which Edgar had lately resolved to perfect and which Mary, before all this occurred, had said that she, too, wanted to master. Plans had bubbled forth. They could publish a journal! Prose and poetry and prints! They could appeal to Zola, to Mallarmé, to anyone to give them stories and poems and essays! The prints could illustrate the prose, or not. They would sell the journal in bookshops. Did Mary want to collaborate? Yes, she did. Overhearing, Caillebotte offered to underwrite the journal. An idea had become reality in one evening. But now Edgar had no idea whether or not Mary even wanted to see him, let alone conspire together on a project.

This letter was a welcome excuse. He needed one. To visit Mary without an excuse would suggest that he intended to answer her question. To visit her with Bracquemond's offer would suggest intent of another sort, one far less dangerous.

Happy now, he flagged down a fiacre to ferry him to his appointment to paint the hideous woman who believed that she could dictate the terms of her portraiture.

Chapter Thirty

Before Mary embarked on her trip with her father, she attended the Paris Salon. Once again, Abigail Alcott Nieriker's submission to the Salon had been accepted. She had painted a portrait of a beautiful young Negress, a yellow scarf covering her hair, her white blouse slipping from one shoulder. To Mary's eye, little, if anything, distinguished it from the many other portraits in the exhibition, but Abigail was pleased with herself and it had received a special commendation.

"Of course, compared to your triumph, this is nothing," Abigail said, taking Mary by the elbow and promenading with her from the "N" room to the concession, where they took a table near the windows that looked out onto the palace gardens. The day was Paris-gloomy—rainy and gray and damp—but they ordered a pot of tea and settled in. Since both Mary and Abigail worked every day, and since Meudon was fifteen minutes outside Paris by rail, their visits were now unhappily infrequent. Mary had not even traveled to Meudon to see Abigail and Ernest's new rooms. Now Abigail was talking on and on about decorating and the scarlet curtains she had ordered and the antique furniture she was coveting and the recent acquisition of a too-grand Louis XIV mirror that took up one entire wall of their parlor. Hers was a far easier life than she had ever lived or expected to live. Best of all, she said, she was free to do as she pleased, and what she was pleased to do was paint, which she did all day when she wasn't walking along the river or writing at her new desk. She couldn't believe that life had turned out so well for her. She was married to a man she loved, she painted all day, and she had been accepted to the Salon. Ernest was devoted and kind and adoring and ... Abigail set down her teacup and said, "I've not stopped talking. Forgive me. Tell me everything. Tell me about Monsieur Degas. I can't believe I didn't ask about that first thing. I don't know what is the matter with me."

"There is nothing to tell. Edgar is nothing like Ernest. He is not devoted and he is not kind and he is not adoring. He is difficult and quarrelsome and he cares not a jot for me."

"But I saw—"

"What you saw was an egregious error in judgment on my part."

"But he looks at you like he looks at no one else."

"Looking is not loving."

"It was love. I would swear it."

"You can swear it, but if it is, it is the kind of love that destroys. He isn't good, Abigail. He is brilliant, but he is not reliable."

Abigail ducked her head. Mary was certain she was thinking of Ernest, who was nothing if not reliable. Abigail looked beautiful today, if a bit weary. She was wearing a new dress, a gray pongee silk trimmed with bunches of forget-me-nots, with a matching pelisse and a bonnet lined in blue. The empire waist was lined with a bow, which Abigail kept touching from time to time, her hand fluttering from her lap to the bow and back again.

"Lydia keeps trying to make a romance too," Mary said.

"And not you?"

"I don't need a romance."

"But he helps you?"

"He helped me, yes," Mary said, emphasizing the past tense, trying to close further discussion because she couldn't talk about Edgar anymore. He infuriated her. Within a second, he could turn from one kind of man into another, and she didn't know which one was real.

"What else does Lydia say?"

"Nothing. She doesn't know and she won't know. Not about this. This one I'm living alone," Mary said, though she feared she wasn't. From time to time, Berthe's and Edgar's *This Is Paris* reared its gossipy head. She wondered what people were saying, what they were thinking. She didn't know. But it didn't matter any longer. She had come to her senses. She and Edgar were colleagues, and like many of the others whom she rarely saw, she would rarely see him. He had come by briefly last week to propose that they still collaborate on printing. He hadn't apologized, nor had he broached the subject of love. He had said merely that Bracquemond was committed to the project and was she still interested? She hadn't yet decided what to do. "Besides, Lydia hasn't been well lately. I don't like to burden her with any of this."

"She'd be furious if she knew you were in pain and hadn't told her."

"Then don't tell her," Mary said, smiling.

"And what about all the rest?" Abigail said. "How do you feel after your exhibition?"

"Battered."

"Do you know, Mary, I've been thinking. You have probably shown more pictures in Paris than any other American woman."

The thought stopped Mary cold. It was probably true. She couldn't think of anyone else who'd ever shown as many pictures.

"And you are braver than I am too, Mary. You knew the press was going to tear all of you apart and you exhibited anyway. This is safe," she said, nodding toward the palais's interior. "One can hide here, easily. But you? You took such a chance."

Mary hadn't felt courageous. For the past month she had felt frightened and nervous and exposed. "You are too kind, Abigail. And I'm glad you are happy. Happy you have everything you want."

Abigail reached across the table and took Mary's hand. "There is something else."

Mary studied her friend's face as the sun glimmered through the thick mist, noticing fatigue and a pallor she hadn't observed before.

Abigail broke into a smile, and the tiny lines under her eyes crinkled into a serene happiness.

"No!" Mary said.

"Yes. The doctor says November."

"But you're older than—"

"Not too old, he says. I'll be more tired, and soon I'll have to confine myself to Meudon, but you'll come see me, won't you, to relieve my boredom?"

"Of course," Mary said. "When I get back. Of course I will." She willed herself not to worry. Berthe Morisot was nearly the same age as Abigail, and things had gone fine for her.

"I'll keep painting as long as I can, but the doctor says I will have to stop if my ankles swell." She made a face.

Mary laughed. They paid their bill and went outside, where the sun had broken completely through the clouds. They shared a fiacre, the driver dropping Abigail at the Gare Saint Lazare before driving Mary on to the Avenue Trudaine.

She started up the long flights of stairs to share the news with Lydia, who would be thrilled. Lydia wanted a child, but her time for that was long gone. No doubt if Lydia had married and conceived she would have died during the pregnancy, her body too taxed by illness to carry the burden of the child. Being childless was Lydia's central pain, Mary thought. For a moment she considered hiding the news, but Lydia would be furious if she believed she'd been protected.

Chapter Thirty-One

W hat have you done to her, Robert? She is on the verge of collapse."
       "Don't be ridiculous."

"You have pushed her beyond reason."

"I hardly think so. I am the one in my seventies. She is only thirty-five, for God's sake. Why aren't you worried about me? I'm tired too."

"You are not the one who has lost a dozen pounds and looks as pale as the sheets."

"You exaggerate."

"I do not."

Katherine and Robert Cassatt were breakfasting in the garden of the Hotel Gibbon, in Lausanne, Switzerland, having left Mary sleeping in her adjoining room. The Rue du Petit-Chêne was steep, but its rise was too modest and its situation too far from the lakeshore to view Lake Geneva from the hotel's gated garden. To enjoy the lake, one needed to picnic on its idyllic shores, a proposition Robert had made last night, shortly after Katherine had arrived on the steamboat from Divonne-les-Bains, where she had accompanied Lydia for the waters while he and Mary had been traveling. But Katherine had taken one look at Mary on the dock and declared that Mary was going back to Divonne with her, and if Robert didn't want to come he could stay alone in Lausanne.

Under no circumstances was Mary to be forced to explore the steep hills and plunging ravines of the little city in the August heat.

Their argument, which had ceased last night only for sleep, had resumed with their morning coffee in the garden, continued through the baguette and omelets, and had not yet concluded.

"Did you at least let her work?" Katherine asked.

"We could hardly have stopped the carriage at the top of Little Saint Bernard Pass for Mame to paint the landscape. And she doesn't do landscapes, anyway. Why are you so cross?"

"She is *sick*, Robert."

"The scenery was spectacular," Robert said, going on as if he hadn't heard Katherine's objections. Café tables covered in white linen dotted the rectangle of lawn in the shade of the fragrant linden trees, where guests were breakfasting in the morning cool. Plans for excursions on the lake were being discussed in French and English. (The Italians were not yet up.) "Mame and I were the very first ones to cross the pass this summer. Little lakes of snow still lay on the ground. In July! Snow! You and Lydia should have come with us. The carriage driver was so adept. Down the mountain into Val D'Aosta he had to keep the brakes on the entire way or the horses would have run away with us over the edge and into the abyss. It was thrilling. And besides, we had to go that way, didn't we, if we wanted to see something of the countryside? Mary was in heaven in Varallo. All her friends gave her party after party. Blame them for her exhaustion!"

"Whether she is thirty-five or sixty-five, she should be your priority, not parties and alpine vistas. You should have seen that she was tired and brought her home immediately."

"But we had to travel down to Milan to catch the train, and it would have been a waste not to have seen the sights there. And I needed her fluent Italian if I was going to make any sense of the city. But I do agree, the train ride from Milan to Lake Maggiore and then the carriage ride over the Simplon Pass was very tiring. I myself could use a good week here to recuperate."

"This trip was to have helped Mary. You know how exhausted she was after the exhibition. And yet you dragged her all over Europe, just to please yourself. You were only supposed to see her friends."

"She could have said something. I was on the verge of canceling the trip myself, but I didn't want to disappoint her."

Katherine sighed and pushed away her coffee cup. The experiment in family unity had imploded, just as she had feared it might. Last night, Mary had hardly been able to say a civil word to her father. "I'm taking her with me today. You can come with us or you can stay, but to be honest, I wish you would come. Lydia isn't better, despite the waters, and now, due to your neglect, I fear for Mary as well."

"No one is as bad as all that, Katherine. Do find it in yourself not to exaggerate, won't you? Can't we be pleasant? We haven't seen one another in a month."

"Fine. You can stay. But I'm going upstairs now to pack Mary and we're leaving on the two o'clock steamer."

Katherine rose from the table and left her husband to bake in the rising August sun. The man understood nothing of women. Throughout their marriage, he had remained as staunchly oblivious to need as when they had first met, though it occurred to her now that perhaps Mary's sudden vulnerability after the exposition had been what had prompted him to propose this trip in the first place; had Mary been her usual stalwart self, he would not have been able to manipulate her into being his tour guide.

Upstairs, Katherine slipped into Mary's room, parted the curtains to let in a sliver of morning light, then set about packing Mary's dresses into her steamer chest, moving quietly, hoping the light and her activity would awaken Mary slowly. After a while Mary did stir, and Katherine pulled a bell for the maid to bring breakfast. They sat at the open window and admired the fine view of the blue lake and the soaring Alps,

Katherine drinking coffee while Mary nibbled on buttered rolls and jam. Mary's gaze, usually so direct and commanding, fell on her mother with a weariness so heavy that Katherine reached across the table to take her daughter's hand.

"He's a demanding child. I don't know how you do it, Mother," Mary said.

"I didn't, darling. You did. It was good of you to indulge him, but now it's time for me to take care of you. I'll finish packing your things and then we're off. It's the easiest trip, just an hour by boat, and then we can stay as long as you like in Divonne with no demands on you whatsoever. Lydia will be so happy to see you."

"Oh, Mother, I couldn't work. A sketch here and there. I'm so behind. This time last year, I had half a dozen canvases finished. Last time I had two years; now I will have only half a year to work for the next exhibition. Shouldn't we just go back to Paris today?" A sharp edge of panic amplified the fatigue in Mary's voice, making Katherine wonder how, in so little time, Robert had managed to decimate their energetic daughter's resolve, for there was no mistaking it: Mary, as much as she might speak of work, had no energy for it.

"You will get so much more done when we return if you are rested."

"I suppose." Mary looked out over the lake again, her gaze indifferent and unfocused, betraying no pleasure in the magnificent view.

Katherine rose from the table and emptied the dresser drawers into the trunk, worried by how little opposition Mary had brooked, further evidence of her diminution. "And Monsieur Degas's new journal can wait. Don't let thoughts of him push you to think of returning before you are ready."

"He's not in Paris."

"Has he written?" Katherine kept her voice even to avoid igniting an even more difficult conflagration than the one she had anticipated over returning to Paris. Mary was so circumspect about her relationship with Degas that Katherine was often left wondering whether one day he would ask Robert for Mary's hand in marriage or disappear forever. Either outcome seemed likely.

"Yes, of course he has. He always writes."

"How is he?"

"He claims health."

Katherine waited for any other bit of information that might help her to understand the relationship between her daughter and that incomprehensible man, but as usual, Mary offered no hint as to their personal intimacies. Not even in this vulnerable state did Mary yield a clue. Of course, Katherine realized then that she was just as bad as Robert, taking advantage of Mary's infirmity, but she'd been driven to it. Oh, how difficult it was to have an unmarried daughter with uncommon friendships.

"I'll finish and then you can bathe, Mary. If we hurry, we might make the noon boat, but don't rush yourself if you haven't the energy. Two o'clock will be just fine, and it will give us time for luncheon in the garden before we go."

After her mother left, Mary rang for water and let the maids douse her shoulders and back in the shallow bath. The cascade, the copper tub, the light angling in through the window slats, all reminded Mary of Edgar's bathers, and once again, she pushed away the memory of his latest letter, which she had hidden in her purse from the prying, gentle concern of her mother.

Château de Ménil-Hubert, près Gacé (Orne)

Tuesday

Ma chère,

I have considered and reconsidered your question, and find myself at a loss to convey to you how much you mean to me. Your regard, your friendship, your elegant taste, your quick tongue, your reserve, your lively brush, all foster an affection and respect for your being unparalleled by anyone else in my acquaintance. Is this love? Tell me, my dear, before the universe smites me for my neglect of you. You are to me what no other woman is. I miss you. Paris misses you. Art misses you. You are unfair to leave us so long bereft of your company. When you come home, I will come to see you and we will talk.

We must make plans on your return for our journal. I'm so delighted you've agreed. *Le Jour et la Nuit.* Do you love the title? As you know, Caillebotte has agreed to finance us, and Bracquemond is eager to instruct us on all the elements of printmaking. Pissarro is in. We will be a merry four, transforming the world with shadow and light.

Your Edgar

The letter had been forwarded to her in their little rented villa in Varallo, and she'd read it on the hillside while her father napped on the porch in the afternoon heat. Of course, Edgar had waited until she had left Paris to speak of the question, suspended between them like the mists hovering above the tumbling creek rushing through Varallo's treed couloirs. He could have said any of this to her in person in June, when she had finally assented and they had planned the great project for when she returned to Paris, but of course he hadn't. He had sent this letter to torment her, to avoid being with her when he confessed whatever it was that he might be feeling. Letters were his shield, though this note lacked the usual winning mockery his other letters employed to such great defense. She didn't understand how he could be so affectionate in correspondence and so withdrawn—punishing, even—in person. But even this reality came with its contradictions. On the last day of the exhibition, after supervising the carter's stowing of their canvases to be delivered back to their studios, he had kissed her on the cheek, though he had offered no apology to Berthe or to her for his rudeness.

And then nothing. She had met with him to agree to the journal, then left Paris without seeing him again.

While she toweled off and dressed, the maids withdrew, coming to her assistance only to tighten her corset, which had grown looser over the past month as she thinned under her father's obstreperous demands. He had constantly changed the itinerary, refused to leave the hotel room for days on end, then proposed innumerable outings and museum visits that required rushed parades through overcrowded exhibitions, complained that nothing was as it once was, and offended any Americans they met. After days of dithering, they finally boarded the train for Lausanne, where they were to have changed cars for Paris. But in Lausanne, her father declared himself infatuated and disembarked, shouting for the porters to search the baggage car for their trunks, commandeering a cab on the tortuous streets to take them to a hotel, any hotel. Beside herself, Mary had telegraphed her mother in Divonne to meet them in Lausanne lest she lose her mind. She didn't even think her father questioned why her mother had come; his self-absorption prevented him from questioning a universe that met his needs, accepting any serendipitous blessing as his due.

Looking in the dresser mirror, Mary pinned her wide-brimmed hat to her hair, piled carelessly upward in the heat. Every bone in her body felt heavy. She couldn't remember ever once feeling so exhausted. The last thing she needed was to faint, and she believed she might. Never had she felt so fatigued, not even in Chicago, when the fire had raged. Overwork, the excitement of the exhibition, her family coming to stay with her, all had taken their rightful toll in these past two years, but they were nothing compared to the demands her father and Edgar imposed.

Both men exhausted her. Each was impossible to please, to understand, to assuage. They claimed love, yet showed little. Seduced as she had been by her father to undertake this miserable trip, she was now wary to yield to Edgar's charm, curdled as it was by his own question: *Is this love?* Did he suppose she was to answer, to instruct, to persuade him that the qualities he admired in her equaled love? And what of his other mention of love? Did she love the title? *Day and Night?* In other words, did she have the same amount of affection for a potential art project as he might or might not have for her? It passed intolerable. It was a shabby letter, elusive and teasing, no matter how proud he might be of his little missive.

She took the letter from her purse and tucked it in the lining of her trunk, where her mother would never look for it. The clock said ten thirty. The noon boat, then.

She placed her hairbrushes and combs in the trunk and shut it, locking it with the little key she kept on a chain around her neck. The project, the journal, would take time from her painting, and it would mean that she would be working at Edgar's side, attempting to master the tricky planishing and etching to make something of beauty and mystery. The thought of the necessary intimacy, late hours, and shared meals frightened her now, but she suspected fatigue robbed her of perspective. She had grown incautious in the spring. She would not make the same mistake again.

From her month traveling with her father, she had learned never to say yes when she meant to say no, although having to relearn that lesson shamed her. What was it about a father that could reduce a daughter to infancy in mere moments? She heard him through the door to their adjoining room, proclaiming to her mother that after undergoing so many social demands on the trip, he would appreciate a little solitude. He would stay on in Lausanne and return to Paris when it suited him.

"Mother?" she said, opening the door to their room. Her father sat by the open window in an armchair, the white lace curtains billowing with the morning breeze. He was reading the English newspaper, his trousers crisp, his hair oiled and combed, his upward glance disinterested and casual.

"You see?" he said, looking up from his paper. "The bloom of health."

Chapter Thirty-Two

Degas dangled a screwdriver from his right hand and confronted the structure of lead pipes before him: two would-be legs, one curved by a vise, the other straight as a plumb line; a small crossbar masquerading as a pelvic bone; a backbone driving skyward; and canted clavicles. How to make a girl? At night, unclothed women paraded through his sleeping mind, not the women of Salon masterpieces, marbled and pristine, iconic and untouchable, ideations of sainted, unclad womanhood, but spectral women made of flesh, dirtied and troubled by hard work, eminently touchable, vulnerable, secret. They twisted and turned in their private ablutions, combing their hair, climbing from a tub, inspecting their feet. Or they danced and danced, their muscles knotted, dreading the *abonnés'* arrival. Or they plunged their blued hands into deep sinks of scalding water, the copper pipes banging overhead. No Madonnas, his, just women as he imagined them in their intimate moments or at their work.

He set down his screwdriver, went to his cabinet, and pulled open its doors. From a drawer, he retrieved his private work, work he never showed anyone, excepting Manet or Alexis Rouart, who would not condemn him. The world could hardly stand a picture of a nude woman squatting in a shallow tub, let alone these brutally naked, mercilessly rendered, shamelessly commercial women. Yet these prints were his antidote to insanity. Drawing the starkly etched, vulgar forms soothed him, somehow. Cartoonish, exaggerated, puerile in their clinical accuracy, he rendered prostitutes in no romantic terms: women selling their naked flesh to clothed men. What he loved about this particular obsession was its emperor's-new-clothes sensibility. There were twenty thousand legal prostitutes in Paris, and yet if exposed, these prints would engender a censorious public rage from which his career would never recover. What was it about the world that it could not face the reality it lived?

He locked the prints away and turned. The frame, unfleshed, iron-boned, sexless, awaited him. Memory. He had made so many drawings of Marie, drawings that would have to revive themselves so he could make her into something so true, so specific, so bestial that her beauty could not be denied. A hundred times the girl had shed her clothes to plant herself in the posture her muscles had memorized, returning again and again to his studio, allowing him to circle her as an animal stalks its prey, to peer at her from every angle, decent and indecent, as she abandoned herself to his rapacious scrutiny. Later, he made small studies of her in wax, anticipating this effort, this terror. He loved the way wax molded and unmolded, the way it taught him how to see. That his obsession had manifested itself in the malleable, the tactile, the dimensional, had come not just from the need for challenge, that vain and lovely ambition in which he so often indulged, but from something much more disquieting. His eyes, the fickle, traitorous, necessary organs of his work, had now begun to steal from him the mass of things, their shape-ness, their roundness, their solidity. Edges wavered and blurred and doubled until forms became hallucinating shape-shifters, liquid impersonators of what had once been reliable, immutable matter. Were it not for his hands, he would no longer see anything clearly, though his vision focused and unfocused of its own accord, a variable that made everyone doubt his affliction. Any moment or day or week, he could see, and the next he couldn't, reinforcing the only blessed truth: that it is the mind that sees, and the vehicle of its perception is not singular. Touch, as much as vision, fashions an image, and in homage and capitulation to this truth, he stood now before his crude iron skeleton surrounded by waiting boxes of wire, wood chips, cotton batting, wax, and clay, materials he hoped his memory would fashion into a confabulation so realistic, so solid, that no canvas could rival it.

He picked up a knife, slit open the boxes piled around the floor, and pulled from one a nest of coiled wire. He dragged a canvas bag from the corner and undid the drawstring, plunging his hands into its depths and scooping out a waterfall of wood chips he let spill to the floor. He donned a pair of gloves and snipped pieces of wire. Then he secured the thick chips of wood to the center pipe with the wire. To keep the wood from slipping, he had to twist the wire ends tightly, and through the gloves he could feel the sharp points pressing against his fingers. It was tedious, clumsy work. He had to bend over to work on her; she was not life-size, nor was she small enough to set on a table. From time to time, he stood up and stretched, his hands linked behind him in an unconscious parody of the figure he was endeavoring to create. It took two dozen wood chips to cover the entire length of the spine, and when he was finished it was past noon.

He uncorked a bottle of wine and poured himself his midday glass to have with his cheese and baguette, liberally buttered by Sabine and wrapped in cheesecloth that morning to keep fresh. Sitting, eating, he thought that he did not mind so much that his mercurial eyes had driven him to this. Only a fool would think he had turned to such an expression out of desperation. He had turned to it because it was a way to replicate life.

It was only now, as a burst of sunlight brightened the studio, that he allowed thoughts of Mary Cassatt to drift in. In these times of intense concentration he stayed away from everyone, eschewing even dinner invitations and salon evenings, an excuse he would use when Mary demanded, as she had every right to, the reason he had not yet responded to her note announcing her return from her trip. The real reason was that she made him nervous, which no other woman did. That he spent much of his time with unclothed models, who did all he asked and more, he did not let figure into his thinking. That he sometimes relieved the ache of his desire in brothels, he ignored too. No intellectual challenge there. Mary was both vulnerable and independent, and that combination proved seductively paralyzing. At the exhibition, surrounded by her paintings, Mary, in her pride and terror, had been irresistible. Her exquisite artistry, her fierce tenacity—he had not lied in that letter. He had finally succumbed to the impulses he generally throttled in her presence. To his surprise she had tasted not like one of the brutal women of his dreams or the resigned women of the brothels, vulgar and fecund, but as familiar as himself, comforting and inviting. The thought that he might one day be physically unable to see her terrified him. To touch her, to feel the mass of her, solidified the lurking desire he had so often suppressed. And then the dressing-down had begun, and all his fears of marriage and entanglements reared before him and he escaped, brutally, using the tool of unkindness.

He had missed her, though, and so he had written that letter, promising to talk. He had to, of course, if they were going to proceed with *Le Jour et la Nuit.* She had seemed eager enough in the exchanges he had purposefully kept public and brief before she left with her father. And now he was going away for October to the house of some friends. But what did he know of talking about love? If he could paint love, he would. If he could sculpt it, he would. If he could sketch it, he would. But talk? Would that he had not written, would that he had instead let silence wring from Mary's memory that moment of sublime intimacy.

Sighing, he rose. He pulled a roll of batting from its box. Eyeing the torso, he measured with his memory the proportions of Marie's body. With scissors he cut the batting into pieces and swaddled the wood-draped piping, using rope to secure each blanket of cotton in place. It took some time to fashion the inside of her. He felt almost foolish, for the work was clumsy, like the discarded mistake of a demented

Michelangelo, crafted not of marble but of ignoble wire and stuffing. There was something so subversive about her, something so seditious, Degas thought, that he wished he could, when finished, expose her innards to the world. But her plebian core would be his glorious secret, his own little rebellion against those who believed art existed only in the realm of the pure and sacred.

As the afternoon light fell across his peculiar creation, he wondered how much ingenuity it would take to flesh out his little dancer, his little statue, his little, little girl. He had more boxes: clay and beeswax and filament and cotton and silk and ribbons and paintbrushes and a single pair of a child's ballet shoes. No more exciting challenge or balm existed for him now. She was *of* him; she was his, she was his very soul. Tilting his head to the side, studying the mess of wire and wood and cotton with the sharply angled lenses of his failing eyes, he wished he could intuit Mary the way he hoped to intuit this girl. It was a shame that a woman of flesh was not a made thing, though he did not know what he would change of Mary, given the chance. Perhaps it was the curse of all artists to wish to fashion everything to their will. Perhaps it was the ruination of their lives, the way nothing could be controlled and nothing could be fixed, not even one's own desire. It was this tension that might keep him alone forever. He was master in his studio, even as he was uncertain and afraid, and this comforting thought drove him back to his work, which he would not finish until long after the sun had gone down.

Chapter Thirty-Three

One early November morning, Degas arrived at Mary Cassatt's studio bearing several paper-wrapped packages bound together with a length of knotted twine. He had sent no note to announce his visit. He just appeared, a bearded ghost in a gray coat and top hat, with gifts he wordlessly handed to Mary. She set the packages on the paint-scarred table that held her palette, adorned this morning with fresh dollops of scarlet lake, ultramarine, and lead white.

She would still be in Divonne if Lydia hadn't rallied. When Mary had arrived with her mother on the steamer from Lausanne, Lydia was weaker than Mary had ever seen her. On the hour-long trip over, her mother had explained that Lydia was in trouble, but Mary had not imagined such peril: Lydia's skin had grown waxy and pale; she had to fight for breath after climbing just a few stairs; and her face, hands, and feet were swollen beyond measure. The doctors, in despair, ordered Lydia to stop taking the waters and to merely rest in hopes that immobility might conquer what the famed waters had not. Every day for weeks, she rested in the far corner of the wide veranda overlooking Lake Geneva, the illness again waxing and waning without discernible reason, at least none the doctors could ascertain or explain. While Lydia napped, Mary took up her sketchbook and made studies of the other invalids: their entwined hands folded on their laps, the curve of their enfeebled bodies at rest, the anguished ministrations of their loved ones. Several weeks into their stay, her mother bent over Lydia's reclining figure to adjust her blanket, and Mary sketched them, seeking to capture the closed circle of maternal devotion and love, her mother fighting inchoate dread, her sister attempting to conceal her misery. Upon returning to Paris early in October with the slowly recovering Lydia, Mary had done nothing but paint mothers and their children. Earlier this week she had hired a young model and her infant child and positioned them in a stream of sunlight. She had painted the mother bent over the infant cradled in her lap.

It was this canvas she was finishing now.

Mary did not invite Edgar in, but left the door open, and after a moment's hesitation, he followed her inside, taking care to shut the door behind him. She paid him no attention as she took up her palette and resumed staring at the canvas. After some minutes of consideration, she dipped a hogs hair brush into the scarlet lake and lead white and mixed them together, but not thoroughly; she wanted both colors to show when she laid down the paint, to echo the stripes of the mother's dress. The painting needed only last touches. Mary felt Edgar's presence but fought to ignore him. He remained quiet; she couldn't even hear him breathe. She shut her eyes, remembering the light of southern France, her mother's heartache, the vivid blue of the sky. And in an instant she was on the veranda, once again observing their private moment. With that revival came motion. Mary touched her loaded brush to the curve of the mother's elbow, then to her cheek, then to a splash of sunlight on the floor, attempting to mimic the reflections of true light by balancing the deep rose of the mother's skirt in unexpected places. Mary's movements became flourishes, born of instinct; she made quick decisions with her arm extended and her brush skimming the canvas, her gaze darting as her brush did, the two now one. Stepping back, she dipped her brush into the jar of turpentine, quickly blotted it on a rag, and touched it once again to her palette, swirling the ultramarine and rose until they purpled. This she applied to the mother's cheek, the folds of the baby's arms, a strand of the mother's hair, and finally the underside of the windowsill. She worked on, deepening the values, hoping to achieve that elusive unity of tone so necessary for cohesion. Time evaporated: an hour, a minute; it was impossible to know.

She stepped back and laid down her brush.

Edgar came to stand beside her. He smelled of the ocean and the country whence he had just come, of the autumnal rain that was beginning to gather outside, of the chasm of their separation. On his lavender glasses flickered the gray light of the clouding day.

"My God," he said. "It's glorious. Perfect. You have found your obsession."

She looked once again at the canvas, not as the artist but as a viewer, to see the whole of it: the sunlight through the window, the touch of the mother's cheek to the child's, the lazy rapture of their entwined arms and half-closed eyes, their moment of eternity, of future memory, of the present made immutable.

"You've painted love," Edgar said. "You must always paint love. You must never paint anything else. You have found it. Your obsession is love."

He was right. Here was love—light and color and affection sprung from her brush, desire and innocence in every stroke, and something more, something real, something absolute.

A moment passed, and then another. "And what of you? What will you paint?" Mary said.

"I will paint what is real."

"And love is not real?"

"It is when you paint it," he said.

Mary sidled past him, intent on emptying the turpentine, washing her brush, scraping her palette, all things she would abandon at the slightest encouragement if he would only grasp her wrist or whisper, *I missed you.* It was exhausting to have to constantly be on guard, especially since he changed so often from intimately confiding to a kind of amused diffidence that disarmed her, making her trust him once again. Outside, the skies opened and rain drummed on the Boulevard de Clichy and pedestrians dashed for archways and pressed themselves against doors.

"Aren't you going to look at what I've brought you?" Edgar said, gesturing to the abandoned packages.

Mary took up her palette knife, sawed through the twine, and tore open the paper. Inside lay a stack of ten copper plates, an assortment of burins, and a brush. The tools of the printmaker.

"For the journal," he said. "Though perhaps you don't want to now, after everything."

She gathered her things and strode out the door and down the hallway, leaving Edgar behind. She set the turpentine jar in the sink and dropped her brush and palette knife into the liquid, spattering her smock. She scraped the palette under the running water and scrubbed its surface with a sponge soaked in turpentine. When everything was rinsed, she dumped the turpentine and took everything back to the studio. Edgar was standing where she had left him.

"We can work together in my studio," he said. "I have the press, the acid, everything we will want, everything we will need."

She threw the empty jar at the wall. It shattered and fell to the floor.

Edgar flinched but went on as if she had not just tried to take off his head. "This is for us, for our future," he said.

Mary unbuttoned her smock. She would lock him in the studio; she didn't care. She reached for her coat and hat. Outside, the rain continued to fall. She pinned the hat in place, found her umbrella.

Edgar said, "You must understand. Mine is not the language of love."

He walked toward her and unpinned her hat and handed it to her. He went out into the hall and returned with the broom and dustpan from the *portier's* closet. The glass made a tinkling sound as it tumbled into the receptacle. He shook the broom so the slivers would fall too. He was fastidious. When he finished he returned everything to the closet and then came into the room and took her hand.

She remembered now what had started everything: a careless remark, cruelly made. An avalanche of coldness when she asked him if he was capable of love. The essential question, Mary thought, that one had to ask of anyone. She wasn't certain what Edgar wanted, whether he even thought of happiness. But for far less, far more had been forgiven in the world.

Chapter Thirty-Four

Berthe Morisot, standing at her easel in her studio, picked up her brush, then set it down again. She was inspecting her canvas of two women in a boat in the Bois de Boulogne, which she'd done in the summer. But she couldn't concentrate. Yesterday, a tittering laundress, her basket piled high with her delivery of freshly laundered linens, had relayed to Berthe the latest, that Édouard Manet hardly left his studio now for the embarrassment of the cane he'd had to take up, and worse, that he had grown infatuated with little Isabelle Lemonnier, Madame Charpentier's enchanting sister, and was writing letters of scolding affection to the poor girl, who had no idea what to do with missives of such attentive devotion from a man her father's age. Berthe had turned the laundress out, stunned by the societal depths the tentacles of gossip reached in Paris, so that even her laundress was privy to her brother-in-law's indiscretions. She knew what Édouard was thinking: that by wooing youth he could defy the disease that had rendered him a tottering, ill man, but he seemed not to possess any shame at all, even though infatuations were a far worse embarrassment than the cane. But what infuriated her most was that he was paying attention to Isabelle so that he didn't have to pay attention to himself, a distraction of such misguided idiocy that she could not contain her anger at him. She'd given up Thursdays, claiming Bibi, which allowed her to keep some balance, though the gossip found its way to her anyway. But she knew Édouard, and she knew that he would forsake care in order to fool himself into believing that he was healthy.

Again Berthe took up her brush and palette and studied the canvas. In the summer she had painted this picture of two women boating, working in a rocking rowboat as Julie cried from shore, the nurse endeavoring but failing to distract her, paint tubes tumbling while the portable easel pitched from side to side, even though Berthe had braced it against the gunwale. The loose, sometimes frantic brushstrokes had been executed as much to get back to Julie as to capture the scene before the light changed. Motherhood forced such limitations. Now she studied the painting again to see whether she needed to highlight the brilliance of the water to keep the sense of impermanence in the canvas, the of-the-moment shower of light she'd been reaching for.

But it was impossible to think clearly. She supposed her roiling fury with Édouard had something to do with the isolation of raising a toddler. Darling as Julie was, she extracted all Berthe's energy, even though the nurse came daily to give her time to work—so much time that Berthe believed she could produce enough canvases to make a respectable showing in the exhibition next year, an accomplishment that belied the predictions of her non-artist friends, who thought a child would certainly, finally instill a more normal spirit in her. Those friends, who had feigned indulgence at her "pastime," disappeared soon after she took up her palette again, though Berthe thought it was entirely possible that the reason they had deserted her was that she had no doubt lost her charm in the process of producing a child. She had certainly lost her beauty. Julie was the little star now, charming people with shy smiles on the street, seducing shopkeepers, who indulged her with treats, and braving the adulation of the occasional overbearing matron who clearly needed a grandchild to quell the maternal acquisitive siege of middle age.

Even the attentive Auguste Renoir had abandoned her; he'd become society's darling, their appointed portrait painter extraordinaire, in no small part due to the Charpentiers' generous patronage. Auguste had so many commissions now and so many invitations to stay at people's summer homes that he was beginning to complain of exhaustion. One would think that in gratitude to the Charpentiers for the waves of money now coming Auguste's way he would feel obliged to intervene for poor little Isabelle Lemonnier, or at least warn them all of Édouard's chronic faithlessness. Apparently, though, Auguste felt no such obligation.

Now only Stéphane Mallarmé came to visit Berthe, to talk of poetry and remind her of an intellectual life, a life not taken up with the diapering and feeding schedule of a baby. On occasion, Mary Cassatt extracted herself from Degas's clutches to pay Berthe a visit, but Mary's hands were so blackened by ink and her conversation so concerned with printing presses and plates that Berthe felt exiled from art, no matter her afternoons of work. To be fair, Berthe babbled too, but about Julie and little else, and so Berthe believed it was entirely possible that she had become insufferable.

But Édouard was not insufferable. He was pitied in his infirmity and visited daily by hordes of women who made it their singular business to drown him in their collective silken and lace-framed décolletages. Édouard liked an admiring audience and he certainly had one now, though how he could paint when he was crowded in on all sides, forced to chatter and amuse, to flatter and flirt, was a mystery to her. She needed privacy. She always had.

Eugène stuck his head in after tapping at the door. "Darling?"

"Mmm?" Berthe said.

"Mother sent a note. She's planning a family dinner for next month, for all of us, including Gustave. She has to book him weeks in advance now just to get him to show his face. She wants us to convince Édouard to go to Meudon for the summer, for his problem with his legs." They had taken to referring to Édouard's affliction that way, in order not to have to say what it really was.

"Do you think Édouard can tear himself away from that impertinent Isabelle Lemonnier?" Berthe said. "And doesn't Suzanne ever tire of his little dalliances?"

"Not as much as you, it would seem," Eugène said.

Berthe affected a preoccupied glance at her canvas, at the boats and the way they seemed to be rocking, and Eugène apologized for the interruption and shut the door.

When his footsteps had completely receded, Berthe sighed. Her husband was far too nice to be treated so badly. After a minute, she picked up her brush and looked again at the canvas. No, it needed nothing. It was already what it was meant to be.

Chapter Thirty-Five

Late in November, a pink-bordered envelope from Meudon brought Mary the long-awaited announcement of Abigail Alcott Nieriker's delivery of a baby girl, named after Abigail's famous sister, Louisa, and with it the unhappy news of a postpartum illness. The hand was Abigail's, but shaky, and it requested Mary's presence at her bedside as soon as possible. Though the language was not dramatic, the request, for the even-tempered Abigail, was. Within half an hour, Mary was on her way to the Gare Saint Lazare to catch the train for Meudon.

Mary had never made it out to visit Abigail in Meudon, despite her promises. After the unproductive summer, her exhausting travels with her father, and Lydia's lingering illness, Meudon, for all its proximity, had seemed too far: A visit would consume a day, a day in which she would lose a chance to work. She had decided to wait until after the baby's birth, when Abigail was past her confinement and ready for visitors, but now Mary regretted the delay.

The Nierikers had taken rooms in a large house behind tall wooden gates that shut the house off from the street. The parlor overlooked a side garden that lay brown and fallow this time of year, but through a great window at the rear of the parlor the red-roofed houses of the village, the wandering Seine, and in the distance, Paris, all floated like a welcoming mirage. Mary envied Abigail painting at that window.

"Abigail's been sleeping all day," Sophie Nieriker said. Louisa Alcott was still too ill to come for a promised visit, and in her absence Ernest's sister and mother had come to help with the baby, who slept in a cradle in the nursery. After showing her to Mary, Sophie ushered Mary into Abigail's bedroom, where Ernest stood next to his wife's bed. Abigail was sitting up, nested in a pile of pillows, her cheeks flushed, her skin a bluish white, her eyes shut against even the dim light of a tallow candle burning softly on the linen-draped table at her bedside.

Ernest leaned over and whispered into Abigail's ear, "Darling, Mademoiselle Cassatt is here."

Abigail's eyes fluttered open, her gaze vague and distracted.

"Your baby is beautiful, Abigail," Mary said. "She looks like you. She has such a pretty mouth."

Abigail nodded, a film of disinterest glazing her eyes before they fluttered shut.

Ernest said, "But you feel better today, don't you, darling?" In his grief, he looked older than Abigail, who had once confided to Mary that her husband was fifteen years younger than she was. Mary felt his youth acutely. He was speaking out of hope.

"Oh, yes. Better," Abigail said, but her voice was thin and reedy.

"Abigail," Mary said. "You must get well so you can paint again. We all need your beautiful paintings. And you've made such a pleasant home. I must come back when you are well again, and we'll have tea in your exquisite parlor."

Abigail did not respond. Her breathing became fast and shallow. Mary waited to see whether or not she would reawaken, but she did not.

Outside the bedroom, Ernest took Mary by the elbow and said, "The doctor says she will get well. At least, he says, she cannot get worse."

"What does he do for her?"

"He does nothing. He hopes, with us." Ernest pulled his handkerchief from his pocket. "Abigail was very frightened about the delivery. She boxed up all her things, some for her sisters, some for her friends. She asked me to bury her in the cemetery at Montrouge if something happened. Abigail wants, should she not survive, for me to send the baby to her sister Louisa in America."

"She'll get better," Mary said, but even as she said it, she mourned what insipid things were said in the face of grief.

Ernest's gaze met hers, hope shining in his glassy eyes. "You'll come back?"

"I'm so sorry I didn't come before."

"You didn't know." His eyes drifted to the nursery. A wet nurse was bending over the crying child, undoing the buttons of her dress. "Do you know that Abigail refuses to see the baby, so as not to make the child love her?"

Her mother, leaning over Lydia; Abigail, making the kind of dreadful sacrifice only a mother could make.

Mary reached for Ernest's hand, but he turned away before she could grasp it and hurried back into Abigail's bedroom.

Mary walked back to the station in a rising wind; the cold air, smelling of snow, funneled off the Seine and whipped up the sloping hill. All she could think about was Abigail, so happy at the Salon, so thrilled to be getting all she had hoped for. This was the danger of being a woman. Childbirth could take everything from you, even your chance at happiness. Mary waited in the small railway salon on a slatted wooden bench, its curved back biting into her spine. Other passengers began to gather in the station, and as the train steamed toward the platform, Mary waited until they had all pushed forward before finding a seat as the doors closed.

Mary, occasionally accompanied by Lydia, took the train weekly to Meudon until a telegram arrived at noon on December 29, saying that Abigail had died at nine that morning and that the funeral was to be on December 31. On the bitterly cold New Year's Eve, an American minister said prayers in the Nieriker parlor and read scripture over Abigail's coffin as the baby cried in her mother-in-law's arms. The attendees, only a few—a Miss Plummer, the Nieriker family, and Lydia and Mary—climbed into the carriages and followed the hearse to the Montrouge Cemetery. Along the way, onlookers raised their hats in mournful respect. At the graveside, the coffin was lowered in a relentless wind. They tossed in their hothouse flowers, their petals stripped by the wind, and went away.

1880

Chapter Thirty-Six

"My God," Edgar said, "you've been in the acid. We might choke to death in here one day. They'll find us, you and I, dying for our art."

Mary's copper drypoint plate fell into her lap, and she shuddered to think of the ruin a soft-ground plate would have incurred in the fall. "Couldn't you knock or say hello instead of bellowing the second you step inside? And I haven't been in the acid. The cover must be off the basin."

Edgar opened a window to ventilate the fumes, secured the cover, then wiped his glasses with a cloth. He'd been gone since midmorning, painting a portrait, leaving Mary to work alone. Her comings and goings from his studio had become so frequent that he had given her a key. At her studio, dust covered everything: her easels, her tables, her brushes and jars; all her tools had begun to sour from neglect. That room seemed lifeless now compared with Edgar's, where his muttered asides and dramatic entrances and exits over the winter months had enlivened the lonely hours of work in the frosty gloom. Depending on her mood on any given day, her studio could seem either refuge or jail, but never before had it been as at Edgar's: a theater, at once dramatic and collaborative, a bazaar of imagination and instruction, an escape.

"I'm so tired of this woman, I'm not sure I can continue," Edgar said. "She is such a bore."

"Will you finish?" Mary said. Sometimes he didn't, especially when he didn't like his subject.

"Yes, but I'll only have to start another portrait, while you get to experiment all day."

She let his complaint pass without argument. Lately, Edgar's comparison of their relative economic freedoms had become a dirge. She had given up reminding him of her need to maintain the expenses of her studio or the fact that he kept a box at the Opéra.

"Are we printing tonight?" he asked.

She indicated the five finished plates lined up on the table, the product of days of work. As it turned out, they were not the merry four of Degas's imagination, but rather an intent two. Camille Pissarro, who had planned to work beside them, contented himself with sending his work in from Pontoise, taking critique by letter, while Félix Bracquemond, after spending only several hours instructing them over the course of a week, had abandoned them to their fate.

Mary said, "We can print tomorrow if you are too tired."

"We can't lose another day."

And so began their daily adagio, working toward their self-imposed deadline for the publication of Le Jour et la Nuit, set to be published in conjunction with the next exhibition on April 1. This was their intimacy—not a bodily intimacy, but a communication of minds. He had not pressed her for more than caresses and kisses, beyond which she was not certain she would go, anyway. What mattered was this moment, and moments like it.

They had rearranged Edgar's second room to accommodate the new project, pulling the intaglio press from the wall so that they could each work a side. Now they covered a table and the floor with layers of butcher paper to protect it from the huge pots of sticky ink and profusion of rags needed for the laborious process. Bracquemond had warned them that the consumption of supplies would be enormous before they produced a print of any quality, and indeed the expense had been prodigous. Mary had poured her earnings from Alexis Rouart's purchase of *Woman in a Loge* into boxes of copperplate and ink, also piled under the table. Vessels of acid were stored up against the wall.

"How many states do you want to pull?" Edgar asked, dropping a sheet of watercolor paper into a tub of water.

"The usual. Four or five," Mary said. She pulled on her waterproof gloves, opened a jar of tacky ink, and smeared the plate with the thick paste, adding drops of thinner to achieve the consistency she wanted. Then she worked the ink into the bitten grooves with her gloved hands until it penetrated them. She wiped the plate several times, examining it to ensure that the flat areas were clean. She laid it on the press as Degas placed the wet paper on top of the plate. Mary slipped a second sheet into the water to bathe.

Degas piled several sheets of felt on top of the paper and turned the crank, and the bed rolled under the drum roller. Mary pulled the print free of the felt and smiled at the result. The impression was exquisite, the light tender, the dark fierce: It was Lydia, smiling, seated at the Opéra in a loge, the print an echo of the original oil, which was an echo of all the studies Mary had made of her beforehand. It pleased her that she could make print after print from this one plate, iteration of iteration of iteration, keeping Lydia well forever, trumping medicine, trumping time. She wished now that she had thought to draw a picture of Abigail; Monet had painted his beloved Camille swathed in her shroud just after she died, a ghostly, haunting image he had brought one night to the Manets'.

Love and art: too much, it seemed, for a stingy universe to bestow.

"Mary?"

"I'm sorry."

The waltz required perfect timing to keep the rhythm; any hesitation in the process and the plate might dry out, making the next impression too light. She floated the finished print onto butcher paper while Edgar increased the pressure of the rolling drum to compensate for less ink. He laid down a new sheet of blotted paper, bundled the paper and plate in felt, and rolled the bed through again, producing another Lydia. After five pulls on the first plate, Mary declared it spent and inked the second. Twenty-five times Edgar turned the press bed: five impressions for each of the five plates. When they finished, Mary peeled off her gloves and recapped the ink pot; Edgar laid the last print on the papered floor next to the others. Each one was a version of Lydia, the first pulls vibrant and alive, the last pulls ghostly and pale.

"Which do you like?" Edgar said.

She couldn't choose. To choose might maledict the future: vibrant Lydia, faded Lydia; Abigail, taken from her child.

Edgar touched her hand. "You shouldn't grieve so. Lydia has been well for months now."

"Hardly plural. Two, only." Lydia had taken a turn for the worse in November, just as Abigail was failing; she had forced herself out of bed so that she could visit her.

"The last time I saw Lydia," Edgar said, "she looked herself again."

In the window, inky with the winter evening, their outlines were etched into the plate glass, light against dark.

"If you like, I'll draw the two of you together," Edgar said. "We will make a plate and then put her in the journal. She will be eternal. Do you think Lydia would like it?"

"Lydia loves everything about you."

"And you, mademoiselle?"

"Yes," Mary said, smiling. "Lydia loves everything about me, too."

Edgar laughed. "I want to show you something."

"Not the mystery behind the fortress of boxes?" Edgar had built a wall of wooden crates, partitioning off a part of the room he had then forbidden her to enter.

Unlike Edgar, who was forever working on other things, Mary hadn't painted in months, hadn't been back to her own studio to work except to retrieve, on occasion, something or other. She had become smitten with the journal, with printing, but Edgar was a polymath, able to paint, print, sculpt, draw, and etch, moving between each medium without hesitation.

"You must promise to say nothing. I can't bear a word of criticism." He shoved aside the stack of crates and pulled a tarp from an odd structure of pipe and wire and stuffing.

Mary looked at him.

"She's a dancer," he said, "but I have no idea if she'll turn out. I'm going to build her from clay and cover her with wax. I'll show her at the next exhibition. You must tell no one. I don't want half of Paris clamoring to see her."

Mary couldn't see how he would make a dancer from the jumble of materials he had nailed to a wooden platform. She wanted to ask a thousand questions.

"Promise you'll tell no one," he said, covering the structure with the tarp and shoving the boxes back into place. He turned and looked at her, vulnerable. He was proud, like a parent. Obsessed, something he had declared she was with the prints, albeit with great admiration. And perhaps she was. The process of printing was addictive, the challenges absorbing. The difficulties of drawing on the copper had refined her work. An eloquence of line had emerged, an arabesque so fluid it evoked the best of the Japanese prints she admired. And there was something else. Working next to Edgar had changed her eye. He would look at her work, pointing out places where the line was weak, and say, *You may draw a straight line crooked, but it must give the impression of being straight.* Or, *Art is an artifice; it is made up of sacrifices.* Or, *Nothing in art must appear accidental, even the action of it.* And she had understood him.

But he had never shown her anything of his own work in progress before. Though he had warned her he wanted her to say nothing, she searched anyway for the thing to say that would encourage him, as he had encouraged her, to help him, as he had helped her. But what could she say that would match *You've painted love*? She could think of nothing.

He would never accept a pronouncement. He was a genius, but to tell him that would only earn his derision. He was a visionary, but he would likely expel her from his studio, plates and all, for declaring him so. He was unique, but he would only say that everyone was unique. And the thing was such a jumble now. Only he was able to see whatever it was to become.

"You must have dreamed her," Mary said.

Edgar lifted his gaze, his face becoming rapt. "She's modeled on a *petit rat*, but I don't know where this idea came from. It just appeared. One day, I saw her. Every bit of her."

"A gift."

"This one is," he said. His voice carried a trace of wonder. He stood by the barricade he had built between the world and his dancer. As far as Mary knew, he had never made a large sculpture before. The studio was littered with small forms he had crafted from wax, dancers and horses, but neither he nor anyone, to Mary's knowledge, had ever tried to sculpt a wax statue as large as the one Degas was attempting.

"You'll tell no one?"

His problem, Mary thought, was that he was in love with the thing he was about to create. And there was nothing like love to terrify a person.

"Edgar," she said, kissing his cheek. "What a silly thing to say to me." And she gathered her things, and he his, and they walked out into the night.

Chapter Thirty-Seven

The plaster in the Manet family's new apartment at 39 Rue de Saint-Pétersbourg still had not dried, as it had not in many of the buildings so recently erected in the Quartier de l'Europe. A heavy dampness hung over the dining table. Though the pastry had already been served and consumed, they were still at table: the Manet sons, their mother, Suzanne, Berthe, and Bibi, who had been retrieved from the nurse's care and was cruising from lap to lap to be petted and kissed. Édouard was painting watercolors, inking pictures of women's legs peeking out from underneath taffeta skirts, his brush occasionally flipping out of the saucer of colored rinse water and rolling among the coffee cups and dessert plates. His mother suffered his antics and did not even complain when his tray of watercolors clattered to the floor and the overworked maid had to be called in to mop up. Tonight, as always, he carried all the sparkle, despite the ravages of illness on his gaunt face.

At dinner, Édouard would speak only of his upcoming solo exhibition, fending off all attempts to get him to discuss the summer. The Charpentiers, who seemed not at all alarmed by his sudden affection for Madame Charpentier's younger sister, had offered Édouard a show at their new gallery on the Boulevard des Italiens. Édouard hoped the Charpentiers' influence might even extend to persuading the Salon jury to award him a medal this year. The thought now occurred to Berthe that Édouard might have been paying attention to Isabelle not to court her, but to inveigle her older sister and brother-in-law to offer him this exhibition. But that kind of subterfuge seemed too underhanded for Édouard. He was careless in love, but not treacherous. It was more likely that the young Isabelle had entranced him of her own accord, unaware of her effect on him.

Édouard, in a celebratory mood, had spent the past few minutes teasing Berthe about the fifth impressionist exhibition, set to begin in a few weeks, on April 1, timing that would coincide with his own opening.

"We'll be competing, dear Berthe. Who will win? I predict that hundreds—nay, thousands—will flow through the doors." Which doors, he wouldn't say. "The streets will not be able to handle the surge of traffic. A parade will ensue."

Berthe didn't want to deny Édouard his ebullience. He deserved his own show, and not one financed by himself, as he had done so long ago for the World Exhibition. The excitement was also serving, for better or worse, to distract him from his ailment, and she wondered if it might not be an even better strategy than the hydrotherapy his mother wanted him to take.

"Have no doubt, there will be a parade for you, Édouard," Gustave said. "Especially after they see the portrait you're painting of that little Isabelle."

Gustave seemed to have forgotten that he was here to serve as ballast for the family's argument that Édouard should take the treatment the doctor was prescribing. He had left his office early that afternoon to pay a visit to Édouard's studio, and he was now full of drunken praise. "Not that anyone would deny our darling Berthe her due. Her exhibition will no doubt be a triumph." He raised his glass to Berthe, but then said, "But that Isabelle, she shines. What is this now? Your third, fourth picture of her?"

"She does shine, doesn't she?" Édouard said. "Quite an excellent little model. I'll submit that picture to the Salon."

"Couldn't you give me the painting?" Gustave said.

"If I give it to anyone, I will give it to Isabelle, if she will allow the gift."

Berthe looked across the table at Suzanne, who had made not even the slightest remark of unhappiness at Édouard's proclamations. If Berthe had been married to Édouard, she would have thrown a plate at him by now, but Suzanne instead seemed to be preoccupied by the maid's coming and going, handing her plates to clear and brushing crumbs from the table.

"Isabelle would shine at the Salon," Gustave went on, awash in memories of the enchanting pictures of her.

"The Salon is the only place for her," Édouard said.

"I don't see why you continue to care about the Salon, Édouard, when they hate you so much," Berthe said. Her tone was sharp, and everyone at the table turned to look at her.

"They don't hate me." Édouard dipped his pen into the ink bottle and drew, in quick succession, a series of booted feet, ankles and calves exposed, raised skirts above. Never had Berthe seen him execute anything so charming so quickly. "They just don't love me yet."

"Perhaps you ought to stop courting everyone, Édouard."

"Are we still speaking of the Salon?" Eugène said.

Berthe made a quick, shameful glance at her husband.

Édouard said, "Not to worry, Eugène. Berthe is only worrying about my legacy. She fears I will die having misjudged who and what is right for me. Don't you, Berthe? You fear for me, don't you?"

Bibi had made her way around the table, and was now pulling herself to standing on Berthe's lap. Berthe straightened her daughter's dress and was about to say that yes, she did fear for him, when Eugène answered Édouard instead.

"My wife only wishes to ensure that you don't tire yourself by overwork. Isn't that right, darling? That is all that matters to us. How well you are, Édouard."

"Yes," Berthe said. "You must watch your health. As your mother and Suzanne have been trying to say all night."

"Is that what you are worrying about, Berthe? My health?" Édouard asked. "You oughtn't, you know. I'll be well by Christmas if I go to Meudon for the summer."

"You'll go, then?" Suzanne said.

"I don't know."

"But you must." Suzanne reached her hand through the remaining china and crystal to take his, but Édouard, engrossed in his drawings, either didn't or chose not to see her gesture.

"Yes, Édouard, you must," his mother said.

"What I love about Isabelle is that she demands nothing. She lets me amuse her. She makes me forget." Édouard laid down his brush and looked at Berthe.

Berthe knew she ought to be quiet, to let Eugène answer for her again, but she couldn't help herself. "That girl, at seventeen, is hardly the salvation you want her to be," Berthe said. "What does she know of the needs of a man who is ill and is behaving as if he isn't? If you do not go to Meudon because you do not want to be separated from this girl, then you are making a very silly mistake, Édouard. One none of us will ever forgive you for."

Suzanne stared. Madame Manet brought her napkin to her mouth and waved the maid away. Bibi began to cry and Berthe hugged her daughter to her chest. Berthe knew she had revealed herself, but she couldn't help it. The man would flirt himself into an early death and everyone would let him. Distraction due to ambition was one thing, but distraction due to infatuation was another thing entirely.

Eugène's voice broke into the hollow that had followed her outburst, his voice rising above his daughter's whimpering. "Berthe is right, Édouard. All any of us at this table care about is your well-being. You require health more than you require the company of a charming innocent. Of that, you have had plenty in your life."

On the way home in the carriage, Eugène said, "One day, sooner rather than later, Édouard is going to die. You should prepare yourself, darling."

It was crueler than she had expected, but it was far kinder than she had a right to. In the hazy light of the foggy evening, Eugène looked like Édouard when she had first met him, when he was healthy and knowing, willing to wait, willing to convince her.

Chapter Thirty-Eight

The soft light and warmth of the March morning was a much needed respite from the Parisian drear that had cooped the Cassatts inside their flat during one of the worst winters any of them could remember. After several months of rising good health, Lydia had been afflicted with a stomach neuralgia so fierce that she expressed a fear that she might die. It was unlike her to give in to the same alarm the others guarded so stealthily, and for days, the doctor had come and gone, his prediction of recovery careening between doubtful and optimistic.

But this morning Lydia had risen from bed and nested herself in the parlor, declaring herself completely well and insisting that she wouldn't tolerate anyone wasting the glorious Saturday on her account; everyone had to go out or suffer her severe disapproval. It took Lydia an hour to convince her mother that a brief sojourn would not be a breach of parental vigilance. Giving in, Katherine decided to roam the sandy paths of the Tuileries and admire the children sailing their wooden boats in the fountains; Robert and Degas were to meet, as previously planned, at the races at Longchamp in the Bois de Boulogne, having recently forged a tight kinship over horseflesh; Mary, also a lover of horseflesh, was also going to the *bois*, but to ride rather than to watch the races. Since leaving Pennsylvania, she had not been able to afford a riding horse, but the new monthly stipend from Aleck meant that in addition to the family's carriage, she could rent a horse from the livery stable on the Champs-Élysées and ride in the *bois* on the trails through the linden and oak forests as often as she liked.

It was a week away from the exhibition and Mary was looking forward to some exercise. She had exhausted herself putting together the journal, but it was at the printers now and there was little else to be done. At the livery stable, she rented her favorite mount, a dappled gray mare, and trotted in a long train of carriages of race-goers and other pleasure-seekers to the gates of the reserve, where she skirted the traffic and headed for the riding paths. For two hours she rode through the forests and meadows, the spring mud flying up and splattering her skirt. When the horse was spent, she angled toward the water troughs on one of the lakeshores. The park was crowded and it took a moment before she recognized Gustave Caillebotte trotting toward her. His handsome, austere figure was well seated on his Arabian, and he was impeccably attired in his fastidious, almost militaristic riding clothes.

"Mademoiselle Cassatt." He dismounted and led his horse beside hers to the trough. "What a pleasure."

"The pleasure is all mine," she said, pulling off her gloves. "Why aren't you at the races this morning?"

"I prefer to ride rather than watch someone else have all the fun."

"Edgar and my father are in the stands. They'll come home poorer, I fear. At least my father will."

He pulled off his gloves too, and stood beside her, ill at ease. He was always in control, and his nervousness surprised her. "Monsieur?"

"You must forgive me, Mademoiselle Cassatt, but I feel I must say something to you. I want you to know that I tried to persuade Edgar, but he wouldn't listen. Of course he never listens, at least not to me, but I did try very hard to dissuade him. At first, I was so shocked, I didn't know what to say, but then I found my tongue. I even scolded him, if you can believe that, which he didn't take all that well. But I'd already given the printer a deposit, which he now refuses to return. The balance was due yesterday. That is how I found out. Can you imagine? I was at the printer, ready to write a bank note, when the man told me. Edgar hadn't even the consideration to write me a letter to save me the trip. Of course I went over to his studio immediately. I couldn't believe what he had done, but he confirmed it. That blasted man always does exactly as he pleases, no matter what it means for anyone else."

"Forgive me, Monsieur Caillebotte," Mary said, "but I don't know what you are talking about."

A cloud passed over the sun, casting a cool shadow over the lake, dulling the reflection of the trees in the water. Mary knew the answer Gustave would give before he gave it, but something inside her forced her to ask for the details, to wait for them and to hear them in this awkward way, pushing poor Gustave beyond apology to merciless message bearer.

"Edgar didn't tell you. Of course he didn't. I thought for certain you knew. Edgar has called off the publication of *Le Jour et la Nuit*. I don't know whether or not Monsieur Pissarro knows, but it would be just like Edgar not to tell him, either."

Heat blossomed in Mary's face. In the telling, the news was somehow worse. She was embarrassed she had coerced him, but that did not stop her from extracting more. "Exactly what did Edgar tell you? Can you remember?" she said.

"That he wasn't ready."

The last time she had seen Edgar was on Wednesday, when she had run a final plate through his press, an etching of a young toddler wearing a wide-brimmed hat. It was to be the last print to go into the journal. *Innocence*, Edgar had said. *The picture of it.* His kiss bidding her farewell had betrayed nothing other than preoccupation. He was terribly sorry, he said, but he had to leave right away. He escorted her out of his studio, saying that he was awfully busy with a commission but that he would see her on Saturday, and then again on Monday for the hanging of the exhibition. He had pressed her hand into his on the street and disappeared.

"I saw Edgar on Wednesday. He said nothing to me." He should have come to the house, to the studio, should have sent a note, should have told her before he told anyone else.

"It's inexcusable. It's just like Edgar to be so careless of other people. It is as if he believes he is the only person affected by these decisions of his." Gustave went on complaining about Edgar's cruelties, but Mary hardly heard him. She was looking at her ink-stained fingers, thinking of the hours she and Edgar had spent together, the backbreaking work of the press, their long discussions about which prose should accompany which print. There had been not the slightest indication he was wavering from their plan.

"I must be getting home," Mary said.

"I shouldn't have told you. Not here. I've ruined your ride, ruined your morning."

"It's not your fault," Mary said. She pulled on her gloves, mounted and clicked to the horse, and trotted out to the road. She wanted to gallop back to the stables, but the slightest misalignment in the cobbles, the least fright from a carriage, and the horse would stumble. She disciplined herself to keep to a walk and finally reached the stables, where she handed the reins to a groom and hired a hack for home.

"What is the matter, Mary?" her mother said. "You've been restless since you got back from your ride. I thought the exercise would have calmed you."

For an hour, Mary had been pacing in the parlor, stopping at the window on every round to look down onto the Avenue Trudaine.

"Mary?" Katherine said.

Mary turned from the window. "Pardon?"

Katherine exchanged a look with Lydia.

"You've been pacing like a caged lion," Lydia said.

"Have I?" she said. She pulled back the curtain and looked out onto the street. "Here they are. They're coming."

Katherine called to Anna to prepare coffee as the sound of footsteps echoed up the stairwell. The two men, after climbing the five sets of stairs, paused at the doorway to catch their breath and remove their hats. Robert headed straight to his club chair, where his papers awaited him in a neat pile. Edgar hovered at the doorway, holding the brim of his hat.

"Oh, Robert, where are your manners? Do invite Monsieur Degas in," Katherine said.

Robert sank into the chair. "I'm exhausted, Katherine. You can't expect a man to remember all the societal niceties when he is tired."

"I apologize for my husband, Monsieur Degas. You'll come in, won't you?" Katherine said. "Anna is bringing coffee and we have a lovely dinner planned. We would love to have you stay."

"That is very kind of you, madame, but I cannot. I have an engagement, and I am already late." Degas raised his hand and edged out of the doorway, barely meeting Mary's eyes as Anna bustled in with the promised coffee.

"But, Edgar," Mary called. "Lydia wants to show you the print you gave her. She's had it framed. Haven't you, Lyddy? It's all she could talk about all afternoon."

"It was?" Lydia said.

"She's very eager to show you how lovely your print looks," Mary said, feeling no compunction about using her sister as bait. "She won't even share it with us but has hung it in her bedroom. Go get it, darling."

Obediently, Lydia rose and disappeared down the hallway to her bedroom.

"Do have a cup, Monsieur Degas," Katherine said.

"Yes, have one, have one," Robert said. "You've been tiresome and distracted all day. A little coffee will do you good."

After a moment's hesitation, Edgar offered his hat to Anna, who set it on the entry table. He sat in a chair next to Katherine, nodding at Mary as if they were mere acquaintances. He crossed and uncrossed his legs and then accepted the proffered coffee cup, set it on the table, and folded his hands in his lap.

Mary said, "I met Monsieur Caillebotte today when I was riding in the *bois*."

"Now, there's a young man who understands money," Robert said, dropping a lump of sugar into his coffee. "Even if he is French."

"Mary, you didn't tell us that you met Monsieur Caillebotte," Lydia said, returning, the prized print cradled in her arms. "I like him so much, don't you, Mother?"

"Gustave is a fine young man," Katherine said, passing Mary coffee. "We should invite him to dinner."

Mary accepted the coffee and then set her cup on the table too. "Tell me, Edgar, were you ever going to say anything, or were you going to keep it a secret?"

"Edgar has a secret?" Robert said. "Well, no doubt he has. I've never met a Frenchman who didn't have dozens of them. Must have been what made him so jumpy all day."

"I didn't tell Pissarro either," Edgar said.

"Monsieur Pissarro lives in Pontoise!" Mary said, her voice rising. "I saw you last week. All you had to do was tell me. There are a thousand ways we could have worked it out." She was remembering the canceled exhibition, his preemptory action, his thin excuse. She had been impotent then, too, in the face of his resistance. "I have just three paintings ready."

Robert and Katherine glanced at one another and recognized the marital tone: the implied ultimatum, the private conversation carried on in public.

"What is the matter?" Katherine asked.

"Your problem, Mademoiselle Cassatt," Edgar said, "is that you worked on only one thing, while I had other projects. You should have been more prolific."

Mademoiselle Cassatt. He hadn't called her Mademoiselle Cassatt for a year.

"How could I have been?" Mary said. "I sacrificed everything for that journal. On a promise you made. You saw me. I was at your studio every day. When could I have done more?"

"What is all this, Mame?" Robert asked.

"Edgar is pulling out of the journal, Father. He told Monsieur Caillebotte not to pay the printer."

Lydia shifted in her chair and reached for her mother's hand; as she did the print slid off her lap to the floor.

Robert leaned back in his chair and crossed his legs, assuming a professorial air, immune to the currents of emotion running through the room. "In business, Edgar, people meet their obligations."

"This is not a business, Robert; this is art," Edgar said.

"But when you commit to a project, when you involve other people, when it involves investment, it is a business, no matter what the commodity," Robert said.

Mary winced at her father's use of the word *commodity*, but Edgar said, "Yes, our *articles* are for sale, but only when we are ready to sell them. I am justified in withholding whatever I choose from the marketplace. I cannot compromise my work merely to benefit another person."

"But Mame is not just another person, is she?" Robert said. "She's Mary. Your friend. And I don't know what else."

"Robert!" Katherine said.

"I never believed you selfish before, Edgar," Mary said, "though everyone warned me."

"I can't produce the journal if I'm not ready," he said.

"But what has to be ready? Everything is finished. Everything is prepared. There is nothing else to do." She stood and went to the window. The curtains had caught the cooling breeze and billowed into the room. The journal, when published, was to have showcased her work, to have catapulted them both into a wider audience. What a nightmare the past year had turned out to be: the tedium of her trip with her father, Abigail's death, Lydia's frequent illnesses. The only bright time had been working with Edgar, and now what had that gotten her? "This is all I have," she said. "This is what this year has been about for me."

"I am not responsible for your work or your happiness," Edgar said, rising. "I cannot apologize for doing what is right for me. I see that I have hurt you, which is unfortunate."

Lydia said, "But you don't mean this?"

"I am afraid I do," Edgar said, and was out the door before anyone could say anything else.

"Well, that's the last of him, I imagine," Robert said, snapping open a newspaper and staring into it.

The wind began to chill. Lydia crossed the room and shut the window, and the sailing curtains stilled.

Chapter Thirty-Nine

Edgar:

What he does not tell her:

That sometimes he cannot sleep at night because he is dreaming of gouache, lithography, pastel, monotype, charcoal, oil, etchings, plates, wax. That he wants to stop and start time at his prerogative so that he can revel in the bounty of materials, can challenge himself and experiment without time passing because the day isn't long enough. That the circus or the Opéra ballet or the café chantants or dinners with friends or the delicious masculine embrace of the racetrack devour his evenings and Sundays but in between there is only work. That some days he looks up and hours have passed and he is late for one thing or another and he races to the café or the friends or the theater and what he leaves behind is unfinished work, and he thinks nothing he makes will ever be finished. That he must make careful calculations in order to produce his *articles* because he is not gifted, he is not prescient, he is not an auteur, he is only a draftsman, a servant, a plodding poseur who wishes to excel. That he is hampered by the infernal blur in his eye he fears will only spread. That the arrangement of legs on a group of dancers or the color of skirt sashes or the depth of the stage or the bend of a laundress's back or the line of her apron confounds him and has to be worked and reworked. That these problems haunt him, and he fears that he has lost his touch. That he has to struggle with each canvas, though he has already painted many. That with each beginning he is again a beginner. That each composition requires its own rules. That his experienced yet flawed eye needs repetitive correction. That color is still changing, though no one believes him and no one believes that what he sees and what he used to see are so different that it is as if he were seeing the world through an ever-changing, ever-blurring, ever-achromatic prism. That the Sturm und Drang about their annual exhibition is always a struggle when people—Renoir, Monet—defect to the Salon seeking its false external confirmation, hoping to find in the cloistered snobbery some validation, when validation ought to be internal, personal, private, and he can't understand why they don't believe in themselves. That art is a confection—it is true only when it is false—and their attempt to render natural light negates the filter of the eye and the brain. That the endless haggling over apartment rental and lights and hanging takes up so much time that he thinks of never exhibiting again, but there is no economic salvation for the artist who does not show. That the inglorious details of buying and selling and the oppression of the Bank of Antwerp intrude and force him to ask Durand-Ruel for money in order to pay his housekeeper, Sabine, and to eat. That the process of selling art is so repugnant, so commercial, yet so necessary that he submits to it and tries to do so with integrity and inclusiveness, but the others like to complain and exclude artists they believe inferior, which is just like the Salon jury, but they can't see the hypocrisy because they are so taken up with themselves. That one must believe in oneself enough to attempt to surpass Rembrandt or Ingres or Delacroix. That this striving is always on his mind, this making a mark, this elevation of art to the sublime, the real, the relevant, the necessary. That he is unequal to the task—every day, he believes this—and doesn't know where to place himself in the world or history or the future. That the red herring of pride interferes with real work because the real work is lines and more lines and the willingness to stand before the canvas, the sculpture, the pastel, the easel, the subject, the window, the model and construct form and shape and light and color. That such courage is only the beginning. That there is the essence of the thing that struggles to make itself known, and you don't know what it is when you begin, that you discover it as you work. That is the secret that critics and laypeople do not understand. That nothing is clear to the artist until the art reveals itself, and it is a mystery where art resides before it is expressed, even though he can recount each step and each choice and each calculation he made; it is this riddle of art that eludes him, even as it infuses him as he works, even as he rejects it because he applies tenacious deliberation to his days and the tension between what he knows and what he doesn't know abounds. That he doesn't want to believe the muse exists, though she does—of course she does— for he cannot account for the music of his composition; even as he follows the golden ratio and the laws of tonality and perspective there is the in-between, wherein his brush works and color plays and it is magical and true and beguiling and it comes from him and *not* from him. That he falls in love with every new confection and doesn't want to let it go, though he must, to pay bills, to live, to eat, to drink, to go to the Opéra, to travel, to buy oil, charcoal, paint, canvas, wax, fixative, frames, nails, lumber, saws, brushes, turpentine, poppy seed oil, needles, plates, silk, and now his latest, his most exciting: tulle and tarlatan and even a skein of real hair, and this new project—more than the etching, more than the puzzle of black and white that delights Mary Cassatt—absorbs him, and he would like to tell her that he is not fickle, that he is not flighty, that he is not mercurial, that he is helpless, that inside him is a pirate who plunders his desire and twists it and distracts him from a single scheduled purpose with deadlines and demands and expectations to explore the unexpected, the rare, the difficult, and he has already mastered the etching, so therefore it is boring. That he needs to prove himself only to himself. That work is never finished, because some other beguiling insight is always out of reach, lurking, taunting. That he defected because he has to make money, has to meet commissions, and he could not find the time to devote to his avowed goal of *Le Jour et la Nuit*. That this is not true, not really, because the truth, ever elusive, is that he cannot slow down his mind for other people, nor for the arbitrary requests and obligations and responsibilities he has imposed on himself, because deadlines are malleable, and he is sorry that he committed himself to Mademoiselle Cassatt and that she believed him and made a religion of the print and the paper and the press but he is past that now or not yet ready or the process no longer intrigues him, all possibilities that he cannot parse, not for her, not for anyone, not for himself. That the conundrum is that he is who he is, and this defection is not personal or disloyal or a breach of trust. That the non-elusive truth is that she has never failed him. That he can't think of a moment or a gesture or an act wherein she betrayed or disappointed him. That even her anger over Berthe was an attempt to persuade him to kindness. That she cheers him, she delights him, he respects her. That she looks at him sometimes as if she sees through him, but he knows himself to be opaque, because he has painted himself that way, and it is only her desire that makes her believe she understands him, when even he cannot escape the murky dungeons of his own soul.

Chapter Forty

Mary:

What she does not tell him:

That sometimes she cannot sleep at night because she dreams of texture and shadow, of prints and plates, of ink and burin, of perspective and foreshortening, of light shimmering and colors colliding, of juxtaposition and contrast, of press and pressure, of mordant and hydrochloric acid, of damp and dry paper, of depth of line and shallow, tiny scratches, of third, fourth, and fifth states, of the craft of dimension, of detail and restraint, of the uncommon, the difficult, the true, the sublime. That not enough time exists to accomplish mastery, though she wants it, she dreams of it, she aches for it. That some days she rues the tyranny of the clock, a devil that instead of recording hours steals them from her, impeding her progress, handicapping her, because she needs time, she is not quick, she is not cavalier, she is not prolific; she is studied, careful, deliberate, cautious, even, though no one would believe her—they think her courageous and adventurous, and while it is possible that this is true, they do not know with what reflection she approaches her art even as she strives to be free. That she is hampered by her fear of being irrelevant even as she is determined not to be. That her father's doubt nags at her, that to have to maintain resistance to skepticism even in her own home exhausts her. That suddenly the fear that she is not gifted, not skilled, not talented overcomes her and she has to bury the unease so as not to alarm her models and make them question her and in so doing drift away and lose the expression or even the desire to please her and she needs them to want to please her for she does not paint out of doors, she does not paint vases or flowers or rivers, she paints people, she seeks to portray their inner lives, and they will not show them to her if they do not believe she can reveal them. That color and light are all she has in the world by way of tools. That though her sharp mind does her well, it can only be deployed through brush and beauty, for she would not be welcome to run a railroad, a bank, a university, though she believes she could if given the chance, though no man would give a woman such leave, but in art all is allowed if one frees oneself of prejudice, which is why she needs the madding rabble of the impressionists in their quarrelsome disagreements, because they never say to her face that she is a woman, though she is one and sometimes, sometimes, she yields and it is this that troubles her, for Edgar is necessary to her and *gratitude* is not the word to describe her relief that he came to her and rescued her because she had been on the verge of quitting, there were days when she thought *I can't fight them anymore* and surely there was some grand, divine bon mot in the universe that would convey to him what it meant that he had shared his courage, intellect, and artifice with her, that he had befriended her, that he had given her her sight. That she has had to find a way to say that she needs him without capitulating to the romantic, though as a woman she does sometimes capitulate, for what is more desirable in life than someone who knows you, who finishes your sentences, who challenges you, who gives you what you need, who considers you an equal, who makes your days fuller, brighter, better, and this to her is romantic, it is the heart of romance, a mirrored mind, a matched soul, twinned yearnings, reciprocal intellects, and why this should frighten him she doesn't know, because it does not frighten her, though if he came to her and said *I am yours* what would she say, because Abigail died for love and what other woman has survived marriage intact, childless, free to pursue that which is selfish, because art is selfish of necessity, it is selfish by its nature, it is selfish because art is the thief of time, and love also demands time but then wilts into something other, something institutional, something obligatory, like Berthe's unholy imbalance of motherhood, sisterhood, and marital obligation, a nightmare of subterfuge Mary could never countenance but admires for its honesty because Berthe's desire is for art, it is fully for art, as is hers, but somehow Berthe has managed to love if illicitly and while Mary has painted love and seen love and been admired for seeing and painting love, somehow she has not managed to have love. That it confounds her that her life must be devoid of love to have art. That it confounds her that this must be the choice. That she remembers her avowals and declarations and certainties from not so long ago, when she was young and her goals seemed distant and a monastic life necessary to achieve them and she had not hesitated to announce her firm renunciation of the encumbrances of womanhood, but she'd been young then, not yet in love, not yet torn apart by desires so palpable they cause her pain. That it was the pain that surprised her, that it was the love that surprised her, that it was she who was in need of the love that astounded her. That life is ungovernable, even for a disciplined soul like hers, and betrayal its practical joke.

Chapter Forty-One

I see nothing."

"Is this a statement? Is he mocking us?"

"Of course he is."

"It's the emperor's new clothes. He wants us to praise it to show our idiocy."

Mary Cassatt and Gustave Caillebotte, pretending to study Berthe's paintings in the room closest to the apartment foyer, eavesdropped on four art critics crowded around an empty vitrine in an apartment on the Rue des Pyramides. It was Tuesday, the opening day of the exhibition, and the spectacle of the empty glass container seemed to have arrested them all. Somewhere upstairs, hammers were pounding to the grating dissonance of rasping saws and the occasional loud thud. The building was still under construction, and this apartment, like all new apartments in Paris, smelled of the ubiquitous wet plaster. Outside, on the street, people were going about their business, not at all enticed by the large green posters with red lettering tacked to the kiosk outside that announced the exhibition. It might have been the blackening downpour, but Mary feared that the public had perhaps grown indifferent, or had tired of the new and different, or that the yearly change of venue was too difficult for them to follow.

"This is the Wandering Jew of exhibitions," one of the critics said, as if he had read Mary's mind. A nervously thin man, he was thumbing through the catalog, smudged in places where the pages had been put together while still wet. "One year here, one year there. Who can find them?"

"Just tell us, will you, what the catalog says this case is supposed to display?" another said.

"It's Degas, right?" The one critic turned several pages and read. "Ah! A little dancer of fourteen years."

"Well, then, that hypochondriac Degas is telling the truth after all. Maybe he really can't see if he believes there is a piece of art in there. Or he's finally gone mad. Such a shame, really, though I'm sure that Manet will keep drawing enough laundresses and prostitutes to bore us all."

"Why Georges Charpentier has opened a new gallery to extol the virtues of these idiot rebels is beyond me."

"Manet has never exhibited with these bottom-feeders. I hear he's sending something to the Salon again this year."

"I heard that Manet can't even stand up anymore. A touch of Neapolitan fever."

"More than a touch, I'd say, if he can't stand up."

They focused again on the vitrine.

"I heard Degas made the dancer out of wax and that she wears a real dancer's dress and shoes."

"A wax sculpture? Are you certain? Not stone?"

"Yes. Wax."

"Ah, that's it, then. The sculpture melted. That's why it's not here."

"Don't believe it. He has made this phantom up. Or it is invisible. Or he means to goad us with its absence."

"This is why they call themselves the 'independents.' In addition to being independent of taste, they are independent of the need even to show us their work."

En masse, the critics abandoned the vitrine and wandered into the room where Mary and Caillebotte tried to appear as if they were engrossed in Berthe's canvases, hung alongside Gustave's. In a barely suppressed stage whisper one of the critics glanced their way and said, "Why does anyone ever come to shows like this? Why don't they just go to the Salon, where they'll be assured of some quality?"

"Well, as you can see, hardly anyone has come, except for us and those poor souls."

"Dear God. I have to rub my eyes after looking at these things. This Monsieur Caillebotte is in love with the color blue. All he can paint are green sheep and blue cows."

Mary glanced at Gustave, but he shook his head, warding off any sympathy. The critics went on discussing his supposed failures, which included timidity and an inability to completely free himself from artistic rules without actually making up new ones, except where they applied to color, which the man obviously felt free to violate at will. After disparaging Gustave a while longer, they drifted to Mary's display in the same room. She had but one wall this time. Gone was the private room, the special showcase, the profusion of canvases, along with any vestige of her pride. Even to her own eyes, her work looked orphaned. Yesterday, she had gone to the printer to retrieve the originals of her prints to fill out her meager showing of just three oils and one pastel. She quickly framed several of the prints, choosing to show the ones of Lydia in all five states, another of the little girl Degas had called innocent, and several others hung together as a series, but they were lost in this setting. Small, inconspicuous, they hardly drew the eye. Though her oils were few, she did like two, *Tea* and *On a Balcony*, but they were not as evocative as her portraits from the year before. The other, a portrait of Madame J, was the least accomplished of all of them. The critics, strutting about the exhibition as if they were the gatekeepers of all that mattered, did not hold back their criticism.

"This portrait is nonsense. There is no dimension to the figure. It's as if Mademoiselle Cassatt painted a blob on a divan. I daresay she's copying Manet in his love of black, but her execution is flat."

"It's evident why. Look at what else she is showing. So many prints.

No wonder she's lost her sense of dimension. And they're not very good, are they?"

"As opposed to that dilettante Caillebotte, Mademoiselle Cassatt doesn't actually break the rules, does she? But she doesn't execute very well, either."

Caillebotte put his hand on Mary's shoulder, but she shook the kindness away, unwilling to draw attention to herself or to be an object of pity to her friend, whom she herself had nonetheless tried to comfort only a moment before.

The critics spent another half hour taking in the rest of the exhibition before they withdrew, complaining of Monet's absence, since they had wanted to see what the lover of color was going to display, then agreeing that the only way to deal with the disaster of the morning was to repair to a café where they could collectively deconstruct the calamity that was the avant-garde.

"I will never forgive Degas," Caillebotte said as they watched while the critics, who had not recognized them, took a last look at the untenanted vitrine before they exited. "Why does he push for these exhibitions and then not bring his work?"

"I don't know," Mary said.

"He will ruin us with this capricious blindness to deadlines. Did you see how they mocked that vitrine? No one will be able to get past that glass charade. Do you know? Has he even finished it?" Caillebotte said.

"I don't know. He only showed her to me once, when she was nothing but a skeleton. He kept her hidden from me after that."

"And the noise. I should have pushed harder about the choice of the site."

It was as if no one had supervised anything, Mary thought now. Somehow, even the paintings were not hung to best advantage; though they had all taken great care, it looked as if they had hired the construction workers upstairs to do the job for them. As if to solidify this impression, a huge bang from the floor above made them both jump.

"You would have risked another argument with Edgar," Mary said. "You already incurred his wrath this time about the posters."

"Why is he such a plebian about things like this? We put names on the posters so that people know who we are. It's not elitist; it's a device to draw people in. Otherwise we could be any group of artists who wanted to exhibit. How would people find us? And why does he care when he doesn't even bring in the cataloged art? No one told him what to bring. He alone decides what to show and then he doesn't even show it. The man drives me out of my mind. Tell me, did he apologize to you about the journal?" Gustave said.

"No." She had not seen Edgar since Saturday, when she learned of the demise of *Le Jour et la Nuit*. This year, there had been no party on the eve of the opening. And Degas had avoided seeing her by not being here to hang what work he had sent in when Mary had been hanging hers.

"It pains me that the man paints so well. Doesn't it you?" Caillebotte said. "He has talent like no one else."

"Brilliance incarnate," Mary said and sighed.

Throughout the morning and afternoon, the crowd remained sparse, ablated by the heavy rain or by indifference. At one in the afternoon, Caillebotte reluctantly left Mary behind to meet someone for luncheon, but she stayed, unable to tear herself from the disaster. It was good to be free of Gustave's fury, though his anger had been validation, too. Every once in a while one of her fellow artists dropped by to see how things were going, but Berthe and Pissarro stayed away. Berthe had the excellent excuse of Bibi, and Pissarro the unfortunate excuse that a train ticket in from Pontoise was too dear for him. Mary wandered listlessly among the rooms, eavesdropping on the rare visitor, hearing again and again that her work was uninteresting and dull, the prints too small to make an impression, implying that her lack of quantity was somehow an indication of a lack of quality. She feared they were right. Over the past year, her work had paled. In this setting, exposed to the public, the prints appeared amateur. And next to Edgar's work, her prints were less finely detailed, less dense, less remarkable, a judgment she had been spared today because Edgar hadn't yet brought his in, but when he did, she was certain everyone would point this out.

Toward evening, Mary left the chilly apartment for the rain-swept streets, uncertain where to go, not wanting to return home and face her family or to go to her studio, grown dusty with disuse. *Paris is raining.* Since last year's triumph, everything had changed except for two things: The rain was coming down steadily and she had once again quarreled with Edgar.

She raised her umbrella, crossed the street, and walked a block to the Grand Hôtel du Louvre, where the doorman put her into a covered fiacre.

Chapter Forty-Two

Edgar's disconsolate "Come in" trickled through the locked door, and Mary let herself in with her key as the encroaching darkness strangled the last gasp of light from the sky. A single candle burned in the gloom, revealing the familiar disarray of Edgar's studio. Mary unpinned her sodden hat and hung it on the rack with her coat and dripping umbrella. Next to the door, narrow crates, presumably holding Edgar's canvases bound for the show, awaited the arrival of the carter.

She found Edgar in the back room, sitting on one of his paint-spattered chairs, his hands resting on his knees, staring at his little dancer, who was barely illuminated in the waning light of another candle. Beyond him stood the press, pushed into a corner and smothered with a dust sheet, forgotten. Edgar offered not even the slightest evidence that he had heard Mary come in. His eyes stayed on the girl, as if he were afraid she was going to pirouette away. Even in the deep gloaming, Mary could see that the statuette was a marvel. For weeks, she had wondered whether Edgar had finished her, but he had revealed nothing; knowing what it was to be in the middle of something, she didn't inquire. But here the girl was: finished, gorgeous, a triumph. What had once been a crude skeleton was now a *petit rat*. Nearly four feet high, she was neither doll-nor life-size, diminutive, but not miniature, stunningly rendered in the malleable and fickle medium of beeswax. Outfitted in bodice and dancing shoes, cloth stockings warming her legs, a skein of cascading hair falling down her back, she stood defiant and proud before her maker, arms twisted behind, fingers entwined, chin thrust forward, every detail, from her marvelously rendered fingers to her knobby knees, crafted in convincing particularity.

"Caillebotte must be livid," Degas said, his voice flat. "Has he sent you to tar and feather me?"

"He did, but he wouldn't have if you hadn't placed the vitrine before you brought her in. The critics were thrilled to find a way to skewer you. I can only imagine what they'll write. Of course you'll deserve it."

"Is this why you've come?" Degas said. "To scold me?"

"Don't your promises mean anything?" she said.

"About what? The journal? I tell you, it's nothing."

"Nothing? Everything to you is nothing. Why didn't you tell me? Why let me be embarrassed by hearing it in the *bois*, at the horse troughs, of all places, from Gustave? I was humiliated. I don't understand why you pulled out. Everything was set."

The fluttering candle magnified the sunken hollows of Edgar's eyes as he turned to look at her. He seemed far away, as if he had heard nothing of her outburst. She had rarely seen him so distracted, and certainly never in his studio, where he was always the master. She began to wonder whether he was ill, whether some disease of the mind had suddenly rendered him simple.

"I couldn't publish those prints."

"Why not?"

"Because they weren't good enough." He was speaking distractedly, studying the sculpture as he spoke.

"Whose? Yours or mine? Be honest," Mary said. "You owe me that. Did you not publish *Le Jour et la Nuit* because my work was inferior?"

He turned, finally, and fixed his gaze on her. "You are wrong about your work," he said.

"But not about my failure."

"Look around, Mary. Nearly every single one of my canvases for the exhibition is still here. I am late for everything. What was the journal anyway? Just an idea that didn't work out. Nothing else. It means nothing. It's not a failure."

She threw up her hands. "I've gone backwards. I want to pull all my work off the wall. I'm embarrassed that anyone has seen it."

"Then do it!" His raised voice echoed off the walls. "What are you whining at me for? What do I have to do with your work? It's your work, not mine."

Mary turned and sat down, the glimmer of the candle fading now, and with it all her vague dreams of a life lived beside this man, strange and indistinct as they had been. The flame trembled in its puddle of molten wax and went out, rendering the studio a place of shadows and depth. Edgar, at once reticent and irreverent, generous and selfish, careless and careful, was a terrible man to want, as terrible a man as Édouard Manet was for Berthe. What was it about genius that sabotaged happiness? What was it about desire that betrayed?

"My God," Mary said. "We aren't good together, you and I. You have a masterpiece but I have so little to show for the year that I am ashamed of my work. I lost something working with you. Something of myself. Something essential. Something I cannot abandon."

"You lost yourself."

"The trouble with you is that you care more about art than you do about love."

"So do you."

"But I don't abandon anyone."

"You abandoned yourself." Degas wrenched himself around to face her. "Besides, I have no masterpiece."

"She is standing there in all her glory."

"She is a failure." He fumbled with matches and relit the candle. "Look at her, Mary. Really look at her. Renoir was here this afternoon, the bastard, wanting to argue with me about something or other. He took one look at her and said her proportions were off. It would be like him to undercut me out of spite, but I think this time he meant well. I was about to take her to the Rue des Pyramides, but now . . ." Edgar's voice trailed off in despair. All the anger was gone. He was near tears. Mary had never seen him this raw. He was like a father who had lost his only child. Distractedly, he knelt down beside a large dress box that was hiding at his feet in the shadows. He pulled from it two green ribbons, one narrow and short, the other wide and long. He tied the narrow one in a bow around the girl's braid, and the second, wider sash around her waist, taking time to tighten the knots and fluff out the bows as fastidiously as any costumer at the Opéra. Then he lifted from the box a billowing, layered froth of a tutu, which he pinned into place under her newly beribboned waist. The skirt fell to her knees in a spume of tarlatan and tulle that Mary was certain he must have stolen from the dressing rooms backstage at the Garnier. With these unlikely additions his genius revealed itself. The stockings sagging on her legs that Mary had thought were cloth were not cloth but wax; the shoes and bodice that she thought were wax were not wax, but canvas and satin smeared with wax; neither was the girl's hair wax but instead a waxed fall of real hair. Only the tutu and ribbons were what they appeared to be: arresting flourishes on a breathtaking apparition. All else was illusion.

When he was done straightening the many layers of the marvelous skirt, he stood and fixed his gaze on Mary. "Look at her. I mean really look at her."

Mary could not speak, the dressed statue was so remarkable.

The rain had stopped now, and in the courtyard the echoing clatter of dinner plates and conversation from the other apartments swelled the night with domesticity. Edgar began to shout, his face haggard and pained. "For God's sake, Mary, with her clothes on, what do you think? Is Renoir right or when she is dressed does she appear in proportion?"

In the three years since she had known him, he had never once asked her to critique him. "You want my opinion?"

"My God, Mary, don't torture me." He sank onto his chair once again.

Fending off apoplectic admiration and an avalanche of envy, Mary circled the statue, attempting to see what Edgar said he couldn't see, a notion that seemed to her a great apostasy. It was almost impossible to look past the intricate details, the astonishing surprise of the ribbon and tutu, the brilliance of Edgar's extravagant conceit, to see the dancer as a structure, for essentially, this was what sculpture was, even one as unorthodox as this. Form was a matter of precise measurement. Without the underpinning of accurate scaffolding, no piece of artwork succeeded. But for all of that, art was instinct, too. One *felt* the balance or imbalance. The revelation was something akin to a religious experience: You didn't know the truth and then you suddenly knew it, and because of it everything was transformed. In the dim light, the little dancer was a silhouette. It was this trick of the light that aided Mary.

"Monsieur Renoir may be right." It was almost gratifying to be able to point out his misstep, but she couched it slightly to spare him. "Her head is too small. Not by too much, but off, slightly, at the crown, and here, at the forehead, where it slopes too steeply."

Degas crumpled forward, his hands to his knees. "My damn eyes. I didn't see it. Why didn't I see it? Both you and Renoir. Dear God. She is flawed."

"It was only the shadow that revealed it. I still think she is gorgeous. Perhaps no one else will notice."

"I can't bear to let anyone see her." He was echoing her words, all her worries about failure, but he was not aware that he was. He eyed a large crate that loomed in the corner, awaiting the blemished girl he would not now send.

He shifted his gaze and studied Mary. "You see? I have no masterpiece. We are equally bad for one another."

In the swelter of the moist heat, sweat beaded on her forehead. Mary realized now that as she had studied the girl, she had unconsciously opened the top buttons of her shirtwaist to the angle of her collarbones. Degas's gaze drifted there now.

"Do you know that this is the first time you treated me as your equal? The first time you didn't yield to me?" he said.

"I was furious with you."

"I want to draw you." His raw voice crackled through the heat, his desire clear: He did not wish to draw her as he had before, chastely—the curves of her clothing, her head and hands, the line of her long neck, her corseted, clothed waist. He wished to draw her in the most intimate way, to trace the unclothed rise of her breast, the curves of her thighs, the circles of her buttocks. "You are to me what no other creature is. We are the same mind, Mary. We are the same soul, occupying two different bodies."

"We are not," she said.

"You are the only woman I can tolerate in the world."

"That is not praise."

"Why would I flatter you? I respect you too much."

"This is how you show your respect?"

He rose from his chair and padded to the window. He lifted an open box of pastels from the sill, where he had placed them to let the sun blunt their color, but he seemed to think better of it and set aside the deadened chalk for a new box. Of course. For this, he would want the noise of color, the punctuation of high pigment, to set this drawing apart from any other, this carnal drawing of intimacy. It was no secret that he was unkind to his models, but Mary knew he would draw her differently, with something akin to reverence.

The little dancer stood impassive, inscrutable, imperfect, her eyes hooded, blind. An indifferent witness. Certainly she would tell no one. His little dancer had become to him something beloved, wept over, treasured. Mary studied Degas's hands, fallen to his sides. These were hands deft enough to create an airy confection from the lowly medium of wax, perceptive enough to fashion a curious thing of strange beauty, and inventive enough to create what no one had ever dreamed of creating before and might never create again. He would never betray this girl, would surely never part with her, wouldn't expose her to a world when he thought her less than perfect. Mary felt herself yielding, or wanting to yield. She wondered whether this would be the way that Edgar would finally, truly see her. And what was virtue in a warm studio on a rainy night in Paris, when possibility seduced and intimacy beckoned? Over the years she had believed there had been no one else for him, at least no one he had ever revealed, and certainly no one else for her.

She went to him, her footsteps slow and measured. He had never seemed more essential to her. He was stripped of his defenses, his armor, his mocking wit; his need, naked and pure, beguiled. But more than his mind, here was his soul, asking for her. She would need help with her buttons; he would need to unlace her corset, help free her of her bustle. These were skills he no doubt had perfected in his life, though she didn't know for certain, didn't know what happened behind his doors when models visited.

He kissed her. He put his hand to her cheek and kissed her for a very long time, affection transforming to need, then to hunger, then beyond, to a place where she had no will. She did not resist, though she thought she ought to because she was not a woman to let herself be seduced. She was not a woman who made undisciplined choices. She was none of these things, yet here she was, being all those things and more. His hands began unbuttoning her shirtwaist. He pulled it off, unhooked the sash at her waist, unbuttoned her skirt. It fell to the floor. He did not stop kissing her. He asked her to turn. She did. He unhooked her corset. She held it to herself while he disrobed, first his smock, then his shirt and pants. He untied her petticoats and they, too, dropped to the floor. He pulled over the tarp that had covered the girl and spread it on the floor, and in that moment she thought she should stop, but she didn't. She kneeled on the floor with him and then she lay down beside him and he took her corset from her.

"Are you certain?" he said.

She could not bring herself to answer, but she meant no just as much as she meant yes, and in that noisy silence he kissed her again and then there was no more no. There was no drawing, either. There was only clumsy touch and willing surrender, timeless discovery and shocked astonishment, and when it was over, the fear that she had been enticed forever into the tangle of him.

Chapter Forty-Three

In the first days after their encounter, Degas chose not to see Mary. He wrote to her that he was much taken up with getting his canvases to the exhibition but that he would come to see her soon. He then spread the task over several days, hoping that Mary would understand that he did not yet wish to see her, and that his note was not an invitation to come and help him with the hanging. Because the exhibition was now open, he had to hang his paintings while visitors strolled among the rooms, and the startling sight of an artist with a hammer bewildered many of them.

"Who do you think hangs them?" Degas spat, after a man made a disagreeable number of comments of increasing stupidity. The inquirer gaped and then hurried away, grumbling to the woman on his arm about the arrogance of artists. Degas turned back to his task but was interrupted again when someone else said, "Could you tell me how you get your ideas? Because I'm trying to paint, and I don't know where to start."

Degas turned in a rage, only to find Édouard Manet leaning on his cane, mocking hilarity enlivening his haggard face.

"You are trying to get yourself killed is what you are trying to do. I nearly threw this thing at you," Degas said.

"I'm here to kidnap you. Where the hell have you been? Why didn't you come to my opening party?"

He had forgotten all about Édouard's party. That was the night he had been with Mary. "I took ill. How did you know I'd be here?"

"When you weren't home, I went looking for you at Mademoiselle Cassatt's. She said you would be here."

"Why didn't you ask Sabine?"

Édouard shrugged. "Oh, Sabine told me. I'm just very fond of Mademoiselle Cassatt. As are you, I might point out. That one is crooked," he said, pointing with his cane at a canvas that Degas had just hung and which was perfectly straight. He made a dozen other comments of questionable helpfulness until Degas finished hanging the last of his canvases, gave the ticket seller the hammer, and announced that he was done.

"And what about the dancer?" the girl asked.

"She won't be coming," Degas said.

"Caillebotte must be thrilled," Édouard said.

"Caillebotte is no longer speaking to me."

"You must be more careful with your friends, Degas. We've just lost Duranty." They had gotten the news only yesterday, when it rippled through Montmartre like a gunshot: Duranty, dead.

It took Édouard an enormous amount of effort to descend the stairs. Outside, he navigated the cobbles of the sidewalk, stumbling every once in a while and wincing from the pain. They had not gone fifteen feet before Édouard said, "I'm afraid we'll have to use the carriage."

In the past, Édouard would have scoffed at taking a carriage for a walk of less than two miles; he loved walking as much as he loved women, and Degas felt this loss for his friend as keenly as he felt all the others. They climbed into the carriage, which he had kept waiting on the corner in case, for the brief trip to the Charpentiers' gallery, La Vie Moderne.

There, Degas fell into rapture. "My God, Édouard, you will never paint an untrue painting in your life." The vibrancy of the oils and pastels, all of them newly done in the past year, belied Édouard's condition. Degas was relieved that no siege of illness could ever dim this man's

facility with a brush, no matter that he was falling into the hell of an illness he still would not acknowledge. "You are the incarnation of modernity. You are one of us, Édouard. I don't know why you've refused to
exhibit with us all these years. Everything about your work is a revelation."

"Your paltry little exhibition is a cloister, effectively separating new
art from the Salon," Édouard said. "I wish to force the Salon to acknowledge us. I've sent in two pieces this year and I have every belief they'll be
accepted."

Degas rather doubted the Salon would take them; he feared his friend
was far too optimistic. The Salon jury enjoyed nothing more than belit-
tling him at every chance.

Édouard's admirers delayed them, emitting congenial laughter and
gasps of praise when they greeted him, a joyful clamor that resonated in
the small gallery, where the number of visitors, Degas was not surprised
to see, exceeded theirs by too many to count. While Édouard was gathering compliments, Degas fielded jibes about his empty vitrine from not a
few attendees and managed to fend off more with an icy stare. When
Édouard finally exhausted his need to hear how wonderful he was, he
went with Degas for luncheon to the Café de la Rochefoucauld. En-
sconced at a small table far from the window so no passing friends could
find them, Édouard lolled on the bench that lined the long wall of the
café, one elbow hung nonchalantly over the lip of its back, his despised
cane forgotten on the bench beside him. The dreamy wash of too much
wine soon gave him the appearance of loosened serenity. During the
meal, they discussed his canvases. Édouard's pastel of Zola's wife had
been a favorite of Degas's.

"I have to say, Zola gushed over it. I delivered it myself to Meudon
when it was finished," Édouard said. "You should have seen him argue
with me when I asked him to lend it back for the show. He adores it."

"Zola will never return to us," Degas said. He was glad for this time
with Édouard alone, not only because his sociable friend usually

preferred to wallow in a scrum of sociability but because he was rarely given to tête-à-têtes. Also, this time with Édouard helped him to avoid thinking any more about Mary. "Zola won't, in a spasm of appreciation, join our circle again. He has his own now. He and Maupassant meet at Café de la Paix. Don't try to woo a writer with your talent, Manet, despite how much you think your poet friend Mallarmé loves you. Writers despise us, and none too secretly. You'll never get Albert Wolff to write you a good review. Leave the writers be. Art is one thing, literature another."

"Maupassant doesn't despise me," Édouard said, smiling and taking another sip of wine. "It's you he can't stand."

"You are the worst kind of bourgeois, Édouard," Degas said. "You are an artist who wants to be loved. You love to be loved, even more than you love art. Why do you chase glory? Don't you understand how fickle the world is? How little declared love means? Not only does the world not care about you, but those who you think care about you do not care. You are alone. We are born alone and we die alone and in between any dalliance or declaration that is made is a temporary respite from the damnable truth. You dream of love, but there is no love. It doesn't exist." By the end of his speech, Degas was aware his voice had risen, but he could not help himself; Édouard could infuriate him.

Unoffended, Édouard reared up from the bench, leaning over the marble table and the scattered remnants of their meal. "Dalliance? What is this? Edgar Degas, speaking of love? What has happened? A man who doesn't believe that love exists is a man wounded. Has someone broken your heart?"

Degas fiddled with the stem of his wineglass, furious. It was maddening how one's secrets always made themselves manifest. And the relentless Édouard would delight in sniffing out the cause of his rant. "What do you know of broken hearts?" he said.

"Everything."

Édouard's gaze slipped away, and Degas wished he had thought of another way to best Édouard. The poor man would never be free of his obsession with Berthe. After the birth of Julie, Berthe had made a religion of her marriage. The others, Isabelle Lemonnier and Méry Laurent, were nothing to Édouard but feeble variances of Berthe.

"Ah, I know," Édouard said, coming to himself. "You cannot seduce the brilliant Mademoiselle Cassatt."

Degas endeavored not to change his expression or tone. He hearkened back to that moment when he and Édouard had first seen Mary at the Salon. Now he would have to imply that he had taken Mary in order to convince Édouard that he had not. "You are dreaming."

"Well, I suggest that you stop dreaming and make love to her or any other woman as often as you can. Death puts an end to all that, you know. Start now. If you cannot persuade her, and I doubt that you can, I see plenty of women here who will cost you a franc, but what is that when there is such pleasure to be had?"

Degas ventured a comment that any other human being would think was cruel, but that he knew Édouard would find funny. "Really, Édouard, do you want me to end up like you?"

"Yes. Then I wouldn't be the only man in Paris suffering such embarrassments."

"For God's sake, just say it. It's syphilis, isn't it?"

"If I don't say its name, then it doesn't exist."

The two things that didn't exist in their world: syphilis in Édouard's, and love in Degas's. But of course they were both deluded, something they toasted with the kind of enthusiasm that only old friends could muster.

In the two hours they had lingered inside the café, the sky had grown a dull purpled blue and verged now on yet another spring rainstorm. Before summer came, it was conceivable that Paris would drown. Degas put the exhausted Édouard in his carriage and watched it trundle down the avenue in the direction of Pigalle. Not until the carriage was out of sight did Degas pull off his glasses and wipe his eyes. More than his sorrow, he was furious at the ingratitude of Paris officialdom, all the imbeciles who had made Édouard suffer over the years, for the man felt every slight in his bones, despite the unending adoration of the public. Édouard was greater than any of them knew, and the world would not come to its senses before they lost him. They would never understand the enormity of their privation until after he was gone; only then would they mourn all the paintings he would never paint after the syphilis worked its grim end.

He had declined a lift in Édouard's carriage because he had put off dealing with Mary for far too long. If Édouard loved to be loved more than he loved art, then what did it mean that Degas loved art more than he loved love, as Mary had accused? In their relationship of three years, he and Mary had affected a certain restraint of commentary that he had relied on to define things. Now that there was no restraint of any kind, Degas worried that he would not be able to keep himself hidden. He would have to define his desire in a more precise way, one that might render him more vulnerable than he wished. To make Mademoiselle Cassatt a more intimate participant in his life would be to make himself subject to the pathologies of humanity, to which he was already more than prey. Subject to love, whose exact nature he questioned, he would be as incapacitated as Manet, who was besotted with Berthe and enfeebled by the myriad afflictions of love, not merely the deterioration the physical act had visited on him, but the other confusing and obligating connections that stole one's independence. And wasn't he already troubled enough? In the stormy gloaming, the muted colors of the city were blending into one another, becoming the color of evening, though it was only three or four in the afternoon. Someday this washed darkness would be all that he would see. Wasn't that frailty enough? Why love a woman and therefore risk losing her when the world was such a fickle place?

Just go and ask her, he thought. *Just go and say, Do you think we should?*

But his language was not the language of love, as he had once tried to tell her. His language was the language of incision, and if he dared to go to her home, dared to knock and ask for an audience, dared to declare what he thought she might want him to declare, he would fumble the words. He would say, *I can marry you, but I have no confidence.* He would say, *I fear love as I fear art.* He would say, *You cannot hold my nature against me.*

No gaslight yet lit the streets and only a few passing carts with their swinging lanterns brightened the deepening gloom. Practice for his dark future. He shuffled forward, one uncertain foot in front of the other, toward home.

In her studio, Mary watched the afternoon light dim on the Boulevard de Clichy. That morning, when Édouard Manet had come looking for Edgar, she had worried, suddenly, that Edgar had been indiscreet, that Manet's visit had been a foray to discover whether or not Mary displayed any sign of her compromise. But Manet had been nothing but charming, as always. He sent his driver up to the studio to ask her to come down to the carriage because, he said to her when she climbed in, stairs were now too much for him, a fact he shrugged off as if he had said that it was a shame that the weather was threatening. Where was she keeping Degas, he wanted to know. He needed to see Edgar now. When she told him where she suspected he was, Manet asked her to come too, as he was planning to force Degas to go with him to see his exhibition, but Mary told him she was working, that she planned to go soon with Berthe, and that she was very happy for him.

After Manet had gone, Mary returned to her studio. Aside from the terror that she might become pregnant, the other worries of entanglement with Edgar had bubbled to the surface almost as soon as he had left her at her door. He had walked her home, but they had had little to say to one another, and he had let her climb the five flights of stairs to her family's flat on her own, unwilling, she was certain, to face her family. Since then, she had heard nothing from him except his note that he would be too busy hanging pictures to come by, a feeble excuse of such transparent panic that she had torn it up.

What had she been thinking? How had she allowed it to happen? What odd creature had taken over her body? In the past few days, there had been moments when she had nearly buckled remembering the unexpected pleasure of his touch. Once she caught her image in a mirror and discovered that she was blushing. The embarrassment was too acute. She couldn't dismiss the fear that she had disappointed him, that her body had dissatisfied, her inexperience had alarmed, her bashfulness had annoyed. Each day that passed without a note or a visit worked a paralyzing fury in her. She could not erase what had happened and wasn't sure she wanted to. The days passed at a glacial pace, and his silence chilled any wonder that remained. Edgar? The man who could hurt her with just a look? The man who would lift her up and then just as swiftly cut her down? The man who made promises he never kept? He was maddening: generous at one moment, self-serving the next, incapable, it seemed, of any sustained devotion.

And yet.

The dissonance of her situation kept her from work, which had already been compromised for far too long. The past three days she had come every morning to her studio in hopes that habit would revive the muse that had inspired last year's extraordinary portfolio. But the room's neglected disarray, its echoing emptiness after the circus of Edgar's comings and goings, even the different light, once serenely familiar but now perturbingly foreign, engendered not comfort but unease. She occupied herself with sweeping and dusting, taking inventory of her brushes and supplies, counting her blank canvases, sorting her paint tubes, but the domestic flurry was of little help. From time to time, she had to keep herself from dashing to the exhibition and pulling everything of hers off the wall, restraining herself with the hope that the disaster of her showing would soon be forgotten, erased from all memory but hers. And daily she returned to her family, whose questions she could not answer. Where was Edgar? What had happened? Had he apologized? Had he changed his mind?

Lydia, always observant, asked her what the matter was.

He is being difficult, Mary said.

Surely he'll come round to see you soon.

I doubt it, Mary said.

He always comes back.

Perhaps not this time.

When Berthe came to collect Mary for Manet's exhibition, the first thing Berthe said was, *My dear, take care. It's you who has to keep on living.* Mary did not know how Berthe knew, but if anyone would see, it would be her.

Mary decided that she would not contact Edgar. She would avoid anywhere he might be. She would wait him out. This would be her act of courage, confronted with such a morass of difficulty. Edgar's would be to face her. She half-expected never to see him again. But if he did come, he would need to persuade her that his passion had meant more than a momentary respite from the devastation of his failure, that it was not need that had driven him but worship of her, which, she decided, would be the only acceptable absolution in these circumstances. He had only to come. It was a small thing to expect of a man who had made love to her. She would give him a month, knowing his reticence. He had only to decide that he wanted to.

Chapter Forty-Four

Y ou don't want to marry, do you? All that complication and commit-
ment? The obligation and boredom?"

One expected such bluster from Degas; one waited for it, prepared for
it by rehashing old conversations, as Mary had done, planning the perfect retort to any forthcoming imagined parry, but when he arrived at
Mary's studio door two weeks after their affair and this was what he said,
her hoarded armory was no answer for a proposal that denied itself in the
asking.

It pleased her that he looked terrible. Through his glasses, his eyes
were dull, and his skin had become pallid in his isolation. No one had
seen him. This was reported to her all over Paris. He had even skipped
his night at the Opéra, a development that gratified her, for he never
missed a performance. Since their encounter, she had taken more care
than usual with her appearance. It was a matter of pride: She would make
him sorry if, or when, he finally chose to see her. So when she opened
the door this morning and it was he, she preened just a little, because the
reflection in the mirror that morning had been especially kind.

And then he spoke.

She slammed the door in his face.

He opened it and stepped inside.

She could not, she discovered, bear to be near him. She crossed to the
windows and stood in the comforting warmth of a ray of morning sun.

He stayed by the door and held his hat in his hands. "That was a shabby thing to say," he began. "I apologize."

It had been a very long time since Edgar had been to her studio, and he looked around now, as if surprised to see a canvas on an easel, a palette prepared, and Mary at work.

"I meant to say that I will marry you if you wish."

"That is the kind of proposal a woman never wishes to hear."

"And what kind of proposal is that?"

"The kind the speaker is sorry to have made." There had been some relief. She was not with child. The overwhelming solace of that reprieve fed her indignation now.

"I am not a normal man. Surely you have come to understand this."

"What do I care of normal? Surely you have come to understand that I have never been a woman who wanted a quotidian existence. But none of this has anything to do with love, does it?"

"Édouard is dying."

"You cannot prevent his death by marrying me."

He looked up then, savaged.

"The world is not that kind, Edgar."

Degas stared at her, aghast, and she let him suffer for a minute before she shook her head.

"The point is, Edgar, that we don't know what to do with one another. And I can't trust you."

His face, already mournful, collapsed into hapless need. She was shaking. She put her hand on the windowsill to steady herself. He remained uncharacteristically still, arrested at the doorway, where he could just as easily leave as stay. The light from the window fell on his glasses and concealed his eyes. It was all him now. With a swift denial, he could controvert the difficulties of the situation, could refute the realities she perceived, could persuade her of the depths of his devotion. In the long silence, the noises of the street reached into the room, as if to remind her that time was passing, that life went on, that the ordinary really did reign. She could not remember a longer silence between them, but she would not break it. He had to declare himself. She wasn't even certain what she wanted him to say, but she wanted him to say something final, because she was tired of the uncertainty.

He shifted on his feet. "Perhaps if we were different creatures," he said, "less alike."

She heard her voice breaking. "It seems a strange reason not to love one another."

"I didn't say I didn't love you."

She waited for him to steal her courage by saying next that he did love her. She might do anything then, if he did. She might even disappoint herself. She looked at him, but his gaze faltered. Only for a moment, but it was enough.

"Good-bye, Edgar," she said. "You can fix your dancer. I know you can. It will only take love."

He hesitated a moment, then opened the door and left.

She waited at the windows until she saw him step onto the street. She did not want him to see her. She moved to the canvas and tacked to its edge the study she had made of Lydia last night. The only solution to heartbreak was to paint the thing she knew she would never have. *Paint love*, he had once said. He had at least given her that. She squeezed paint from the tubes and took up her brush and began, as if she had never known him.

1881–1883

Chapter Forty-Five

Ayear later, on the sidewalk at 35 Boulevard des Capucines, Édouard Manet waylaid Berthe Morisot under one of the leafy maples that lined the street, persuading her to come into his closed carriage so that they could talk in private, away from the stream of people, friends and otherwise, entering and leaving the building. Today was the opening day of the sixth of the impressionists' exhibitions, hung in rooms at the top of the building, whose wide windows let in the most extraordinary light, an ambient shimmer that showed Berthe's canvases to perfection. The whole of the exhibition glimmered: Degas was finally showing his dancer and the place was alive with astonishment; Mary Cassatt's canvases exceeded anything she had ever done; Pissarro's usual array of bucolic landscapes impressed with their mastery; and Monet and Caillebotte and Renoir had seceded over yet another argument with Degas, who had organized the show around his favorites and had seemed, somehow, to push the show away from technique and into a celebration of modernity. Manet thought he was even a little sorry he had not eschewed the Salon this year to show with the impressionists, but he quickly dismissed the thought. He was thrilled to have been accepted to the Salon: two pictures, promised to be beautifully hung.

Berthe wore a straw bonnet trimmed in silk and decorated with a spray of flowers at the crown that deepened the black of her hair. The breeze had teased a few tendrils from her loose chignon and they played around her face, softening the sharp darts of her cheekbones that defined her beauty. Édouard resisted the overwhelming urge to whisk her to the station to board a train to Italy. He would alert no one until the deed was done, until life was what it could have been, had he been less circumspect: a flowered refuge in Venice or Madrid, Berthe painting beside him, the air exquisite, their days filled with the intoxications of body and soul. He rubbed the head of his cane, restless. It would take only a word to his driver.

Berthe studied him. He could hide nothing. She tucked the loose hair under her bonnet and said, "Eugène is coming back for me soon." After years of searching for a position, Eugène had a chance in the Finance Ministry. "He is going to pick me up after his interview."

"Upstairs there are a dozen people who will recognize my carriage."

"You cannot frighten me. I won't leave with you. If Eugène comes, we will tell him you were keeping me from the wind."

"If he gets the job, he will no longer be an embarrassment to you," Édouard said.

"That is unfair."

"And also true."

"We are leaving Paris, Édouard. We've decided. I've come into some money after my grandfather's death, and we are leaving."

Édouard fought to keep his voice under control. "Where are you going?"

"Not far. Bougival. But it is out of Paris." The plan had come to her after the dinner when Eugène had made his point, just over a year ago. *Prepare yourself, darling,* indicating that he understood everything about her and Édouard. But the lack of money had been an impediment. Now that she had come into her inheritance, and Eugène had a chance at a job, she could repair the damage, could endeavor to worship Eugène in all his frailty and peculiar moods, as wives did, she supposed, when they loved their husbands. She had wanted to go farther, to the south, far enough from Paris with its terrible weather and impossible longings, where the sunshine might scrub Édouard from her memory, but those plans seemed impossible now that Eugène might have a job.

"You would leave me when I am ill?"

"Bougival is not that far. And you will be in Meudon again. We will see you in the summertime as we did last year." Édouard had relented, finally, to treatment, and had spent last summer taking baths at Belleville, where he had chafed at his exile and painted in the garden. The treatment seemed to have done him some good, or so he claimed. "But this is the last time you will ever see me alone," she said.

"This is ridiculous. A half hour by train from the Gare Saint Lazare is no distance at all."

"It is enough to keep us from being expected at your mother's Thursdays, enough to keep you from dropping by, enough to keep me from the pain of you."

Tears gathered in his eyes.

"Please, don't pretend you are an innocent. If I am to live with my husband and treat him as one, you will have to face the truth, not play with it."

"Motherhood has made you unkind."

"It has made me chaste."

"The virgin Berthe."

"Don't make me be cruel to you."

It was perhaps a mark of his illness that he surrendered, when he never would have before. He climbed out with his cane and stood guard outside the carriage, waiting until Eugène arrived to collect her. He spent several minutes in solicitous conversation about Eugène's job prospects and the exhibition before he said good-bye to them both, walking them to their carriage even though his legs bothered him. He planted his cane on the sidewalk, his legs astride, his top hat and morning coat impeccable as he stood there, resolute, lifting a hand as they drove away.

Chapter Forty-Six

"It's too much pudding, Father," Mary said.

"Now, Mame," her father said. "Not even you can be this quixotic. The last time you received bad reviews we had to resuscitate you. Now you are lauded in every review, are celebrated as the epitome of 'grace, delicacy, and femininity,' and you say the praise is too much. I will never understand you."

"That is because you are not an artist."

"What does Edgar say about your triumph?"

"I have no idea." She'd been saying this to queries about Edgar for a year, though she saw him everywhere. They talked. They visited. They critiqued one another's work. She modeled for him. He painted her. But everything had changed. Had she noticed anything, everyone asked her? Was Edgar being as vile to her as he was to everyone else? She always said nothing, only gave a vague shake of her head and smiled what she hoped was her most enigmatic smile. "Ask him yourself when you see him," she said, determined not to imply any intimacy other than the mostly public friendship they continued.

"But when will we see him again?"

"He is coming for dinner next week."

"And who else is coming?"

"Everyone."

"Everyone? God help us. You know I disapprove. You will exhaust Lydia gadding about Paris with her like you do."

"We do not gad. Lyddy, do we gad?"

"Oh, I think we do." Lydia was knitting in the parlor, smiling through the open doorway at her father and sister.

"We do not," Mary said. "We attend the Opéra, parties, openings, salons. None of this is gadding."

"Then what do you call it?" her father said.

"Living."

"And what do you call rejecting a tidal wave of praise?" he said.

"Reason."

"It is unreasonable," her father said. "Isn't it, Lyddy?"

"Entirely unreasonable." The brisk click of knitting needles raced along in the parlor.

Lydia, newly well and thriving, had become Mary's constant companion in Edgar's place, charming artistic Paris with her generosity and observant intelligence, rendering even Émile Zola an admirer, no mean feat for the sister of the *Américaine*. Sometimes Louisine, on her frequent trips from the States, joined their trips to museums and shows, and together they mourned Abigail, whose husband had indeed sent Abigail's infant to the states to live with Louisa. Mary's joy at her sister's burgeoning strength compensated for that sorrow, and far exceeded her happiness at this year's redemptive success at their exhibition, which she nonetheless relished far more than she would ever let on. On the first day, she sold everything, even pictures of the family, which she then had to buy back when they protested. The memory of last year's failure receded, and in its place resided only the normal, quotidian terror that every artist faced.

Degas's dancer, delayed a year, her head reconfigured, caused a sensation, as she ought to have done. Whistler, who had come from England for the show, stood before the now occupied vitrine and uttered unintelligible croaks of adoration. That so many critics called her ugly only fed Degas's pride in his creation. Caillebotte, fed up with Degas's "antics," as he called them, had not exhibited this year, furious with him for turning the impressionist exhibition into a realist exhibition, or so he said.

Mary's paintings were the fruit of the summer. Her brother Aleck, his wife, Lois, and their children had come from the States to spend the summer with them out in the country, where they had rented a house. Mary painted all summer long: Lydia crocheting in the garden, Lydia drinking tea, Lydia seated on a bench, mother and infant embracing, her mother reading to her grandchildren, her brother in his austere magnificence, her nephew playing a violin, babies and their mothers recruited from the town, painting after painting about love. She painted love into the autumn and through the winter, and when the pictures were hung in rooms on the Boulevard des Capucines and the reviews poured in praising her work and Pissarro and Berthe and even Édouard Manet declared her pictures sublime she did not think about Edgar, except that, of course, she did. Her art had soared after she had broken with him in the most essential way, a convoluted outcome that haunted her.

But Lydia, dear Lydia, thrilled to be well, went everywhere with her; they crisscrossed Paris in the family carriage; they gadded about.

"Do not try me so, Mame," Robert said. "Just accept your well-deserved praise for the sake of your father's heart and allow me to rest for once in the thought that you are pleased with your efforts. Give me that, at least?"

"All right," Mary said. "For one moment, I will let you believe that I am well pleased."

"My God, you are a lot of trouble, darling," he said, and kissed her.

Chapter Forty-Seven

Later, when Mary looked back, she marveled at the equanimity of the year after her triumphant exhibition, though had she been paying attention, she might have seen Caillebotte's desertion of that same exhibition as the harbinger of all the pain to come.

After the summer of 1881, when Mary's other brother, Gardner, made a trip to Paris for the first time since he'd been a child, and they rented Coeur Volant in nearby Marly-le-Roi, and all had seemed well for a good long time, rumbles of disquiet began to reverberate through the ranks of the impressionists. Caillebotte wanted to eject all Degas's pet artists: Raffaëlli, Forain, and Zandomeneghi. It was a matter of principle, Caillebotte said. They were terrible artists, and Degas was a stubborn, power-mongering fool. This was what Caillebotte told Pissarro. "Monet and Renoir might return to exhibit with us," he opined, "if we could just rid ourselves of the trash Degas drags around behind him." Pissarro tried to quiet the exasperated Caillebotte, but Caillebotte was out for blood. Retaliation or no, the thing was settled in his favor. Degas's favorites were out, and Monet, Renoir, and even the outlier Sisley were back in. That Degas withdrew in protest only served to embolden Caillebotte, and he managed somehow to keep Gaugin, Degas's other darling. Then he called on Mary.

"You are asking me to choose against Degas?" Mary said.

"Hanging one's pictures on a wall is not a political act."

"Don't be ridiculous. Of course it is. It always has been and you know it."

"He has not been good to you."

"Don't use the past against me, Gustave."

She withdrew. Mary could not side against the man who had invited her into the world in which she now thrived.

But soon little of that mattered. Lydia took a turn. In the winter, Lydia and her mother journeyed to the South of France, to Pau, where the warm weather and the Pyrenean springs were said to heal anyone. Her mother was in need of a cure too, for her heart had begun to trouble her. It had been little things at first: occasional dizziness and having to pause on the stairs for breath. Then the palpitations started and a hacking cough that never ceased. Something about the air in Pau was good for Katherine, but not for Lydia. When they returned in the spring, just as Mary renounced exhibiting, they all hoped that another summer back at Coeur Volant visiting with the Manets, who had taken a house in nearby Versailles, would heal Lydia, but instead she began to drift in a haze of illness and pain.

In October Lydia took to bed. Mary stayed up nights with her, sitting at her bedside, reading her poetry to distract her from the pain. The doctors prescribed arsenic and morphine, but it did not forestall the nausea and headaches. Lydia slipped in and out of consciousness, her swollen hands worrying her coverlet in feverish restlessness, her skin darkening, her befuddled mind causing her from time to time to cry out some vague endearment, directed at no one specifically but cherished by all her hearers as meant for them. In a single moment of clarity, she begged to be buried in Marly-le-Roi, and the family, stupid with hope, said, "Don't be silly; you'll be well soon, our darling girl." When hope failed, they brought her back to Paris in a rented victoria, propped up against the padded red leather seat and swaddled in blankets for the slow ride into the city. As they approached the outskirts, it began to rain.

At home, in her own bed, Lydia rallied, reviving their unreasonable hopes, but the next day she succumbed. She just left them—no lovely last moments, no farewells, no lingering laughter to treasure. The air in the bedroom, heavy with heat, pressed down on them, and for a good while they all sat weeping at her bedside, not believing that she had gone. Mathilde and Anna, who had been vigilant with tea and sandwiches that no one would eat, opened the bedroom window to the rainy Paris afternoon to let Lydia's soul fly away. Katherine bathed her body. Robert stood and sat and stood again. In the past month, he had prayed that he might die instead of Lydia, but his plea had failed, and from that moment he lost faith in the rescuing power of grace. Katherine thought of the boy they had buried in Germany and could not finish the bathing. Mary took up the cloth and washed her sister's lifeless legs and arms. They changed the sheets under Lydia and combed her hair and put on her prettiest day dress. They tied a ribbon in her plaited hair. Mathilde went to the store to buy black-bordered stationery and black bunting that she draped on the door. Mary wrote a note to the funeral home to come the next day. Robert went to the telegraph office and sent a note to Gardner and Aleck. They were both in the States, but Aleck was about to board a boat for Paris. Then there was nothing else to do. They sat into the night with the candles burning, contemplating a lifetime without Lydia, the girl they all adored, and they thought, *Where will we find love now?*

At the small cemetery at Louveciennes, next to Marly-le-Roi, in the shadow of Versailles, the January wind bristled through the denuded trees shading the clay grounds, whipping small pebbles and dust into the air. They had waited to bury Lydia until Aleck and his family arrived and the holidays had passed. Katherine, her face veiled in black, wept on Robert's shoulder, who stood shakily against the dual onslaught of grief and winter. Mary stood beside them, with Aleck and his wife, Lois. Lou-isine Elder stood with Edgar. Handkerchiefs clutched in their gloved hands, they each threw a flower onto the mahogany casket before it was interred in the little raised vault, far from Paris, far from home. The scrape of the casket sliding onto its shelf in the tomb was lost to the wind. The flowers blew onto the clay. Mary picked them up and laid them again on the casket. The grave workers shut the door, sealing Lydia in. Mary stood back as Katherine and Robert and Aleck and Lois walked back to the family carriage.

"Are you coming?" Robert called.

"I'll travel with Louisine and Edgar."

The open hearse followed her parents' carriage out the drive. Mary watched it go, relieved now to be apart from her family, whose heavy sadness she could no longer bear. She pulled off a glove and placed her right palm on the cool, new stone and leaned into the vault.

Lydia was to have lived, to have kept her company after their parents died, to have eased her old age, to have charmed her until they both died at the same moment in the same blessed place, together, two unmarried sisters of two married brothers, comforting one another in the passing years, astonished at the affronts of age, shocked at the mordant relentlessness of time. Now the great gulf of the future, vast and empty, would have to be faced alone. Language yielded no word to describe what it was to lose her beloved sister. Mary laid her cheek on the cold stone and closed her eyes against the chill.

Edgar and Louisine each took her by an arm and steadied her as they walked to the carriage and helped her to climb in. All the way into Paris, Edgar held her hand and would not relinquish it.

Chapter Forty-Eight

Bougival was not far enough, after all. As it turned out, Berthe and Eugène saw Édouard all the time. The rail line, as Édouard had warned, turned out to be no obstacle. So Eugène and Berthe moved south to Nice, where she painted and tried not to think of Édouard, not when she was using the pastel easel he gave her for New Year's, not when she agonized over composition or color or models, not when she rose and not when she retired, not when she breakfasted and not when she dined, not when she attempted the waters of the Mediterranean nor when she painted the wildflowers on the hillsides, not when she painted the beach and not when she drew the charming houses climbing the steep streets. She tried but she did not succeed, could not exercise the emotional fidelity that Eugène deserved, though she never once mentioned Édouard unless he wrote. Then she affected, in the most offhand way, a slightly bored voice of informality as she slit open his prettily decorated envelopes and related to Eugène the little trifles Édouard always wrote to her, all the while searching the letter for some opaque indication of his devotion. She tried not to reveal the catch in the back of her throat as she mourned any mention of his dwindling health. Sometimes she had to keep herself from booking passage back to Paris to comfort him; she especially had to resist the day he wrote to tell them of winning the Legion of Honor from the state, the coveted prize from the Salon he had desired for so long. They traveled to Italy, where Julie fell ill, and when she recovered they returned to Bougival for the summer and again spent the warm months chastely visiting the Cassatts and Édouard and Suzanne and Madame Manet in Rueil, just four kilometers away. She virtuously doted on her brother-in-law and cared for him and admired his landscapes and still lifes, all that he had energy for now. They painted Julie side by side while everyone ignored their affinity, watching from tea tables set up in the garden. Then suddenly it was the fall and Édouard and Suzanne and Madame Manet left and Berthe stayed behind in Bougival, because to be near Édouard was to love him and she could not stand the pain of him, she could not, even as he began to fail in earnest. When Berthe received the news of Lydia's death, she rued her decision to save herself from the abyss that was Édouard, but she stayed on in Bougival, until the spring of 1883, when the terrible happened and she rushed back to Paris.

Chapter Forty-Nine

As Édouard traveled the middle distance, somewhere between mortal depletion and immortal plenty, he felt the light trickling away. It seemed that he would not be able to survive the ambush of the last prescription, written for him by a quack he had visited in hopes of a last-minute cure. The quack had given him rye ergot, promising it would shut down his pained nerves, but instead insects began creeping up his skin, and his limbs burned and swelled and he suffered from unrelenting cold. And soon after, the skin on his feet and legs began to pucker and desiccate and blacken. And then the doctor took off his leg. Gangrene, he said, though Édouard heard the condemning diagnosis through the gauzy haze of suffering and could not protest. His fight was over and he knew it and he could not speak.

This mortal lucidity did not surprise him. Life, he now knew, was a fleet sprint from birth to death, revealed at twilight to be astonishingly brief. This truth arrived as a terrible certitude, his lost days sparkling like gems of squandered clarity. Enlightened as he was by the affront of the finite, he could not imagine why humanity suppressed this verity. What had once seemed so necessary evanesced too: the struggle and the striving and the wild gabbling of intellects arguing about brushstroke, subject matter, color, all now revealed to be mere taste, preference, choice. He hoped, though, that his paintings might endure, but this no longer troubled him as it had troubled him in life. All of it was vanity. The question of what life is, of how one should live one's days, and to what one should pay attention no longer puzzled him, either; it was as clear as light. He saw, on this unexpected brink, the certainty of what life should have been: a life with Berthe. Though he once thought this selfish indulgence, he knew it now to be honest. Love was not the obligation to Suzanne and Eugène that he and Berthe fulfilled out of chivalrous fastidiousness. While loyalty was no shabby stepsister, a form of love some claimed superior to all others, it was not *love*. Love was not, either, the sum of all his casual distracting dalliances, which was the reason he was dying, all the willing women who had made him feel alive and joyous spurring this ironic death. Nor was love the more justifiable of his infidelities, rooted in the sincerest, if briefest of affections. Love was instead an affinity so pure he wept as he thought of it. That cleaving to Berthe would have been further infidelity, disloyalty, and betrayal, he found oddly incongruous, but he could not help the ways of the universe.

Now he grieved for his beloved, who must witness the agony of the gnawing, voracious pain that clawed at his flesh. She wept at his bedside and claimed his mortifying hands, her unabated grief coursing through them, the fragments of his life ebbing as she mourned with abandon, forgetting decorum, forgetting that she was betraying herself. Her grief sanctioned their ardor. I love you, she said. I love you.

He could not speak, but he wished he could tell her the comforting truth that seemed to be reserved only for the dying. Though his soul trembled at her sorrow, her endless tears soothed his pain and hastened his mortality, and he wished, upon crossing over, that he could voice his utter astonishment at the grandeur awaiting befuddled humanity, wished he could return and suffer all the folly again to whisper, *It is love, my frightened ones. Love.*

Sitting at Édouard's bedside, watching the light leave him, Berthe could not stand the injustice of losing the man she loved. She could not purge the horrors of the agony of his dying. She could not imagine a world that did not succumb to grief in his absence. Afterward, when five hundred people came to his funeral and his illustrious friends carried his coffin to the mournful dirge of bagpipes to Passy, where they laid him in the earth outside the village of Berthe's birth, there was still not enough grief in the world to mark his passing. The cemetery inhabited a hill behind high walls, and the sun shone on the grave where she vowed that she would one day be buried too, not knowing that Eugène and Suzanne would be buried with them and they would all be entangled throughout eternity. Eugène's unknowing revenge would be that he would haunt her, for he was Édouard's pale ghost, a muted wash of the ebullient and clever man she loved.

A year after his death the École des Beaux Arts, the Academy, the Salon, put on a display of all of Édouard's work. All his genius was acknowledged, from his first radical canvases to his last masterpiece, *A Bar at the Folies-Bergère*, painted before the final onslaught of pain. They all helped: Renoir and Monet and Degas and Mary Cassatt, whose attentions and kindness forged an even greater friendship. But friendship was not love. Nothing consoled Berthe. Life, she knew, would drag on with childhood illnesses and exhibitions to attend and paintings to paint. She would adore her child and tend her husband, but love, that elusive prize, had left her now. What a horror it was to be mortal, she thought, subject to such appalling weaknesses and needs. What a horror it was to be alive.

The Rest of Time

Chapter Fifty

The struggle that had seemed so essential, the yearning for transcendence, the doubt that had plagued her, fell away in the face of success. Mary had become the artist she had wanted to be by dint of hard work and perseverance. And what was left was work, the work she had chosen: the pleasure of the puzzle, the technical questions of execution, the choice of composition and color, nothing different than before except that now she understood that pain was the foundation of art—not always its subject, but always its process. To be in pain was to be in the work. But no longer did she fear it meant failure. She knew she would succeed eventually with a canvas. She knew that if she stayed with it long enough, through the blindness, she would finally see what it was meant to be. She knew that she would find its soul. Pain was the essential ingredient.

Would she call this newfound calm patience? Perhaps. But patience based on confidence born of the struggle that had now faded away. Degas, too, fell away. Like a waxing and waning moon, he came in and out of her life, full of affection and respect one moment, spouting trouble and discord the next. Even when he was in Paris, he wrote her notes of praise for her painting, of news of the Opéra, the ballet, Sarah Bernhardt, of his aghast horror at the Eiffel Tower's startling appearance on the skyline, of his travels around France and to England, of the insolence of the upstart van Gogh, of his bafflement with Pissarro's and Monet's continuing infatuation with the countryside, of this and that and more, an endless stream of letters he sent when he was not at her door asking her opinion on this, inviting her to an exhibition of that, behaving as if he were her dearest friend, which he was on some days and others suddenly wasn't, when none of her opinions on anything were valid and her company was neither needed nor wanted, and he would disappear for months at a time without notice. She never knew what to expect, and so she guarded herself, as others had learned to do.

Louisine Elder married a wealthy American named Havemeyer, who indulged her love of art, buying her canvas after canvas on Mary's advice. She asked Mary, from time to time, how it was with Edgar, and Mary made brave answers of independence and indifference, but Edgar's cutting tongue set loose on one of her paintings or proffered opinions could set her back so much that she wouldn't be able to paint for days, sometimes weeks. Mary often wondered whether, had she given in, had she allowed herself to become irretrievably entangled, had she been willing to submit to a lifetime of uncertainty, they might have found a way to be at intimate peace with one another. The question came to her at the oddest times. Well, perhaps not so odd. They came when she was with her nieces and nephews. Her brothers and their families came often to visit and so Mary had, over time, the pleasure of a revolving coterie of children who managed in their most endearing moments to make her wonder about the child she might have had. Fleeting, but unsettling, the question rebounded throughout the years to bedevil her. Why was so little in life ever truly settled? Not the happenstance of things, but the why of things?

The work came to her in an endless profusion of possibilities. There were a thousand ways to paint a mother and her child, for in each familial bond there was a unique tie that found its expression in a particular gesture. It was what he had taught her, so long ago. Gesture. Made, not spontaneous. Studied, not accidental. The signifier of a unique truth about a life, or two lives. The gift of Degas.

He was losing his eyes. There could no longer be any question about that. Over the years, his work grew both freer and more coarse, especially his pastels. Everyone liked to say how bold his work had become, how vivid the colors, how brave the stroke, but she knew it was because he no longer had the sight for refinement. She was certain that what he saw and what he put on the paper were two different things, a trick that the mind always played with artists, but this was a nastier kind of betrayal. A more sighted Degas, a younger Degas, would have recoiled at the blind turn his wavering eyes had taken. She tried not to tell him, though sometimes she broke down and suggested that he might not be seeing what he thought he was seeing, that what he put on paper might not be what he thought he was putting on paper. But she struggled because he had no patience for prevarication; over the years he had not once hesitated to devastate anyone whose work he considered inferior. It was, he always said, a point of the defense of art. She gave up, finally. For what more could she have said? *Stop working, because the thing you have most feared has arrived*? What would he do? How would he live? Would she have wanted him to warn her? Would she have even believed him? Would he believe her? And in the end, who was she to say? If the work was different due to the failure of retina and macula, was it not still art? She would not jury his or anyone else's work. Just her own. Perhaps in this lay their true difference. She would not devastate him as he had devastated her.

Time marched on, years of industry vanishing one after the other, marked only by her work and the needs of her father and mother, grown dearer to her since Lydia's death.

Her father, so proud of her work that he spoke of little else, died next. *Everything is failing.* Or so her father prophesied. *A body coming to its end,* he wrote Aleck, just a month before he died.

And so the decade of the nineties went, with more deaths.

Gustave Caillebotte, who had returned to painting after abandoning art and its exhausting politics in favor of sailing and designing boats, succumbed to death before he even reached the age of fifty, in his will leaving to the Louvre all his collected paintings, ensuring that the new French painting would be preserved for the public, a last, prescient act of passion, for Manet's prices had soared after his death, and Monet couldn't keep up with the demand for his work. Now living without financial care in a house in Giverny, the first house he owned, Monet was besotted with his garden.

Berthe, who had outlived Eugène by only three years, died of pneumonia, moving from health to death in three swift days of astonishing suffering that left her sixteen-year-old Julie in the bereft hands of Berthe's dear friends Mallarmé and Renoir and her sister's children, one of whose friends later married her and made a life from painting. And only three months after Berthe, Katherine died, having outlived her invalid daughter and husband, having struggled for years for air, having fought a failing heart far longer than anyone believed she could.

Mary buried her parents near the new country home she had purchased north of Paris in Le Mesnil-Théribus, the Château de Beaufresne, moving her father and sister from Marly-le-Roi, so that they could all be together once again. And then the Dreyfus affair happened and Degas was beyond terrible, and she could tolerate him no more. Or so she thought. Months after their break, friends invited them both to dinner and he said something gracious and she forgave him, and so on and on it went. She lived between Paris in a new apartment on the Rue de Marignan and at Beaufresne, and he lived in Montmartre. They shared a friendship of intervals, of deep contention and torturous reconciliations, of unspoken need and concealed regard, but a life lived, essentially, apart, though it seemed wrong that two people who had survived so much together could not find some way to comfort one another.

Edgar Degas could find his way around Paris in the dark. He had to, because the black sun floated in his vision now all the time, plaguing his days. Lately Mary Cassatt had begun to query him about color, whether or not he had given up on subtlety, whether he had decided that saturated colors were best after all, whether he really wanted such a strong orange, such a hard turquoise, but he did not know what she was talking about and told her so, somehow forgetting that this had been his deepest fear. The colors he applied were muted, as they had always been, as he had always preferred, but she insisted that he couldn't quite see what he was doing, that he was choosing more vibrant tones, implying that he was losing his grasp, implying that he was unaware of his choices. She let it go, but the implications bothered him, and he ignored her for months, only to woo her back with a kind word about her work. He was always saying nice things about her work, except when she indulged her worst bourgeois tendencies and painted something so commercial it was as if she were begging for money.

It was difficult to see lines, though. This he did not doubt. They doubled and tripled under his hand so that he had to retrace them again and again. Sometimes they were not clear at all for some reason, and he had to outline his figures in black to ground them, which he had done sometimes in the past, but now found a necessity. Or the forms he was after, the precise curve of a shoulder, the long line of a neck or an extended leg, would not materialize from the canvas. No matter the medium—oil or pastel—he indulged that need, one he could not remember being such an imperative before. He could not remember lines being such trouble. The technique of his youth began to leave him. But people rarely listened when he complained of his eyes. They believed him a hypochondriac, still. And he wouldn't tell Mary, because she would only go on about color again.

The exhibitions ceased. After the contretemps of 1882, when Caillebotte seized the reins, there was only one other, in 1886, and he and Mary had exhibited then. They held it at the same time as the Salon, a last statement of their belief in their own significance. But the fire of it all was gone. The State had given control of the Salon to the artists, and so there was little left to rebel against. The dealers Durand-Ruel and Portier bought and sold their work now. The art world had changed, and whether or not their exhibitions had had a hand in altering it was a question he could not answer.

He filled his evenings and Sundays with visiting the Rouarts and the Halévys and their children. He asked one of the young women to marry him, and she pretended his question was a joke. Sabine died and a woman named Zoe Cloisters came to care for him. The city of Paris argued about Dreyfus, a Jewish army captain who had been accused of being a traitor. Everyone in Paris took sides for or against the man. Degas was against him. Everyone said the opposition was de facto anti-Semitism and not about the man's betrayal, that what the opposition disliked was the man's Jewishness. Degas stayed opposed to every writer and artist in Paris, and lost many friendships, even his dear friend Halévy, who was a Jew himself. Even Zola supported the captain, writing an article in the newspaper against the government's prosecution, so he lost him, too. And Mary Cassatt was beside herself with fury at him. For years, she had wavered in and out of his vision, his life. Now she forgave him nothing. Friends frequently reunited them, but Mary was sharp now. That yielding young woman had become an old woman who yielded nothing.

Chapter Fifty-One

After Berthe Morisot died, Julie Manet, who had begged Degas to teach her how to paint, asked him one afternoon about Mademoiselle Cassatt.

"Oh, once we were great friends."

"Once?" Julie asked. "Is this what happens when you grow old? Don't you wish to see everyone you ever knew, to say everything that should be said?"

"No," Degas said. "What happens is that you no longer have the energy for talk."

"How sad," Julie said.

He had to turn his head to see the whole of her, but he could make out her beautiful cheekbones and long hair, a silhouette that reminded him so much of her mother he had to look away to hide his dismay. Where was the Manet in her that had once caused him so much trouble?

"Tell me, Monsieur Degas, did you love Mademoiselle Cassatt?" Julie asked. "Everyone wonders."

"Do they?"

"Of course. People say lots of things about Maman and Uncle Édouard, too."

"Ignore people, Julie. I always do."

"Why didn't you marry her?"

"She didn't want to marry me. And it would have been a marriage

only of the mind. That was all I had then. A mind for art." Which wasn't
completely true.

"Maman was married. She had time for love."

"Yes," he said quietly. "She did."

"Did Mademoiselle Cassatt love you?"

"It's possible," he said.

"But don't you know? You would know, wouldn't you, if she did?"

How did he not know the answer to that question? It seemed to him
suddenly that this was the essential question, the question of their lives.
Why didn't he know? Shouldn't he know? And if he did know, would it
change anything about now, about the end, when the hours were beginning to pass like bitter pills, one after the other, God playing a joke, making him suffer, draining him of light? Would his life be better if he and
Mary Cassatt had ever once said I love you? Or even said it a thousand
times? *I didn't say I didn't love you.* How those words had come to haunt
him. Why hadn't he said it outright? Would she have then said that she
loved him? And what would have happened then? Would she have married him? Would they have enjoyed dulcet days, surprised by devotion?
Back then time had seemed elastic, eternal; the choices, endless. This
was the shock as the end loomed: that one paid too little attention to
the moments when life was asking questions. One had to pay attention.
One had to think, *Why not be brave? Why not take a chance?* Regret was
the stepchild of unheeded desire, and now he might never know. But if
he asked her, if he visited her at her apartment or begged Julie or someone to take him to see her, far away in Mesnil-wherever-it-was that she
lived now, what would he learn?

That perhaps he had been a fool.

And what man wanted to learn that?

"She has her life," he said.

"I don't think she is happy."

"Isn't she?" he asked, trying to suppress the surge of joy that ran
through him.

"Monsieur."

"You reproach me, but you have everything ahead. You don't know."

Daily he limped to the Café de la Nouvelle Athènes, but no one was there to argue with him anymore and so he limped home. He wandered the streets, hardly able to see anything, remembering his way, remembering light. The restless flaneur, walking because he could no longer paint.

Then the worst cruelty: They forced him to move his studio. They were going to tear down his building. Haussmann's reach was long, even though he no longer held office, but the man had influenced everything, and nothing of old Paris would remain. It was an affront, having to move. Someone said the *Little Dancer* was falling apart, but he couldn't find her, because she was buried deep in his packaged things, left disorganized in his new studio because he could not see to organize them. He wanted to work. He played with wax in an effort to feel his way to something, anything, to at least feel himself at work, but he had to abandon the lumps of uncooperative wax in disgust, as he once had abandoned many things.

He attended art auctions. He could see none of the canvases for sale, but he wanted them all. He had to have them. He bought and bought, borrowing money to pay for them from Durand-Ruel, who in turn bought more of Degas's work, work that had sat for years in his studio. Degas took his treasures home from the auctions and did not even unwrap them.

Zoe died. Alone, he spent his days walking. He walked and walked and walked. He did not know what he wished to find except the hours filled. He no longer even tried to work. He was old and he felt old and everything was too much. He forgot to wash and eat. Sometimes he did not even rise from his bed.

Chapter Fifty-Two

She didn't lose the light until late, not until long after Degas had lost his. Not until after she broke her leg in a fall from her horse. Not until after she fell so deeply in love with Japanese prints that she would see her style irrevocably influenced, finding in the flat planes of the Oriental art something so pure and interesting that even her brushstroke altered. Not until after she had traveled Europe with Louisine and her husband, helping them to purchase a museum's worth of paintings. Not until after she earned Degas's scorn by designing murals for the great Chicago exposition, fulfilling a commission she was proud to have received. Not until after she traveled one last time to the States to visit America and to see her paintings exhibited in Philadelphia. Not until after her brother Aleck died. Not until after the pains in her leg struck and the doctors diagnosed diabetes. Not until after she began to inhale radium to cure it. Not until after Matisse and Picasso infuriated her by making a mockery of art. Not until after she traveled down the Nile with Gardner, his wife, Jenny, and their children, a trip to ease her loneliness.

She may have begun to lose the light when Gardner died after returning to Paris from the boat trip, felled by some bacterial infidel of Egypt. Or it may have begun when the Germans started marching through Alsace-Lorraine and she had to flee for a time to the South of France, leaving her chateau and all her Manets and Monets and Pissarros and Degases and Japanese prints vulnerable to the marauding Germans.

Or it may have begun when she last visited Degas, after hearing of his peripatetic wanderings through Paris, and had seen for herself the lonely, pained man he had become.

Yes, she believed, that might have been the moment. Shock could do that to a person, couldn't it? Who knows what the human body will do? It might even blind you when you cannot stand what you see.

He lived now at 6 Boulevard de Clichy, where she had once had her studio, so long ago. The tree-lined boulevard had gone from backwater unsophisticate to busy avenue, but it still carried the shabby patina of Montmartre, the unpolished edges of the little village it had once been. Even so, much had changed: Automobiles weaved among carriages; the trees had grown up to block the light; and newer, taller buildings had replaced the lowly two-story houses and open lots and chicken coops from her time. Neither was 6 Boulevard de Clichy the same building where she had once toiled; it was instead a new and anonymous sandstone building butted up against a brick monolith, all of which, she knew, Degas must hate, even though artists' studios, equipped with north-facing window walls and attached living apartments, stamped the area as uniquely, once and forever, the artists' quarter of Paris. She had heard he had four floors. At the entrance on the third floor, at No. 3, she stopped to catch her breath. She knocked and waited a long while before the shuffling sound of slow footsteps approached the door.

A wraith answered the door: an old man with unkempt white hair and a snowy, bushy beard. He wore an ill-fitting threadbare woven coat, baggy pants, and slippers on his unsocked feet. His skin had grown translucent, creped and spotted here and there under his eyes, which were glassed behind thick lenses smoked black. Through the opaque glass it was impossible to tell if he betrayed shock at her unheralded arrival or if perhaps he just needed a moment, as she needed one, to accommodate the mark of time. She had not written him to tell him she was coming to visit, not when he could not see to read her note. She stepped forward, took his hands in hers.

"Is it you?" he said.

"It is."

He felt his way into a cluttered parlor, a pathway it seemed he had traversed a hundred times, expertly dodging dusty tables and chairs piled with dishes crusted with dried food. Here and there stale half-eaten loaves of bread hibernated in their paper wrappers. He sank into an armchair while she lifted a pile of unread mail from the cushion of another and sat down too. Behind this room was another room. A spiraling private staircase provided navigation to the upper floors. Sunlight filtered through the stairwell, attesting to better light upstairs, where, she thought, he must have his studio.

"Do you remember?" Mary said. "My studio used to be here, at this address?"

"Did you hear my sad news? Zoe left me. She abandoned me."

"She didn't abandon you, Edgar. She died."

"Well, she's gone, either way." He turned his head as if to look for her, though his gaze drifted.

He was thin, his clothes hanging from his shoulders.

"Are you eating, Edgar?"

"The cheese vendor on Rue Lepic takes care of me. He gives me a baguette and slices me some cheese and makes my change for me." He fingered the damask cloth of the armchair. "What color is this? I can't remember."

"It's gold."

"Is it?"

"Have you even had coffee this morning?" Mary said.

"Pardon?"

"Have you eaten today?"

"I can't remember. I don't think so."

No one had told her that it was this bad. They had written that he followed funeral processions, that he was dependent on walking sticks, that he could roam in circles for hours about the streets, but not that he wasn't eating. She wondered whether anyone had checked on him recently.

"You must see my new work," he said.

"You have new work?"

Upstairs, in a high-ceilinged studio that any artist would envy, the usual disarray had mushroomed into complete disorder. Crates were heaped in a jumble, with barely any room to walk between them; boxes of wax lay open and dried out; molded figures vaguely resembling his old dancers and horses lay half-done, abandoned, or finished, the figures imperfect, barely reminiscent of his previous obsessive perfectionism; hundreds of papered-over canvases lined the walls along the floor—it was impossible to know what they were, for no identifying label marked the paper, just his address and that of an auction house; a forest of cylinders storing rolled-up drawings leaned against one another in the corners.

On his walls hung many of the paintings he had long loved: drawings and oils by Delacroix and Ingres, a number of primitives by Gaugin and one extraordinary canvas of a vase of flowers; two early Renoirs, before he prettified everyone and made Degas furious; print after print by Pissarro of his countryside villas and gardens west of Paris; studies and oils by Édouard Manet, including one of Berthe Morisot in mourning, just before she married Eugène. And framed by all the others hung a single oil of hers from the eighties that he had adored and had to have: *Girl Arranging Her Hair*, hung in the exact center, surrounded by dozens of her prints—all the prints from the journal that was never published—of her mother and father reading the newspaper, Lydia at the Opéra, her mother reading to the grandchildren, her mother knitting. Her family, her old life, their old life, resident with him.

There was no new work. He had wanted to show her this.

"I made sure that you were here. I made certain." He turned, unsteady on his feet, shuffling, his unseeing gaze hidden behind those black glasses. "Do you remember when we were together? I'm afraid I wasn't very kind to you. But I don't know what would have been," he said, suddenly defiant. "I cannot say."

Even now, years and years later, he would not define what they had been to one another.

"Where is your little dancer?" Mary said.

"I don't know. I've lost all my friends," he said. "They leave you, don't they, when you are old and infirm? I've lost everyone. Sabine. Zoe. Caillebotte, Manet, Berthe, Achille. Where do they go? And Halévy died, but we had broken with one another long before, over Dreyfus."

"As did we, if you'll remember."

"You forgave me, though. It's odd, isn't it, how none of that matters now?"

"I think it still matters."

"I must be nearer death than you."

They went downstairs.

"I have my car and chauffeur," she said. "We can go somewhere nice to get something to eat."

They drove to Rumpelmeyer's, the celebrated café on the Rue de Rivoli. The doorman opened the door for them and shuttled them inside, two old people who no one recognized anymore.

During breakfast, Degas talked about old Paris, the winding streets and the dark misery of it all; he talked of his mother, who had died when he was thirteen, and how he missed her still; of his dead sisters and their daughters and sons; of his dead brother, Achille, and his living brother, René. He often lost his way; Mary reminded him what he had been speaking about and he talked on. He picked at his eggs and salad, pushing them around on his plate, sipping his coffee, misplacing the cup on the saucer from time to time. When they had finished eating, Pierre drove them across Paris, through the Place Vendôme, past the palatial Opéra house, approaching Montmartre through the twisted triangles of streets, the new white cathedral of Sacré Coeur sailing above the butte. The Germans were in Alsace-Lorraine, but as yet had not touched Paris, though Mary wondered if they might, if food would be as short as it was in the Prussian War, if Degas would be stuck here, defenseless, having to fend for himself in an upturned world. At his studio, they ascended the stairs together, his walking stick making sharp noises as he planted it before he climbed each step. Who had chosen this ghastly building for him, Mary wondered, without either gas or elevator?

She walked him inside to the parlor, to his chair, grasping his elbow. She was reluctant to let go of him.

Degas's myopic gaze searched for hers and he said, "I never loved you, did I?"

It was then, certainly, that the light dimmed.

Then he pulled off his glasses and kissed her. Her lips softened and opened to his. His hand rose to her cheek and still the kiss went on. He was forgetting, she thought, that they could have spent a lifetime doing this.

After a time, he pulled away slowly, his brown eyes cloudy with blindness. Then he sank into the armchair and closed his eyes. In his sudden sleep, age veiled any vestige of his former self: his savage vitality, his mirthful savoir faire, his ruthless devotion to principles no one else believed in and which had made his art as masterful as Velasquez's or Titian's.

She covered him with a blanket and went back upstairs, into the studio that was little more than a storage room with the best art of the nineteenth century hanging on its walls. She had not seen the little dancer in decades, but she knew she had to be here, hidden, perhaps, behind boxes, as he used to hide her. Surely someone would have taken care of her in the move, set her somewhere she couldn't be harmed. Squeezing through narrow aisles between piles of boxes, Mary headed for the back of the long studio, where a dustcloth draped an upright figure. She pulled off the cover, removing it inch by inch, careful not to pull too hard. And there she was: his little girl, his made woman. She was in pieces. Her arms had broken off and lay at her feet. Her tutu had grown ragged and moth-eaten. The ribbon tying her hair, once glossy and jaunty, drooped in a dull frown; dust grayed the black velvet ribbon around her neck. Broken, neglected, she had been rotting for years.

Faint, Mary reached out to the statue to steady herself, then snatched her hand away, lest she harm the little dancer further. The detritus of Degas's obsessions surrounded her. A satin ballet slipper, its long ribbons tucked inside the shoe, lay on a marble-topped table, as if he had unearthed it to paint a dancer again. A spray of brushes of all sizes and shapes wrapped in paper spilled across the same table. On the shelves beneath, palettes lay one on top of another—oval and rectangular, small and large. He had not scraped the dried globules of paint from them, as if he had set down each one intending to pick it up again in a moment.

A life mask, rendered in gray plaster, stared up at her from the clutter. It was Degas when she had fallen in love with him: heavy lidded, long nosed, his once piercing gaze rendered blindly benevolent by the opaque clay. It must have been done when his bust was sculpted in the early eighties. She stared at his face frozen in time, all of who he had been to her preserved now in plaster. She stroked the contours of his cheeks, the lilting wave of his hair, his half-closed eyes. *Edgar.*

She turned away.

Downstairs, she woke him. "Tell me, is your niece, Marguerite's daughter Jeanne, still in Nice?" He had mentioned her sometimes in his letters, his young niece, training as a nurse in southern France.

"I don't know. They say she's working in a hospital."

"Do you know which one?"

"Which one?" he echoed.

She touched his hand. "I'm coming back, Edgar, but not for a few days. You'll be careful, won't you, until I'm back?"

"You'll come back?"

The next day, Mary took the train to Grasse with Mathilde and found Jeanne in a hospital on the harbor in Nice. It took no time to convince her to come to Paris to care for her uncle. She returned with Mary and Mathilde, and they went immediately to Edgar's apartment. Mary waited outside the door while Jeanne went in to greet her uncle and to tell him she had come to live with him.

"How did you know," Mary heard him say, "that Zoe died?"

"Mademoiselle Cassatt told me."

"She did? How did she know?"

"She is here, Uncle. She was here with you a few days ago."

"Was she? Isn't that strange?"

From the doorway, Mary beckoned to Jeanne. "It's best if I don't come in."

"He'll want to thank you," Jeanne said.

"He has nothing to thank me for."

"Don't you want to say good-bye?"

"I already did."

"Are you all right?"

"Not at all," Mary said, and kissed the girl on the cheek, then picked her way to the bottom of the stairs, where Mathilde and the chauffeur were waiting to take her back to Mesnil, alone.

Chapter Fifty-Three

Yes, it was then that the light dimmed. The moment Edgar wondered whether he had ever loved her. Later, at his funeral, the light barely penetrated at all. They buried him in the cemetery in the shadow of Montmartre, so that he would always be at home.

Mary put down her magnifying glass. The night had completely fallen now. The lights in the studio were on; she didn't know how. No doubt Mathilde had come in and seen her reading the letters and retreated. She wished she hadn't because she could have used her help; she wasn't quite certain what she had read. Some of the lines had faded, and even his latest letters, written in Jeanne's hand, recalled a past unfamiliar to her. Sometimes she had to remember what she had wanted. It was the meaning of a life, wasn't it, all that desire? But desire for what? Lately, she was waking up at night gasping for air, and in those strained few moments when it seemed that she might not be able to catch her breath, the past opened up to her in one shining image of color and light that by morning had receded and left her only with a sense of wonder. It was the heart that saw what your mind hid from you. Perhaps, as Edgar so reverently believed, it wasn't the mind that saw, after all.

Mathilde must have stoked the fire, too, for it flickered and flared with a savage, comforting warmth. Well, it was over now, all of it, or it soon would be. How odd it was to survive nearly everyone, to be the last, to be the one who might tell everyone the tale, though no one would ever care now, she thought. For what was lost love? It was the story of every-one's life. Hers, Edgar's, Berthe's, Édouard's. A multiplicity of confusion, a multiplicity of pain.

The letters had scattered: in her lap and on the divan and on the floor. Her memories. His. How slowly she moved now, what effort it took to gather them up. It seemed it was the work of her lifetime.

Was it a crime to burn memory? She didn't know. *Memory is all we have*, Degas had once said. Memory is what life is, in the end.

She would be ash herself, soon, like all the others. She thrust the letters one by one into the fire. The flames took their time consuming the inked pages, turning indigo and vermillion and ocher, a dazzling radiance that penetrated the opaque wall of blindness that in the end had stolen from both of them their beloved avocation. How odd it was that in burning their lives—burning memory—color and light returned to her.

The pages burned on and on. And in those flames the years evapo-rated, the things unsaid and foregone, the misunderstandings and mis-conceptions and subverted hopes, the things that would now never be said.

Paint love, he had once said to her. *You must always paint love.*

In this, she supposed he had given her all he could give.

And what had she given him?

She didn't know. She didn't know.

Acknowledgments

I would like to thank the following individuals: Marly Rusoff, agent extraordinaire, and Michael Radulescu, her wonderful partner in literary excellence; Kathryn Court, the editor from heaven; Tara Singh, the assistant editor from heaven; John Pipkin, who read an early draft and is somehow still my friend; Rich Farrell, who read a later draft and gave me confidence; Kelly O'Conner McNees, who buoys me when I am down; Rena Pitasky, who introduced me to the concept of the golden ratio; the Thomas J. Watson Library, at the Metropolitan Museum of Art; Emily Walhout, at the Houghton Reading Room of Harvard University, who sent me copies of Miss Plummer's articulate letters on the death of Abigail May Alcott; Richard Kendall and Patricia Failing for answering questions about Degas; Michael Erickson, OD, my ophthalmologist, who explained macular degeneration and its symptoms to me; Annabelle Mathias, of the Musée d'Orsay, who signed her life away to get me past the receptionists at the museum after I left my identification back at my rented Paris apartment; Portia LaMotte, who wrote several letters in French on my behalf so that I could make the appointment at the Musée d'Orsay to see the contents of Degas's studio; Scott Cohen, Kathryn Court's able assistant, who went beyond the bounds of duty and found Portia for me; Dennis and Kathy Hogan, old friends who always drive me around D.C. when I go there for research; Julie Hill Barton, who arranged for me to stay at her in-laws' home in the San Juan Islands during one of the final pushes, and my son, Miles, who kept me company there; Sue and Doug Barton, who lent me said home (a thousand thank-yous); Kathleen Doron, who recommended the great apartment in Paris; Jennifer Otte Vanim, at the Philadelphia Museum of Art, who opened the storage rooms for me so that I could see Cassatt's first Mary Ellison portrait; the faculty and staff of Vermont College of Fine Arts, in particular Douglas Glover, who taught me that "repetition is the heart of art"; and my husband and children, who let me disappear from time to time without complaint when deadlines loomed.

Author's Note

In doing research, I never have any idea what I will find that will prove relevant to a story. I spent ten days in Paris retracing the impressionists' steps, searching out their studios, haunts, and homes. I walked every inch of Montmartre and the boulevards below, getting a sense of atmosphere and distance and viewing the actual buildings in which they lived, occasionally sneaking into those same buildings and trespassing up and down private alleyways. (I did draw the line at going to the city planning department to see whether I could verify which buildings were original, but I feared my meager language skills would be no match for the French bureaucracy.) The most remarkable moment, however, occurred in the basement of the Musée d'Orsay while I was viewing artifacts from Edgar Degas's studio. The museum had received some things, though unfortunately not everything, from his studio after his death. I requested to see all I thought they had: his eyeglasses, palettes, brushes, and pastel and paint boxes, all of which were marvelous and inspiring to see and gave me some of the small details I was after. But then the assistant curator said, "There is a mask. Do you want to see it?" We were struggling along—my bad French, her better English—and I wasn't quite certain what she had said in her heavy accent. "Yes, of course," I said, not knowing what it was she was going to show me. Then she pulled the mask out of the cabinet and laid it on the table. This was the gift, the one surprise I always hope I'll stumble on. Upstairs, waiting in line earlier to eat in the dining room, I had viewed a stone sculpture of Degas that had been executed in the early 1880s. This mask, in beautifully preserved gray clay, was the impression of his face made for that sculpture. In contrast to the stone carving, there was something much more real and startling about the mask. Perhaps it was the absolute repose of his face, relaxed for the impression, or perhaps it was the material itself, but in that study, I saw Edgar Degas as I had never imagined him, even after viewing numerous self-portraits and photographs. The moment was breathtaking. The mask ultimately gave me an important moment at the end of the story I would not have had but for this serendipitous gift.

I am indebted to myriad books on art history, biographies, exhibition catalogs, guidebooks, etc. Of particular note are Nancy Mowll Mathews's *Mary Cassatt: A Life*; *Degas Through His Own Eyes*, by Michael F. Marmor; *Edgar Degas Sculpture*, National Gallery of Art; *Degas*, by Roy McMullen; *Degas: Letters*, edited by Marcel Guerin; *My Friend Degas*, by Daniel Halévy; *Manet*, by Henri Perruchot, translated by Humphrey Hare; *The Shop-Talk of Edgar Degas*, by R. H. Ives Gammell; and *Berthe Morisot: The First Lady of Impressionism*, by Margaret Shennan.

The reviews quoted in chapter twenty-eight are contemporary reviews published in various journals and newspapers. I translated them from French with the help of a grammar text, Google Translate, a French dictionary, and my two years of college French. Any mistakes of translation and interpretation are mine.

The letters in the book are fiction, though I read many Cassatt and Morisot family letters to determine sentiment and whereabouts. One phrase of Robert Cassatt's—"a body coming to its end"—is paraphrased from a letter he sent to his son Aleck and which was quoted in the Mathews book.

The three lines in italics in chapter thirty-six are taken from the book *The Shop-Talk of Edgar Degas*, and are purported to be actual quotes of Degas.

Abigail May Alcott was called May Alcott during her lifetime;

however, in the book I refer to her as Abigail because the juxtaposition of Mary and May in the text was too confusing.

I used the contemporary titles of paintings, but over time, paintings' titles can change. The following is a list of those painting titles referred to in this book that have changed: Manet's *Portrait of M. Faure, in the Role of Hamlet* is now known as *Portrait of Faure as Hamlet*; Degas's *Portraits in an Office (New Orleans)* is now known as *The Cotton Office of New Orleans*; Cassatt's *Portrait of a Young Girl* is now known as *Little Girl in a Blue Armchair*.

A PENGUIN READERS GUIDE TO

I ALWAYS LOVED YOU

Robin Oliveira

An Introduction to
I Always Loved You

"Mary thought that the art of love might just be blindness: the willingness not to see the truth of anything, to blur life's sharp edges and drift on an impression of one's own making, to act as if the life you lived was the life you wanted" (p. 196).

Paris, 1877. Mary Cassatt is at a crossroads. An American expatriate, Cassatt has spent the last several years in Europe, studying painting and working to establish herself as an artist. When none of her pieces are accepted into the annual École des Beaux Arts Salon, she is crushed and contemplates returning to America. But soon after, Cassatt meets her idol, Edgar Degas, a forceful and charismatic man, who overturns all her plans.

A few days before they are introduced, Degas notices a lone woman at the Salon. "The mystery woman was not beautiful . . . but

2

her strict self-possession appealed for its singularity alone" (p. 25). He attempts to speak to her, only to lose her in the crowd. So when a friend presses Degas to meet an ardent admirer, the usually unflappable artist is stunned when Cassatt turns out to be the very woman he had pursued.

Although he had never met her in person, Degas had been struck by Cassatt's work. He invites her to abandon the Academy and exhibit the following year with a nascent group of renegades who call themselves the Impressionists. "You will no longer have to subject yourself to the parsimonious Salon jury; you will paint what you wish to paint" (p. 43).

Instead of giving up art, Cassatt finds herself sipping champagne with members of Degas's coterie, including Claude Monet, Camille Pissarro, Édouard Manet, and Auguste Renoir. Cassatt longs to throw herself into new paintings and live up to Degas's faith in her talents, but complications unexpectedly arise.

Cassatt's father, mother, and invalid sister, Lydia, announce that they are leaving Philadelphia and will soon join her to live in Paris. The news brings Cassatt both joy and anxiety. She dearly loves her family—especially sweet-tempered Lydia—but she is expected to find and furnish accommodations that will satisfy both the family's budget and her father's capricious tastes.

Two women buoy Cassatt during this difficult time: Abigail Alcott, a friend and the sister of Louisa May Alcott, and Berthe Morisot, the only other female Impressionist and Manet's sister-in-law and former mistress. Morisot tutors Cassatt on how to navigate the fractious Impressionists and, in particular, cautions her against succumbing to Degas's charm. "You haven't known him long enough to know that his regard can easily be withdrawn" (p. 93).

Initially, Cassatt is reluctant to think ill of Degas—and all Paris knows that Morisot herself is still in love with her husband's brother. Why should Cassatt listen? Soon enough, however, she discovers the truth behind Morisot's cryptic warning. Nothing—and no one—is more important to Degas than his art.

Painstakingly researched and dazzlingly rendered, *I Always Loved You* is a bravura performance by the *New York Times* bestselling author of *My Name Is Mary Sutter*. Through the dual prism of Cassatt and Degas's unconventional romance and Morisot and Manet's tortured affair, Robin Oliveira awakens a bygone Paris animated by the indelible personalities and passions of the men and women who changed art forever.

ABOUT THE AUTHOR

The *New York Times* bestselling author of *My Name Is Mary Sutter*, Robin Oliveira holds a BA in Russian and an MFA in Writing. She lives in Seattle, Washington.

A CONVERSATION WITH ROBIN OLIVEIRA

Your previous novel, the New York Times *bestseller* My Name Is Mary Sutter, *was also set in the nineteenth century. What is it about this period that captures your imagination?*

The nineteenth century, in human terms, is fairly recent, and in historical terms is well documented in both the details of everyday life and historical events, rendering research relatively easy. I'm very interested in mixing fact and fiction, in setting my fictional characters in a realistic, historically accurate landscape. Nineteenth-century guidebooks, newspapers, photographs, diaries, street maps, etc., are all readily available; earlier centuries' are less accessible. My characters adhere to real train and boat schedules, museum hours, and eat at contemporary restaurants. There is something grounding for me in having my characters operate in the same circumstances as those who lived in the nineteenth century. And I suppose I have a romantic notion of life then, which is probably less based in reality than I'd like to think.

What inspired you to intertwine Cassatt's story with that of Édouard Manet and Berthe Morisot?

In the structure of a novel, a subplot expands the main plot by contrasting and mirroring the story arc of the main characters. That is to say, the subplot comments on, reinforces, and delineates the main story by illustrating a different approach to the same conflict. In *I Always Loved You*, one of the conflicts is impossible love between soul mates. Once you undertake a study of the lives of the Impressionists, the pairing of Cassatt/Degas and Morisot/Manet is quite obvious. I am but one of many students of Impressionism who have recognized the parallel dynamics between the two couples. From a writer's point of view, I was thrilled to discover the connection, because it served my literary needs very well: their differing circumstances and approaches to their similar predicament presented the perfect plot and subplot.

As a writer, it must have been fun to write the scene in which Degas and Zola debate the superiority of their respective art. Zola says, "Here is the difference between writers and painters. You are handicapped by your medium, paint, whereas a writer is a savant of sorts, using our more facile medium of words to inquire about and observe any subject. . . . Words reign" (p. 77). Do you agree with the argument he expresses?

I believe that paint is as facile and powerful a medium as words. The Impressionists revealed their own politics and views on contemporary society just as Zola's essays and novels did; their themes mirrored one another. Zola's realist novels *L'Assommoir* and *Nana* commented on modern life in the same way the Impressionists' paintings did. No one can look at Degas's *In a Café* and not understand his politics, nor can one look at any of Pissarro's peasants-at-work paintings and not recognize his socialist leanings. Painters and writers alike were commenting on modern life with equal force.

The Impressionists both reviled and revered Zola. A compatriot of change, he was one of the first to champion their exhibitions, but he was often severely critical and arrogant in his critique; he also cruelly portrayed his childhood friend Cézanne in the novel *L'Œuvre*. I gave Zola those words in *I Always Loved You* to show that this conflict became an essential element of their interactions.

After Mary Cassatt's first exhibition with the Impressionists, she is crushed by an abundance of negative reviews, including one that said, "The work of Madame Mary Cassatt betrays a preoccupation with attracting attention, rather than an attempt to paint well" (p. 200). Are they based on the original reviews or are they verbatim excerpts?

All the reviews are verbatim excerpts, with the caveat that I was their translator and, since I am not a native French speaker, may have made some errors. Wherever possible, I include the actual documents that pertain to whichever piece of historical fiction I'm writing. For instance, in *My Name Is Mary Sutter*, I hunted down the original Sanitary Commission report on the Union Hotel Hospital, which took some doing. In the case of Mary Cassatt's reviews, there was such a plethora of available authentic contemporary reviews that I deemed invention irresponsible. And the critics were so creatively insulting! I don't think I would have been as original. And I loved that some of the critics also got her name and marital status wrong. That irked Cassatt and certainly would have irked me. Furthermore, the critics differed so greatly from one another in their opinion of her work; it was a pleasure to reveal Cassatt's varied critical reception. I couldn't have altered the reviews in any way that would have improved on the originals.

Lydia Cassatt suffered from a painful and lingering illness that goes unnamed in the novel. Does history record what it was?

It is believed that Lydia Cassatt died of what was then called Bright's Disease. This disease title encompassed several conditions of inflammation of the kidneys, but the specific illness that afflicted Lydia cannot now be accurately identified from this distance in time. Nephritis, chronic pyelonephritis, or hypertensive nephrosclerosis are all possibilities. Modern treatment offers a variety of medications and antibiotic and, in the worst cases, dialysis, but these treatments were unavailable then. Lydia's symptoms progressed and led to renal failure and premature death.

Degas's losing battle with macular degeneration is one of the most tragic aspects of the novel. How many years did he live after he was no longer able to paint?

It is difficult to know exactly when Degas gave up painting, but the decline is generally believed to have been complete by 1909. Prior to that, he had begun to work only on very large canvases and smaller wax sculptures (*Edgar Degas*, Rizzoli). He died in 1917.

Is there any documented proof that Cassatt and Degas had—however briefly—a love affair?

The only documented proof would have been a letter or, failing that, a diary entry that we could authenticate. Since Cassatt burned all their letters before her death, there is no way of knowing for certain what went on between them on any given night of their lives, just as we cannot know for certain what happens in the lives of our neighbors or friends. What we do know is that they shared an uncommon love of art and one another that kept them emotionally tied until their deaths, despite the volatile nature of their relationship. My portrayal of a night of passion is, of course, conjecture, but given the nature of friendships between men and women, I believe it is well within the realm of possibility.

In your Author's Note, you write about being in Paris and unexpectedly seeing a clay mask taken of Degas's living face. What are some other highlights of your research trip?

There were many other wonderful moments, especially in the basement of the Musée d'Orsay. Aside from the startling mask, the most poignant objects were the series of Degas's increasingly darker smoked eyeglasses, which highlighted for me how great his visual handicap was and its inexorable progression. Of equal importance was finding Degas's last studio and apartment, where he lived and worked in his last years and where he died. I visited Morisot's and Manet's common grave at the Passy Cemetery; they rest together in the same grave with Suzanne, Manet's wife, and Eugène, Morisot's husband and Manet's brother. This eternal connection cemented for me how intimately entwined they were in life. Cassatt's footprint in Paris is less defined, but I was thrilled to look up at the Avenue Trudaine apartment and imagine her life there, as well as walk in her footsteps to her first separate studio, which, ironically, was situated on the site of Degas's last studio.

What are you working on now?

Another historical novel. I can't really talk about it as it's still taking shape, but it will begin in the nineteenth century and take place in Albany, New York, Saint Lucia, Paris, and St. Petersburg, Russia.

QUESTIONS FOR DISCUSSION

1. In Robin Oliveira's novel, it's clear that Mary Cassatt and Edgar Degas genuinely loved each other. Might they have found happiness in marriage? Would their art have been diminished or elevated by the relationship?

2. It seems extraordinary that one organization, the École des Beaux Arts, once held such power in determining what was considered "good" art. Yet in our own era, an exhibition at the Museum of Modern Art will attract more reviews and attendees than any show in an independent gallery. Does this kind of official validation ultimately have a positive or negative effect on art, literature, music, and other creative commodities?

3. After she meets Degas, Cassatt thinks, "People were always asking artists that inane question. *Don't ask me how I do what I do.* . . . But hadn't she asked Degas the same thing in his studio?" (p. 112) Why are we drawn to understand other people's creative processes?

4. Mary Cassatt's father, Robert, is indifferent to the needs of anyone beside himself. To what extent did his attitude toward the women

in his family influence Mary's attitudes toward marriage and her relationship with Degas?

5. While Mary Cassatt is still struggling to make her name, her father asks her, "What is the purpose of any endeavor if not to make money? And how does an artist tell whether or not he is successful?" (p. 130) How would you answer his questions?

6. As depicted in Oliveira's novel, many legendary artists—not to mention the writers Émile Zola and Stéphane Mallarmé—were part of the same circle. How did their association help them achieve success? Do you think all of them would have achieved fame independently?

7. Degas treated his "rat," Marie, quite cruelly while she modeled for his wax sculpture of a ballet dancer. Does great art justify the collateral damage of its creation?

8. The novel intimates that Édouard Manet married his father's mistress and that Berthe Morisot married Édouard's brother, Eugène. Do you empathize with their decisions?

9. So many of Cassatt's later paintings capture the love between mother and child. Yet she herself was childless. Do you think she could really understand this particular form of love? Why or why not? If you were a woman living in an era when childbirth put your health—and often your life—at risk, do you think you would have been willing to take that chance?

10. Manet died at the height of his powers, whereas Degas lived for years unable to create. In your opinion, which artist suffered the worse fate?

11. To whom does the novel's title, *I Always Loved You*, refer?

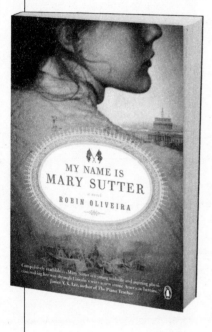